Rooted in Dishonor

Peter Tyzack

This book is a work of fiction. Any resemblance to actual events or persons, living or dead, is entirely coincidental.

"Rooted in Dishonor," by Peter Tyzack. ISBN 1-58939-932-3 (softcover); 1-58939-933-1 (hardcover).

Library of Congress Control Number: 2006937377.

Published 2006 by Virtualbookworm.com Publishing Inc., P.O. Box 9949, College Station, TX 77842, US. ©2006, Peter Tyzack. All rights reserved. No part of this publication may be reproduced, stored in a retrieval system, or transmitted in any form or by any means, electronic, mechanical, recording or otherwise, without the prior written permission of Peter Tyzack.

Manufactured in the United States of America.

To Sandy,
for giving me the will to finish this book

**"His honour rooted in dishonour stood,
And faith unfaithful kept him falsely true."**

"Idylls of the King"
Alfred, Lord Tennyson (1859)

Resident at Beaumont Castle

Lord Quentin de Courcey, head of the de Courcey family
Lady Annabelle de Courcey, his wife
Catherine de Courcey, his eldest daughter
Philip de Courcey, his youngest son
Paul de Courcey, a relative of the family

Servants

Mr. Johnson butler
Dwyer
O'Mahoney
Sweeney

Mrs. Hughes cook
O'Brien
Dunne
O'Halloran

Guests attending the Sevastopol Reunion Dinner

Colonel Charles Howard, Chief Constable of Hampshire
Florence Howard, his wife
Sir Henry Rawlinson, a local landowner
Elizabeth Rawlinson, his wife and one of Quentin's daughters
Alexander de Courcey, Quentin's eldest son
Geoffrey Montagu, a friend of Alexander

Harrison Montgomery, a friend of Alexander

Inspector Everett Parsons, a friend of Alexander

Major George Fitzherbert, a brother-officer of Quentin

Captain Cecil Ashton, a brother-officer of Quentin

George Hamilton, a local doctor

Anne Hamilton, his wife and one of Quentin's daughters

Joshua Harding, the local vicar

Andrew Robertson, the family solicitor

Rooted in Dishonor

-1-

9th September 1880

Lord Quentin de Courcey drank deeply from his silver goblet and gazed languidly and contentedly over his domain. The view from his bedroom to the west was one he especially enjoyed, particularly at this time of the year when the trees in the Great Park began changing to their multifarious shades of Autumn. Reaching majestically to the sky, they symbolized for him the might that was England and the steadfastness that had always been his family's by-word. The proud de Courceys were as deeply rooted in England as the trees themselves. A family of soldiers, always ready to answer their country's call.

He took another long swill of claret. And by God, he thought, if need be he would answer that call again. Even at his age.

Enriched with the alcohol his blood pounded through his body, coloring the rich matrix of prominent arteries visible in those parts of his cheeks that were not hidden

1

behind his heavy moustache and thick Dundreary side-whiskers. Such a display of hirsuteness was now rarely seen, but Lord Quentin had worn his hair in this shaggy manner since the style first became fashionable in the late eighteen-fifties, and it was unimaginable to those that knew him that he would ever change. In his opinion a good show of hair was a fine manly sight, and it would have surprised and angered him to know that there were those of his acquaintance who saw something peculiarly sensuous and feminine about the manner in which he gently stroked and tugged at the long strands of hair that hung from his face and from under his chin.

Straightening his shoulders, still broad and powerful in spite of his five and fifty years, he raised his glass in a silent toast to the ancestors that had owned Beaumont Castle since the days of William the Conqueror. Those Normans certainly knew how to fight, he thought. With a few thousand of them we would have seen off those bloody Russians.

After a few more moments swaying in further contemplation of those dreadful years in the Crimea he crossed the room to refill his goblet from the decanter on a small rosewood table. The table was covered in elaborate carvings that were copies of the exotic sculpture from the Surya temple at Konorah, and it required more than a casual glance to realize that they represented men and women engaged in a startling panorama of acts of human congress. Like the matching figures on a silver cigar box lying on the table they were mementos of a brief regimental tour in India.

He briefly allowed his fingers to stroke the figures on the box before taking a cigar and lighting it, then turned to glare through the clouds of smoke at the three-quarter length portrait above the fireplace. As ever his glare was met by the serene gaze of his wife. How little, he thought, she had changed since the portrait was painted just after their marriage thirteen years before.

"Damn you, Annabelle," he muttered darkly in a voice already heavy with drink. "Damn you for your beauty and your cold heart."

He emptied the goblet in one long swig, and finding the decanter empty tugged angrily at the bell-pull near his bed. They would know in the kitchens what he wanted at this time in the afternoon, especially with guests in the castle.

As he turned back towards the fire-place he heard the sound of a man's laughter coming from the direction of the stables below his window.

It was the laugh of someone at ease with the world, and Quentin warmed to the sound of it. Beaumont had been a sadder and lonelier place without such laughter, and he blessed the good fortune that had brought this young man to England. Seeing the tall, strong body moving around the castle and watching the confident way he handled a horse had been like reliving his own past. And it provided such a contrast to the two weakling sons that had been the fruit of his own loins.

He smiled in appreciation as he saw the effortless way his nephew slid from his saddle. But his expression darkened once more and his fierce eyes narrowed as he watched the young man reach up to grasp the waist of his riding companion, and he saw how Lady Annabelle maintained her hold on his shoulders long after she had dismounted.

"Just remember you're still my guest, my dear Paul," Quentin muttered threateningly, the cigar clenched firmly between his teeth. "You may go so far, but by thunder if you abuse my hospitality I'll have the skin off your back."

For a few moments he gazed down on the two figures. Then he broke wind loudly and turned away from the window as Johnson entered the room with a fresh decanter of wine.

Not for the first time that afternoon Paul de Courcey gazed into Lady Annabelle's green eyes and felt a burning desire to kiss the inviting mouth that smiled up at him. If the damned game-keeper had not disturbed them earlier in the copse there was no knowing what he might have accomplished. But he knew he had to be patient and keep a firm control over his passion. She was a prize worth waiting for, and he could tell she was weakening. Her eyes made that quite clear to him, and his experience told him that when it came to matters of the heart a woman's eyes never lied.

He had seen the figure watching them and knew only too well that this was no place for love-making. There would be plenty of other opportunities for that, and in the meantime it was vital he did nothing to annoy Quentin. He was already greatly indebted to him, and he had no intention of allowing any foolish indiscretions to upset his own ambitions.

It was just unfortunate that his uncle possessed such a beautiful and desirable wife.

"Don't look now, my dear Annabelle," he whispered, "but I do believe we are being watched."

He winked and offered her his arm as they made their way slowly towards the castle. Then almost as an after-thought he turned back towards the stables.

"Smith!" he bellowed. "Wake up you idle man and stable these horses."

He waited until he saw movement in that part of the loft where the grooms slept, and watched in disgust a slovenly figure climbed slowly and reluctantly down the wooden ladder to the stable floor. Then he spun on his heel and returned his attention to his more engaging companion.

"I'll never understand why Quentin tolerates that man, Annabelle," he said as they strolled across the lawn. "He's the most disgusting drunkard it's ever been my misfortune to meet. You can smell his breath from five paces and I doubt he bathes more than once a year. If that's an example of a sergeant in the British Army it's no wonder the Crimean War was such a disaster. Not that I'd ever dare say that to Quentin."

The unshaven and disheveled object of his scorn shuffled in his long dirt-encrusted coat across the stable yard to where the two horses waited patiently to be stabled. Through his blood-shot eyes Smith glared at the departing figures until they had reached the path leading to the front of the castle. Once he heard the sound of their footsteps on the gravel he cleared his nose and throat noisily and spat a large ball of phlegm in their direction.

"And what would you know about bloody soldiering, Mr. fine-and-dandy bloody Paul de Courcey," he hissed. "I've got my beady eyes on you. Just give me 'alf a chance and I'll 'ave you back on that bloody boat to America. And that's no idle bloody threat."

Smith watched until the pair disappeared from sight around the corner of the castle before grasping the horses' reins and leading them into the stables.

"Come, my beauties," he whispered affectionately as they nuzzled against his shoulders, "Smithie's got some sugar lumps for you to 'ave with your oats."

In another room overlooking the stables Captain Sir Cecil Ashton sat thoughtfully sipping wine at his desk. He had been looking forward to this visit to Beaumont for several weeks. It was always a pleasure to meet up again with old army chums like Quentin and Fitzherbert. There were few enough like them any more. But before allowing himself to engage in the serious business of pleasure he had a few letters to write. Using the impressive embossed stationery that was always provided at Beaumont was always a useful ploy to gain further invitations, and in his present parlous financial state he needed plenty of those lined up for the winter.

He checked the addresses on the envelopes against the list he had brought with him to ensure that no one had been missed. With any luck, he thought, this batch of correspondence would see him through the New Year.

Satisfied with his afternoon's work Ashton decided it was now time to get down to some serious drinking. From what he had seen since arriving there were some damned fine-looking women around. Quentin certainly knew how to pick his servants. And that suited Ashton admirably. No longer able to afford the pursuit of women of his own class, he had come to see the advantages of bedding the lower orders. They were more fun between the sheets, less demanding outside them, and if they got themselves pregnant they made less fuss about it.

He smirked at himself in the mirror as he brushed his short dark hair and combed his neat moustache. Then he inspected his teeth before pouring a liberal dose of cologne into his left palm, rubbing his hands together and patting them against the cheeks of his slim hawkish face. He was pleased with what he saw. In spite of a debauched life-style he had managed to maintain a trim figure for a man already into his fifties, and he knew how important that was if he wished to continue his success with women.

"By gad, but you're a dashed handsome feller, Ashton," he muttered as he tugged gently on his shirt cuffs and adjusted his monocle, fondling the green ribbon that secured it to a button on his waistcoat—the ribbon that had come from the hair of the big-busted blonde barmaid at Epsom. No doubt Quentin would enjoy hearing the story of that wild night, he thought, as he made his way along the corridor leading the short distance to his host's room.

ଙ୍ଙ୍ଙ୍

The report in the *Times* made agreeable reading for Inspector Everett Parsons. In his summation the Old Bailey judge had been more than generous in praising the Metropolitan Police and their colleagues in the Irish Special Branch. The nation, the judge had said, should be grateful to them all. Parsons had played a relatively small part in the operation, but he was nevertheless proud of his contribution, and confident that the death sentences awarded to the bombers would make other Irishmen think twice before terrorizing the streets of London.

By the time the Portsmouth train had reached Guildford he was reading the report of the final day's play at Kennington Oval in the first cricket Test Match between England and Australia. Parsons had a strong dislike for most of the games forced upon him at school. His rotund figure was never intended for the rigors of the playing fields. But he had always loved cricket. It was a game in which brawn played a relatively small part, and it was also one of the better English sporting traditions. A game for all classes to enjoy on the village green, be they lords of the manor or humble blacksmiths.

From all accounts the Test Match had been an enthralling contest. After Murdoch, the Australian captain had scored a marvelous one hundred and fifty-three runs to save his side from what looked like an innings defeat, the impossible had almost happened. Requiring only fifty-seven runs to win, England had slumped to thirty-one for five before Dr WG Grace had salvaged a famous victory. Whoever would have thought that the Australians could run us so close, Parsons mused, as almost without thinking he turned the pages of the newspaper to the Court Circular. During the recent Irish crisis it had become second nature for him to scour these pages for the engagements of prominent figures in society who might have been possible Fenian targets.

It was only then that he saw the announcement.

Sevastopol Reunion
Lord de Courcey will host a dinner
at Beaumont castle on 9th September
to commemorate the twenty-fifth anniversary
of the fall of Sevastopol. Members of his
family and officers of the 18th Royal Lancers
will be in attendance.

Parsons cared little enough for the landed gentry and the manner in which they lived. As a policeman he was only too aware that the protection of their rights and privileges was given undue priority in a country where even in 1880 obscene differences in wealth still divided the social classes. Nevertheless, to his shame, on this occasion he experienced an over-riding sense of pleasure from reading this particular notice. It was not every day that he was included amongst the guests at such a gathering. His late father, an old soldier himself, would no doubt be proud to think that his son was moving in such exalted military circles.

Not that anyone would ever have associated Parsons with a military family. Only five foot six inches in height and with small hands and feet, he had a gentle aesthetic appearance that he had chosen to accentuate in recent months by allowing his unruly dark curls to grow to his shoulders. It was a decision that had not been well received by senior officers in the Metropolitan Police. Prominently ex-army in its composition, the ruling echelon at Scotland Yard regarded a military appearance and bearing to be highly desirable qualities for a policeman. More so, it appeared to Parsons, than any ability to apprehend criminals. His appearance was nevertheless somewhat extreme, and had earned him the nickname of "Professor" amongst his colleagues. It was a title that secretly pleased him, as for sometime whilst a science student at London University he had intended pursuing an academic career.

It was unfortunate that his only traveling companion was asleep. Had he been awake Parsons might well have been able to steer the conversation discretely towards the event at Beaumont and could casually have announced that he was on his way there. But for much of the time since his ill-mannered entry into the crowded compartment at Clapham Junction station the man had been dead to the world.

Parsons and his fellow passengers had been deeply engrossed in their newspapers at the time, and had not been amused when the bulky figure had entered the compartment and swayed around in their midst while attempting to squeeze a large battered leather case into the luggage rack. Eventually, without a word of greeting or apology, the man had slumped into the seat opposite Parsons, tilted his brown bowler-hat over his eyes and fallen asleep, oblivious to the hostile faces around him.

After allowing an appropriate period of time to elapse, Parsons had lowered his newspaper and subjected the man to closer scrutiny. Although much of his face was covered either by his hat, his thick matted hair or his unkempt whiskers, it was still possible for Parsons to see traces of breakfast in the man's moustache. This piece of evidence, together with the stained reefer jacket with missing buttons, suggested an ill-managed bachelor existence, while the florid complexion and briefly glimpsed blood-shot eyes indicated a propensity for alcohol. To Parsons' satisfaction this latter observation was borne out as the train left Surbiton by the man removing a dented hip-flask from his pocket and taking a furtive gulp from it.

At Guildford the emptying of the compartment had momentarily disturbed Parsons' traveling companion. But after resorting to his flask again as the train left the station he had slumped once more into a deep sleep, accompanied this time by a raucous open-mouthed snore.

Finding it no longer possible to concentrate on his newspaper, Parsons had turned his attention to the rolling countryside, watching the farm laborers and their families struggling to bring in another poor harvest. A series of wet summers during the past decade had been disastrous for British farmers, nowhere more so than in the arable areas of southern England. To make matters worse their traditional markets had been eroded by the cheap wheat that could now be shipped across the Atlantic in fast steam ships from the highly mechanized plains of North America. Land was no longer a safe investment, and the aristocratic families that had long relied upon it now sought to replenish their fortunes by marrying into the new wealth of commerce and industry and the New World. In spite of its pedigree, Parsons imagined that the de Courcey family would be managing no better than others. But he would be able to judge that for himself soon enough. The train was fast approaching Beaumont Station on the edge of the South Downs.

-2-

"I*'m sorry I disturbed you.*"

In the process of retrieving his bag from the luggage rack Parsons had accidentally woken the sleeper and knocked off his bowler hat.

"Where the devil are we?" grunted the man, his voice thickened by the effects of drink and sleep.

"We're approaching Beaumont Station," replied Parsons, keeping as much distance as possible between himself and the whiskey on the man's breath. "Have you much further to travel?"

"This is my station, you fool."

The disheveled figure struggled to his feet.

"Get out of my way," he blustered, pushing Parsons back into his seat as he struggled to retrieve the battered leather case from the overhead rack. "I'm traveling to Beaumont Castle to see my old friend, Quentin."

Parsons was both surprised and dismayed at the prospect of spending the weekend in such disagreeable company. It was

13

far from what he had been expecting. But he could not fail to be impressed by the reception committee awaiting them on the platform provided by the station-master and his staff.

"A good day to 'ee, gentl'mun," announced the station-master gravely in a rich Hampshire accent and with an admirable display of dignity. "Welcome to Beaumont. I hope thy stay at the castle will be a pleasant one."

The broad-shouldered, ruddy-faced countryman was an ill-match for the chocolate-coloured coat with salmon piping that was the uniform of the London and South Western Railway. But he was clearly proud to wear it, and gave what passed as a plausible imitation of a military salute to the two passengers after they descended from the train. Parsons smiled in acknowledgement of the dignified greeting, but gracious as the reception was he could not help thinking it an extravagant waste of manpower to maintain a railway station like Beaumont almost entirely for the convenience of a single family. However, such had been the demand from the rapidly-expanding railway companies for suitable land that many landowners found themselves in a position to negotiate very favorable terms and special privileges. Such privileges frequently included the provision of their own private railway stations.

"Thank you, station-master," he replied with appropriate gravity. "Can you tell me if transport has been arranged to take us to the castle?"

"Indeed 'tas, sir. Please be good enough to follow me. Get the gentl'muns' bags now and look sharp about it."

His last sentence was addressed to the two strapping young country lads who had been waiting patiently in line behind him. Dressed in a similar though less ornate uniform they practically fell over one another in their rush to pick up the cases and follow the station-master and the two passengers along the platform.

After such a reception Parsons was mildly disappointed to find there was no landau and liveried coachman to greet them, merely an untidy young groom with a pony and trap. However, he was pleased to see the pale youth who had accompanied the groom. It was his old school friend, Philip de Courcey.

Philip had always been small and slight, but he seemed paler and thinner now than Parsons remembered. Leaning against the wheel of the cart, his sallow features and sunken grey eyes made an unflattering comparison with the healthy glow on the faces of the two porters. His hand felt limp in Parsons' grasp, but his smile was warm and welcoming, transforming the gloomy expression momentarily and bringing life to his wide, sensitive mouth.

"Everett, how g-good to see you ag-gain after all these years," he said, with the nervous stammer Parsons remembered from school and a solemnity that seemed out-of-place in one so young. "I hope I f-find you well."

"I am indeed, Philip," Parsons replied, pumping his friend's hand, "and I trust I find you in good spirits."

"As well as can be expected living in this d-desolate place," Philip said mournfully. "Apart from an abundance of f-fresh air there is p-precious little else to recommend it. B-but you will see for yourself what I mean."

Philip smiled self-consciously as he turned to Parsons' companion, who had been scowling at them both during the exchange of greetings.

"Forgive me, sir," he said politely, "b-but I don't b-believe we have met before."

"Major George Fitzherbert of the 18th Royal Lancers, young man. I served with your father in the Crimea."

If Fitzherbert had been intending to impress anyone with his pedigree, the desired effect was lost in his pompous-sounding slurred tones and unsteady posture. Nevertheless, it had the effect of leaving Parsons and Philip speechless and they said nothing more as the groom and the two porters loaded the trap with the cases.

There was little opportunity during the journey for further conversation. Philip sat in the front of the trap with the groom, leaving Parsons to share the rear-facing seat with Fitzherbert and the luggage. The gentle rocking motion of the trap soon sent Fitzherbert back to sleep, and to Parsons' disgust the drunk's body continually made contact with his, and occasionally his head rested on Parsons' shoulder. As a consequence Parsons found himself having to strike a balance between shrugging his shoulder hard enough to keep Fitzherbert at bay, but not so hard as to send the lifeless figure spilling out of the cart.

Beaumont village could never be described as a rural idyll. Even at the height of summer any such descriptions of villages such as this were merely the romantic notions of the group of poets and artists who made but fleeting visits to the countryside and had no intention of staying. The eyes of such people were blind to the grinding poverty of the farm laborers and their families, and their miserable lives in cottages with crumbling walls, dank thatches and outside earth privies. The idealized village inns that they painted or eulogized did not portray the sullen groups of laborers as there were this moment in Beaumont, watching the progress of the trap as it jostled along the muddy lane.

One man Parsons noted in particular. He wore a long brown coat and wide-brimmed hat, and he glared with undisguised hostility towards them. As the trap passed he cleared his throat noisily and spat into the mud at his feet.

In stark and obscene contrast, the castle dwarfed and dominated the village from its high vantage point. As the trap climbed slowly between the long avenue of oaks it became increasingly clear why it had been such an impregnable fortress for over eight hundred years. Not as large as many Norman castles, the tall crenellated walls nevertheless managed to convey a threatening appearance even in the pale sun of the Autumn afternoon; and as the trap crossed the drawbridge into the shadow of the twin towers of the barbican Parsons found himself shivering involuntarily.

Philip's elder brother, Alexander, awaited them outside the main entrance to the castle. Taller than Philip, but at twenty-two only a year his senior, his serious gaunt expression made him appear much older. He was dressed soberly in a black suit, with a white cotton shirt and black silk cravat, an apparel that only served to reinforce the gloomy impression conveyed by long, lank hair, brooding dark eyes and hollow cheeks.

"Thank you for coming, Everett," he said quietly as they shook hands, but he failed to hide the sadness in the eyes that but briefly engaged Parsons.' "And you must be Major Fitzherbert. Father's often spoken of you. You're welcome, sir."

The words sounded anything but welcoming, and it was clear to Parsons that whatever Alexander had learned from his father about Fitzherbert had been far from his liking.

"Don't let us stand here talking," Alexander continued. "I know how tiring the journey from London can be. Please come inside and take some refreshment. Leave your luggage in the trap. Johnson will see that it is taken to your rooms."

Parsons had been watching his friend as he spoke. There was a flatness in the tone of his voice and a lethargy in his movements that indicated that Alexander was in no mood for company. This was not the enthusiastic boy he had known at school, or even the carefree young man who had invited him to Beaumont when they had met but a few months ago in London.

He followed the others up the steps towards the thick oak door with its rounded Norman arches, passing as he did the elderly grey-haired servant in claret livery who had stood motionless behind Alexander when they arrived. Johnson's superior expression during the introductions had conveyed the impression that he had little regard for shabbily-dressed ex-army officers and young men of undistinguished ancestry, and it never ceased to surprise Parsons to see how some servants adopted the same attitudes of superiority as their employers.

Johnson acknowledged the instructions with a slight inclination of his head before walking slowly down the steps towards the trap.

"Get the gentlemens' cases, Dunne, and be quick about it," he ordered in a stately voice that all but concealed his Hampshire roots, managing in that one short sentence both to demean the young groom and question the credentials of the owners of the luggage. But whereas there might be some doubt about the right of Fitzherbert and Parsons to call themselves "gentlemen' there was no doubting Dunne's position at the bottom of the servants' hierarchy.

There speaks a man with little affection for his fellows, thought Parsons, feeling a sudden surge of sympathy for the young groom. At the top of the steps he turned to watch Dunne struggling with the luggage, and noticed for the first time the heavy bruising on the left-hand side of the boy's face. Had Johnson been a younger man Parsons would have the thought him to be the likely cause of the wounds, but he doubted whether the old man still had the requisite physical strength. But there were doubtless others who would per-form that task for him.

-3-

The entrance hall was a cold and gloomy place, with no rugs on the floor to muffle the sound of their footsteps on the large stone slabs. The only light came through the open door, and in the semi-darkness the display of muskets, swords, bayonets and pistols on the oak-panelled walls was far from welcoming.

"You have quite an armory here, Alexander," said Parsons, attempting to initiate a conversation.

"My father's playthings," the young man replied dismissively. "There are far more in the Great Hall. If you're interested in such things I'm sure father will be glad to tell you about them. Philip and I are a great disappointment to him. Even with such heroic names as ours we fail to share his passion for killing. But, of course, Major Fitzherbert you must be an expert on that."

The major's inebriated expression showed little change, and at first Parsons thought him oblivious to Alexander's sarcasm. But his abrupt reply suggested he was only been too

20

aware of what had been said and had merely chosen to ignore it.

"Where is your father?" he demanded. "I'll leave you boys to your own amusements. I feel in need of a drink."

"He's p-probably in his bedroom with Captain Ashton," interjected Philip, anxious to avoid any further unpleasantness between Fitzherbert and his brother. "It's upstairs and along the corridor to your left. You can't miss it. There are a set of antlers on the door."

Philip directed Fitzherbert towards the wide stone staircase in the center of the hall. Then walking past it into the corridor beyond he invited the others to follow him.

"C-come on you two. Let's go to the D-drawing Room for some refreshments."

After helping themselves to tea and plates of thinly-sliced sandwiches Parsons and the de Courcey brothers joined the two other men already seated near the fire. Both were friends of Alexander who had arrived with him from London on the previous day.

"Everett, this is my good friend Geoffrey Montagu," Alexander announced with some pride. "Those of us familiar with his work believe him to be a poet of great promise. He allowed an appropriate pause before making his next triumphant statement. "Perhaps even a new Byron."

Parsons turned towards the tall figure lounging in a chair opposite the fire. Like Alexander he was dressed in a somber dark suit. Montagu made no attempt to rise to shake the hand that Parsons offered, merely acknowledging his presence with a cursory glance before resuming his melancholy contemplation of the flames. No doubt, thought Parsons, such a haunted expression was the appropriate hallmark of an aesthete. For to be compared to Lord Byron, the poet and social reformer who had died in 1824 supporting the Greek people in their struggle for freedom from the Turks, was praise indeed. But, on the other hand, Parsons reminded himself, there had been a darker side to Byron.

Alexander had in the meantime moved to the side of the chair where the other man sat stiffly. "And this is Harrison Montgomery," he said. "Harrison is a writer from Canada. Geoffrey and I met him recently at one of Bernard Shaw's lectures.'

Montgomery rose to accept Parsons' out-stretched hand, the strength of his grip belying his slim frame. This, and the steel-grey eyes set wide over the asymmetric pugilistic nose, suggested to Parsons that the Canadian had followed other less sedentary pursuits than that of a writer.

"I'm pleased to make your acquaintance, sir," said Parsons. "Of what do you write?"

"Mostly about the early days in North America before the arrival of the white man. I believe that's what you gentlemen would call romantic fiction."

The voice was unmistakenly transatlantic, but one with an unattractive flat timbre. Like Montgomery's heavily oiled hair it created a less than favorable impression; and Parsons found himself uncharacteristically, and for no reason he could readily explain, feeling a dislike for the man.

"I confess I'm not a great reader of modern American fiction," he replied politely, "and I know little about the early days of America, either in fact or fiction. But I'll be sure to look out for your books in future."

Montgomery made a pretense at a light laugh in response to what he took to be an attempt by Parsons at humor.

"I'm afraid my reputation is not as great as Alexander implies," he said. "My fellow countrymen don't yet appear ready for home-grown authors. They still prefer to import what they consider to be superior work from these shores. That's one reason for my visit to England. It seems essential for any serious writer to visit here and absorb some of the culture that has produced such great literary figures. And in the course of this education I was fortunate enough to meet Alexander and Geoffrey."

Montgomery smiled gratefully towards his newly-found friends, but it seemed to Parsons that there was a trace of cynicism in his words.

"And what of you, sir," the Canadian enquired. "What are your links with the great de Courcey family?"

"Very tenuous these days, I'm afraid," replied Parsons. "But some years ago Alexander, Philip and I were all at the same dreadful boarding school."

Parsons smiled towards Montgomery.

"I sincerely hope you don't have such institutions in Canada," he said. "There are many Englishmen who swear by them, of course, but I think we three would willingly have foregone the experience."

Parsons waited for the laughter to cease before continuing. "As you can see I'm some years senior to my friends," he said. "In fact Alexander was my fag for a year."

Montgomery looked puzzled at the expression.

"A fag," explained Parsons," is a sort of servant. Like officers have in the army. But believe it or not a fag at an English public school often leads as harsh a life as any lowly domestic servant. In Alexander's case I didn't thrash him as much as was customary. So he decided I wasn't such a bad fellow. And in due course we became friends. Unfortunately over the years we went our separate ways and lost contact, that was until a few weeks ago when I met him at an exhibition of Impressionist paintings. That was when he was kind enough to invite me here for the celebration."

"Ah, the Impressionists," said Montgomery. "You must tell me all about them. In Canada we are rather out of touch with such avant-garde ideas."

"I'm sure there'll be time enough for that later, Harrison," said Alexander, unexpectedly dutiful. "But I think it's time we were thinking of dressing for dinner."

From his bedroom Parsons bedroom could see the square towers of the barbican through which they had earlier entered the castle. Beyond the west wall of the castle the last rays of September sunshine bathed the upper branches of the trees and cast long shadows across the grass lawns. How different, he thought, was this timeless view from that of the smoking chimneys he could see from his small office in Old Scotland yard.

There had been a welcoming fire in the grate when he reached his room. His case had been unpacked and his evening clothes lay ready for him on the bed. The only other light in the room came from a small oil-lamp on his bed-side-table, and until then he had not realized that there was no gas lighting in the castle. He knew that this form of lighting had not yet reached many country areas, but he was nevertheless surprised to find that such a notable house as Beaumont was still without it.

Although generally a quick and meticulous dresser Parsons struggled in the flickering lamp-light to put on the unfamiliar evening dress. It was one he had borrowed from a more socially-conscious colleague with a trimmer figure, and in consequence found himself wearing a jacket with sleeves that were too long and trousers that cut uncomfortably into his waist. As he struggled with his white bow-tie and squinted at his dim reflection in the mirror he was forced to admit that his colleagues' choice of a nick-name was very appropriate. The small round glasses with their thin metal frames that he wore for close work conveyed a wise, owlish appearance, and the receding hairline that concerned him so much only served to further emphasize what was already a prominent forehead. No one would ever readily take him for a policeman.

He frowned at the sight of the bulging waistline spilling over the waistband of his trousers. Although he might walk regularly between his lodgings in Camberwell and his office, he knew he was fast losing the battle to control his weight. But the prospect of ever having to cut back on any of his culinary pleasures dismayed him, and he certainly had no intention of starting while at Beaumont. This visit had been eagerly anticipated for too long.

Sherry was being taken in the Drawing Room when Parsons arrived. Across the corridor in the minstrels' gallery above the Great Hall a string quartet was playing a lively selection from Gilbert and Sullivan. Feeling rather self-conscious in his ill-fitting dress suit he was pleased to find Philip standing alone by the door.

"Where's your father?" he enquired. "I'd imagined that he'd be here to greet his guests."

"Father doesn't have t-time for such social niceties," explained Philip. "We don't expect to see him before dinner. He'll still be upstairs d-drinking with Ashton and Fitzherbert. He relies on Annabelle and cousin Paul to do the entertaining."

Philip nodded in the direction of a tall man with dark curls who was deeply engrossed in conversation with his auburn-haired companion. They made an especially handsome couple, even in the midst of such an elegant gathering.

"Is Annabelle a friend of your sisters?" asked Parsons.

Philip laughed ironically.

"I suppose you might d-describe her as that. But my eldest sister, Catherine, can't stand her. No, she's more than a friend. Annabelle is my step-mother."

Parsons was greatly surprised to learn that Lord de Courcey had a beautiful wife who seemed but a few years older than himself. But he felt it inappropriate to say so to Philip.

"Why should that be surprising?" he said. "I can see she's many years younger than your father. But surely that's not so uncommon."

"You'll see what I mean, Everett. Just w-wait until you meet father."

A loud unmistakably military-sounding voice interrupted their conversation.

"Philip, my dear boy," the voice boomed, "we haven't seen you for weeks. How are you? And who's your young friend?"

"T-this is E-everett Parsons, sir," said Philip, his stammer more pronounced than before. "E-everett, this is Colonel and Mrs. Howard. C-colonel Howard is our Chief Constable."

"I'm honored to meet you, sir," said Parsons, thinking how alike the two Howards were, both of them tall, amply proportioned and wearing expressions that suggested a lack of cerebral activity. "You also, ma'am."

"You must be one of Alexander's bohemian friends we hear so much about."

Mrs. Howard's voice was as loud and over-bearing as her husband's. She would have made an excellent drill-sergeant, thought Parsons.

"I'm sorry to disappoint you, ma'am," he replied meekly, "but I'm only a simple policeman."

"S-simple policeman, indeed," said Philip, eager to impress the Howards with the caliber of his friends. "Everett was one of our schools finest scholars, and now he's a detective inspector in the Metropolitan Police."

An identical expression of disbelief appeared simultaneously on the faces of both Howards. It was abundantly clear that police inspectors in Hampshire were made from a different mold than that which had produced Parsons.

§§§

A break in the music and the opportune appearance of Johnson to announce that dinner was served enabled Parsons to escape from the Howards. He mumbled an excuse about having to look for his name on the seating plan and then joined the end of the procession led by Lady Annabelle and Paul de Courcey as it filed across the corridor to the Great Hall. The quartet had resumed playing, and the rollicking notes of *The Roast Beef of Old England* accompanied them all to the dinner table.

The Hall looked magnificent, lit only by candelabra on the long dining table and a huge log fire at the far end of the Hall. The silver tableware and fine glass reflected these lights a thousand-fold, while shadows flickered across the high beamed ceiling. In the shadows at each side of the table, visible only by their pale faces and white aprons, the servant-girls stood motionless, waiting in silence until each diner had reached their appointed place. At a sign from Johnson the musicians stopped playing, an expectant silence fell on the assembled company, and a tremulous voice offered a short prayer of thanksgiving for the food that was to be served. There followed the scraping of chairs as first the ladies and then the men took their places at table, and with another signal from Johnson the servants sprang into action laying the white china plates bearing the de Courcey crest. At the same time the musicians resumed playing with a selection of country airs.

℘℘℘

There were only nineteen at table. Far fewer than Parsons had imagined there would be. The announcement in *The*

Times had implied a much larger gathering. Not that he was too concerned about that. He had no great love for large social occasions, preferring instead good food and wine and the company of a few friends. He was also pleased to find himself seated at Lady Annabelle's end of the table, well away from Lord Quentin and his military clique. From what he had already heard about his host and from his earlier encounter with Fitzherbert he had formed a firm impression that he would be far from comfortable in their company.

Now that he was closer to Annabelle he found her even more beautiful than he had first thought. She had unusually pale green eyes, a full sensuous mouth, and long auburn hair that looked especially fine in the light of the candles. Her low-cut black velvet dress complemented her slim white shoulders and tantalizingly offered a glimpse of small well-rounded breasts. It took all of Parsons' control to stop himself from staring at them.

"You must be one of Alexander's friends." Her unexpectedly husky voice interrupted Parsons' reverie.

"I am indeed, my lady. My name is Everett Parsons. I knew both Alexander and Philip when they were at school, although they were some years my junior."

"Please call me Annabelle. Everyone else does. Titles have their place. But not amongst friends."

She smiled sweetly at Parsons, flattering him to think himself a friend of hers on such a short acquaintance. To his embarrassment he felt his cheeks flushing and was grateful that the darkness concealed what was for him an unexpected display of emotion.

"Everett," she said. "Such an unusual name. I don't believe I've ever met anyone called by that name before."

"It was my mother's choice," Parsons explained. "She was always a great lover of art, especially the Pre-Raphaelite Brotherhood. John Everett Mills was one of the group, and my mother was especially fond of his rather sentimental studies of pretty children."

Parsons found himself blushing again. It was somewhat of an irony that his dear late mother should have chosen to associate anyone as graceless as himself with paintings of such beautiful people. How blind can a mother's love be?

He noticed that Annabelle was examining him in a mildly amused fashion. No doubt the same thought had crossed her mind.

"Let me introduce your dinner companions, Everett," she said gaily, enunciating each syllable of his name for a fraction longer than normal. "The gentleman on your left is George Hamilton. George is our doctor, and is married to Anne, one of Quentin's daughters. Opposite you is Geoffrey Montagu, one of Alexander's clever friends. But I expect you've already met him."

Parsons turned to shake the hand of the doctor, a well attired man in his forties with short, dark hair that was greying at the temples and a neatly trimmed moustache.

"I've already had the pleasure of meeting Mrs. Howard," explained Parsons. "She was kind enough to think that, like Montagu, I was a poet."

"I can see what she means, Everett. You do have a sensitive face. But do tell me, what is your profession?"

"I'm a policeman," said Parsons, aware once more that his color was rising.

"A policeman," she trilled. "But that's wonderful. You and Charles should have a lot to talk about."

That seemed highly unlikely, thought Parsons. The problems of policing town and country in the modern world called for very different approaches—indeed the majority of rural police forces did not think it necessary to establish criminal investigation sections. And judging by the Chief Constable's earlier reaction Parsons thought it unlikely he would ever be recruited by the Hampshire police force.

Annabelle continued her introductions.

"I expect you've already met Harrison Montgomery, one of Alexander's creative friends. But I don't think you've had the opportunity to meet another visitor from across the Atlantic, our long lost cousin, Paul."

"It's truly a great pleasure to meet you, Everett."

The soft, lazy drawl was quite unlike Montgomery's. And unlike Montgomery, Paul appeared to Parsons to be someone who had always enjoyed the good things in life. It was written plainly over his finely chiseled features, dark hazel eyes, carefully groomed side-whiskers, and even white teeth. And it was obvious in the ease and confidence of his behavior.

"To my untutored ear it appears that you are not from the same part of North America as Mr Montgomery," commented Parsons.

"You're very observant, Everett," said Paul, giving more attention to his well-manicured nails than to Parsons. "I come from Georgia, from what we were once proud to call the Confederacy. Mr. Montgomery, I believe, is a Yankee. From New York, if I'm not mistaken."

"Now then, Paul," said Annabelle, patting his hand gently, "that didn't sound very complimentary to poor Harrison. As it happens he's a Canadian, and not one of those nasty Yankees you detest so much. But if you can't say anything nice about him, perhaps you should concentrate on those closer to your heart. Like me, for instance."

She bestowed one of her melting smiles upon him.

"That, Annabelle, will be my pleasure," he said, immediately losing interest in Parsons and turning his undivided attention to his hostess.

To Parsons' immense disappointment the food at dinner was plain country-fare. Pea Soup, Jugged Hare and College Pudding served with a brandy sauce. The de Courceys it appeared were not extravagant hosts. His interest in food was legendary amongst his colleagues, and he had tried their patience to the limit during the past few weeks by describing in great detail the culinary delights he was anticipating at Beaumont.

The conversation at the far end of the table was becoming increasingly noisy, dominated by Lord Quentin's imposing voice. Even from a distance and in the dim light of the candles he appeared a formidable character, with an aggressive jaw line and fierce, dark eyes that glowed like coals in the candlelight. Occasionally he leant back in his chair to allow someone else to speak, and at such times he tugged gently on his long Dundreary whiskers. The gesture, thought Parsons, was surprisingly feminine for one so demonstrably masculine in his appearance. The whiskers were so long that they brushed the lapels of Lord Quentin's dress jacket.

Parsons had seen many paintings of men from a generation or so before who had worn their hair in such a fashion, but this was the first person he had seen in the flesh. It was not a fashion he found at all attractive, and he thought it unusual for a man with a military background like Lord Quentin to sport such a rakish style.

"Lord de Courcey appears to be enjoying the evening," Parsons commented to his neighbor, the doctor.

"He's drunk, if that's what you mean," Hamilton replied in a matter-of-fact voice, as though it were normal behavior for his host to be in that condition. "He's probably been drinking all afternoon with his chums and will probably continue drinking long into the night. He has an amazing constitution for one of his age, I'll say that for him. But the way things are going I can foresee trouble tonight, and if you take my advice you'll seek the safety of your room as soon as you can after dinner. Events tend to get out of hand here on evenings like this."

"I'm intrigued," said Parsons, warming to the doctor's blunt appraisal of their host, and reckoning by his calm demeanor that he was a methodical man who could be relied upon in a crisis.

"You'll see what I mean. Just remember what I said and keep well out of it."

"Is that Captain Ashton sitting next to his lordship?"

"Captain Sir Cecil Ashton, to give him his full title. Another so-called hero of the Crimean War. What a collection! Quentin, Ashton and Fitzherbert. No wonder it was such a disastrous campaign. I can only assume that the Russian commanders were even more disorganized than our own. It just saddens me to think that our brave soldiers were led by such incompetent fools. None more so than these three."

As if to illustrate his point there was another loutish outburst of laughter from the head of the table. This time Colonel Howard was to the fore.

"There's another military buffoon for you," confided Hamilton.

"You mean the Chief Constable," said Parsons, trying to control the grin he could feel spreading over his face. It felt good to have his opinion of a senior policeman so amply corroborated.

"Chief Constable indeed. My dog knows more about policing than Howard. He was only given the job because Quentin has influence in the county and likes to surround himself with old soldiers. You'll find them everywhere on the estate. He pays them a pittance. But most of them have nowhere else to go. Quentin, of course, knows that. He's an exploiter and a bully and I pity any poor devil who has to work for him."

"But that surely doesn't apply to Colonel Howard. He was a senior officer."

"That's perfectly true. But from what I know he has no money of his own, and it isn't easy to keep up appearances on the meager pension he receives from the War Office. He needed a job as much as Smith in the stables. Apart from that it must be very convenient for Quentin to have the local Chief Constable in his debt."

♕♕♕

Parsons knew only too well from his own experience that there were many advantages to be gained from having senior officers in one's debt. He had seen enough of the patronage that existed in the Metropolitan Police to know how the system worked. But he thought it unwise to raise the issue with someone of such short acquaintance, even though he felt sure the doctor would agree with him.

Parsons fondness for good food was only exceeded by his love of fine wine, and he had felt confident before he arrived that he would find the cellar at Beaumont well stocked. From what he had sampled so far he had once again been mistaken.

"I had imagined that there was an excellent wine cellar at the castle, doctor," he said diplomatically, declining Johnson's offer of a second glass of claret.

"Not any longer, Parsons. In the past it was the envy of the county. But when it's consumed at the rate it has been for several years, I'm afraid it becomes a case of quantity rather than quality. This inferior claret is probably a recent vintage that has barely recovered from its journey across the Channel. I'm just hoping that Quentin hasn't finished the 'forty-two Noval.'"

Parsons could only pray he had not. To sample a port of that quality would be enough in itself to have made the journey worthwhile.

At that point Hamilton became engaged in conversation with the lady on his left, and Parsons took the opportunity of listening more intently to the quartet as it played a selection of rousing waltzes by Strauss. When he closed his eyes he imagined how magnificent a grand ball in the Great Hall would be. He could see in his mind's eye the ladies' dresses swirling as they spun with their partners to the romantic melodies. Even though he knew himself to be an awkward dancer he imagined himself partnering Annabelle, the two of them spinning faster than every other pair, and he the envy of every other man. Overcome by the power of the music and unaware of what he was doing he began tapping the waltz rhythm on the table with his fingers.

"You seem to be enjoying the music, Everett."

Paul's drawl interrupted Parsons' reverie. Opening his eyes he found himself the object of the American's close scrutiny. For a moment he was foolish enough to think that his thoughts had been transparent, and for a second time that evening he found himself blushing.

Annabelle was now talking with Montagu and it was the turn of the luckless Montgomery to entertain the formidable Mrs. Howard.

"Is this your first visit to England, Mr. de Courcey?" Parsons asked after an awkward interval during which he composed his thoughts.

"It is, and I would be greatly sorry were I ever to leave these shores again."

"I'm gratified to hear that," said Parsons. "What in particular has made such a favorable impression on you?"

"Practically everything. There is such beautiful countryside here and Lord and Lady de Courcey have been unbelievably hospitable to me. Quentin treats me almost like a son and has told me I can stay here as long as I want. You can have no idea what it feels to be part of a family again.

"It must indeed be a welcome experience," Parsons said, surprised to hear of Lord de Courcey's paternal instincts, "but how did you lose touch with your English family in the first place?"

"It all happened several generations back. The actual circumstances are lost in the mists of time. But my great-great-grandfather ran away from Beaumont after a row with his father," explained Paul. "He was the youngest son and by all accounts the black sheep of the family. One day he went to America and never returned. In those days it was a pretty wild place, so when his family never heard from him I imagine they thought he'd been killed by Indians—if indeed they cared anything about him at all."

"But he obviously survived and prospered," said Parson, acknowledging the elegant man beside him.

"From what my father told me my ancestors were a pretty tough lot, and from what I've seen since I've been here it runs in the family. Early this century my people settled down to farm in Georgia, where over the years they built a fine house and ran a successful plantation. We'd be there to this day were it not for the war against the damned Yankees.

Parsons was surprised to hear the bitterness in Paul's voice. The civil war in America, after all, had been over for fifteen years.

"And afterwards?" he asked.

"Nothing," said Paul. "The Yankees made sure of that. They burnt down the house, destroyed our cotton, and to use their mealy-mouth words they *liberated* our blacks. I was away at the war at the time, but from what I learned afterwards it broke my parents hearts. And when I returned after being incarcerated in a filthy Yankee prison-of-war camp all I had to remind me of my past life was my parents' gravestone."

"What a terrible story," said Parsons sympathetically, noticing how across the table Montgomery was doing his best to ignore Mrs. Howard's monologue and to focus instead upon Paul's story. "What did you do then? Did you have other family?"

"I was alone in the world, with no money, and very few prospects in a country dominated by Yankee carpet-baggers. So I decided to trade on the only things I knew well. I had been brought up a gentleman, and while I was in the camp I developed a knack with the cards. So I became a professional gambler, working the riverboats on the old Mississippi. They were good years I can tell you."

He gave Parsons a knowing wink and lowered his voice.

"I'm sure you follow my drift. It's perfectly true what they say about hot-blooded southern belles. And after the war there were more of them than there were eligible young beaux to satisfy them. It was a wild time I can tell you."

He seemed particularly pleased with his achievements and flashed his immaculate teeth at Parsons.

"It's hard to imagine what made you give up such an attractive way of life and come to England," said Parsons innocently.

"It was fate, Everett. Fate. Quite by chance I met an Englishman at the card table one night who came from around these parts and knew of the family. As ours was such an unusual name I thought they might be relatives of mine. I had no ties, I was curious about my roots. So here I am."

"What a remarkable story. And what a fortuitous ending. To my shame I know very little about the history of your country, even as recent an event as the civil war. Perhaps you can spare me some of your time during my stay to educate me."

"That would give me great pleasure, Everett. But I can do better than that. I'm not what you would call a literary man, but in New York I picked up a book about the civil war intending to read it on my way over here. We front-line soldiers didn't always understand the higher strategies of the war, so I thought I would learn something from reading it."

He gave Parsons another of his expansive grins and lowered his voice.

"Unfortunately I got distracted by a poker school on the ship and never opened the book. You're more than welcome to borrow it. When you've read it you'll probably know more than I do about the war."

Dinner was drawing to a close. The dishes had been cleared and cut-glass decanters of port were circulating clockwise around the table. When they had arrived back with Lord Quentin and he was satisfied that everyone's glass was filled he rapped loudly on the table with his knuckles.

An instant silence descended upon the Great Hall as he rose to his feet.

"Ladies and gentlemen," he announced. "The Queen."

There was a scraping of chairs as everyone rose to their feet, the anthem was played by the musicians, and Parsons was delighted to find that the Noval was every bit as good as he had hoped.

A few minutes later the toast was the 18th Royal Lancers and their heroic exploits at the Battle of Sevastopol. This was followed by the stirring sounds of *The Brave Lancer,* the regimental march of the Lancers and loud cries of "The Regiment!" from the head of the table as the toast was drunk. Parsons, like the majority of the guests, made only a token response to the toast, content merely to enjoy the fine wine.

The decanters circulated once more, allowing the gentlemen the opportunity to recharge their glasses as the ladies prepared to leave for coffee and chocolate in the Drawing Room. But before inviting them to withdraw, Lord Quentin rose to his feet once more.

"Ladies and gentlemen," he boomed, resting his hands on the table and thrusting his chin forward belligerently.

From the way he swayed it was clear that he was drunk, but not so drunk that he had lost control of his speech. Hamilton was right, thought Parsons. The man could hold his drink.

"I appreciate your presence here tonight," he said slowly, enunciating each word with care, "to help my friends and I celebrate the famous victory that brought the Crimean War to such a successful conclusion."

He paused briefly to allow his remarks to be enthusiastically received by those around him, frowning at Fitzherbert when he continued slapping the table with the palm of his hand. Then he continued.

"But there is another matter of a more personal nature I would like to mention before the ladies leave us."

An ominous silence fell over the table. Even a stranger like Parsons sensed the tension in the room. Whatever was coming was unexpected. Even Johnson, he noticed, looked anxiously towards Lord Quentin at this obvious break with tradition.

"The future of the de Courceys and a great estate like Beaumont is not just my concern," Lord Quentin continued. "It is a matter of national importance."

There were a few muted cries of "Hear! Hear!" from Ashton and Fitzherbert, but only a growing sense of unease showed on the faces of the family.

"For some time now I have become increasingly concerned with the provisions of my will."

The anxiety around the table was now palpable; and as though savoring the reaction, Lord Quentin allowed several seconds to elapse before continuing. He inclined his head towards a man sitting half-way along the table who had hitherto been hidden from Parsons.

"I have asked my solicitor, Andrew Robertson, here tonight not just because he is a good friend and faithful servant to the family, but because at eleven tomorrow morning in the Library he will read the terms of my new will."

Lord Quentin seemed pleased with the devastating effect of his dramatic announcement and his eyes swept the table seeking the reactions from individual members of his family. Apparently satisfied with what he saw he resumed his seat and announced that the ladies might now leave the table.

The strained silence continued as Annabelle led the other ladies from the table, interrupted by jeers from Ashton and Fitzherbert when Alexander, Philip and Montagu chose to join them.

"That should give them something to talk about over their cocoa," said Lord Quentin in a voice loud enough to be heard by everyone. "Now you can fetch the brandy, Johnson. The night is young, gentlemen, and there are pleasures yet in store."

-4-

ord Quentin led those who had remained to the far end of the Hall where a semi-circle of leather arm-chairs had been arranged around the large stone fireplace. While they settled into their chairs Johnson brought decanters of brandy, glasses and cigars and placed them on strategically placed occasional tables that were within easy reach of everyone. At the other end of the Hall the musicians had finished packing their instruments, and their footsteps could be heard descending the wooden stairs from the minstrels' gallery and into the corridor leading from the Hall to the rear of the castle. While this was happening Johnson extinguished the candles on the dining table. The Hall slowly faded into darkness and an expectant silence descended on the group around the fire.

Lord Quentin's deep voice, coarsened by hours of drinking, cut into the silence.

"This is a favorite haunt of mine at this time of night," he announced, "I share it with my ancestors and a few personal mementos."

He gestured around him to family portraits now barely visible in the flickering light of the fire and to a halo of bayonets above the fireplace.

A few curious eyes tried to penetrate the darkness, but most, like Parsons, sat back in their chairs awaiting with curiosity upon the pleasures that had been promised.

"By a process of elimination you must be Inspector Parsons."

Parsons found himself the object of his host's penetrating gaze. Seated contentedly next to the fire with a cigar in one hand and a glass of brandy in the other, the consternation that he had caused at the end of the dinner seemed already far from Lord Quentin's mind. To the casual glance he appeared the epitome of a country gentleman innocently enjoying the company of friends. But the fierce eyes that had fixed upon Parsons were those of a man not to be trifled with.

"That is true, your lordship," Parsons replied, "and as this is my first chance of speaking with you I would like to take this opportunity of thanking you for inviting me to Beaumont. It is a great privilege."

"Damned if I did," Lord Quentin snorted. "You're Alexander's guest not mine. Though a fine host he's turned out to be. But in his regrettable absence allow me to introduce you to some of your fellow guests."

The words were flat and cold, the dismissive tone uncharacteristic of a father talking of his eldest son. Any illusion of a jovial host had gone. For a few moments Lord Quentin's eyes locked with Parsons,' then his gaze moved slowly around the remainder of the group.

"The gentleman on my left is Sir Henry Rawlinson. Henry is the husband of my daughter, Elizabeth."

The small, plump figure with a few strands of fair, wispy hair brushed sideways across his balding head lifted a limp hand and waggled his fingers in Parsons' direction.

"Pleased to meet you, dear boy," he said.

Lord Quentin continued with the introductions.

"I believe you have met my old friends, George Fitz-herbert and Charles Howard, but not this scoundrel, Cecil Ashton."

Ashton raised his monocle to inspect Parsons, the green ribbon attached to it visible against the white of his ruffled shirt. An expression more akin to a sneer than a smile flitted across his face.

"Charmed, I'm sure," he drawled.

"The two serious-looking gentlemen on your left are the Reverend Joshua Harding, our spiritual guardian; and Andrew Robertson, who cares for our more secular needs. As I mentioned at dinner, we shall be hearing more from Robertson tomorrow.

The vicar's bulbous, restless eyes engaged briefly with Parsons.' He smiled shyly but said nothing, a man apparently of nervous disposition who was uncomfortable in the present company. No doubt, thought Parsons, he had been given instructions to appear at dinner for the sole purpose of saying Grace. Like so many priests in rural Anglican parishes he would be at the beck and call of the local land-owning family which paid his small stipend. In this case that would be the de Courceys.

In complete contrast, Andrew Robertson seemed a man well satisfied with himself, confident in both his professional and social standing. Immaculate in his evening suit, he drew contentedly on his cigar.

"I understand you're a detective, young man," he said with the assured tones of a man of the law.

Being called a young man by someone less than ten years his senior did not endear Parsons to the solicitor. Nevertheless, his style and manner of speech made a favorable impression. Unless he was mistaken, this was the caliber of man Parsons had frequently seen in action at the Old Bailey. Such talent seemed wasted in a country practice. Unless, of course, it was something other than professional ambition that kept him in Hampshire.

Parsons' thoughts were interrupted by Lord Quentin.

"Of course, you will know our two transatlantic visitors, Mr. Harrison Montgomery and my nephew, Paul."

Montgomery sat on the opposite side of the fireplace to Lord Quentin, Paul de Courcey on Parsons' right. They both nodded amiably towards him, but he sensed that Paul was not pleased at being included in the same *transatlantic* package as Montgomery.

"I believe you are to be congratulated, inspector, for your part in sending those damned Fenians to the gallows."

To Parsons' surprise it was Ashton who spoke. It appeared he was better informed than Parsons had imagined such a dilettante to be.

"I'm pleased to say I did have a small part to play in the recent police operation," he replied, noticing with some pleasure how his standing within the group seemed to have improved markedly as a result of Ashton's observation. He was especially pleased to see the look of surprise on the faces of Fitzherbert and Howard.

"And have you come to Beaumont to protect us?" asked Lord Quentin, with a snort of laughter that was immediately echoed by Fitzherbert and Howard.

"I'm sure neither you nor anyone else here is in any danger," Parsons observed, "although I did think the announcement in this morning's paper was a little unwise in view of the recent Irish outrages. I'm sure you're aware that in the past there have been Fenian attacks on social gatherings such as this."

"And which announcement would that be?" demanded Lord Quentin.

"The announcement in the *Times*, your lordship, giving information about this dinner."

"That's none of my doing," Lord Quentin said angrily. "I've no wish to inform the whole damned world how I spend my time. Does anyone else know about this?"

He glared at the faces around him seeking an answer, but no one replied.

"I'll speak with Alexander and Catherine about this in the morning," he said sternly. "It's probably an attempt by one or other of them to impress their friends. It can't be Philip. He has none to impress."

Lord Quentin laughed heartily at his own joke, releasing the slight sense of unease that had arisen from the news of the mysterious announcement.

"Hang all Fenian bastards! Hang all bog-trotting Irish-men! That's what I say."

It did not surprise Parsons to hear such sentiments expressed by Fitzherbert, increasingly slumped in his chair and rapidly becoming the worse for his day's drinking.

"Excuse my ignorance, but will somebody enlighten me as to who these Fenians are I keep hearing about."

Having no wish to allow the likes of Fitzherbert to vent their prejudices, Parsons seized the opportunity to provide Paul with an answer.

"The Fenians were a band of legendary warriors, Mr. de Courcey," he explained. "The name was adopted by the Irish Republican Brotherhood when it formed in 1858. In America you have a similar organization which calls itself the Fenian Brotherhood. They are both devoted to the same cause. Irish self-government. No doubt with your own problems after the civil war it probably escaped the attention of most people that the American Fenians launched a series of raids against Canada, hoping that such actions against our North American possessions would encourage us to grant Ireland its independence. It seemed an unlikely tactic to me. But perhaps they thought the American government would help them, seeing that many in Britain had been sympathetic to the Confederate cause during the civil war. Needless to say, no help came and the raids proved ineffective."

"Well I'll be damned," said Paul. "I'd no idea my country was the center of revolutionary activity against the British Empire. On the other hand it doesn't altogether surprise me. Yankees are capable of undermining any stable civilized society."

"You're better versed in American history than you would have us believe, Parsons," said Montgomery quietly.

But there was a antagonistic edge to his next words, which were directed at Paul.

"Do I take it, Mr. de Courcey, that a Southern gentleman's idea of what constitutes a civilized society is one based on the ownership of slaves?"

The question was greeted by a hostile silence. Either Montgomery was a brave man, thought Parsons, or as a Canadian visiting England for the first time he was oblivious to the sympathies of the English upper classes. The expressions on the faces of Lord Quentin, Colonel Howard and Paul were particularly vehement. But surprisingly it was Sir Henry Rawlinson who was the first to speak.

"I have never had any wish to own slaves," he said pompously, "but I do believe in a natural order in society. Some people and some classes are better able to govern and provide leadership. Aristotle believed that. Such leadership requires breeding, often only acquired over many generations, and if it is the right kind of leadership every class will respect it. The majority of us," and at this point his glance included everybody except Montgomery, "know the value of a gentlemanly education; and I believe that in this country we have schools and institutions that have produced an ideal which is the envy of the world. Don't you agree, vicar?"

The question came as an unpleasant surprise to Joshua Harding, and his nervous reaction made it clear that he was unhappy at being drawn into any discussion that was at all controversial.

"Yes, what's the Church's attitude towards the question of class, Mr. Harding?"

Andrew Robertson's question sounded innocent enough, but there was a condescending smirk on his face.

The vicar thought deeply before replying, and stammered nervously when he eventually spoke.

"The Church, of course, b-believes that our time on Earth is b-but a preparation for eternity. In this life we must all accept the p-position in which the Good Lord has seen fit to place us. I can do no b-better than quote the words of the b-beautiful hymn we sang in my humble church last Sunday:

The rich man in his castle
The p-poor man at his gate
G-god made them high and l-lowly
And ordered their estate.'"

He paused to wipe beads of perspiration from his upper lip with a large white handkerchief.

"Of course, the Church has n-nothing against any man seeking to improve himself, p-providing he adopts the traditions and b-behaviour of a Christian gentleman."

The vicar looked across the fireplace hoping to find approval from his patron.

"Well said, vicar," bellowed Lord Quentin, clapping his hands together slowly in mock applause. "I'm glad to know you're not considering joining the ranks of the Evangelicals in the Church of England. There's no place for socialism in the Church.

Harding wriggled with pleasure at this praise. For his part, Parsons squirmed with embarrassment at the Christian message he had just heard. Like many with an interest in science, his religious beliefs had foundered on the discoveries of Darwin, and he found the sort of sanctimonious senti-ments expressed by the vicar to have no place in a civilized society at the end of the nineteenth-century.

"And would it be Christian gentlemen of the sort you refer to who meted out justice to Johnson Whittaker?" asked Montgomery cynically.

"Who the hell is Johnson Whittaker, Montgomery?" demanded Lord Quentin, infuriated by the sarcastic com-ments of someone he clearly regarded as a social upstart.

"He was a mere black man, Lord Quentin," Montgom-ery explained condescendingly. "One of the token few ad-mitted to the United States Military Academy at West Point after the civil war. By all accounts he was an exemplary stu-dent, but that was not enough to prevent him from being shunned by his fellow white cadets. Earlier this year he was attacked by three of these cadets, who slashed his hands, face and ears with a razor. As one of these so-called gentlemen said, it was how they treated hogs in the South. Whittaker identified his attackers, but none of them confessed, and since it was assumed that white gentlemen-cadets would never lie he was accused of faking the whole incident to discredit the Academy."

Montgomery allowed himself a wry smile before con-tinuing.

"Justice was finally seen to be done," he said bitterly, "when Whittaker was court-martialled and expelled."

It did not surprise Parsons that he had not heard the story before, news such as this was unlikely to be published in any of the London newspapers. He was disappointed, nev-ertheless, to learn that even in America, a country that had boasted equal rights for all its citizens, and had just fought a long and bloody war to free its slaves, the same prejudices existed as did in England.

"I pray to God that the day never arrives when the word of a black is accepted before that of a gentleman," said Paul, his voice trembling with emotion. "We have our own way in the South of dealing with uppity niggers and no-good carpet-bagging Yankees."

"And so do we, Quentin," slurred Fitzherbert. "Tell them about Jamaica."

Lord Quentin's expression turned to stone. He gripped the arms of his chair so tightly that the whites of his knuckles were visible even in the half-light. For one moment Parsons thought he was going to strike Fitzherbert, although Fitzherbert was far too drunk to realize the reaction his words had caused. The controversial governor-ship of Jamaica might now be past history, but it was clearly still a taboo subject in Beaumont.

"What happened in Jamaica, Quentin?" asked Paul innocently.

"It was all a long time ago, Paul," Lord Quentin replied coldly, "and it is not something I wish to talk about now."

It was understandable that he should feel so, thought Parsons. The episode had been a national scandal and had made Lord Quentin a *cause celebre*. About fifteen years before he had been stationed in Jamaica with his regiment and had become acting Governor when the previous incumbent had unexpectedly died. Shortly afterwards there had been a rebellion of black farmers which had been ruthlessly suppressed by British troops. In the course of the following weeks over four hundred black people were massacred and at least six hundred flogged, including women and children.

Although a Royal Commission had white-washed the whole affair, there were still those who demanded Lord Quentin's prosecution for murder. However, a much larger and more influential group somewhat surprisingly led by middle-class intellectuals, thought he should be exonerated and rewarded with a seat in Parliament. Eventually the furor died down and on his return from Jamaica Lord Quentin had retired from the Army and slipped quietly away to the country. The message to the world, however, was clear. In order to control its Empire the British ruling class would employ any measures they saw fit to pacify those they considered to be lesser races.

Such sentiments were obviously still shared by the majority of the men sitting around the fire.

"You've nothing to be ashamed of, Quentin," said Ashton. "We all know that the only way to command the respect of people like Irish, blacks and even our own soldiers, is to have the skin off their backs. Without the lash we'd soon have lost control in the Crimea."

A murmur of support from all but Montgomery, Hamilton and Parsons was acknowledged by Lord Quentin refilling his glass and emptying it in one long swig. The dark, brooding expression that had settled on his countenance gradually lifted.

"Gentlemen," he said loudly and unexpectedly, "a toast to the ladies. God bless them. Gentlemen, raise your glasses. The Ladies!"

The toast was echoed with varying degrees of enthusiasm by all, but there was a general sense of relief that discussion of the uncomfortable subject appeared to be over.

"That seems to be an appropriate point at which to take my leave. My own lady is waiting and we have a long journey ahead. Thank you, Quentin, for a most enjoyable evening."

Colonel Howard rose to his feet and was followed by Sir Henry Rawlinson, Doctor Hamilton, Robertson and the vicar, all of whom made their various excuses. For a moment Lord Quentin looked irritated and Parsons anticipated another outburst. Then he realized who it was that had chosen to leave.

"Of course, you married men have your responsibilities," he said understandingly. "You, of course, are excused, vicar. And you Robertson. You'll need to keep a clear head tomorrow. But I forbid anyone else to leave."

Parsons watched the group hurrying across the Hall, thinking how anxious they were to escape. Recalling Hamilton's earlier warning he was on the point of leaving himself when Lord Quentin spoke again.

"Well, gentlemen," he smirked. "We've reached the hard core at last. First, another brandy all round. Then the treat you've all been waiting for."

With his refilled glass in his hand Lord Quentin walked towards the door the servants had used when entering and leaving the Hall during the course of the dinner. His unsteady progress was the first indication that the long day's drinking had begun to take its toll.

"Johnson!" he bellowed, "we're ready now. You can send them in."

He resumed his seat, rubbing his hands and winking at Ashton and Fitzherbert.

"How many hosts offer their guests after-dinner entertainment of this quality?" he asked.

With a rustle of petticoats the six maid-servants who had been waiting at table entered the room and filed into the center of the semi-circle of chairs. They lined up nervously opposite the fire-place. They had changed out of the prim black dresses they had worn earlier into low-cut evening gowns that allowed a generous view of their pale shoulders and breasts.

"Don't you think my Irish fillies look beautiful in Annabelle's castoffs?" purred Lord Quentin. "Take your pick, gentlemen. They're all available to you tonight, except for young Claire."

As he spoke he rose to his feet again and swayed towards the girls, making his way slowly along the rear of the line. He stopped behind the smallest and youngest girl. She stood with her head bowed, her long, dark curly hair hanging forward, and her eyes averted from the lecherous gazes that were now directed at her. When Lord Quentin placed his hands on her shoulders she shuddered visibly.

"Claire has been in England for only a short while," he explained, "and it is the rule of the house that all new girls must be broken in by me."

His hands left the girl's shoulders and moved slowly down her arms.

"I've been saving Claire for this special occasion," he whispered.

As if to demonstrate his intentions he began to fondle her breasts. The girl gave a small whimper of protest, but then fell silent. She made no attempt to move.

Parsons knew that what few laws existed to protect servants from unscrupulous employers were inadequate and frequently ignored, but never had he imagined finding young servants so openly abused. In London it was not uncommon for working class women to be driven into prostitution by economic necessity, frequently as a result of unwanted pregnancies terminating their employment. Young girls in over-crowded tenements were also frequently subject to degrading treatment, often at the hands of members of their own family. But he had never expected to find similar behavior in the home of one of the country's foremost noblemen. This was like an obscene return to the Middle Ages with the Lord of the Manor exercising his *droit de seigneur.* He had seen enough for one evening.

"I have no stomach for this, Lord de Courcey," he said, surprised by his own boldness. "I never expected to find such unseemly behavior in so noble a house. You will excuse me, but I think it is time that I retired."

He looked at the others, hoping to find their consciences touched by his words. But he saw only lechery and disinterest in what he had said. Ashton and Fitzherbert leered at him, their faces made even more grotesque by a surfeit of drink and the prospect of a night's debauchery. Paul de Courcey sat quietly smoking his cigar, seemingly amused by the whole episode. Only Montgomery appeared to be having second thoughts, his eyes flitting uncertainly between Lord Quentin, the girls and Parsons.

In the hope that Montgomery might join him Parsons waited for a few more seconds, but seeing that the Canadian had turned his gaze towards the fire he realized that he was on his own. Turning on his heel he hurried across the Hall, the jeers from Ashton and Fitzherbert and Lord Quentin's parting words ringing in his ears.

"Go to your cold and empty bed, young man, and think of what you're missing."

The chorus of laughter that followed was the last sound Parsons heard as he left the room.

-5-

As he entered the Drawing Room Parsons was almost swept to one side by the departing figures of the Howards. Judging by the infuriated expression worn by Mrs. Howard she was not at all pleased with her husband's behavior during the evening, and from the crestfallen-look on the colonel's face he knew he would be hearing about it during the journey home. They were followed by the tall thin-lipped lady who had sat on Hamilton's left during dinner, who brought in her train the now timorous-looking Sir Henry Rawlinson. Like Colonel Howard, Sir Henry had the look of a man under sentence. They made an unlikely couple as they hastened along the corridor. Lady Elizabeth Rawlinson was a foot taller than her husband, and her long rangy strides made it difficult for him to keep up with her as she hurried out of the room.

Inside the Drawing Room Robertson, Harding and the Hamiltons were taking their leave of Lady Annabelle and Catherine. There was no sign of Alexander, Philip and Montagu.

58

Parsons warmed immediately to the small, bubbly figure of Anne Hamilton, the youngest of the de Courcey sisters. She was the most attractive of the three and seemed to be the only one with a sense of humor.

"I can never understand what men find so fascinating to talk about that keeps them so long at the dinner table. I don't mean you, my sweet," she said, patting her husband's arm. "But did you see the expressions on the faces of Charles and Henry? Didn't they look like two naughty schoolboys."

She burst into a peel of laughter that Parsons found reassuringly pleasing after his recent experience in the Great Hall, but she stopped when she realized that Annabelle was not sharing her joke. But even Anne Hamilton would find the situation less than amusing, thought Parsons, if she had known what entertainment her father had provided for his guests.

Lady Annabelle now seemed quite a different person to the one Parsons had spoken with at dinner. The sparkle was gone from her eyes and the downward slope of the corners of her mouth had robbed her lips of their voluptuousness. Thinking that she might be tired after such a long evening Parsons hastened to make his excuses. Catherine had just wished them both a brusque good night and he knew it was usual for people in the country to retire well before midnight. He was quite looking forward to his bed himself, in spite of what Lord Quentin had said. But Annabelle would have none of it, and as Catherine left the room she beckoned him to wait.

"Is Paul still with the others?" she asked.

"He is, Annabelle."

"Do you think he will be long? I'd like to speak with him before retiring."

Parsons would have liked to assure her that she would not have long to wait, but he could do no more than mumble a few words about his uncertainty about Paul's plans. It seemed an outrage to him that Paul should choose to abandon this beautiful woman for a servant. But from his earlier conversation with Paul he realized that this smooth-talking Southern gentleman was something of a Don Juan, although he had no intention of mentioning that to Annabelle. He was grateful, therefore, when she thanked him, wished him good night and went back to her chair by the fire. As he left the room she was gazing wistfully into the flames.

Parsons was up next morning at seven. There was no sign of any hot water for his shave so he decided to take a brisk walk in the fresh air, hoping it might help him forget the unpleasant memories of the previous evening.

He now understood what Hamilton had been referring to at dinner and why the married men had chosen to leave the room when they did. He was angry with Alexander. Why had his friend not warned him of what to expect? And how much did Colonel Howard, the senior policeman in the county, know about what went on? Was that what Hamilton had meant when he said it suited Quentin to have old army cronies around him? Was he witnessing yet another example of a high-level conspiracy of silence?

He had decided to leave Beaumont that morning. By remaining any longer he felt he merely condoned what was happening. At breakfast he would find out the time of the first convenient train to London.

He strolled through the barbican and over the drawbridge. Then he turned north, thinking as he looked up at the bleak walls of the castle of the many evil deeds committed within them over the centuries. It seemed that little had changed.

Large grey clouds were gathering in the west and the wind was gusting through the trees in the Great Park. There would be rain before long. At the north-west corner of the castle he turned away from the walls and continued his walk into the trees. Birds chattered around him as he walked. Did they sense the change in the seasons? Were they, like him, preparing to leave Beaumont?

After walking for about twenty minutes he turned back, and when he had reached the castle continued along the walls until he reached a large wooden gate near the north-east tower. The gate was open, and there was a large wooden stable block some twenty or thirty yards beyond. Inside the stables the young groom who had driven the cart on the previous day was feeding the horses.

"Good morning, Dunne," said Parsons, as he strolled into the stables. "The horses look well under your care."

The boy touched his cap.

"A good day to you, sir," he replied in a soft Irish brogue, lowering his head quickly to avoid further eye contact with Parsons. Since the previous day the bruises on the boy's face had ripened and Parsons was about to ask Dunne how he had received them when he heard a noise above him.

A scruffy, unshaven man was glowering down at him from the hay loft. The man appeared to have been sleeping in the loft as there were pieces of hay in his hair and on the dirty open-necked shirt he was wearing. His face seemed familiar to Parsons. Then he remembered. This man was one of the crowd sitting outside the inn on the previous afternoon. Parsons recalled him spitting on the ground as they rode past. It was not easy to forget such a look of undisguised hostility.

" 'is lordship don't allow 'is 'orses out without 'is permission," the man said rudely in a coarse Cockney accent.

"Please don't concern yourself about that," replied Parsons. "I'm only taking a stroll before breakfast and was just passing the time of day with Dunne."

"Dunne's got no time for passin' the time of day. 'e's got work to do. An' 'e knows what 'e'll get if these bloody stables ain't clean before ten. So I'll thank you to leave 'im be."

This disgusting creature, thought Parsons, was no doubt one of the ex-soldiers Hamilton had referred to at dinner. His name, if he recalled correctly, was Smith. He considered giving Smith a piece of his mind but thought better of it. In all probability it was Dunne who would suffer if any further time was wasted. Smiling sympathetically at the boy Parsons continued on his way. One question at least had been answered. There seemed little doubt where the boy's bruises had come from.

The wind freshened as he entered the castle and he felt the first signs of rain. Heavy storm clouds were now darkening the sky to the west. He would no doubt get a thorough soaking driving to the station in an open trap.

The hot water arrived just after Parsons had returned to his room.

"I'm sorry to be keeping you waiting, sir," said the young maid as she placed the jug on the wash-stand. "But what with the extra work last night we're a bit behind this morning. We was also thinking that you young gentlemen might be wanting to lie in your beds a wee bit longer this morning."

"And why should that be," asked Parsons coolly.

The girl giggled.

"To be sure you'll be knowing what I'm meaning, sir. Weren't you there yourself last night?"

Parsons looked more closely at the girl. In the Hall after dinner she had been standing at the end of the line furthest from him. Like her freckled face, her body was small and round, but the tight ginger curls he remembered from the previous night were this morning tucked inside her white mob-cap.

"What's your name?" he asked.

"O'Halloran, sir."

"Well, O'Halloran, what happened to you last night?" he asked.

"Nothing, sir," she said. "It's rare that anyone picks me. Praise be they go for the thin ones like O'Brien and O'Mahoney." She giggled again. "There are some advantages to being on the fat side."

She busied herself around the room for a few minutes before speaking again.

"Will you be wanting any washing done, sir? If you do, you can leave it in the laundry basket." She pointed to the basket in the corner of the room. "I'll be collecting it after breakfast."

"I've none, thank you," replied Parsons. "I'm leaving this morning. But I would appreciate someone cleaning these boots before I go."

He gave her the brown ankle-length boots he had been wearing on his walk.

"Certainly, sir. I'll see you have them back straight after breakfast when I come to take your chamber-pot and your shaving-water. Now you'll have to excuse me. I've other gentlemen to see to."

She curtsied and left the room.

Catherine de Courcey and Andrew Robertson were already at breakfast when Parsons entered the Dining Room. They were seated on opposite sides of the table and as far away from each other as possible. Which of the two, Parsons wondered, was avoiding the other.

"Good morning Miss de Courcey, Mr. Robertson," he said cheerfully. "I see you are both early risers."

"Good morning, Inspector Parsons," replied Robertson. "It's good to see you looking so sprightly this morning. You are obviously not suffering any ill effects from last night. I'm usually an early riser. There are not many solicitors of my acquaintance who can afford the luxury of lying abed. Apart from Lord Quentin's will I've other papers to work on this morning. Miss de Courcey is also a busy person."

He received no acknowledgement of the engaging smile he had given Catherine when speaking of her responsibilities. From her reaction it was as though he had never spoken.

"A large house such as this needs constant supervision," he continued, "and Lady Annabelle allows much of the burden to rest on Catherine's shoulders. As you can imagine the last few days have been especially busy."

Catherine continued to allow his remarks to pass without comment, but she finally acknowledged Parsons presence.

"You'll find a selection of cold meats on the sideboard, inspector," she said. "If you want a hot breakfast you must ask one of the girls."

It was clear from her tone that she would consider it a great inconvenience not only to the girls waiting at table but also to herself if he were to ask for anything other than what had already been provided.

"Thank you," he replied. "I'm sure the cold meat will be sufficient."

Parsons recognized the two servants from the previous night. It seemed particularly obscene to him that they should be expected to continue with their duties as though nothing unusual had occurred. As he took his meat he offered them what was intended to be a sympathetic glance, but their faces remained expressionless. Perhaps they were less concerned about what had happened than he.

"What time do Lord and Lady de Courcey normally rise?" he asked Catherine, trying to learn a little more about her unusual family.

"You won't see either of them until much later," she replied coldly. "Probably not before the will is read. They both take breakfast in their rooms. Philip and Alexander are also late risers, and from what I have seen so is Geoffrey Montagu. And judging by what I imagine Major Fitzherbert and Captain Ashton to have drunk during the course of the afternoon and evening I'll be surprised if you see either of *them* before luncheon. So I expect your only company at breakfast will be Mr Montgomery and cousin Paul. Now you must excuse me. I have work to do."

She got up abruptly and swept out of the room with neat, quick steps, her small head with its meticulously combed hair held high on ramrod-straight shoulders. With keys jingling on the chatelaine attached to the belt of her somber black dress she looked every inch the housekeeper. Perhaps, thought Parsons, that was how she regarded herself.

Her tone had been matter-of-fact, almost dismissive. How much, he wondered, did such an efficient woman with an intimate knowledge of what went on in the castle know about her father's behavior. Yet if she knew of it, it seemed inconceivable to him that she approved. And if Catherine knew, then surely Annabelle did as well. Was she not greatly offended and upset by his behavior? Was that the reason for her sadness when he saw her in the Drawing Room? Or was it more a concern for what Paul might be doing?

As Catherine had predicted, Montgomery and Paul were the next to arrive for breakfast. They both looked tired, but whereas Paul retained his charm and good humor Montgomery was quiet and had little to say.

"I've brought the book I promised you, Parsons," said Paul, placing it on the table. "I had a quick look at some of the photographs while I was dressing. There's even one of our prison camp and some of our Yankee guards. You can see quite clearly the sort of scum they were."

For the moment it appeared that Montgomery would take the bait and say something. But he thought better of it. It was too early in the morning and he was probably in no state for an argument.

"Thank you," said Parsons, "but there won't be time for me to read it. I've decided to leave this morning."

"I'm sorry to hear that," said Paul good-naturedly, "but you're welcome to take it with you. You can return it later. I've no plans to go anywhere."

Ashton, the next to arrive, was surprisingly full of life. His arrival precipitated the departure of Robertson, who murmured something as he left about the need to work on his papers. But it was clear from the way his face darkened when Ashton arrived that he had taken a dislike to him.

"What a night," said Ashton, smirking at everyone and tweaking his moustache. "I never realized that Irish women could be so entertaining. You have to hand it to old Quentin, he's a fine judge of young fillies. How was your night, Parsons? Did you fall asleep reading the Police Manual?"

When his taunt went unheeded he turned to Montgomery.

"Isn't that your girl?" he said loudly, with a nod towards one of the two girls who were waiting table. "Don't be bashful, old boy. We're all men of the world here." He winked at Paul. "Well, all except Parsons perhaps."

Having heard enough of Ashton's humor, Parsons was about to leave the table when Alexander arrived. He sat well away from everyone else; pale, uncommunicative and sniffing irritatingly.

"Has anyone seen Montagu this morning?" he asked morosely, but in such a low voice that it appeared he was talking to himself. "He wasn't in his room when I looked."

No one replied. Even if they had heard him it seemed they were little concerned about the whereabouts of Montagu.

Parsons rose from his seat and went to sit by Alexander.

"Do you know the times of the London trains?" he asked.

"There's one every two hours, at ten past the hour," replied Alexander. "The next one will be at ten past ten. Why do you want to know? I hope you're not planning to leave us, Everett."

"I'm afraid I must. I'd hoped to stay longer, but I find I can't afford the time."

"I hope it has nothing to do with last night, Parsons," sneered Ashton. "I hope our little games didn't offend your sensitive disposition.

"Your *'games,'* as you call them, are not my idea of how any gentleman behaves," replied Parsons angrily. "I had mistakenly assumed that when I came here I would be in the company of gentlemen."

In danger of losing his temper—something that rarely occurred—Parsons felt it was time to leave. He appeared to be in a minority when it came to deciding what constituted decent behavior.

"Excuse me," he said, "but I must pack if I'm to catch the next train. Alexander, can you please arrange transport to take me to the station?"

Alexander beckoned to one of the girls.

"Find Johnson, O'Mahoney," he instructed. "He's probably giving father his breakfast. Tell him I want the trap outside the main entrance at nine thirty."

The girl curtsied, and was just leaving the room when Johnson appeared at the door. The old man was obviously in a state of shock. His eyes bulged and his mouth gaped in a vain struggle for words.

"For God's sake, Johnson," exclaimed Alexander. "Whatever is the matter?"

The old servant stared blankly at those sitting around the table as though they were all strangers to him.

"It's your father, Master Alexander," he finally managed to splutter. "There's been a terrible accident. Your poor father is dead."

-6-

10th September 1880

*J*ohnson *looked helplessly at the faces around him. The shock had* drained all the color from his face. He swayed unsteadily on his feet so much so that Parsons thought he would fall. He hurried across the room, took the old man's arm and led him to one of the vacant chairs at the breakfast table.

He was at first unhappy to sit at the same table as members of the family and their guests, but realizing his predicament Alexander told him firmly to be seated. With reluctance Johnson did as he was told.

Taking a seat besides the distraught old man, Parsons asked Alexander to send one of the girls for some brandy. The old man's features were set like a mask; his mournful expression had become even more pronounced and the lines on his face were more deeply etched.

"Where did you find the body?" asked Parsons quietly, when he thought the old man had recovered sufficiently to answer questions.

"In his bedroom, sir. I was taking him his breakfast at the usual time."

Johnson rested his head in his hands. His voice was barely audible as he struggled to find words to describe what he had seen. After a few seconds he continued.

"I knocked on the door like I always do." He glanced furtively, first at Parsons then at Alexander, unsure and uncomfortable about what he was about to say. "His lordship never likes me going into his room without knocking if he has company."

"Go on Johnson," said Parsons quietly. "This is no time to worry about his lordship's indiscretions."

"There was no answer, sir. That was unusual. His lordship's generally such a light sleeper. But I knew his lordship had drunk a lot yesterday, so I waited a while. Then I knocked louder. And when he still didn't reply, I went in."

"What did you see."

Johnson clasped his hands tightly together as though praying and stared into the distance.

"It was dark in the room, sir," he explained in a voice heavy with emotion. "So I put down the tray on the table near the window and opened some of the curtains. I could see then that the drapes around the bed had still not been drawn."

"Does Lord Quentin sleep in a four-poster bed?"

"He does, sir. It was his father's and before that his grand-father's." He looked at Alexander as he spoke, as though this information was somehow relevant to the next in line. "Very proud of that bed your father was, Master Alexander."

Johnson was finding it increasingly difficult to speak. His voice wavered, and Parsons frequently had to lower his head to hear what the old man was saying. He was clearly in a state of shock, but regardless of that Parsons felt he had to press him further.

"Go on please, Johnson," he prompted. "What happened then?"

"I coughed loudly a few times, sir, but his lordship still didn't wake. By then I was getting worried, as I couldn't hear any breathing. So I opened the drapes."

O'Mahoney returned just then with a decanter of brandy, and after a confirmatory nod from Alexander, poured Johnson a generous measure in one of the empty breakfast cups. With shaking hands he raised the cup to his lips and took a long gulp, spluttering and coughing as the spirit hit the back of his throat. To the impatient Parsons it seemed an eternity before Johnson was able to speak again.

"His lordship was lying on his back, sir. At first I thought he was asleep. So I called his name several times. I called louder each time. But he never moved. So I reached out to shake him. But he was cold, sir. He was stone cold."

He looked despairingly at Alexander.

"Your father was stone cold, Master Alexander. He was as cold as the grave. I knew then that he was gone."

Johnson buried his face in his hands and, much to everyone's discomfort, began to sob uncontrollably. A servant crying in one of the public rooms was not something anyone had experienced before. No one spoke, and for several minutes the only sound in the room was the old man's pitiful weeping.

Eventually Johnson stopped crying. With an effort he sat straight up in his chair and looked shamefacedly towards Alexander and then Parsons.

"Is that all?" Parsons asked him.

"Yes, sir."

"Did you come straight here after that?"

"Not at once, sir. I went to Master Alexander's room first. When he wasn't there I thought he would be at breakfast."

"Why didn't you go to Lady Annabelle's room?"

"That wouldn't be proper, sir. It's not my privilege to wait on her ladyship. And in any case Master Alexander is the head of the family now."

As the new will had yet to be read it remained to be seen who was head of the house, thought Parsons. But for the moment that was a problem that could wait.

"Alexander," he said, "will you come with me to your father's room?"

Alexander nodded nervously.

"Good man," said Parsons encouragingly. Then he turned to Paul.

"Mr. de Courcey," he instructed, "I'd like you to go to her ladyship's room. Tell her that her husband has had an accident and that Alexander and I have gone to investigate. Don't tell her any more than that. Ask her to get dressed and go to the Library. After that find Catherine and say the same to her. Mr. Robertson is working in his room and I think we can leave him there for the time being. He'll go to the Library in his own good time."

"What about me, Parsons?" snapped Ashton, irritated that he appeared to be ignored in Parsons' arrangements.

"I'd like you to remain here until you hear from me. You as well, Mr. Montgomery."

"And what if I don't choose to."

Ashton was clearly doing his best to be unhelpful.

"I'll remind you, Captain Ashton, that I'm a police inspector, and no longer just a fellow guest."

Parsons knew he ran the risk of sounding overly officious, but he was left with little choice if Ashton was going to be difficult. It also gave him some satisfaction to have the upper hand with Ashton, tenuous though that might be.

"Sit down and shut up, Ashton," said Paul. "We can do without your clever remarks for the time being."

Parsons caught Paul's eye, grateful for the unexpected support.

"What about Philip, Montagu and Major Fitzherbert? Shall I check their rooms?" Paul asked.

"Leave that to me, Mr. de Courcey," replied Parsons. "I'll check their rooms after I've seen the body. If any of them come down to breakfast before I've seen them, Captain Ashton, ask them to wait here."

Ashton said nothing. His only response was a surly nod.

Parsons was pleased to see that Johnson was slowly regaining some of his former composure. The discipline of years was gradually overcoming the effects of the short emotional outburst.

"I know it won't be easy, Johnson, but as far as possible I'd like all the servants to carry on as normal. Do you think you can cope?"

Johnson sniffed a few times then nodded his head.

"Well done," said Parsons. "Now this is what I want you to do. When the other members of the family arrive have them shown straight to the Library. Neither you nor any of the other servants is to discuss with them what has happened. I'll tell everyone as soon as I get the chance."

Parsons turned to the Irish girls.

"Is that clear?" he said.

They both nodded.

"One other thing, Johnson. Where's the key to Lord Quentin's room?"

"It's still in the door, sir. It was always on the inside of the door. His lordship sometimes locks the door during the night."

"But he didn't last night."

"No, sir, the door wasn't locked.

Beaumont Castle had been built in the shape of a hollow square. The public rooms and kitchen area occupied the bulk of the ground floor. Family bedrooms and those of any guests were on the first floor. Lord Quentin's room was in the north-west corner of the castle, directly above the Library.

"Who is in the room on either side of your father's?" asked Parsons as he and Alexander hurried from the top of the main staircase along the corridor towards Lord Quentin's room.

"No one ever uses this one," said Alexander, pointing to the door on the left of his father's. "Father never wanted anyone sleeping in the room next to his. Major Fitzherbert's is the nearest room that's ever occupied. That's the room directly across the corridor."

"I haven't seen Fitzherbert this morning," said Parsons. "I'll leave his room until after I've seen your father's."

There was no mistaking Lord Quentin's room. As Philip had explained the previous afternoon, the antlers on his door were visible several yards away.

The room was still in partial darkness as Johnson had opened only the curtains on the side of the room furthest from the door.

Unsure of what he might find Parsons told Alexander to remain at the door and walked across the room to draw the remaining curtains. It was only then that he realized that the storm that had been threatening during his walk had now broken and heavy rain was pounding against the windows.

Lord Quentin's room was large, about twice the size of his own, and there was a degree of sophistication about it that was a far cry from the crass militarism in other parts of the castle. There was a handsome bookcase filled with books and a selection of fine watercolors of landscapes and sporting scenes. Above the fireplace a thick velvet curtain matching those of the windows concealed what he imagined to be a large painting or a mirror. Parsons had previously seen paintings and statues hidden from view in this way in Italian churches during the period before Lent. But the fashion seemed incongruous here.

There were two other doors leading off the room. One led to a small, dark dressing room, the other to a water closet. He gave them both a cursory inspection but found nothing untoward.

A large, four-poster bed was the most dominant item of furniture. As Johnson had said, there were heavy drapes at the foot of the bed and along both sides. On the side of the bed nearest the door these drapes were still in place, and Parsons recalled how Johnson had explained that he first crossed the room to place his tray on a table near the windows before drawing the drapes nearest him.

Parsons walked around the bed until he reached the position he imagined Johnson to have been standing when he had peered anxiously into his master's bed. Whatever the old servant had been expecting, it could not have been anything as terrifying as what he had found.

Lord Quentin lay on his back in the middle of the bed. His trousers were still fastened and his braces still attached to them, but the gold studs had been removed from his dress shirt, revealing a broad chest thick with grey hair. As he had approached the bed Parsons had seen Lord Quentin's jacket lying across the arm of a sofa, his white bow-tie folded carefully on top; and at the side of the sofa his shoes and socks had been arranged neatly, a black silk sock rolled up and placed inside each patent-leather shoe.

He had been spread-eagled and held in position by lengths of rope tied to his ankles and wrists and then to the thick wooden bedposts at each corner of the bed. The ropes were not so taut that Lord Quentin would have found it impossible to move, but taut enough to prevent him from being able to sit up.

His long hair and thick whiskers at first hid the fact that a further length of rope had been fastened around his neck to form a noose, and like the rope attached to his wrists and ankles it had cut deep into his flesh. It was this rope that appeared to have been the cause of his death, as on closer examination the free end of the rope disappeared under his pillows and in between two columns in the wooden head-board. From there it stretched along the floor under the bed, and as far as Parsons could see there was sufficient rope laying under the foot of the bed for someone to have stood there and tightened the rope around Lord Quentin's neck. However, with some of the curtains still drawn around the bed it was not clear to him at this stage what actually had happened.

Judging by the crumpled state of the pillows and bed linen and the way in which the rope had tightened around his ankles and wrists, Lord Quentin had struggled desperately for some time before he died. His long hair and his whiskers were tangled and matted as though he had been shaking his head from side to side; and his bulging, sightless eyes, so fiery when Parsons had last seen them, now showed only the terror of his last moments. Parsons reached over to touch his right hand. It was stiff and cold.

He walked back to the door where Alexander had been waiting patiently.

"Your father met a violent death," he said, " and the manner of his dying may distress you. Are you quite sure you want to see him?"

Alexander nodded dumbly and followed Parsons back into the room. His expression changed from amazement to horror when he saw the body and during the short time during which he struggled to comprehend the nature of the tragedy. His breathing quickened and for one moment Parsons thought his friend was going to be sick. But Alexander made no effort to touch his father and showed no sign of grief. The sniffles that Parsons had first taken to be tears were no more than the effects of the cold that Alexander appeared to have caught during the night.

He stood motionless at the side of the bed for several minutes, his eyes focused upon his father's face, and when he finally spoke his voice was high-pitched and bordering on being hysterical.

"My God, Everett," he said, "this is like a vision from Hell. What do you think could have happened? Surely father would not have done this to himself."

"I've never seen anything like this before, Alexander," Parsons admitted, "and I'd like to reserve my judgment about the cause of your father's death until I've carried out a more thorough inspection. As you say it seems unlikely that it was an accident. Nevertheless, that's how I'd like you to refer to it when you join the others downstairs. I'll be down as soon as I can, but before then I want to check the other rooms and speak again to Johnson.

Parsons did not say that he also intended to speak to Claire, the young girl Lord Quentin had boasted about taking to his room. At this stage he was unsure how much Alexander knew about his father's intimate relations with the Irish servants.

"I'm fine, Everett. Don't worry about me," said Alexander, although his voice still sounded unnaturally high-pitched. "You know where Fitzherbert's room is. Philip and Montagu have rooms at the other end of the corridor. You'll find Philip's directly opposite you, Montagu's is on your left. If you want to call the servants just pull that bell-cord by the side of the bed. Someone should be here within a few minutes."

Parsons pulled the bell-cord as soon as Alexander had gone, imagining as he did how it would cause alarm in the kitchen area below. Lord Quentin's death would no doubt by now be common knowledge amongst the servants, and the last thing they would be expecting was a summons to his room.

While he was waiting he drew back the curtains from the mysterious object above the fireplace, half expecting to see a portrait of Lord Quentin or one of his ancestors. To his surprise he discovered it was instead a portrait of Lord Quentin's young wife, Lady Annabelle. There was no date or signature on the painting, but it appeared to have been painted several year ago. Annabelle looked younger and her hair was longer, but it was not unknown for artists to flatter their subjects, especially if they were women. Annabelle's appearance, therefore, gave no obvious clue to the age of the painting, but whatever age she may have been when the portrait was painted, she had always been a beauty. As Parsons gazed up in admiration he was struck, as he had been the previous night at dinner, by the similarity she bore to the sensual red-headed beauties that were so often the subject of the Pre-Raphaelites. Considering the origin of his own name it struck him as an unusual coincidence.

But why should it be that Lord Quentin kept such a charming portrait of his lovely wife hidden from sight. Was it because they had become estranged? Or was he so ashamed of what occurred in his room that he wished to prevent even her portrait from witnessing it?

-7-

Johnson's nervous knock on the door interrupted Parsons' contemplation of the painting. Judging by the anxious expression on the servant's face as he entered the room it was clear he had half expected to see a ghost. Although heavy lines still etched the corners of the old man's mouth and his deep-sunk eyes, it nevertheless seemed to Parsons that in a remarkably short time Johnson had regained much of his former composure. He had probably no choice. In his position as the senior servant there would be little enough time for public displays of grief.

He joined Parsons at the side of the bed with obvious reluctance. It was clear he would have preferred to remain by the door, but that was not where Parsons wanted him. He felt sure the servant had more to say about his master's death than he had offered a short while ago in the Dining Room. Parsons was especially irritated that Johnson had not seen fit to mention the bizarre state in which he had found Lord Quentin, and he wanted to observe the servant's reactions when confronted with the body.

"Is this exactly how you found the room, Johnson?" he asked, permitting an aggressive tone to creep into his voice.

"Yes, sir," replied Johnson timidly.

"So Lord Quentin was lying exactly in that position, with his hands tied so, and with a rope around his neck?"

"Yes, sir."

"And you didn't think that was sufficiently unusual to mention before?"

Johnson didn't answer.

"Answer me, Johnson. Why did you say that his lordship had had an accident. It can't be everyday that you find him in bed with his clothes on, trussed up like that."

Johnson still did not answer and his eyes avoided Parsons' inquisitive stare. It was a full minute before Parsons spoke again, and by then the truth had dawned upon him.

"Am I to assume you've seen this thing before?" he asked.

There was another lengthy silence before Johnson finally spoke.

"Yes, sir," he said, his voice barely audible.

"How often?" demanded Parsons.

"As often as his lordship took one of those Irish whores to his bed!"

The bitterness in Johnson's voice inferred that if there was to be any blame for what had happened, much of it could be attributed to the Irish girls. But Parsons was unclear whether he was actually blaming them for Lord Quentin's death or for making a fool of a man who was old enough to know better.

"Did you ever ask the Irish whores, as you call them, what went on in here?"

"No, sir. It was none of my business."

Parsons could sympathize with his dilemma. Even the most trusted servants were seldom in a position to question the follies of their employers, even if they did foresee the possible tragedies that might ensue.

"We'll speak more about this later, Johnson," he said sternly, "but for the moment you can go. But I want to see the girl that Lord Quentin was with last night. I believe her name is Claire. Tell her that if I'm not here when she arrives she's to wait for me. Is that clear?"

"Yes, sir," said Johnson, and hastened gratefully to the door.

"Just one other thing," said Parsons, as Johnson was about to leave. "I wish to talk to all the servants later. Before then I want you to provide me with a list of their names. In the meantime you are to keep our conversation to yourself."

As Johnson had said, the key to Lord Quentin's room was still on the inside of the door. Removing it and locking the door behind him Parsons crossed the corridor.

Fitzherbert's room was still in darkness, and as he entered a rancid smell of vomit assailed Parsons' stomach. Hastening across the room he drew back the curtains and opened the windows. Below him in the stables the work continued in spite of the weather and the tragedy that had unfolded within the castle. It was possible that the news had not yet reached the grooms. But he doubted it. The servants' grape vine would work better than that.

Fitzherbert lay diagonally across the bed in a semi-foetal position. He was still wearing the trousers and shirt he had worn the previous night, but his other clothes lay scattered around the room where they had been discarded. His mouth was open and he was snoring loudly, his face barely inches away from a pile of vomit on the green candlewick bedspread. It was fortunate for Fitzherbert that he had slept on his side, thought Parsons. Had he laid on his back the drunken oaf might well have choked.

Parsons approached the bed, intending to wake Fitzherbert, when he noticed the dark stain that had spread over the bedspread under the sleeping man. The smell of urine confirmed that Fitzherbert had also soiled himself.

Let the pig stew in his own juice a while longer, thought Parsons as he left the room. No doubt even Fitzherbert will feel some kind of remorse when he wakes. He only pitied the poor girl who would have the task of cleaning the room.

Left to him Fitzherbert would be doused with a bucket of cold water and told to clear up his own mess. But he knew no servant would ever dare to suggest that.

Across the corridor Claire was waiting outside Lord Quentin's room, her child-like face a picture of misery. Tears filled her large brown eyes and trickled slowly down her cheeks. It was enough to soften harder hearts than his. But he counseled himself against any such feelings. For all he knew this distraught angelic-looking girl could be a murderer.

Once inside the room Parsons could not fail to notice the quick, apprehensive glance she gave towards the bed.

From where they were standing the body was still not visible as the drapes on the side of the bed nearest the door were still closed. Before confronting her with the body there were a few preliminary questions he wanted to ask.

"Where do you come from, Claire?" he asked gently.

"From Ballycarra in County Mayo, sir. That's in the west of Ireland. All of us girls come from those parts. The land there belongs to the de Courceys."

Her voice had the same soft timbre as the groom. Theirs were the sort of voices he had come to associate with a gentler race of people than dwelt in his own country; and he found himself asking by what right the de Courceys and their kind could up-root girls such as these and impose such abominable servitude upon them. He forced himself to stop romanticizing. He needed to retain his objectivity. The philosophizing could come later.

"I see," he said. "And how is it you all happen to be here?"

"Lord de Courcey's agent arranges it, sir. He offers some of the girls and a few of the men the chance of working over the water. Very few refuse him, sir. Not only is he a powerful man, but life in Ballycarra is not so great that many of us would choose to stay there."

"And are you aware of the full extent of your duties before you come?"

"Nay, sir" she said softly, her eyes avoiding those of Parsons.

He walked over to the bed and pulled back the drapes, keeping his eyes on the girl as he did. At the sight of Lord

Quentin's body she put both her hands to her mouth and her eyes opened wide in horror. Then she crossed herself and muttered a few words in a language that Parsons could not understand. She began crying again. Her small body shook pitifully, and he found it difficult to imagine that what he was seeing was anything other than genuine grief. Nevertheless, he reminded himself again of the dangers of being deceived by a woman's tears.

He drew back the curtain again and waited patiently for the girl to stop crying. There were other questions he wanted to ask and he wished to avoid her being further distracted by the gruesome sight on the bed.

"Please tell me what happened after I left the Great Hall last night," Parsons asked when he felt he had regained her attention.

She sniffed several times and wiped her face with the edge of her white apron.

"The gentlemen chose which of the girls they wanted, sir. Then his lordship told us all to leave the Hall and not to go to the gentlemens' rooms until midnight."

It had been about eleven when Parsons had stormed out of the Hall. By midnight Lord Quentin would have been confident that all the visitors had left and, with the exception of those remaining in the Hall, everyone else would have retired for the night. From what Parsons had seen this was exactly what had happened, with the possible exception of Lady Annabelle. When he had gone to bed she was still in the Drawing Room.

"Do you remember which girl went with each of the gentlemen?" asked Parsons.

She nodded nervously several times.

"I think I do, sir," she said, concentrating for a few moments. "Mr. Paul chose Katy Dwyer and poor Maggie Sweeney went with the gentlemen who was very drunk.

That would be the disgusting object across the corridor, thought Parsons.

"Go on," he said.

"The other American gentleman picked Mary O'Mahoney and Patricia O'Brien went with the thin-faced gentleman with the monocle."

"Thank you, you've done well. What about you? Was Lord Quentin waiting for you here at midnight?"

"Aye, sir, he was."

"What was he doing?"

"He was sitting there drinking."

She pointed to the button-backed sofa. Next to it was a small table with a decanter and glasses, Johnson's breakfast tray and the set of gold studs from Lord Quentin's shirt.

"What sort of mood was he in when you arrived?"

"He was quiet, sir. I think he was very drunk. He kept falling backwards onto the chair every time he tried to stand up. If Mary O'Mahoney hadn't been with me I don't know what I'd be doing with him."

"What on earth was O'Mahoney doing here?" demanded Parsons, surprised to hear that any of the other girls had been present. I thought she was with Mr. Montgomery."

Claire blushed.

"Sure, wasn't it my first time with his lordship," she explained. "And wasn't his lordship liking things done in his own way. Mary only came to help."

"What were these things, Claire?"

"Do I have to tell you, sir?" she pleaded. "Can't you be asking Mary?"

Her voice was shaking and had dropped almost to a whisper.

"You can be sure I'll ask Mary later," said Parsons firmly. "But I want you to tell me what happened,"

The girl sighed.

"We took off his lordship's shoes and socks, his jacket, and his tie and we helped him onto the bed. Then Mary got some rope from his dressing room and we tied his hands and feet."

"Just like they are now?"

Parsons pointed to the body.

"Aye, sir."

"And what about the rope around his neck?"

"Mary tied that, sir. Then she coiled it through the head-board and put the end of the rope in his lordship's hand."

So he was holding the end of the rope that was attached to his neck. Whatever for?"

"So he could pull on it, sir. Mary said he liked choking himself while..."

Her voice tailed off into a series of sobs.

"While what, Claire? While what?" Parsons said impatiently, running his short fingers through his hair.

"While the girls were lying with him, sir," she said tearfully. "That's what Mary told me he liked. I don't understand it, sir. I don't understand."

She began crying loudly again and her shoulders shook uncontrollably.

"I see," said Parsons to himself. But he didn't see at all. His own sexual encounters had been few and each of them mutually disappointing. They had not prepared him for anything like this. At such a time he wished that one of his more worldly colleagues could be present.

He took a clean white handkerchief from his trouser pocket and offered it to the girl. At first she looked at him in disbelief. Then she wiped her eyes and blew her nose loudly.

"And did you...lie with him last night?" he asked.

"Nay, sir. I did not. After Mary left the room he asked me for another drink. Then he told me to take the studs from his shirt. And while I was doing it he fell asleep.

"So what did you do then?"

"I waited a wee while. Then I went to find Mary and asked her what I should do."

"And what did she say?"

"She told me to take the rope out of his hand and make sure the rope around his neck wasn't tight. Then she told me to leave him. She said he was getting to be an old man and he drank too much. She said he often went to sleep when she was with him. And when he did she always left him like that."

"She left him tied to the bed," said Parsons incredulously. "Whatever for?"

"Because he liked it, sir."

Parsons felt himself floundering. This was something completely outside his experience. Whatever sort of depraved tastes did Lord Quentin have? Did he really enjoy such things, or was he, perhaps, chastising himself for something he had done in his past? Jamaica, for instance.

"So you're telling me he was alive when you left."

"He was that, sir," she said, irritated that he should suggest otherwise. "He was alive right enough. Wasn't he snoring like Old Nick."

"And what time was that?"

"I couldn't be saying for sure, sir. But it was quarter to one when I got back to my room."

"Thank you, Claire. That will be all for now."

As she curtsied and turned to go she noticed for the first time the portrait over the fireplace.

"Jaysus, Mary and Joseph," she said. "It's her blessed ladyship."

"Do I take it you've never seen this painting before."

"Nay, sir. It wasn't there last night."

"Perhaps the curtain was drawn."

He pulled the curtain across the painting for her to see.

"Aye, sir. That's how it was."

"And what about the curtains around the bed," he asked. "Were they open or closed?"

"Open, sir."

"Are you sure?"

"Oh, aye, sir. If they weren't how would we be tying his lordship's arms and legs to the bed."

Parsons locked the door after the girl had gone, pocketed the key, and walked along the corridor to the unoccupied room next to Lord Quentin's. He found it unlocked and, apart from curtains, completely bare of furnishings. And judging by the dust on the floor the room had been unused for some time. Satisfied that whoever had murdered Lord Quentin had not used this room for any purpose Parsons closed the door and continued along the corridor to the south-west corner of the castle to where Alexander, Philip and Montagu had their rooms.

Philip was not in his room. The curtains were open, the bedding thrown back, and the dirty water in the basin and his night clothes on the bed evidence that he had washed and dressed. In all probability he had gone downstairs to breakfast.

The curtains in Montagu's room were still drawn and the room was empty. The bed was still made up and did not appear to have been slept in. But considering that Montagu had been in the castle only a short time the room was exceptionally untidy. Clothes and papers were strewn everywhere.

It was ten fourteen. Soon the Hamiltons and Rawlinsons would be arriving for the reading of Lord Quentin's will. With a preliminary report to prepare for the Chief Constable he would, unfortunately, have to miss that. He had no doubt that Colonel Howard would eventually decide to take charge of the investigation, but before that he wanted Doctor Hamilton to examine the body. But first he wanted the opportunity of speaking to those of the family who were waiting below in the Library.

-8-

The Library was a gaunt oak-panelled room occupying the north-west corner of the castle. Three large windows overlooked the lawns to the west, two more faced north towards the stables. Well-stocked shelves of dusty books covered all the available wall space, except for a space above the ornately carved wooden fireplace that was decorated with a bold display of military weapons and regimental guidons. It was an environment that would have been somber on the brightest of summer days, but when Parsons entered the room it had been made even more gloomy as a result of the storm raging outside.

Watched irritably by Catherine, Alexander paced restlessly backwards and forwards in front of the windows overlooking the lawns. Paul sat calmly smoking a cigar in the corner furthest from the door, with Annabelle nearby making a pretense at reading a magazine. There was, it appeared to Parsons, a marked absence of any sign of concern on the faces of the two women. Either Alexander and Paul had been highly successful in concealing the true nature and seriousness of the incident, or the women were remarkably unmoved by the report of Lord Quentin's accident, involving as it did a man who was father to one and husband to the other.

"Well, Inspector Parsons, what can be serious enough to have called me away from my domestic duties?" demanded Catherine.

Parsons ignored the question. He would inform her soon enough of the gravity of the matter.

"Lady Annabelle," he began, "I'm afraid I have some very bad news for you. You may wish to be alone when I tell you, but I think it will be best if other members of the family are present."

"Whatever you think best, Everett," she replied in a low voice. "I'm sure you're an excellent judge on such matters."

She smiled sweetly at him, a smile he found eerily reminiscent of the one in the portrait in her husband's room.

"In that case, my lady, I'll ask Alexander to fetch Philip from the Dining Room. He can also fetch Mr Robertson. In view of his close relationship with the family I think it will be helpful if he is also present."

Alexander left on his errand with additional instructions for Ashton and Montgomery asking for their continued forbearance and requesting that they remain where they were until Parsons arrived.

Philip was the first to arrive, followed soon after by Alexander and Robertson, and as soon as he had everyone's attention Parsons gave a brief account of Lord Quentin's death. He admitted, when questioned, that it was just possible that Lord Quentin might have taken his own life. But he considered it highly unlikely. However, for the moment he intended keeping an open mind about the possible causes of death until he had carried out a further examination and obtained a medical opinion from Doctor Hamilton. Parsons also explained that as his jurisdiction did not extend beyond the Metropolitan area of London he intended sending a report to the Chief Constable of Hampshire. No doubt Colonel Howard or one of his senior officers would arrive later in the day to take control of the investigations. Until then he would continue with his own enquiries.

"When can we see the body, Inspector Parsons?" demanded Catherine. She was less strident than before, but showed every sign not only of being very much in control of her emotions, but also of wanting to take control of events.

"I'd normally allow that straight away, Miss Catherine," Parsons replied, "but in the circumstances I suggest that the reading of the will continues as planned. That will allow me to write a report for Colonel Howard and seek Doctor Hamilton's professional opinion as soon as he arrives. Until he has seen the body I'd prefer that no one else enters Lord Quentin's room.

"That seems a sound plan," said Robertson. "My business with the family will take no more than half an hour. So if you return by half-past eleven you can tell everyone what you have learnt and when it will be possible for them to pay their respects to his lordship."

Parsons was glad to receive Robertson's support, and to his relief it was advice that was accepted with little demur by the others. It enabled him to take his leave and cross the corridor to the Dining Room.

His reception there was less friendly. Ashton's temper had not improved by being kept waiting, although it cooled dramatically when Parsons had given details of what had occurred. However, he seemed as much irritated by Parsons' refusal to answer further questions as he was about the loss of an old friend. Of the two men Montgomery seemed the most concerned, particularly anxious to know how Alexander and other members of the family had received the news.

After explaining what he intended to do next, Parsons allowed them to leave the room, but requested that they remain in the castle for further questioning. It was a request that did not please Ashton who glared at Parsons through his monocle. When this failed to make any impression he stormed from the room muttering loudly to himself about impudent young upstarts in the police force.

After making arrangements for Johnson to bring the doctor to his room as soon as he arrived Parsons began his report for Colonel Howard. He had instructed Johnson to warn Dunne, the young groom, to be ready to deliver the report when completed to the colonel's house in Bishop's Waltham, a ride that Johnson informed him would take about an hour and a half. On that basis the earliest that Howard would reach Beaumont would be at two o'clock. By then Parsons hoped to be in a better position to impress him with the results of what he planned to be a thoroughly professional investigation. Hopefully that would change Howard's opinion about the competence of long-haired Metropolitan detectives.

Doctor Hamilton arrived at Parsons' room just after eleven. Knowing nothing of the doctor's experience of police work he felt it prudent to explain what he required.

"I need to know how Lord Quentin died and approximately at what time," Parsons instructed as they made their way along the corridor to the dead man's room. "I'd also be grateful if you can disturb the body as little as possible and don't touch anything else in the room. I'd like Colonel Howard to see everything as it was when I first saw it this morning."

Hamilton showed no obvious sign of irritation, although it crossed his mind to tell the bumptious little detective that his medical training in Edinburgh had included a spell in the rougher areas of the city. But his only reaction was a quizzical movement of his right eye-brow at the mention of the Chief Constable.

"I'm sure I can manage to do what you ask, inspector," he said dryly.

Leaving Hamilton to begin his investigation of the corpse, Parsons turned his attention to Lord Quentin's dressing room and closet. There was little in the cramped dressing room other than an oak cupboard, an easy chair and a small table. Judging by the style of clothes in the cupboard Lord Quentin had not been a fashionable dresser. From what

Parsons could see there was not a suit in the cupboard less than fifteen years old. It was what one would expect, he surmised, of a man who had worn his hair in the manner he did.

The water closet was also sparsely furnished. It contained a plunge bath, a commode and a wash stand complete with the basic requirements of a gentleman's toilet. A small window offered a fine view over the lawns and the castle walls to the Great Park beyond. No doubt it was a view that Lord Quentin had enjoyed countless times as he performed his ablutions. The commode had not been emptied for some time. In all probability no one had had an opportunity to clean it since the previous evening when Ashton, Fitzherbert and Lord Quentin had been drinking together.

Back in the main bedroom he found Hamilton peering under the bed.

"Have you any idea how Quentin came to be trussed up like that?" he asked.

Parsons told him what he had learnt from Johnson and Claire.

"That fits nicely with my theory," said the doctor.

He pointed to the heavy bruising on the dead man's neck.

"Quentin was first partly strangled by the noose around his neck," he explained. "Then he was suffocated. You can see from the deep marks how the rope dug into his neck. It seems the rope was long enough for someone to stand either at the side or even at the end of the bed while watching the effects of his work. Whether that was one or both of your girls I'll leave you to find out; but with his arms and legs fastened Quentin was completely defenseless. Judging by the struggle he put up I think he took some time to die. Indeed his killer or killers may even have toyed with him for a considerable time—rather like a cat tormenting a bird it has caught—before performing the *coup de grace* with this."

Hamilton held up one of the pillows from the several that were scattered around the dead man's head and pointed to some faint stains on the white linen.

"These are more than likely traces of the contents of Quentin's stomach," he said in a matter-of-fact way. "Quentin was suffocated with this pillow. Possibly his assailant knelt on him while he was doing it, an action that would cause him to retch even with the rope tightened round his neck."

He looked at the body almost pityingly.

"Even a bastard like Quentin deserved better than this," he said.

"There's no possibility it could have been an accident?" asked Parsons.

"None at all. This was murder at its most foul."

"Could all this have been done by one person?"

"It would have been easier with two, but I believe one person could easily have managed."

"And could that person have been a woman?"

"I see no reason why not."

Nor, from what Parsons knew did he.

"Could Lord Quentin have called for help while he was being strangled?" he asked.

"I'm sure he would've made some sort of noise, but I doubt it would be heard much beyond this room."

And much good that would have done him, thought Parsons. With an empty room on one side and Fitzherbert across the corridor. Some friend he had turned out to be.

"What time do you think he died, doctor?"

"As *rigor mortis* has already set in the murder took place at least seven hours ago."

"That would make the time of the murder between midnight and four-thirty," mused Parsons. "That fits well with what I already know. Thank you, doctor, you've been most helpful. Can you do something else for me before you leave?"

"If it's within my powers, inspector."

"I'd like to know if the servant, Claire, is still a virgin. And if she's not, can you tell if she's had intercourse recently?"

"That shouldn't be difficult, but I'd better get Catherine's permission first. She can be difficult if someone interferes with what she considers to be her domain without first asking. She's not as pliant as most women of my acquaintance. But leave her to me. If there are any problems I'll let you know."

"One last thing, Doctor Hamilton. At dinner last night you tried to warn me about Lord Quentin's after-dinner activities. How much did you know about what went on in this house?"

The doctor did not answer at once and it occurred to Parsons that he might now regret his casual remarks the previous evening.

"It was general knowledge that Quentin was taking advantage of the servant girls, inspector," he said at last. "Men's gossip, you know. But I'd no idea it involved anything as perverted as this."

"Do you think other members of the family knew?"

Hamilton shrugged.

"I've really no idea. It's not something I'd choose to discuss with my own wife. But I can't believe a shrewd woman like Catherine would not have known something about what was going on."

"What about Lady Annabelle?"

The doctor shook his head.

"Quentin and she have lived separate lives for several years now. So even if Annabelle knew anything I doubt she would have cared. It would only reinforce the poor opinion she already had about her husband."

By the time Hamilton and Parsons had reached the Library Robertson had completed his reading of the will. The family, however, remained seated around the table in the center of the room at which the solicitor presided. All heads turned in their direction as the two men entered.

"Take a seat, gentlemen," said Robertson. "You've come just in time. I've just completed my business."

He gestured towards two empty chairs at the end of the table furthest from him.

The family immediately focused its full attention upon Parsons. With one or two exceptions their expressions were cold, but it was impossible to tell whether this was a reaction to his arrival or to something they had learned from Lord Quentin's will.

"Ladies and gentlemen," he said solemnly. "Doctor Hamilton has confirmed my initial fears. I regret to inform you that there is no doubt that Lord Quentin was murdered."

Parsons paused to allow them to digest this dramatic statement. He expected that eventually someone would speak. But they remained strangely silent.

"I've sent for the Chief Constable," he said, after allowing sufficient time for someone to speak. "Unless he is engaged on other business I expect him to be here by two o'clock. Until then I intend pursuing my investigation and hope while I remain in charge I can rely on your continuing cooperation."

The uneasy silence continued for several more seconds, and to Parsons' surprise it was Alexander who was the first to react. He leapt to his feet, sending his chair spinning backwards across the floor. Then he leant threateningly across the table to where Paul and Annabelle were sitting.

"I knew it. I knew my father had been murdered," he screamed. "Not that I can blame anyone for killing him. He deserved to die not only for what he did in his own lifetime but also for all the terrible crimes this family has committed. Maybe others of us will get the same treatment. Maybe we'll all have to pay. How do you feel about that, Paul? Does that change things? Do you still want to be the next Lord de Courcey?"

-9-

The new head of the de Courcey family was visibly shaken by the outburst. But having denied Alexander of his birthright, thought Parsons, he ought not to have been surprised by it. Nevertheless, being addressed in front of other members of the family in such a manner was no way to begin his stewardship.

The faces around the table displayed a mixture of emotions. From some there was disapproval for Alexander's behavior, from others satisfaction at seeing Paul's discomfort. Although Lord Quentin's announcement the previous evening had indicated that his will might contain surprises, Parsons reckoned that very few of the family would have been expecting the title to pass to one whom they had known for such a relatively short time.

Lord Paul licked his lips nervously.

"We all share your grief, Alexander," he said. "No one knows better than I what it is to lose one's parents in tragic circumstances. Believe me then, when I say that I want more than anything to be your friend."

103

He stood up and reached across the table, extending a conciliatory hand to Alexander. But from Alexander's reaction it might just as well have been a deadly snake.

"You. My friend," he exclaimed, through clenched teeth. "Never. No, *Lord* Paul. You may have fooled father and some of the others. But you've never fooled me."

Alexander stormed from the room, leaving the rest of the family to guess what exactly it had been that Paul was supposed to have fooled them about. Parsons had never seen his friend behave like this. Even allowing for the dramatic events of the last twelve hours, Alexander's emotional outburst was completely out of keeping with that of the quiet, gentle boy he had known at school. Alexander, the dreamer; whose only ambition it was to become a poet.

For a moment Parsons was unaware that Robertson was speaking to him.

"Will it be in order for the family to see the body now, inspector?"

"Those who wish may do so," replied Parsons, "with the proviso that I am present when they do. But I should warn everyone. For Colonel Howard's benefit the room has been left exactly as I found it, and some of you may find the manner of Lord Quentin's death distressing."

"What exactly is that supposed to mean, inspector?" demanded Catherine.

Hamilton intervened before Parsons had time to answer.

"You must, of course, use your own judgment, Catherine; but my advice to you and your sisters is to wait until

Charles has seen the body. Anne, I know, would not wish to see her father in his present condition."

The doctor's advice was readily accepted by Annabelle and Elizabeth Rawlinson, but Paul, Philip and Catherine insisted on seeing the body immediately.

"There's nothing my father could do that would shock me," said Catherine, in response to protests from Hamilton and Robertson. And as if to prove that nothing could interrupt her routine she calmly announced that luncheon would be at one o'clock as usual. It would only be a cold buffet, she said. In the circumstances it would be unreasonable to expect the cook to prepare a hot meal.

Five minutes later Parsons accompanied Catherine and Philip into their late father's bedroom. Lord Paul waited outside, acknowledging the immediate family's right to have priority.

Parsons drew back the curtains around the bed, watching them both closely as they approached the corpse. Catherine's thin, pinched face showed little emotion, and after a cursory glance at her father's body and the general state of the bed she turned away. Her dark eyes, so much like those of her father, bore no trace of a tear.

"He lived like a beast, inspector," she said coldly. "And it appears he died like one."

"Have you any idea, Miss Catherine," Parsons asked as diplomatically as he knew how, "how he came to be tied in this fashion?"

"My God, inspector, do you expect an unmarried woman like myself to explain these sexual perversions!"

The bluntness of her answer surprised Parsons. It had never occurred to him that Catherine would assume that the ropes binding her father were connected in any way with some sort of sexual activity. If nothing else, it proved to him that she had known a great deal about her father's behavior.

"Excuse me, inspector, I've work to do," she said abruptly, as though reading his thoughts. She hurried towards the door with quick, neat steps; anxious, it would appear, to avoid further questions.

Philip had also seen enough. Parsons had watched as his lips trembled and his sensitive face fleetingly betrayed a trace of grief. But like his sister, he appeared little moved by the manner of his father's death.

"I was terrified of him all my life, Everett," he confessed. "He was a cruel, sadistic bully, especially to people like me whom he knew to be weak. I don't rejoice at seeing him like this. Nor do I weep."

"When were you last in this room, Philip?"

The question surprised Philip, and he had to think for some time before answering.

"I don't think I've been here since father remarried," he replied. "And that's ten years ago."

"Then you don't know how long Lady Annabelle's portrait has been here."

Philip shook his head.

"I can't imagine at all what it's doing here," he said. "They've barely spoken for years. Annabelle despised him. But it's strange, now that I've seen her portrait here I find myself wondering if there was a side of father none of us ever knew. Look at this room with its books and prints. If you didn't know father's true nature you would imagine it was the room of a cultured, country gentleman with an adoring wife. And what could be further from the truth."

He was right, thought Parsons. There was much about the room that appeared alien to the man he had known so briefly. The man who had been a cruel, sexual deviant in life and whose tortured body now lay on the bed in front of them.

-10-

*I*t *was clear to Parsons from Lord Paul's transparent curiosity that* this was the first time he had been inside Lord Quentin's room. The portrait over the fireplace had made a noticeable impression on him. Considering the apparent closeness between the two men, this unfamiliarity struck Parsons as strange.

"Lady Annabelle is a remarkably handsome lady," he said, by way of encouraging a conversation.

Lord Paul looked at him in astonishment, as though only a connoisseur such as he might be allowed to express such an opinion.

"She is the most beautiful lady it has been my pleasure to meet," he said with great affection. "And I can say that now without fear of offending anyone."

As he spoke he looked in the direction of the body. If Lord Paul was surprised by the state of his predecessor he gave little sign. Nor did he display any sign of emotion. There was, however, a respect that neither Alexander, Catherine nor Philip had shown. But if the haughty gleam in his hazel eyes was anything to go by, there was also a sense of triumph.

"So many people have told me he was an evil man, Everett," he said, his thumbs pressed nonchalantly deep into the pockets of his waistcoat. "But whatever he did in his life he didn't deserve to die like this. He was always kind to me, and in the end he showed me the ultimate confidence and generosity in making me his heir."

"Did that come as a surprise, Lord Paul?"

"Not after what he said last night. He'd told me often enough how disappointed he was with his sons, and from what I know of them he'd every reason to be. I could well understand why he wouldn't want either of them to inherit the title, and his attitude to women made it unlikely he'd ever choose one of his daughters. Of course, I couldn't ever be sure that there wasn't a distant relative somewhere who might have a better claim to the title than me, but he'd said enough during the past few weeks to convince me that he wanted me to follow him. But I never imagined it would be so soon or in such terrible circumstances."

"How do you think the rest of the family will accept you?" asked Parsons. "Was Alexander's outburst merely an isolated incident, or do you think the others share his feelings?"

Lord Paul gave the question careful consideration.

"I know I can rely on Annabelle," he said with confidence. "During the time I've been here we've become very close friends. As far as Quentin's children are concerned, Elizabeth and Anne are probably both neutral towards me. They are infrequent enough visitors here and in their own ways seem happily involved in their own marriages. The boys' feelings are more difficult for me to judge. Philip doesn't seem to have strong feelings about anything; and even after what Alexander said just now, he may still come to accept me in time. In his heart I don't think he ever wanted the title. His interests are in London, not here in Hampshire. I expect the only strong opposition to come from Catherine. From what I've seen and heard she's been more or less running Beaumont since her mother's death and she was closer to Quentin in many ways than anyone else. Perhaps over the years she came to believe she would be the one to inherit, and if that's the case it may take some time before she forgives me. I'll just have to try to be extra charming towards her. Not that that will be easy. She's a difficult woman to get close to, and try as I might I've so far been unable to charm her."

His handsome face broke into a smile.

"And that's not usual, I can tell you," he boasted.

"Did Lord Quentin have any enemies that you know of?" Parsons asked, thinking how self-opiniated and arrogant the new master of Beaumont appeared.

"Not to my knowledge. He was a man with many sporting interests and a few gambling debts. But I believe that's not unusual for English aristocrats. Between you and me the estate has a few financial problems. I don't know the full story yet, but from what Robertson and others have told me Quentin had been living beyond his means for years. But whenever I've tried to find out anything about his past from Annabelle, Catherine or the boys they've always been reluctant to talks. I've learned precious little from anyone else. Since I've been here there have been few visitors. Quentin himself never liked talking about such matters, and you saw what happened last night when I started to probe."

"Perhaps the murder was directed at the family as much as the man. I think Alexander was implying that just now in the Library."

"I heard what he said. But what do you think he meant, Everett?"

"How much do you know about the family's history?"

"Very little."

"But you know the family has estates in Ireland."

Lord Paul nodded.

"Of course I do. Don't take me for a fool. Where do you think most of the servants come from."

"Then you've heard of what is now generally referred to as the Irish Famine."

Lord Paul looked less than comfortable.

"I'm afraid my knowledge of history is very poor," he said irritably. "Especially British history. That's clearly a disadvantage for someone in my position. One of the first things I intend to do is find myself a good tutor. Do you know anyone suitable. I'd pay well."

"I'm sorry, but I don't. But let me at least make a start in your education by telling you about the Famine."

Anticipating that his stay was going to be longer than expected, Lord Paul sat himself on the sofa and waved his arm towards Parsons patronizingly.

"Go on, Everett, old boy," he said with a chuckle. "I can see you're bursting to tell me. But before you start, be a good fellow and draw the curtains around Quentin. If you're going to say anything derogatory about his family I'd rather he didn't hear."

It was a tasteless remark, thought Parsons, and not one he would have associated with the urbane Paul. If it was an attempt to discourage him from talking, he could think again. He was going to get a lecture whether he liked it or not.

Parsons placed his thumbs in the pockets of his waistcoat in the same way that Paul had done some minutes before, and began to pace slowly up and down like a college professor.

"The potato is the staple diet of the Irish peasant," he began, as though addressing a class, "and just over thirty years ago a blight in the potato crop caused a series of disastrous harvests. Countless thousands died of malnutrition and associated diseases. Thousands of others were driven from the land and forced to emigrate. To this day many are still leaving. The majority went to North America, although that is something of an irony as the original blight is thought to have come from there. Not without good reason many Irish blamed the British government and absentee English landlord for doing little to help them in their hour of need. A great deal of bitterness and hatred exists about this even now, especially among groups like the Fenians. To some extent these people have my sympathy, although I don't condone their methods. Atrocities against English aristocrats living in relative splendor in Ireland are one thing, but it's quite another to indiscriminately bomb the streets of London, killing and maiming innocent men, women and children.

"I've heard of one or two things about that," said Lord Paul in a rather bored voice.

He yawned. Then he lit a cigar and nonchalantly blew smoke rings towards the ceiling. It seemed to Parsons that his attention span was short and his interest fading in the history he claimed a desire to learn. Perhaps it was time for a few home truths.

"I imagine the de Courceys were considered by their tenants to be as much to blame as any absentee landlords, although to be honest I don't know the extent of the famine in the north-west part of Ireland where I believe the de Courceys have their estates. But from what I've seen since I arrived at Beaumont they certainly exploit the Irish over here. Perhaps you can see why many will think that Lord Quentin's murder has its roots in Ireland."

"But what about Jamaica? I never got an answer to my question about Jamaica last night. You saw how Quentin reacted."

Parsons explained what he knew about the rebellion in Jamaica.

"Are you seriously telling me the blacks could be responsible for this," said Lord Paul incredulously. "Where I come from they would never dare. We'd string them up from the nearest tree."

Parsons could see what had attracted Paul to Lord Quentin. Apart from a common interest in horses and women, they also shared the same racial prejudices. From what he had learnt so far, the new head of the family might well continue exploiting the Irish servants in the way his predecessor had done. Unless, of course, Lady Annabelle was able to exert a moderating influence.

"To be frank the murder doesn't have the hallmark of a Fenian atrocity," Parsons conceded. "Nor can I believe that after all these years it has anything to do with Jamaica. Strangers would be quickly recognized in country areas like this, especially if they are black or Irish. But I hope I'm explaining what Alexander may have meant when he said the family was being punished for its sins. And as a policeman carrying out an investigation into a murder it's important I keep an open mind.

"Thank you for your lesson, Parsons," said Lord Paul, rising to his feet and stretching. "I've obviously become head of a family with some skeletons in the cupboard. But what English family with any pedigree doesn't have a few?"

He made his way to the door, leaving a long plume of smoke in his wake.

"But enough of that for now," he said dismissively. "It's time for a drink before Catherine's miserable cold platter. Won't you join me?"

"Not for the moment, Lord Paul," replied Parsons. "There are still some loose ends I want to clear up before Colonel Howard arrives."

-11-

Parsons checked his watch. There was still time before lunch for another visit to Montagu's room. If Montagu had returned from his mysterious nocturnal jaunt he might even find the gentleman himself. Failing that the room might yield some clue as to where he had gone.

The curtains had been opened since Parsons' earlier visit. Other than that little had changed. Some of the clothing had been cleared away and the bed-cover had been straightened; but the bed itself was still covered in papers. Montagu may indeed have returned, but it seemed much more likely that a diligent servant had been doing her best to tidy the room.

He put on his spectacles and glanced casually through the papers on the bed, half expecting to find amongst them drafts of some of Montagu's poems. Instead he found papers of a more serious nature: extracts of what appeared to be political essays and speeches. In some of these papers individual paragraphs had been sidelined in red, as if to emphasize particular points.

115

He was familiar with some of the authors. As a student John Stuart Mill had been one of his heroes. A Member of Parliament with radical views on democracy—particularly in regard to women's' rights—Mill's opinions rarely met with the approval of the upper classes. He had died six years ago, but during his life he had been a stern critic of the paternalistic structure of society, believing that everyone had an equal right to happiness, regardless of their background or class.

Intrigued by what he had found, Parsons sat on the bed and began reading the items that had been given special attention.

"Of the working men," he read, *"at least in the more advanced states of Europe, the patriarchal or paternal system of government is one to which they will not again be subject. The working class have taken their interests into their own hands and think the interests of their employers not identical to their own, but opposite to them. The poor cannot anymore be governed or treated like children."*

"The social arrangements of modern Europe commenced from a distribution of property which was the result, not of just partition, or acquisition by industry, but of conquest and violence."

William Morris was another name with which Parsons was familiar. Morris was both a poet and an artist. He had once been associated with the Pre-Raphaelite Brotherhood, but had later turned his talents towards the production of furniture, tapestries and wallpapers. Within the last few years, however, he had become increasingly interested in the political doctrines of socialism, and had strong views about the nature of work.

"Worthy work carries with it the hope of pleasure in rest," he read, *"the pleasure in our using what has been made, and the hope of pleasure in our daily creative skill. All other work is slave's work—mere toiling to live, that we may live to toil. But the total work done is portioned out very unequally among the different classes of society. The class of rich people who do no work consume a great deal, while they produce nothing."*

There was nothing unusual in finding papers such as these in the room of an intellectual like Montagu. These were sentiments shared by many young people. Even he, as a policeman charged with the protection of society, was aware that the wide divisions within British society were a matter of great concern. But whereas most thinking people, like Parsons, hoped for evolutionary change, there were those who wanted nothing short of revolution. Among these was the relatively obscure, elderly German political theorist who had been living in London for about thirty years. Karl Marx. Until recently Parsons had never heard of him. It was only when he was recently searching through the rented rooms of some of the arrested Fenians that he had come across a copy of Marx's *Das Capital.*

Montagu's papers contained extracts from some of Marx's works. One in particular had been marked for special attention with several explanation marks at the side of the page.

"The so-called revolutions of 1848 were but poor incidents," he read, *"small fractures and fissures in the dry crust of European society. However, they denounce the abyss. Beneath the apparently solid surface they betrayed oceans of liquid matter, only needing expansion to rend into fragments continents of hard rock. Noisily and confusedly, they proclaimed the emancipation of the proletariat—which has been the secret of the nineteenth-century—and of the revolution of that century."*

"To revenge the misdeeds of the ruling class, there existed in the Middle Ages in Germany, a secret tribunal called the 'Vehmgericht.' If a red cross was seen marked on a house, people knew that its owner was doomed by the 'Vehm.' All the houses of the ruling class of Europe are now marked with the mysterious cross. History is the judge—its executioner, the proletariat."

At the bottom of the page, written in large red capitals and under-lined several times were the words:

QUENTIN de COURCEY—YOUR DOOR HAS BEEN MARKED!!!

Parsons had thought of Montagu simply as a poet. But like Morris he appeared to be a poet with strong political views. But was he even more than that? Did he support not only the socialism and egalitarianism of the likes of Mills and Morris, but revolutionary anarchists like Marx, whose aim it was to abolish private property and destroy those that owned it. And if Montagu was of such a mind, what of Alexander? Had his recent outburst been more to do with his political beliefs than the loss of his inheritance?

೪೪೪

The small writing desk in front of the window was surprisingly uncluttered. Most of the papers that might have been on the desk appeared to have been thrown into an adjacent waste-paper basket. His curiosity now fully roused, Parsons picked up the basket, tipped the contents onto the desk and began sifting through the papers.

This time the content was different. Here were the discarded drafts of poems he had been expecting. In all probability the words were Montagu's. And from what he read he was scarcely to be compared with the great Byron.

Among these papers he found an unfinished letter that had been screwed up into a tight ball. It was written on Beaumont Castle stationery and from the scrawling manuscript with its exaggerated flourishes and heavy emphasis on capital letters it had been written by the same hand that had executed the poems. In spite of his prejudices against the upper classes, Montagu, it seemed, still clung to some of their trappings. It was a love letter.

"My dearest one," it began,

"After only two days I am missing you more than words can express. What can I ever do to put right what was said in one unfortunate unguarded moment.

As I sit here in my loneliness, the bright September moon fills the room. It comforts me, my love, to know that it gazes upon you. We are both so fortunate to share this miracle of life. Surely what we are creating together can only bring us even closer.

Beaumont is unbearable. With few exceptions the people here know nothing of the world and those who toil in it. Lord de Courcey himself is a monster, an abomination and the devil incarnate. How he could have fathered two such sons as Alexander and"

The letter ended abruptly. But along with the other papers it revealed to Parsons an entirely different side to Montagu than the one he had been led to believe existed. No longer was he merely an aesthetic young poet. He now appeared to Parsons to be driven by quite different motives.

Parsons began replacing the papers in the waste-basket, re-examining them as he did in case there was anything he had overlooked. After a second reading one of the verses looked familiar. It was not, as Parsons had originally assumed, one of Montagu's. Although he was not a literary connoisseur, the words were familiar to him, but for the moment he could not identify the author. He read the verse aloud in the hope that it would jog his memory, but the words only served to conjure up the image of Annabelle. It was a pleasant experience, and for him an unusual one, as rarely did he become distracted by thoughts of the opposite sex. He read the verse several times, relishing the sound of the words.

"She walks in beauty as the night
Of cloudless climes and starry skies;
And all that's best of dark and bright
Meet in her aspect and her eyes."

At the end of the verse there was what appeared to be an unrelated sentence:

"I will be in touch with you soon."

The note was unsigned and undated, but neither the verse nor the postscript had been written by Montagu. The handwriting, although similar, was much smaller, more compact and less flamboyant. But like Montagu's unfinished letter they were also written on Beaumont Castle stationery.

What did the postscript mean? Was there a threat implied or was he, as a policeman, reading far more into the words than they merited? And if it was a threat, to whom was it being made, and why was it associated with the verse. What connection, if any, did it have with Lord Quentin's death? Probably none at all, thought Parsons, realizing that he was now being irrational and allowing his mind to run ahead of him.

He could find nothing in the four small drawers at either side of the desk. It was easy to understand why Montagu had not chosen to use them. The quality of the wood used for the drawers was not good and they had become warped with age. Once opened, they were difficult to close. The bottom drawer on the right proved especially tiresome. He had not been able to pull it out to its full extent and it was now jammed. Parsons grunted in dismay as he was obliged to kneel on the floor to exert the necessary pressure on the drawer to close it. It was then he realized his mistake. The drawer was not empty. It contained a small silver box with Oriental designs.

There was a white powder inside the box. Recognizing neither its smell or taste he poured a small sample onto a sheet of paper, folded the sheet several times and put it in his waistcoat pocket. With luck, he thought, Doctor Hamilton would be able to identify the substance.

He also took the political tracts that Montagu had appeared to consider the most significant, Montagu's unfinished letter and the page containing the verse and the brief postscript. Montagu's explanation for all of these could prove illuminating.

-12-

The wide corridor at the bottom of the main staircase led in one direction to the Library and in the other to the Drawing Room. At right angles to this a narrower and much darker corridor ran towards the rear of the castle and the kitchen area. Parsons was sure he would find most of the servants there at this time of the day, as it was customary in most large houses for them to take their mid-day meal together in the Servants' Hall.

His assumption was confirmed by the sound of women's voices and the clatter of plates, directing him to a large room near the end of the passage. Through the open door he could see Johnson sitting in a high-backed chair at the end of a long pine table. At the far end of this table a large woman with a wild bush of grey hair presided over the meal, and from her ample proportions and ruddy complexion there could be no doubting that she was the cook. The other servants sat on wooden benches on either side of the table; although at one side of the table Parsons noted that Smith sat alone on one bench while four of the Irish girls squeezed together on another.

123

The conversation stopped abruptly when Parsons appeared. Sitting as he was with his back to the door, Johnson was at first unaware of Parsons' presence; and only the unusual silence and the faces of the servants staring past him towards the door drew his attention to the unexpected visitor. It was clear from his frown that Johnson was not pleased to see an uninvited guest in the part of the castle he considered to be his own domain.

He rose reluctantly to his feet.

"Can I help you, sir?" he said icily.

Parsons took a few paces into the room, conscious that he was now in a part of the castle where, especially for guests, the normal rules of decorum did not apply.

"Please sit down, Johnson," he said in what he hoped was a reassuring tone. "I won't keep you long from your meal, but I wanted to take this opportunity of saying a few words to you all about Lord Quentin's death."

He waited for the excited rustle of whispered conversation to stop before continuing.

"For those of you who do not already know me," he said, "my name is Parsons. Inspector Parsons of the Metropolitan Police."

Parsons waited a second time for the ripple of conversation to stop. Then gradually the faces around the table turned once more to face him. All except Claire. Her eyes remained firmly fixed on the table in front of her.

"As I'm sure you already know, ladies and gentlemen," Parsons said solemnly, "a terrible tragedy occurred here last night. Doctor Hamilton and I have now examined Lord

Quentin's body, and I regret to tell you that there can be no doubt that he was murdered."

There was a flurry of movement around the table. Hurried glances were exchanged, but no one it seemed dared speak. For several seconds there was an uncomfortable silence. Then, regardless of a frozen glance from Johnson that demanded she be silent, Claire began to sob.

This time Parsons ignored the tears.

"I've asked Johnson for a list of all your names," he said, "and I intend interviewing you all as soon as I have time. I hasten to add that this is merely a matter of routine and you have nothing to fear. Unless, of course, you have something to hide."

If Parsons had hoped that his last sentence would provoke a guilty reaction from someone in the room, he was disappointed. With the exception of Claire, all eyes had been firmly fixed upon him while he was speaking, and during that time every expression had remained inscrutable.

He looked inquiringly towards Johnson.

"Do you have the list yet?" he asked

"You will have it after luncheon, sir," Johnson said stiffly. "Where will I find you?"

"Either in my room," answered Parsons, "or in Lord Quentin's room with the Chief Constable."

For the time being there was nothing further Parsons could achieve in the Servants' Hall. It was one-fifteen and he was hungry, and anticipating a long, and perhaps acrimonious, afternoon with Colonel Howard he made his way to the

Dining Room. As he left the unnatural silence in the room behind him gave way to an excited outburst of animated conversation.

The atmosphere in the Dining Room provided a startling contrast. There was little conversation. Catherine sat stiffly at one end of the table, flanked by the Rawlinsons and Hamiltons. Lord Paul, Lady Annabelle and Robertson sat at the other end, leaving Philip and Montgomery to confront Ashton and an ashen-faced Fitzherbert across the middle. After his recent outburst it was not surprising to see that Alexander was absent.

Parsons helped himself to a generous portion of cold meat and vegetables and chose a seat across the table from Fitzherbert.

"You were not awake when I called on you earlier, major," he said casually, but in a voice loud enough for everyone else to hear. Whatever excuse Fitzherbert had offered for his absence from breakfast, Parsons wanted him to know that he was aware of the real reason.

Fitzherbert did not reply, attempting as best he could to ignore Parsons while he halfheartedly pushed a few vegetables around his plate. Ashton, however, aware of his companion's discomfort, attempted to divert Parsons attention.

"So what happens now, inspector?" he asked sarcastically. "Have you solved the murder? Which one of us is guilty?"

Catherine's furious gaze, had Ashton been aware of it, conveyed her displeasure at such inappropriate remarks.

"I'm anticipating that Colonel Howard will be here soon," explained Parsons. "When he arrives the investigation will be handed over to him."

The sneer on Ashton's face warned of further unpleasantness, but Catherine pre-empted him.

"I've sent a message to Mrs Williams in the village, inspector," she said. "She'll be here at three-thirty to prepare the body."

As ever she was a model of organization, thought Parsons. But even when it appeared that Catherine was trying to be helpful she appeared cold and distant. He found it impossible to like her.

"Thank you, Miss Catherine," he replied. "I'm sure that will be perfectly in order."

Parsons turned his attention to Philip.

"Is Alexander not eating?" he asked.

"He says he's not hungry. He's still upset and w-worried about G-geoffrey."

"Doesn't anybody yet know where Montagu is?" asked Parsons. It was getting to the point where a search might be necessary, and he wondered what resources the local police might have available. But no sooner had he considered this new problem than Montagu entered the room.

He had neither washed nor shaved and was still wearing evening dress from the night before. Ignoring the astonished expressions around the table he made straight for the food on the side-board and filled his plate. Then he sat next to Philip and began eating with the single-mindedness of a hungry vagrant.

"W-where the hell have you b-been, Geoffrey?" demanded Philip, enunciating the thoughts of everyone at table. "W-we've all been w-worried about you."

"I was walking," replied Montagu, between mouthfuls of food.

"W-walking at night!" asked Philip in amazement.

"Yes."

"W-where, for Heaven's sake."

"Just round the grounds."

As much as Montagu was becoming increasingly annoyed by the persistent questions, Philip was equally irritated by the evasive answers.

"Then you won't know that f-father has been m-murdered," he announced dramatically.

Montagu stopped eating and looked at Philip in disbelief.

"My God, has he," he said, with a thin slice of chicken still hanging from the corner of his mouth.

Either Montagu was a remarkable actor or his surprise was genuine, thought Parsons. From what he could see it was the latter. Not only did his response sound sincere, it was a stark contrast to the reactions of the others when they had first heard the tragic news.

"He was murdered in very unusual circumstances," Parsons said quietly. "I'll want to talk to you later about your whereabouts since dinner last night. So please don't disappear again."

Montagu did not reply. He sat sullenly at the table, all interest in his meal now abandoned. Parsons could sense his unease. But he had more pressing matters to attend to.

Doctor Hamilton and his wife were on the point of leaving the table, and before Colonel Howard arrived he wanted to speak to the doctor again.

He caught up with the Hamiltons in the corridor.

"May I have your opinion about this powder, doctor," Parsons asked, taking the folded paper from his pocket and handing it to Hamilton.

"Excuse us, my sweet," Hamilton said to his wife. "You go ahead. I will join you in the Drawing Room in a few moments."

Hamilton watched his wife until she was safely out of ear-shot before examining the powder. He licked a finger and dipped it into the powder.

"Where did you get this, inspector?" he asked, clearly surprised by Parsons' offering.

"I'd prefer not to say for the moment. Do you know what it is?"

"Certainly," said Hamilton. "It's cocaine."

The doctor was amused by the look of amazement on Parsons' face. There was something delightfully innocent about this young man, he thought.

"Tell me more, doctor," said Parsons. "What is it used for, how is it taken, and what are its effects?"

Hamilton became serious again. He thought for a few moments before replying.

"Cocaine is derived from the leaves of the coca plant," he explained, "a plant that is commonly found in South America. The Indians there use it for pleasure or to withstand strenuous working conditions, hunger or thirst. It acts as an anesthetic by interrupting the impulses in the nerves, especially in the mucous membranes of the eye, nose and throat. For that reason it's often inhaled and frequently causes a runny nose."

Parsons thought at once of the cold that Alexander had developed overnight.

Hamilton continued.

"It causes exhilaration and a sense of well-being, increased mental alertness and relief from fatigue. I believe for those reasons it is popular with some of the so-called creative people."

The doctor's choice of words indicated that he had guessed where Parsons had found the drug.

"In the short term it produces euphoria, but later this leads to symptoms like depression, sleeping disorders, mental confusion, loss of contact with reality, and severe personality disturbances. In large doses it often causes convulsions and even death."

"Could someone under the influence of cocaine commit murder?" asked Parsons.

"Undoubtedly. They might even be unaware of what they were doing."

"I see," said Parsons. "Thank you, doctor. You've been a great help once more. I hesitate to impose on you so much, but have you managed to get Catherine's permission to examine Claire?"

"I have. She was naturally curious and asked me why I was doing it. When I told her it was a police matter she wasn't at all happy. But she eventually accepted my word that it was important. I've arranged to examine the girl in her room this afternoon, and I'll tell you what I find before I leave."

Parsons allowed Hamilton to rejoin his wife. He needed a few minutes to gather his thoughts, and a stroll in the grounds seemed as good a way as any of preparing for what could prove to be a stressful afternoon.

The storm had passed, leaving in its wake the first signs of the approaching winter. The lush grass of the Great Park under his feet was thick with leaves that gusted and swirled in the intermittent breezes that still played amongst the trees. Had not duty beckoned he would have walked happily through the park for the rest of the afternoon. But after only fifteen minutes he turned reluctantly back towards the castle and retraced his steps.

As he reached the drawbridge he could see through the trees the distant horsemen, and as he watched and waited the three figures gradually came close enough for him to identify individuals. Colonel Howard was in the lead, a brown bowler hat wedged firmly on his large head. A policeman wearing a familiar pointed helmet rode a few yards behind. Both of them were draped in long black riding capes to protect them from the elements. The third figure was some distance behind the other two men, and was less prepared for the inclement weather. Wearing only the same cloth cap, thin jacket and trousers he had worn when he had collected them at the station the previous day the wretched groom appeared miserable and bedraggled.

Parsons waited for Howard to reach him.

"Thank you for responding so quickly in such dreadful weather, sir," he said. "I've plenty to tell you, but I suggest you first of all dry yourself and have a bite of lunch. Dunne can take the officer to the kitchen for something to eat. Then I suggest we meet in Lord Quentin's room at two-thirty."

"Good thinking, Parsons," said Howard, his face flushed more than before from the exposure to wind and rain. "Tell me, how are the family taking the tragedy?"

"Remarkably well, sir," replied Parsons diplomatically. "I've been surprised to see how calm and unemotional everyone has been."

"Typical de Courcey pluck in the face of adversity, if you ask me," retorted Howard. "Must be some of Quentin's character rubbing off on them."

It was not the way that Parsons had interpreted the family's reactions. Apathy and dislike were the words he thought more appropriate in describing their response to the death of the head of the family.

-13-

olonel Howard reached Lord Quentin's room at two-thirty precisely, his face flushed even more by the three glasses of claret he had taken with his lunch. Unaware of the finer details of the murder, he was quite unprepared for what awaited him, and regardless of the seriousness of the investigation it was all Parsons could do to keep a straight face as he witnessed the colonel's bewildered expression when first confronted with the body.

"My God," he said, "however did they manage to tie Quentin up like this. It must've taken several of the devils."

With growing disbelief Howard listened to Parsons' account of what had happened, based on Claire's evidence and Doctor Hamilton's examination.

"I'd never imagine Quentin to have involved himself in anything like that," he said, genuinely shocked by what he had heard.

"Nor I, sir."

"Do you think the girl can be believed?"

"It seems altogether too incredible a story for an ignorant girl to invent, and there may well be others who can corroborate her story. But as far as I can tell there seems little doubt that Lord Quentin was taking advantage of the servants. After you left last night he was even boasting of his exploits."

Howard shook his head several times. It seemed he was either still unconvinced about his late friend's perversions or found it too difficult to come to terms with them. For some time he stood at he end of the bed, seemingly unsure of what to do next.

The decision was made for him when the police officer who had accompanied him appeared at the door.

"Stay outside until I call you, Sergeant Brown," he commanded. "We don't want to be disturbed for the time being."

"Can't have the junior ranks seeing their superiors like this," he confided to Parsons after Brown had withdrawn. "Bad for morale you know."

Parsons thought he had never heard anything quite so ridiculous.

"You'll pardon me, sir," he said, barely able to control his anger, "but may I remind you we are investigating a particularly hideous murder. Apart from the Irish girl, Claire, several members of the family have already seen the body, and I imagine what has happened will soon be common knowledge amongst the staff and even in the village. I've already told the servants we will be interviewing them all individually about their whereabouts last night and the sooner we start doing that the better. So keeping Sergeant

Brown in the dark seems an unnecessary waste of police resources."

The deepening color of Howard's face and the furious expression in his eyes told Parsons that his words had not been well received. He had over-stepped the mark and anticipated a severe rebuke. But he was spared for the moment. Much to Howard's increasing displeasure Brown had re-entered the room.

"I thought I told you to wait outside," Howard snapped.

"Doctor Hamilton is here with information for Inspector Parsons," explained Brown patiently, in the voice of a man who has learned to control himself in the most trying circumstances.

"Well, don't just stand there, man. Show him in," ordered Howard, his impatience growing by the second.

Hamilton entered the room, but was given no opportunity to explain the reason for his visit.

"Yes, doctor," said Howard brusquely, "what is it? Can't you see we're busy?"

"I asked the doctor to examine the girl, Claire," Parsons explained patiently, "to establish whether she was still a virgin. Lord Quentin had intimated that she was when he told us last night he had never previously had intercourse with her. Apparently he considered it his right to de-flower each of the Irish female-servants when they arrived at Beaumont. This morning the girl told me that his lordship had fallen asleep before they had become intimate. I think it is important to try to establish what happened here last night, and I'm hoping that Doctor Hamilton's examination will help resolve the matter one way or another. Has it, doctor?"

"I can confirm that the girl is not a virgin," said Hamilton solemnly.

"But can you establish whether she had intercourse last night?" asked Parsons.

"I can't be certain about that. All I can tell you for sure is that she did not lose her virginity last night, but if you want to learn more I'm afraid you'll have to ask the girl yourself. I didn't consider such personal matters as any of my business. Now you must excuse me, gentlemen. It's time we left. I've other patients to see today and Anne is anxious to be home before dark."

Hamilton had previously made clear to Parsons what he thought of the Chief Constable's professional ability and it was clear from the doctor's tone that he was only too glad to have an excuse to leave.

"Thank you, doctor," said Parsons. "Your help today has been invaluable."

Hamilton's nod of acknowledgement as he left gave Parsons hope that the doctor did not associate him with the colonel's unwarranted rudeness, nor had he been included on the doctor's list of incompetent policemen.

"Well, Parsons, what does all that tell you?" Howard demanded, after the doctor had gone.

"It tells me that the girl was not as innocent as I thought, sir."

"And where does that get us?"

"Nowhere in particular, sir. Until I've interviewed everyone who was in the castle last night I'm not speculating about anything."

"That approach may be good enough for you, Parsons," said Howard, his face close enough to Parsons for him to smell the colonel's stale breath, "but I want this cleared up quickly. I already have my own suspicions. I warned Quentin many times about the potential danger of employing so many Irish, but he always laughed it off as foolishness on my part. He said he treated the Irish like his soldiers and he never had any trouble with them when he was in the army."

Sergeant Brown entered the room again.

"There's a feller called Spencer here, sir. Says he's got something to say about last night."

"Do you know this man, Parsons?"

Parsons shook his head.

"Then send him in Brown," ordered Howard, "and let's hear what he has to say."

A tall broad-shouldered man with a military bearing entered the room and stood respectfully just inside the door waiting to be spoken to. He appeared to Parsons to be in his mid-forties, and wore a shabby single-breasted check jacket patched at the elbows, and lovat-coloured breeches. He had removed whatever footwear he had been wearing, presumably because it was dirty, revealing a well-darned pair of thick socks.

"Well, Spencer, who are you and what can you tell us?" Howard asked bluntly.

"I'm the game keeper here, sir," explained Spencer, in a quiet voice with the trace of a Northern accent. "We've been losing too many birds of late, so his lordship instructed me to patrol the grounds regularly at night to see if I could catch anyone poaching."

"And is that what you were doing last night?" Parsons asked, anxious to keep in control of the questioning as much as possible.

"Yes, sir."

"Did you see anything suspicious while you were patrolling?"

"No, sir. Not then. But early this morning when I was coming past the stables on my way to the kitchen for a bite to eat I saw someone coming out of the castle. It was barely light, sir, so I hid in the shadows in case it was an intruder."

"What time was this?"

"I couldn't say exactly, sir, but I'd say it was around five-thirty."

"Did you see who it was?"

"Yes, sir. It was Dunne, the young groom."

"And what's so special about that?" interrupted Howard.

"Well, sir, he's not supposed to be in the castle at night. He sleeps in the stables."

"Quite right too," said Howard, "it wouldn't be right with all those young girls around."

As soon as he had spoken Howard realized how foolish his last remark had sounded, and took refuge in a fit of coughing behind a large white handkerchief.

"Thank you, Spencer, that's been very helpful," said Parsons, after waiting for Howard's coughing fit to subside. "But why have you waited until now to tell us this?"

"Because at the time Dunne being in the castle didn't seem that important, sir. I knew it wasn't right, but I was more interested in getting a hot drink inside me than questioning the lad. And if you want to know why I haven't told you before it's because I've been asleep. After night duty I go home for a few hours, and I didn't hear until late this morning about the girl's involvement in Lord Quentin's murder."

Parsons caught the Chief Constable's eye. Spencer's comments made Howard's attempt to keep his sergeant in ignorance about the nature of the crime appeared to be even more foolish now that the news had reached the village. But Howard was not to be discomfited and reacted with his customary bluster.

"Where's all this leading, Spencer?" he asked abruptly. "What exactly are you trying to tell us?"

From the resigned expression on Spencer's face, Parsons deduced that he had dealt with people like the Chief Constable before. If, as appeared probable, he had served in the army he would have had ample opportunity to develop an ability to remain respectfully silent in the face of provocation from a superior officer.

"I'm not trying to tell you gentlemen anything," he said politely but firmly. "But I did think the connection was obvious, Dunne being the girl's brother."

-14-

*P*arsons' *initial shock at hearing that Claire and the groom* were brother and sister gave way to a sense of failure, a feeling that was compounded by the sight of the self-satisfied expression on Colonel Howard's face. He was furious with himself for not finding out whether any of the staff were related to one another. Such an over-sight would do little to convince Howard of his ability to run an investigation, and he was sure the colonel was unlikely to forget it. What made it even more galling was that he had earlier noticed the similarity in the voices of the two Dunnes.

Howard was galvanized into action.

"Brown," he instructed, "take Spencer, find the boy and bring him here for questioning. If necessary get Smith to give you a hand. I know he won't take any nonsense from Dunne."

"Well, Parsons," he said, when they were alone, "so much for your methodical detective work. I'm always inclined to follow my first instincts, and Brown will tell you I was uneasy about the boy all the time we were riding here. He

140

always hung back as though he was trying to avoid us. It seemed to me all along that he was trying to hide something."

"You're probably right, sir," replied Parsons, humbled by what he had learned and hating to acknowledge that such a pompous ass as Howard might be right.

He watched sullenly as Howard closed the drapes around the bed.

"I'm sorry, sir," he said. "My error was unforgivable. But even now the evidence against the Dunnes is purely circumstantial. Hamilton thinks the murder took place before four-thirty, which is an hour before Dunne was seen leaving the house. And his sister claims she left this room before one o'clock. No doubt one or other of the servants can confirm that."

"Why should we believe any of them, Parsons," said Howard, pacing the room like a turkey-cock. "I shouldn't have to tell someone with your recent experience that the Irish are renowned liars and can be relied upon to stick together through thick and thin. For all we know they're all involved in this. Especially if there's any truth in what you say was going on between Quentin and the women."

Parsons had to accept that Howard could be right. The girls could easily fabricate a story amongst themselves. After all, perjury was common enough amongst criminals. But that was all the more reason why a methodical approach like his would achieve better results than Howard's crude hit-or-miss methods.

After ten minutes Brown returned with Smith and Spencer, holding between them the sorry figure of Dunne. His clothes were still wet from the morning's ride, and he left a trail of wet footprints behind him as he was half-led and half-dragged into the room. As a small man himself, Parsons could sympathize with the groom. He looked terrified, dwarfed as he was by the two burly men holding him. There was blood trickling from his nose and from the corner of his mouth, and he was close to tears. Which of the men, thought Parsons, had been so free with his fists.

There was no respite for the boy. Howard began questioning him immediately.

"Well, Dunne, what have you got to say about this?" he said, dramatically opening the curtains around the bed to allow the groom sight of Lord Quentin's body.

The boy seemed to shrink back into the arms of his captors.

"B'Jaysus, sir, I know nothing about that," he said in alarm.

Howard bent threateningly over Dunne, thrusting his face against the boy's.

"So what were you doing inside the castle last night?" he roared, with all the assurance of a swaggering bully with a defenseless victim at his mercy.

The boy did not speak for a few moments, and when he did the lack of assurance in his reply was palpable.

"I was not in the castle, sir," he mumbled. "I'm not allowed in the castle at night."

Howard stepped back and nodded to Brown. Without warning the sergeant put his full weight behind a violent punch to the boy's stomach. As Dunne doubled up in agony Parsons stepped forward to protest. But he was rudely waved to one side.

"Keep out of this, Parsons," Howard said grimly. "This is my investigation now."

Parsons was no stranger to this form of questioning. The Metropolitan Police could be as rough as any, and he had seen bigger and stronger men than Dunne reduced to tears after a few nights in police custody. But there was something pitiful about the defenseless young groom in the hands of the four large men, and he felt ashamed to be any part of it.

Howard continued his onslaught.

"Don't lie to me, Dunne," he bellowed, "or Sergeant Brown will hit you again. And when he tires Smith will take over."

Dunne's terrified glance flitted from Brown to Smith, and then back to Howard, who had begun pacing backwards and forwards in front of the boy. Eventually he stopped in front of the groom, put his right hand under Dunne's chin and pulled the boy's face towards him.

"As you rightly say," Howard said, in a quieter voice, "you had no business to be in the castle. Yet you were seen leaving this morning at half-past five by Spencer. How do you account for that?"

Dunne said nothing, and finding no sign of sympathy on Spencer's face he looked apprehensively towards Brown, anticipating the next blow.

Howard continued his questioning.

"By her own admission your sister was in this room last night," he said. "And it is my belief that the two of you murdered Lord Quentin."

Howard gripped Dunne's cheeks between the thumb and index finger of each of his hands and pulled the boy's face upwards towards his, forcing him to stand on his toes.

"There may, of course, have been others involved. If there are I'm sure you'll eventually tell us. Won't you, Dunne."

The implication of Howard's threat was as visible as the marks left by his nails on the boy's face. He finally released his grip, allowing Dunne's head to slump forward, and then resumed his pacing.

After several minutes he stopped in front of the boy again and gripped his chin so tightly that Parsons could see the whites of Howard's knuckles. He pulled Dunne's face towards his, re-establishing eye-contact.

"Would you like Sergeant Brown to hit you again?" he asked threateningly.

Dunne attempted to shake his head in spite of Howard's firm grip.

"I didn't do it, sir. I swear to God and all the saints I had nothing to do with any of this. You've got to believe me, sir."

"If *you* didn't do it, then who did?" demanded Howard. "Was it your sister or one of the other servants? Speak up, boy, my patience is running out."

The colonel tightened his grip on Dunne's chin and pressed his red, angry face closer to the boy's.

"Well, Dunne, was it that sweet sister of yours?" he whispered. "Or did *you* kill Lord Quentin in a fit of rage after you discovered he'd taken her virginity? Is that why you killed him, Dunne?" shouted Howard, his voice rising to a crescendo and his saliva sprinkling the boy's face. "Did you kill him because he raped your lovely young sister?"

Fear of another sort appeared in Dunne's eyes. He was now no longer frightened for himself alone. His fear was now for his sister.

"She's innocent, sir," he begged. "I swear by Our Blessed Lady she'd never do this."

"That's what you say, Dunne," screamed Howard. "But why should I believe a Fenian liar like you. The evidence against you both looks damning enough to me, and I'm sure a few days in Brown's tender care will convince your sister she's every bit as guilty as you."

Howard lowered his voice and smirked.

"Brown can be very convincing, you know," he said.

The wretched groom looked desperately from Howard to the body on the bed and then at the grim faces of the men holding him. Then he began whimpering like a child, the tears that had always threatened trickling slowly down his cheeks to mingle with the blood around his mouth.

How ironic, thought Parsons, that the only tears he had seen shed since Lord Quentin's death were those of the two Dunnes.

"I did it, sir." The boy's voice was barely audible between sobs. "God help me. I did it. For sweet Jaysus' sake, take me but don't touch Claire."

An unbearably smug expression appeared on the Chief Constable's florid features. He glanced triumphantly towards Parsons before issuing his instructions.

"Take this Fenian bastard to the cells in Petersfield, Brown,' he ordered. "We'll hold him there for further questioning before transferring him to Winchester for trial. Smith, you organize some transport and then go with Spencer and Brown. We don't want to risk this desperate young assassin escaping."

-15-

onvinced that he was witnessing the arrest of an innocent man, Parsons could, nevertheless, do no more than watch helplessly as Dunne was bundled away.

"Aren't you being a bit premature, sir," he said, mustering as confident a voice as he could under the circumstances. "The evidence against Dunne is far from conclusive and will hardly stand up in a court of law."

"Poppycock, Parsons. You heard Dunne's confession, and I see no reason why he would ever retract it as long as he thinks he's protecting his sister."

"And what makes you think she's guilty?"

Howard regarded the young inspector with contempt.

"It's quite obvious to me that Dunne was involved. Judging by his reaction I'd say his sister was as well. He'll soon talk. It's only a matter of time before we get the full story out of him."

God preserve us from such incompetent oafs, thought Parsons, as he struggled to remain calm. Losing his temper at this point would help neither Dunne nor himself.

"I'm surprised you've reached this conclusion without questioning anyone else, sir," he said, a trace of sarcasm creeping into his voice. "As far as I'm concerned the only person who seems to have an alibi for the time Lord Quentin was murdered is Fitzherbert. And that's only because he was too drunk to stand. For a start we appear to have a political radical like Montagu roaming around all night, probably under the influence of cocaine. We have no idea yet what he was doing. I don't automatically assume he's involved, of course, but on the face of it there's as much circumstantial evidence against him as there is against the Dunnes. So you must at least let me question the other people who were in the castle last night."

"You'll do nothing of the sort, young man," Howard snorted. "This investigation is now entirely in my hands. I want no further assistance from you. My men or I will do all the questioning that's necessary. And I warn you, Parsons, if you continue to interfere I'll have you recalled to London."

It was the last thing Parsons had been expecting. Even allowing for the unfortunate clash of personalities between he and Howard he had never imagined that the Chief Constable would dispense with his services so peremptorily. Under normal circumstances he would expect a county police force without its own criminal investigation department to welcome the experience of an experienced detective like himself. What was Howard playing at? Was he merely trying to cover up his own professional inadequacies and those of his force or was there an alternative motive? Had the fact that it was possible to implicate an Irishman like Dunne so easily played right into Howard's hands? And could it be that the Chief Constable was more aware of what had been going on in the castle than he cared to admit?

The more he thought about it the more convinced he became that Howard wanted to keep him out of the way. A few judicious questions by him could prove embarrassing for the colonel. Perhaps it was time for him to go on the offensive.

"I find it hard to believe there were not others who knew about Lord Quentin's behavior," he said, looking across the room to the body.

"What exactly are you getting at, Parsons?" snapped Howard.

Parsons sensed a trace of unease in the colonel's answer.

"From what I've heard his lordship's abuse of the female servants was common gossip amongst the local gentry. I'm sure rumors such as that must have reached your ears."

He waited as Howard blew his nose loudly.

"As a frequent visitor to Beaumont, sir," he said, adopting the predatory tone he had last heard employed by prosecuting counsel at the Old Bailey, "you had ample opportunity to investigate such rumors, and if necessary put a stop to any sort of behavior that was in breach of human decency or an abuse of the servants' legal rights. Or could it be that you might have availed yourself of the services that Lord Quentin provided?"

It was a wild and desperate shot and one he might well live to regret, but it had the desired effect. Howard was not one to easily conceal what he was thinking. His disquiet turned rapidly to unease. The earlier look of triumph gave way to one of dismay, not dissimilar to that which Parsons recalled seeing the previous evening as Howard was marched out of the castle by his wife. With a sense of relief and a growing confidence Parsons felt his gamble had paid off.

"No doubt any scandal associated with this murder will reflect upon others," he said, pressing home his advantage. "So an early arrest and a convenient scapegoat would be in everyone's interests."

The flicker of panic on Howard's face finally convinced Parsons that he was on the right track. But he was wrong in thinking he could manipulate Howard so easily.

"Inspector Parsons," the Chief Constable said icily. "You are an ill-mannered and insolent young man, and I only wish I had the time to teach you some manners. Your presence here is clearly hampering my enquiries, and I intend to do something about it. As soon as I get the opportunity I will be sending a telegram to my friend, Colonel Wilson, the Metropolitan Police Commissioner, informing him of your insolence and asking him to order you back to London immediately. In the meantime let me remind you that I am your superior officer, and regardless of who you are, where you come from or what you think, you'll do as I say. From this moment you are not to take any further part in this investigation."

Howard had quite unexpectedly and dramatically regained the initiative, and Parsons knew there was no point in protesting. There was little doubt that what Howard proposed doing would succeed. In the final resort it was impossible to get the better of the powerful network of ex-Army officers in the higher echelons of the police.

Without a further word Parsons stormed from the room and headed downstairs. It was only a matter of time before he was officially recalled. But until then, and regardless of what Howard had just said, he had no intention of stopping his own enquiries. If there was to be any miscarriage of justice at Beaumont it would be through no fault of his.

-16-

It was just before four o'clock when Parsons reached the kitchen: a large well-equipped room with two large pine dressers crammed with saucepans and a miscellany of other cooking utensils along one wall and a range of spotless ovens along another. Preparation for afternoon tea were well in hand. Supervised by the cook, whom he now knew to be called Mrs Hughes, two of the girls were making delicate-sized sandwiches on a scrubbed wooden table in the center of the room. From the open doorway where he stood, Parsons could see into the adjoining Servants' Hall where Johnson was seated in his customary place at the head of the table engrossed in a newspaper.

In the silence that greeted his arrival, Parsons approached the ample figure of Mrs Hughes.

"Good afternoon," he said, with what he hoped was a winning smile. "I can see you're very busy, but if it were at all possible I'd like to have a few words with some of the girls.

He consulted the list Johnson had given him.

"Can Dwyer, O'Mahoney, Sweeney or O'Brien be spared for a few minutes?"

"You can't have Sweeney or O'Brien, sir," the cook replied, continuing to bustle and busy herself around the kitchen. "You can see they're helping me with the tea. O'Mahoney and Dwyer are in the scullery peeling the vegetables for dinner. You can talk to them there provided you aren't too long."

She indicated the direction of the scullery with a sideways nod of her head.

"You may rely on me, Mrs Hughes," said Parsons, keeping his smile firmly in place. "I'll be as brief as I can. But it would help me if I had some privacy. Is there anywhere I can speak with each girl alone?"

The idea that any servant should be entitled to privacy appeared a novel one to Mrs Hughes. Parsons watched with some amusement as she debated the question silently with herself, turning her ruddy, round country-woman's face alternately between himself and the direction of the scullery. After much deliberation she granted him the use of the laundry room, which she informed him he would find on the other side of the scullery.

He found O'Mahoney and Dwyer slicing cabbages on a rough wooden table. With its steamy atmosphere and disagreeable smell of boiled vegetables, the room was a living testimony to the way in which English cooks contrived to destroy the flavor of their food.

"I have Mrs Hughes' permission to speak with you both," he explained, when he saw their apprehensive looks.

"She tells me there's a laundry room nearby where I can talk with each of you in private."

Dwyer was the first to react. Placing her knife on the table she went over to the sink to wash her hands.

"'Tis this way, sir," she said, drying her hands on her apron as she led Parsons across the stone floor.

As he passed the table he picked up a piece of raw cabbage.

"I can never resist the heart," he explained to the surprised O'Mahoney. "It tastes so much better before it's cooked."

The laundry room was damp and cold, and in the dimness of the fading afternoon the large wooden sinks and clothes-ringers appeared at first glance like instruments in a medieval torture chamber. Only the wicker baskets of dirty linen and the rows of serried garments billowing on the lines outside revealed the room's true purpose.

The stables were visible beyond the washing lines, establishing the position of the laundry as being in the north-east and coldest corner of the castle. It seemed to Parsons a miserable place in which to work.

Dwyer was the tallest of the girls. She had a long, thin face with freckles. Although there was a sense of imbalance between her wide-set eyes and small, rounded mouth the overall effect was not displeasing. It was an honest enough face, and Parsons found his first impression to be favorable. Had he met her in any other circumstance he would have had no trouble in trusting her word implicitly. But this was not just any circumstance.

"Will you tell me what happened last night after I left the Hall," he asked.

"Aye, indeed I will, sir. And bless you for speaking up as you did. 'Tis a fine gentleman you are, and you'll not be meeting many like yourself in this terrible place."

In spite of attempts to hide his embarrassment, Parsons could feel his cheeks coloring. Flattery was the last thing he had been expecting, and for a moment he lost his composure.

"Please continue, Dwyer," he mumbled.

"Well, sir, after you'd gone they didn't take long to pair us off, and I was thinking to myself that for once my luck was in. Wasn't I chosen by Mr Paul."

"You mean Lord Paul. Since this morning he's the new head of the family."

The girl looked at Parsons blankly. Then her eyes opened wide in surprise.

"B'Jaysus," she said, "so he's the new master. Lady Annabelle will be well pleased. But we'll have to be watching our manners down here, and that's a fact. Miss Catherine won't be taking kindly to the news."

"And why should that be?"

"Because 'twas rumored, sir, that Lord Quentin had made Miss Catherine his heir, seeing he was so disappointed with the two boys. Ach, but it seems Mr. Paul has stolen the march on her."

Parsons wondered if there was any substance in this rumor. Servants' gossip was hardly the most reliable of sources. Nevertheless, he made a mental note to ask Robertson about the contents of any earlier wills. That was always supposing he ever had the chance of speaking with the solicitor again.

"And what happened last night between you and Lord Paul?"

"Nothing, sir," she said, the disappointment in her voice echoed in the down-turned corners of her small mouth. "Nothing at all. When I went to his room he was smoking a cigar. Sure, I could see he was a little drunk, but nothing like others I've seen. To be sure he's a dreadful handsome man, sir, and all we girls think well of him."

There was a barely concealed sigh from the girl before she continued.

"Well, I asked if I could be fetching him a brandy, sir. But he said he'd already had enough for one night. So I stood in the middle of the room feeling foolish and not knowing what to be doing next. You see none of us had been with him before, sir. Since Mr. Paul arrived at Beaumont Lord Quentin hasn't been doing any entertaining."

"Did you spend long in his room?"

"Nay, sir. Sure, after a few minutes he said he wouldn't be needing me and that I should go to bed. To be honest, sir, I'd been looking forward to bedding him. He was such a change from the likes of Lord Quentin and the others."

"And who might these others be?" asked Parsons, hoping to confirm his earlier hunch.

"Two of them were here last night, sir. Sir Henry Rawlinson and Colonel Howard. Of course, they weren't able to be staying last night, weren't they with their ladies."

Dwyer had attempted to enunciate the word *ladies* in the nasal tones of the English upper classes. In that she had failed, but she nevertheless managed to convey quite successfully her opinion of such women.

Parsons wished that the Chief Constable had been present to witness the jubilant expression on his face. Dwyer's comments could be the first step in unraveling a sordid episode involving a group of prominent local figures. It might have little to do with the murder of Lord Quentin, but nevertheless he hoped an opportunity to expose the scandal might arise sometime in the future.

"What time did you leave Lord Paul's room?" he asked.

"Sure now, it must've been quarter after twelve, sir, as I was back in my own room before half past."

"Can you confirm that?"

"Sweeney can, sir. We share a room. She was already getting undressed when I arrived."

"I believe she had been with Major Fitzherbert."

"That she had, sir. And when she went to his room didn't she find he'd been sick all over his bed. So she left him. And fortunate she was, for the man's a disgusting creature, and the last thing any of us would want to be bedding."

"Did you see anyone else on your way back to your room?"

"Nay, sir. I did not."

"Then that will be all, thank you, Dwyer. You can tell O'Mahoney I'll see her now."

Parsons had encountered similar hostility to that shining from O'Mahoney's dark eyes many times before. A policeman becomes accustomed to it. But he sensed that O'Mahoney's reaction to him was not entirely due to his profession. All Englishman would, no doubt, have elicited a similar response from her. And he had little doubt that she considered a small, mild-mannered Englishman such as himself to be fair game, regardless of the fact that he was a police inspector.

"I believe you were in Mr Montgomery's room last night," he said with an exaggerated politeness, hoping to lull her into a false sense of security.

"Aye, that I was."

The absence of the customary 'sir' and the belligerent tone contrasted sharply with that of the soft-spoken Dwyer.

"And did you sleep there all night?"

She tossed her dark shoulder-length hair defiantly, and only then did Parsons notice that she had removed her mob-cap for the interview. It was the sort of defiant gesture very few servants would have dared make.

"And where else would I be sleeping?" she said insolently.

Parsons ignored the provocation.

"I believe you were also in Lord Quentin's room."

"Aye. I was that."

"And what exactly were you doing there?"

"Tying the dirty bastard up like I always do."

"That's no way to speak of your late master."

Parsons knew he was sounding pompous and patriarchal. But he had little time for bad manners, no matter what the circumstances might be. He was also fast tiring of O'Mahoney's bellicose attitude.

Either she read his thoughts or she had decided that it was after all not such a good idea to speak her mind too freely, but her response was quieter and more respectful.

"I'm sorry, sir," she said, "but he was a wicked man, and God will surely punish him for his sins by roasting his soul in Hell for eternity."

The girl was probably right about Lord Quentin's destiny, thought Parsons. Even Catherine had considered her father had received his just desserts.

"Tell me what else you did in that room."

O'Mahoney explained how she and Claire had helped Lord Quentin onto the bed and tied his arms and legs to the bedposts. It was no different to what he wanted when she had been with him before. After that she had left the room. She confirmed that the curtains around the bed had been open and that when she left the room Lord Quentin was snoring loudly.

"What about the painting over the fireplace?"

"Lady Annabelle's portrait. The curtains were drawn across it."

"Did it always remain so when you were with him?"

"Nay, sir. It did not. He liked to be seeing her face when we were bedding him."

"Why do you think that was?"

"'Tis only a guess, sir, for he never said anything to me. He never called her name nor spoke of her, but I'm thinking he imagined it was always she in the bed with him and not any of us."

For a moment it seemed she had forgotten that Parsons was in the room. Did she, and even some of the other girls, he wondered, know more about Lord Quentin than any of his family. Like Philip, he was beginning to think there were sensitivities and emotions that Lord Quentin had kept buried deep within himself. It was too late now for anyone to seek those finer feelings. Lord Quentin was dead.

"Did you see Claire again last night?"

"Aye, sir. She came to Mr Montgomery's room to say that Lord Quentin was still asleep. She asked me what she should do."

"And what was your advice?"

"I told her to see that the rope around his neck wasn't tight and then to leave him. It had happened like that when I was with him before. He was getting too old for these games, especially after a jar or two."

"Why do you think he wanted to be tied like that?"

She looked at him for a long time before answering. Perhaps she felt unqualified to speak on such matters and feared that if she did she would be misunderstood. But he had asked the question, and she could do no more than answer it.

"Lord Quentin was a wicked man, without doubt, sir. He enjoyed hurting people in many different ways, sometimes through their bodies and sometimes through their minds. But I'm thinking that sometimes he wanted to feel the pain for himself."

As O'Mahoney's defiance mellowed it began to dawn on Parsons that not only was she a handsome woman but she was one who also possessed sensitivity and intelligence. It saddened him to think that in her present station in life she would be unlikely ever to fully express those virtues. Her fate was more likely to be a lifetime of drudgery. How often had the de Courceys and those like them failed to appreciate the qualities of those that served them, and how great might be their ultimate penalty for this omission.

But he had no time for philosophizing. His time at Beaumont was too precious for him to waste it. He continued his questioning.

"Do you know what time Claire left Lord Quentin's room?" he asked.

"I do not, sir, but I swear on my dead mother's grave that she had nothing to do with his death."

Parsons would not have expected her to say anything else.

"You said that you stayed in Mr Montgomery's room all night?"

"Until five-thirty this morning, sir."

"And he was there all night with you."

"He was, sir."

"You mean you were awake all night."

"No, sir. Sure we slept some of the time."

She allowed herself a brief coquettish smile.

"Then you can't be certain he was in his room all night."

"Nay, sir. I suppose I can't."

"With whom do you share a room?"

"With O'Halloran, sir."

"What about Claire?"

"She shares with O'Brien."

"And O'Brien was with Captain Ashton."

"That she was, sir."

When O'Mahoney had gone Parsons spent a few minutes completing his notes. He was little wiser about the events of the previous night leading up to the murder of Lord Quentin. With the possible exception of Dwyer, Sweeney and Fitzherbert no one else seemed to have a convincing alibi. At this stage in the investigation even Lord Paul himself would have some difficulty in providing a convincing enough reason as to why he did not have the opportunity to kill his predecessor.

-17-

*A*part from a few wispy clouds drifting aimlessly like soap suds, the sky to the east was clear. This was, however, no reliable indication of good weather to come, as the prevailing wind was from the opposite direction.

Parsons did not normally make a habit of studying washing lines, but as a result of his casual interest in the weather he could not fail to notice the large collection of underwear hanging on the outside lines amongst the bed-sheets and table cloths. The mysteries of a lady's boudoir were there for all to see. They were mysteries that normally would interest him little enough, and he was on the point of leaving the laundry when a few isolated patches of red amongst the rows of ladies' white cotton drawers caught his attention. Such provocative garments, he deduced, could scarcely belong to the Irish servants. He could never imagine Mrs. Hughes allowing it. Of the two possible owners his money was on the fashionable Annabelle, but it would be amusing to see if he was right.

To avoid a chance meeting in the Drawing Room with Howard, Parsons had decided to beg an afternoon tea in the kitchen. Whether it was because Mrs. Hughes recognized in his short, plump body a kindred spirit, or simply because of her good nature, but within five minutes of his request they were sitting together with a large plate of well-stocked sandwiches. The healthy appetites of servants made no attempt to emulate the fastidious conventions of the Drawing Room. Ignoring Johnson's scowls from behind his newspaper, Parsons tucked in with relish.

Mrs. Hughes' description of her own whereabouts during the night were uncomplicated. She had supervised the washing-up after dinner and had then gone to bed with her customary cup of cocoa. Within a few minutes she was asleep. She knew nothing of anyone else's movements. After twenty-seven years working at Beaumont she had come to accept as normal the immorality of some members of the gentry, though she could never condone it. She was a good moral Christian and knew the difference between right and wrong. About Lord Quentin she had little to say that was good, but her loyalty to the family remained unquestioned.

Dwyer had ensured that the news of Lord Paul's inheritance was now common knowledge, and Parsons could sense that Mrs. Hughes was uneasy about the change. She had, she confided, always hoped to end her working life at Beaumont. At this stage of her life there was little chance of alternative employment within the neighborhood. And she was too old to ever consider moving far afield.

It was not until she was on the point of leaving him to begin supervising the preparations for dinner that Parsons plucked up the courage to ask the question he had until then been avoiding.

"While I was in the laundry just now, I couldn't help noticing some red under-garments on the washing line. Do you happen to know to whom they belong? Not, I imagine, to one of the servants."

Her cheery expression had turned to a frown.

"God bless us, sir. I'd not tolerate such a thing," she replied coldly.

Parsons felt he was in danger of jeopardizing his good relationship with this admirable woman. Judging by her expression no gentleman would ever dream of discussing such matters.

"Do you really need to know, sir?" she asked.

Still avoiding her gaze, Parsons nodded meekly.

"They belong to Miss Catherine, sir. Of late she's taken to wearing them. Much to my surprise, I might add."

It was as great a surprise to Parsons, and it reinforced his opinion never to wager on any instinct he might have about a woman's behavior, no matter how certain the outcome might at first appear.

"I see," he said, "and can you relate this change in Miss Catherine's wardrobe to any particular event in her life?"

"Indeed I cannot, sir," she said abruptly, and proceeded to ease her great body out of her chair. "But now you must excuse me. There's work to done."

Mrs. Hughes waddled away from the table leaving him with the clear impression that although he may have lost considerable ground in his relationship with her, she also knew more than she was prepared to say about the changed circumstances of Catherine de Courcey's private life. But with luck, he thought, that information might be gleaned from one or other of her fellow servants.

Parsons had not failed to notice that Johnson had become increasingly interested in their conversation. He had spotted the old man's face peering around the edge of his newspaper on more than one occasion. It was as good a time as any to question him and he moved to the other end of the table where Johnson was sitting.

"How long have you been at Beaumont?" he asked.

"All my working life, sir. I started as a footman when but a boy of fourteen. That would be in the time of Lord Quentin's grandfather. Things were very different then. In those days there were thirty of us servants at Beaumont, all of us proud to wear the de Courcey livery. It was like being part of one great family then. But times change, sir. Times change. Nothing's like it used to be."

Johnson took a slow, wistful sup from his cup.

"They say 'tis the same everywhere these days, sir. Though I only know about Beaumont. Over the years when any of the servants here died or retired fewer of them were ever replaced. And then Lord Quentin began bringing over the Irish. Cheap labor he called them. But if you ask me, sir, his lordship cared little enough about the money and more about how he was to fill his empty bed. Perhaps I should've gone then. But where could I go. I had no friends around here any longer and no family of my own."

The deep lines at the corners of the old man's mouth seemed to sharpen as he recounted the decline of the once-great estate and the loss of the companionship of his earlier days. His tone had become increasingly bitter, but it was not clear to Parsons whether it was Lord Quentin's behavior that had upset him or the fact that he was now obliged to share his responsibilities with the Irish.

"For how long had Lord Quentin been bringing over Irish servants?"

"More than ten years now, sir. It all started not long after his lordship married Lady Annabelle. They were never a match. Everyone knew that. It wasn't long before she locked her bedroom door against him. That made him mad, sir. Wild drunken rages there were. All of us suffered, but his sons more than the rest of us."

"Take your time, Johnson," said Parsons, seeing that the old man was becoming increasingly distressed by these memories.

"He was always a hard father, but he became more violent. Many's the time I've seen him take a whip to those boys. Miss Catherine was the only one who could stand up to him. Often I've seen her shouting at him, and telling him to stop before he killed one of them. I've never had much time for the Irish whores, sir. But at least his lordship quieted down after they came."

The satisfaction of Lord Quentin's sexual appetites may have sapped his physical aggressions, thought Parsons, but it may well have led eventually to his death.

"I believe his lordship was in the habit of offering the freedoms of his home to some of the local gentry," he said, hoping that Johnson would understand the meaning of his question.

At first Johnson seemed reluctant to reply.

"Who told you, sir?" he asked suspiciously.

"That's my business, Johnson. Just tell me if it's true."

Johnson nodded sadly.

"'Tis like I said, sir. Times change."

"How much does Miss Catherine know about all this?"

"There's little goes on here that escapes her notice, sir. I'd say she knew exactly what her father and his friends were doing. But as I said before, she had seen what he was like without a woman."

"And what of Lady Annabelle? Was she aware of her husband's behavior?"

The shadows under the old man's eyes deepened as he looked down into his now empty cup.

"I've always remained loyal to his lordship, in spite of everything. But it upset me greatly to see a fine lady such as she live so sad and lonely a life. His lordship's children never took to her. They had always been close to their mother while she was alive. She was a wonderful person, sir, and always managed to keep this place happy; even with a difficult husband like Lord Quentin. So her children probably resented their father marrying such a young girl so soon after their mother's death. But whatever the reason, it saddened me to see Lady Annabelle so alone."

"But she seemed to be in such good spirits last night," said Parsons, remembering her vibrant beauty and good humor at dinner.

"Everything changed shortly after Mr Paul arrived. I beg your pardon, sir, I should say Lord Paul now. That's not easy for me to accept, sir," he confided. "Not after all these years. But after Lord Paul came it was like seeing her a young bride again, just as she was when she first came to Beaumont. Full of joy and with a smile and a pleasant word for everyone."

There was a sudden look of doubt in his sad, grey eyes.

"God help me for saying this, sir. But Lord Quentin's death means a new life for them both."

Even the servants were thinking that, thought Parsons. And it was true. Annabelle and Paul were obviously very fond of one another and made little attempt to hide their feelings. Were these feelings strong enough to lead to murder? But if their display of affection for one another had been so obvious to everyone, then surely Lord Quentin would have known he was being made to look a cuckold. And if that was the case why did he choose Paul as his heir?

"What about the musicians?" asked Parsons. "Where did they spend the night? I assumed that they had stayed in the castle, but there was no sign of them this morning."

"Miss Catherine didn't want them staying in the castle," explained Johnson. "She said there were already enough people staying here. So after a spot of supper they set off for The Old Crown in Petersfield. It was too late for them to travel all the way home to Winchester."

It came as some relief to Parsons to know that there weren't four other people to add to his growing list of suspects.

"I assume they were professional musicians and had to be paid for playing at dinner," he said. "Who took care of that?"

"Miss Catherine, sir. Lord Quentin left her to run the household. Only the other day she went to the bank in Petersfield. Apart from the expenses of the dinner and the extra people staying in the castle it's also Quarter Day soon. That's when the servants are paid."

"Do you know how much money she collected when she went to the bank?"

"Not exactly, sir. Though I imagine it was as much as three hundred pounds."

"That's quite a sum of money. Where did she keep it?"

"In her room, sir. But I don't know exactly where."

Parsons could sense the old man was becoming restless with his incessant questioning. No doubt he was also becoming concerned about his evening duties. But there were still one or two other questions he wanted answered.

"What happened last night after I left the Hall?"

"After the gentlemen had made their choice of partner, sir, I brought the girls back here and gave them a glass of port."

The barest ghost of a smile flitted briefly across his face.

"I call them whores," he explained, "but I sympathize with any girl who has to spend the night with the likes of Major Fitzherbert."

Parsons was beginning to wonder if his initial judgment of Johnson had been too harsh. Rather than censure, the old man deserved his sympathy. His position at the castle was an unenviable one, obliged as he was to set a standard that belied the morality of the harsh and ungrateful man that he had served so faithfully. Behind the stiff formality Johnson had adopted during his years of service there was probably still a simple countryman with feelings of his own. And with whom could he share them? With the exception of Mrs. Hughes, there would be nobody. The loneliness must have been unbearable.

It was easy to see why Johnson would find the presence of the Irish girls so objectionable. Their background and culture were very different to his own. Even their relationship with Lord Quentin, coerced into it though they might be, could undermine his own position. It was only natural that he should feel bitterly towards them, and that in turn would explain his attitude towards the young Irish groom.

Yet in spite of all this Johnson could still sympathize with the girls. For all his apparent hostility towards them Parsons sensed feelings of an altogether different kind. The feelings of an old man for the daughters he had never had.

"Did you wait until the girls went upstairs before going to bed?" he asked.

"It had been a long day, sir, and I'm not a young man anymore. So as soon as I'd seen that the gentlemen in the Hall had all they required I went straight to bed. Slept like a log, I did, sir, and never heard anything until O'Halloran woke me this morning with a cup of tea."

Although there was still more than an hour before dinner Parsons knew there would be no further opportunity for questions. All the servants were engaged in preparing the meal. He had no intention of eating in the Hall with everyone else. Howard might demand an account of his movements. Instead he made arrangements with Johnson for a meal to be sent to his room. Then he made his way stealthily to the first floor. With luck he might find Montagu in his room.

-18-

It was only after Parsons had knocked loudly on Montagu's door for the third time that a weary voice from within bade him enter.

"Is that you, Alex?" Montagu asked irritably, as Parsons entered the darkened room. "Can't you leave me alone? You must know how tired I am."

As Parsons became accustomed to the darkness of the room he could see that Montagu was struggling to sit up in his bed.

"It's not Alex. It's me, Parsons," he said. "I'm sorry to disturb you, but I want to ask you some questions about last night. Do you mind if I open the curtains?"

Without waiting for an answer he walked over to the window and drew back the drapes; an action that did not meet with Montagu's approval.

"Damn you, Parsons, and damn all nosey policemen. Colonel Howard's already woken me once this afternoon. I told him I can't remember much about last night. It's still a bit of a muddle. If you'll just let me sleep my head might clear."

"I can't wait that long," said Parsons purposefully. "I need to know right now."

He sat at the end of the bed and took out his pencil and notebook.

"You can start by telling me what happened when you left the Hall after dinner. Where did you go?"

Montagu glared at Parsons. For a moment he considered refusing to answer the questions, but after some thought decided to be cooperative. In that way Parsons would leave, allowing him to get back to sleep.

"Alex and I sat for a while in the Drawing Room with the ladies," he explained sulkily. "Then we came up here and drank some wine. Judging by the pain in my head still, we drank too much. God it hurts, Everett. Can't you see when someone's in pain? Why can't you leave me alone, for God's sake?"

Montagu flopped back onto the pillows with his hands over his eyes, as though blinded by the light and exhausted by the effort of talking.

Parsons ignored this appeal for clemency and continued with his questioning.

"What were you and Alex talking about?" he asked.

Montagu reluctantly sat up again and ran his fingers through his long hair.

"What do think?" he said, his tone suddenly becoming aggressive. "If you had any imagination at all you would realize that Alex was pretty depressed after his father's unexpected announcement. How would you feel if your father appeared to be disinheriting you?"

Parsons said nothing and waited for Montagu to continue.

"We talked about that swine for a while. I thought my father was bad enough, but Quentin de Courcey is, or should I say was, in a class all of his own. It's hardly surprising that someone eventually decided to kill him."

Parsons found it remarkable that Montagu's reaction to the murder had changed so quickly. Only a short while ago at lunch he had appeared distressed at the news. His mood now was completely different.

"Was that all you talked about?" he asked.

"No. Eventually we tired of the subject and moved onto more important things. You know what happens after a few drinks."

"You mean you began trying to solve some of the nation's problems."

Montagu nodded, pleased to find he was making some headway with Parsons. He had expected more from someone who had attended university. But what could one expect from a man who had merely studied science and had then decided to become a policeman?

He reflected briefly on the nobility of his own calling. A poet moved on an entirely different plane to that of someone whose vocation it was to poke his nose into other people's business. But Parsons' next words took him completely by surprise.

"Perhaps the answers to these problems reflected the thinking of John Stuart Mill, William Morris or even Karl Marx?" Parsons asked innocently. "Or do you have your own unique solutions."

"What the hell do you mean?" demanded Montagu, now fully awake and sensing that Parsons knew more than he thought.

Parsons showed him the papers he had taken from the room earlier.

"How dare you, Parsons!" Montagu shouted. "Those are private papers! You've no right to come in here behind my back and take them!"

"I've every right. I shouldn't have to remind you that Lord Quentin was murdered last night. You seem to have made your feelings about people like him perfectly clear, and in view of your strange behavior I'm far from convinced you didn't kill him. Where were you last night between midnight and five o'clock?"

"I don't know. I lost all sense of time."

"Why was that?"

"I've already told you. Alex and I were drinking. When you're drinking and talking you lose all sense of time."

"And what about this?"

Parsons unfolded the paper containing the cocaine and held it towards Montagu.

"I'm sure you're aware of the effects of this drug," he said quietly. "But in case you've forgotten let me remind you. Among other things it causes depression, mental confusion and loss of contact with reality. The sort of state of mind in which it would be possible to commit a murder, especially the murder of someone you regarded as a social anachronism. Wouldn't you agree?"

Montagu flopped back on the bed again, pulled the sheets up around his neck and glared at the ceiling.

"Did Alexander take cocaine as well?" demanded Parsons. "Then did you both go to his father's room and murder him?"

Montagu sat up again and glared at Parsons.

"I've just remembered," he said coldly. "Colonel Howard told me I shouldn't answer your damn-fool questions. So I guess he doesn't know you're here. In that case I think you'd better leave before I call him."

Parsons had no choice but to go. When Montagu had said that Howard had already interviewed him he had thought it likely that the Chief Constable would have told him not to answer any further questions. He had, therefore, been pleasantly surprised to find Montagu prepared to talk with him at all. The last thing he wanted now was a confrontation with Howard, who might in the circumstances even place him under house arrests for disobeying orders. For the moment it seemed more prudent to beat a tactical retreat to his room and await his supper.

-19-

It was a small comfort to find a welcoming fire in his room. Next to Mrs. Hughes' sandwiches it was the best thing that had happened to him that day. He pulled the bell-chord, threw his jacket on the bed and settled down in front of the fire to await his supper.

Within a few minutes O'Halloran had arrived with his tray. There was no denying that her small, dumpy frame made her the least attractive of the girls. They had something in common, he thought; and as she had said earlier, there were distinct advantages at Beaumont in being plain. It spared her some of the indignities suffered by the other girls.

She carefully placed his supper tray on the small table by the fire.

"I believe you share a room with O'Mahoney," he said, before she had opportunity to make her curtsy and leave.

177

"That I do, sir," she replied anxiously, concerned by his knowledge of where she slept and concerned as to the motive behind his question.

"Don't look so worried, O'Halloran. I won't bite." he said, attempting to put her at her ease. "I only want to know what time it was that O'Mahoney went to bed. Her own bed, I mean. Not anybody else's."

"I don't know, to be sure, sir," she replied, seemingly oblivious to Parsons' drollery. "I was in bed myself by midnight, and when I got up at six this morning she was still asleep."

"Is that when you normally get up?"

"Sure, 'tis only when we're on early duties, sir. That's when we make tea for Mr. Johnson and Mrs. Hughes, wake the other girls and take hot water to the bedrooms. If it's a cold morning the early girl also has to light fires in any of the bedrooms that are being used. Mr. Johnson decides upon that when he's woken. But 'twas mild enough last night so Mr. Johnson said there was no need for any fires."

"So O'Mahoney was in her bed. And where were the others?"

"Dwyer and Sweeney were asleep in their room, sir. So was Dunne. But I had to fetch O'Brien from Captain Ashton's room. It seems she was in no hurry to be leaving a warm bed for her own cold sheets."

Parsons could see the smile playing on her pert little mouth. The girl had a sense of humor after all. But was there a trace of mockery in her grey-green eyes? Was the joke aimed at him?

Perhaps the Irish girls were as amused by his prudishness as Ashton and Fitzherbert."

"Was I the first person you took hot water to this morning?"

"Nay, sir. We always go first to Miss Catherine's room. Then Mr. Robertson, when he's here. They're both early risers. But I heard you were up and about so I knew you'd be wanting your shaving water."

"Who told you that?"

"Mr. Johnson, sir. He saw you talking with Brendan Dunne and Smith in the stable yard."

"What about Lady Annabelle," he asked, "doesn't she get any hot water?"

"Bless you, sir. Sure her ladyship has her own closet with running water. Mrs. Hughes always arranges for another girl to run her bath and give her breakfast. But that's always much later."

Parsons had learnt nothing from O'Halloran that he could relate to the murder, but it intrigued him to learn that Annabelle had running water in her room. Catherine, in spite of her position in the household, did not.

As the light was now rapidly fading O'Halloran lit a candle on Parsons' fireside table, drew the curtains and left. It was not until then that he saw the telegram on the tray. He had known it would not be long in coming, and the message was much as he had feared.

"To Parsons. Return to London on first available train and report to me at the Yard. Jeffries."

Superintendent Jeffries was Parsons' immediate superior and one of the more able officers in the Metropolitan Police. Had he known the full facts of the case Parsons felt sure he would never have issued such an instruction. From the terse message it seemed more likely that the order had come from a higher authority. Howard had not been boasting when he had threatened to use his influence with the Commissioner.

Dolefully chewing on a pork chop that had grown cold and unappetizing, Parsons reviewed his position. It would have been easy for him to give up the investigation right then. After all what could he hope to achieve in the little time he had left at Beaumont? But that was not his way. He was far more determined than the quiet demeanor and scholarly appearance might suggest. In spite of his soft self-effacing exterior there was steel within, and a professional pride that drove him on when others might have abandoned hope.

The manner of Lord Quentin's death suggested to him that the murderer had some prior knowledge of his sexual inclinations. That in itself did not narrow the list of suspects by many. There seemed little doubt that the servants and some of the family and their guests were well aware of what had been happening. And everyone staying in the castle had easy access to his room at the time the murder was committed.

It also appeared that the murder was premeditated. And that implied a motive. But exactly what that motive was, was far from clear. Did the murderer, or indeed murderers, covet Lord Quentin's title and position? Did that mean the murder was linked to the new will? Or was the murder politically inspired? Was it, as Howard suspected, a Fenian atrocity. Was it the work of anarchists? And if anarchists, could Montagu, or even Alexander, be involved?

He was just beginning to give these issues more serious thought when there was a knock on his door. To his surprise it was Philip.

As soon as Philip had heard of the groom's arrest he knew he had to speak with someone. But he did not know whom. There was no one in his family to whom he felt he could confide, and the idea of speaking with someone in authority like Colonel Howard terrified him. Initially he had thought of Everett Parsons. He felt he could rely on his old school friend, even though he was now a policeman. But that was before Colonel Howard had told everyone not to discuss anything to do with the murder with Parsons. Philip was therefore confused, but felt he had no alternative. He could only tell Parsons. But since this morning he had disappeared. He was not in his room when Philip had called there that afternoon and he had not appeared at dinner. Philip had decided to make one last attempt to find him. If that failed he did not know to whom he could turn. It was therefore with some relief that he heard his friend's voice inviting him to enter.

"Thank God I've f-found you, Everett," he said, after being invited to take a seat by the fire. "I've looked everywhere but you seemed to have disappeared into thin air."

"Well, here I am, Philip," relied Parsons, with cheerfulness that belied his own disappointments. "So why don't you take a glass of wine and tell me what is bothering you."

Parsons could see he friend was worried. There had been a desperation in the Philip's voice, and the flickering light of the fire revealed the worry lines that since this morning had appeared on his forehead and at the corners of his eyes, prematurely aging the hitherto unblemished boyish features.

It was a while before Philip spoke.

"Can I t-trust you, Everett?" he asked.

"I hope so, Philip, provided you remember that as well as being your friend I'm also a policeman."

Philip's anxious expression made it clear that this was a dichotomy that had already given him cause for concern.

"Dunne c-could not have m-murdered father," he said at last, looking blankly into the fire.

"You may be right about that, Philip," Parsons replied, as he carefully speared the last portion of potato with his fork and popped it into his mouth. "But what makes you think so?"

The boy looked helplessly at Parsons and then back to the fire, unable to return his friend's quizzical gaze.

"I d-don't think, Everett. I know. And I know b-because he was with me. He c-couldn't have k-killed father. Do you understand what I'm saying, Everett. Brendan Dunne spent l-last night in my room."

-20-

It was the last thing Parsons had expected to hear, and his horrified expression confirmed Philip's worst fears.

"D-don't look disgusted, Everett," he said indignantly. "Some of us are d-different, you know. Surely all those years at b-boarding school must have taught you that. And didn't we learn in our Classics lessons that the Greeks considered the love between two men to be the highest form of love."

"Schoolboy crushes are one thing, Philip," said Parsons, adopting the sort of moralizing tone that Philip had hoped not to hear. "This is far more serious. Surely you know homosexuality is a criminal offense? And aren't you taking things to an extreme to have a relationship with one of the servants? Someone was bound to find out sooner or later. What about your family? Have you considered how they would react if they found out, and the scandal it would cause?"

"D-damn my family," Philip exclaimed. "What have any of them done for me? What do they care about my feelings?"

183

The angry outburst was unexpected. Parsons had always considered Philip to be quiet and reserved. But those impressions had been based on the behavior of the meek young schoolboy he had known several years before. The adult Philip clearly had stronger and deeper emotions.

The dam enclosing those pent-up feelings once broached Philip could no longer control the emotional torrent that poured forth.

"D-do you know h-how it feels," he whimpered, "to be the victim of a b-bully like my father? A m-monster who took every opportunity to whip me as a young child, and as I got older delighted in watching me flogged by that animal, Smith. Can you imagine that, Everett? A f-father taking d-delight in his own son's torment? It was to m-make a man of me, he said. Well, I was never going to b-be his sort of man, and I'm d-damned if I ever wanted to be."

Parsons could understand Philip's bitterness. To some extent he could even empathize with him. His own father, far from being a sadist like Lord Quentin, believed that strict discipline never harmed any child. And it was only his loving mother who had stood between him and many a thrashing. But any reminiscences of his own would be little help to Philip. With his anger now spent he became enveloped in self-pity, and to Parsons' dismay dissolved into tears.

"I n-never really knew my mother," he sobbed. "She d-died when I was still a child, w-worn out and b-bullied into an early grave by father. My world has always been empty w-without her. There's n-never been anyone for me to love, n-no one to comfort me, and n-no one I could ever confide in."

"You have me now, Philip," said Parsons, placing his arm around his friend's trembling shoulders. "Forget I'm a policeman for the moment. Just think of me as your friend."

In a touching child-like gesture Philip wiped away his tears with the back of his hands. It was as though the years had rolled back, and he was a new boy at school again and Parsons the prefect.

"Thank G-god you're here, Everett," Philip said gratefully. "I knew you'd be able to h-help."

"I can't promise anything," said Parsons, concerned that Philip should now regard the problem as resolved simply by sharing it with someone else. "From what I've learned so far there is nothing straight forward about this case. Even the smallest piece of information might prove to be important. So I think the best thing you can do is to start from the beginning. Tell me more about Dunne. When did this relationship with him start?"

At the mention of the groom's name Philip's expression brightened once more.

"Just over a m-month ago," he explained. "I'd been out riding and was leading my horse b-back to the stables when I saw Smith b-beating B-brendan."

He gave Parsons an incriminating look.

"That's his n-name, by the way," he said. "N-no one ever seems to think that s-servants have Christian names like the r-rest of us."

Parsons knew what he meant. In his experience most of those who employed servants or had any dealings with them were guilty of treating them as though they had no lives of their own, or were indeed even a different form of life.

"If anything Smith is even more s-sadistic than father," Philip continued. "Maybe that's what l-life in the army does for you."

Parsons recalled how the previous afternoon Alexander had spoken in a similar way about his father's career. It was common enough now to hear the younger generation speak disdainfully about the vain glory of the nation's militarism. Among his own contemporaries at university there had been a growing awareness that the country's own pressing problems would never be resolved by expending the lives of scarlet-jacketed soldiers on distant battlefields.

"At first I felt n-nothing more than an overwhelming sense of p-pity for Brendan," said Philip, "and regarded him just as an unfortunate v-victim of a stronger and more violent man. Just like me. B-but then, for the first t-time in my life, I began to feel more powerful emotions stirring inside m-me; and I knew that all I wanted to d-do at that moment was to hold the p-poor boy's battered body in my arms and c-comfort him. I shouted at Smith, b-begging him to stop hitting Brendan, but he ignored m-me. He always knew there was l-little I could do to harm him. Father had always sided with him against m-me. I tried hitting him with my riding c-crop. But he only laughed. Then he seized my arm and squeezed it until the pain made me d-drop the whip. And as he did he p-pressed his f-filthy unshaven face close to m-mine, almost making me s-sick with his foul breath. My God, Everett, I hate that man. How I h-hate him!"

Philip paused, breathing deeply in an attempt to control his outburst of emotion.

"Finally Smith grew t-tired of his sport and p-pushed me down on the ground with Brendan. His face was b-badly cut, so I helped him into his pathetic h-hovel over the stables and fetched some hot w-water from the kitchen to bathe his wounds."

Philip stared at the flickering candle, lost in the bitter-sweet memories of that moment.

"That's how it b-began," he said wistfully. "Two l-lonely b-brutalised boys desperately seeking someone's affection."

There was a long pause before Parsons spoke.

"Didn't you think it unwise to invite him into the castle?" he asked.

"Where else could we go?" Philip demanded. "Into the stables to listen to the snores of that drunken brute, Smith. Or into the park with the animals. Why should we be forced to do either when all we wanted was somewhere warm and quiet to be together?"

Very little of this had any direct bearing on his investigation, thought Parsons. More than anything he desperately needed facts relevant to the murder.

"What time was Brendan in your room last night?"

"From about one o'clock until just after five. I told him he should always wait until he was sure everyone was in bed before coming into the castle, and I always made certain he left before the servants were awake. But I had no idea that Spencer patrolled the grounds at night. It was just our bad luck he saw Brendan this morning."

"Are you prepared to swear all this in a court of law?"

The sense of relief drained from Philip and was replaced by a look of abject dismay. When he spoke again there was a ring of desperation in his voice.

"This is to go no further, Everett. Do you understand. No further. I only told you because I thought I could trust you. Now that you know the truth you must do everything you can to prove that Brendan didn't kill my father. But don't ask me to stand in a witness box and admit to what I did. I couldn't face prison."

"But if you don't speak up for the boy he could hang."

"Don't think I'm not ashamed of being a coward, Everett. I'm not a hero like my father. That's why I need your help. We both need it. You've got to find the real murderer and set Brendan free."

-21-

*A*fter Philip had left, Parsons sat for a long while by the fire trying to decide upon the best course of action. Without new and convincing evidence Howard was never going to change his decision about sending him back to London. Although Philip's story provided an alibi for Dunne, it was of no avail if Parsons was unable to use it. And Philip himself had made that impossible. But perhaps there was another way. Perhaps he could prevail upon Howard by using the influence of others. For instance, someone like Lord Paul. Howard would no doubt be anxious to retain his standing with the new master at Beaumont, and might well agree to a plea from Lord Paul. It was certainly worth a try.

It was just after nine. Dinner would by now be over, but in all probability most people would still be downstairs. There were two options if he wanted to speak with Lord Paul without running the risk of seeing Howard. Parsons could either go to Lord Paul's room after he had retired for the night, or he could send a message asking him to come to Parsons' room. The former might be more discrete, but it

189

presented two problems. Firstly, it would almost certainly be late when Lord Paul went to bed; and secondly, if he had been in the company of Ashton and Fitzherbert it was likely he would be the worse for drink. It was preferable he could be persuaded to come to Parsons' room before that occurred.

O'Halloran answered Parsons' summons almost immediately.

"Have you finished with your tray?" she asked.

"I have, thank you. Be sure to tell Mrs. Hughes that I enjoyed my supper."

He gave her the note he had written.

"Ask Johnson to give this to Lord Paul in person," he instructed. "To Lord Paul. No one else. That's very important. Do you understand?"

O'Halloran nodded, curtsied and left the room, leaving him pacing impatiently in front of the fire. He found it frustrating to be a virtual prisoner in his room at a time when he could be pursuing his enquiries.

It was more than fifteen minutes before Lord Paul arrived.

"This had better be good, Parsons," he said as he settled himself into the chair on the opposite side of the fire. "I've left a lively discussion downstairs for you."

The decision to see Lord Paul at this stage of the evening had been the right one. Although far from drunk he was well on the way. Not that Parsons could blame him for that. It was not every day that one inherited a title.

"I appreciate you coming, Lord Paul," he said, adopting a suitably obsequious tone. "Forgive me for asking, but does anyone else know you're here?"

For a moment Lord Paul stared blankly at him, but then smiled and gave Parsons one of his knowing winks.

"I didn't tell Howard, if that's what you mean. Frankly, I'm pleased to leave his company for the time being. If he hasn't been boasting about his success in arresting the Irish groom he's been telling us how his influence with the Commissioner of the Metropolitan Police was instrumental in having you recalled to London. What's all that about? Let's hear your side of the story."

Seizing the opportunity with relish Parsons explained as diplomatically as possible that he thought the Chief Constable had been mistaken in arresting Dunne. And central to that hypothesis was the fact that Doctor Hamilton believed Lord Quentin had been dead for several hours before the groom was seen leaving the castle.

"I can't argue with any of that, Parsons. But what time did Dunne enter the castle?"

Parsons was thrown by the directness of the question. Without revealing anything that Philip had told him there was no way he could give a definitive answer.

"I can't be sure yet," he mumbled.

"Then how can you be sure he's innocent?"

Lord Paul was beginning to sound irritated. The interview was not proceeding the way Parsons would have wished.

"I can't, your lordship. I'm merely saying that the evidence against Dunne is inconclusive. In the interests of justice, Colonel Howard should make other enquiries before concluding the matter."

"Well, I'll convey your opinion to the colonel if that's what you want me to do. But from what you tell me he already knows what you think."

Parsons could see that Lord Paul was beginning to think that his time was being wasted. A direct appeal to his sense of fair play seemed all that was left.

"I was hoping you'd do more than that, Lord Paul," he said. "I want you to persuade Colonel Howard to change his mind and allow me to help him with his investigation."

Lord Paul stopped examining his immaculate finger nails and looked at Parsons in surprise.

"I'm sorry, Parsons," he said. "I won't do that. I'm not going to interfere in police business. Not only would it be impertinent of me, but telling the Chief Constable of this county the best way to conduct his affairs is hardly the best way for an outsider like me to start his new life here. If Howard is satisfied with his actions, who am I to question them. In due course, when the case comes to trial I've every confidence that British justice will protect Dunne. If, as you say, he's innocent."

Parsons had hoped for better than this. He had also misjudged how Lord Paul regarded his new relationship with Howard. It seemed he was more concerned about how Howard would respond to *his* actions rather than the other way round.

"I wish I had your confidence in British justice, your lordship. I'm sure an Irishman like Dunne wouldn't share it either."

Try as he might Parsons could not avoid sounding sarcastic, and he could see from the way that Lord Paul's eyes narrowed that he had over-stepped the mark. He continued nevertheless. Having gone this far there was little else he could do.

"As an Irishman, your lordship, Dunne is scarcely in the best position to gain any sympathy from an English jury. His confession, no matter how it was obtained, will damn him from the start. Just for one moment try to put yourself in his position. If you had a young sister you thought might be arrested for a murder you knew she was incapable of committing, wouldn't you want to protect her. Especially if, after the way you had been treated, you feared for her safety in police custody. Believe me, your lordship, I'm convinced that it was only fear for his sister that made Dunne admit killing Lord Quentin. I believe he's innocent of this ghastly crime and the murderer is still at large."

Before Lord Paul had a chance to comment there was a knock on Parsons' door.

"Come in," Parsons shouted irritably, expecting to see one of the servants.

He was exasperated by the situation, and in spite of his best intentions was beginning to lose his temper. It was becoming only too clear that Lord Paul was not going to help. He was more concerned in avoiding any chance of upsetting the *status quo* in Hampshire society than anything else.

Immediately he saw Lady Annabelle standing in the doorway Parsons regretted his outburst. She was the last person at Beaumont to whom he would have wanted to have raised his voice.

In acknowledgement of her husband's death she wore a simple black velvet dress, and standing in the half-light of the doorway her naked shoulders and pale face added a vulnerability to her beauty that Parsons found especially appealing. He rose hastily and offered her his seat by the fire.

"I hope I'm not disturbing you, Everett," she said demurely, choosing to ignore his ill-mannered bellow, "but when Johnson told me where Paul had gone I thought I would take this opportunity of bidding you farewell. Charles told us you're leaving early tomorrow, and I'm sure you've realized by now that I'm not in the habit of breakfasting downstairs. This may be my last chance of seeing you before you go."

"You're very thoughtful, Lady Annabelle," said Parsons, blushing not only at her graciousness but also at his own indiscretion, and thinking he no longer had any right to talk to her on familiar terms. "It's been a great honor for me to meet you, and I only wish it had been at a happier time."

Even as he spoke Parsons realized how fortuitous her visit could prove to be. If anyone had influence over Lord Paul it was she. If he could only win her over, all might not be lost.

"I regret to say, Lady Annabelle, that I do not leave voluntarily," he said, anxious not to lose another opportunity of explaining his point of view. "I'm going because Colonel Howard has asked my superior to recall me to London for allegedly interfering in his investigation."

Before Lord Paul could interrupt him Parsons repeated his belief in Dunne's innocence and his plea to be allowed to remain and help bring the real murderer to justice. He would also have liked to tell her that Howard was conspiring to pervert the course of justice to protect himself and others, among them her step-daughter's husband, Sir Henry Rawlinson. But this was pure speculation on his part, and upsetting her unnecessarily would not only be foolish it might also reflect badly upon him later if he were ever proved to be wrong.

"And what does Paul think?" she asked quietly.

"He doesn't wish to upset the Chief Constable by interfering, your ladyship," said Parsons, trying to avoid sounding judgmental.

"Then neither do I. I'm sorry, Everett, but I've every confidence in Charles Howard."

She smiled at him, her green eyes sparkling like emeralds in the fire-light. But there was a coolness in them that he had hoped not to see, and he knew she was not going to help him.

"Charles was one of Quentin's closest friends," she said, almost as an after-thought, "and I'm sure he'll do everything in his power to bring the guilty person to justice."

Soon after they both wished Parsons good night, leaving him with the uncomfortable feeling that, with the possible exception of Philip, his opinions were of little consequence to anyone else. On the other hand Colonel Howard's actions seemed to meet with general approval.

"I'm only sorry we should part like this," he said, as he escorted them to his door, "and I fervently hope you've seen the end of this unpleasantness. Unfortunately, I don't think you have. I believe there's a murderer still at large in the castle. And he or she may well strike again."

Murmuring faint words of thanks for his advice, Lady Annabelle turned in the direction of her room and Lord Paul returned to his drinking companions.

Parsons returned to the fire crestfallen, his mood reflected by the engulfing darkness of the room. Never before in his career had he felt so helpless. Not only was his professional advice spurned by the local police, he was also unable to use the only solid piece of evidence he possessed to try to save an innocent boy from the gallows. And if that was not enough, there was the prospect of having to leave Beaumont when there was every likelihood that a killer was still at large in the castle.

It was this last thought that eventually spurred him into action. If, as he suspected, the murderer was still in the castle, he, or indeed she, might decide to strike again. And if that were to happen during the coming night, he would be ready.

-22-

During the centuries they had occupied Beaumont, the de Courceys had made few structural changes or additions to the castle. It remained much as it was in Norman times: a circle of outer walls guarding the main fortress, which in turn formed a protective square around an inner courtyard. There had been no Baroque or neoclassical embellishments to clutter the original design.

However, over the years the living accommodation had been slowly adapted to meet the family's requirements. Public rooms now filled the north, south and west wings of the ground floor, with the kitchen area in the east wing. The family and guests slept on the first floor in rooms with windows facing outwards from the castle, and a wide corridor connecting these rooms ran in a hollow square around the inner walls. The same pattern was repeated on the floor above, where the servants had more humble abodes.

Set high in the thick walls the narrow windows along the first-floor corridor allowed little enough light to penetrate the castle even on the brightest of days. At night, therefore, with

197

the curtains drawn and only a single oil lamp in each corridor, it was relatively easy to move around with little chance of being seen by hiding in deep-set doorways and shadowy corners.

At eleven-fifteen Parsons left his room and set off to explore the castle. Dressed in his darkest clothes he felt all but invisible, and by walking close to the walls he aimed to minimize the chances of attracting attention from any creaking floorboards.

Starting from his room, and following the west corridor in a clockwise direction he passed Lord Paul's room, then the top of the main staircase and finally Lord Quentin's. Between the stairs and Lord Quentin's room there was an unoccupied room. Fitzherbert, Ashton and Montgomery had rooms along the north corridor, as had Robertson on the previous night. This was the room Parsons imagined Howard would be now using.

Alexander and Philip had rooms in a narrow corridor in the south-west corner of the castle, with Montagu's room between theirs and the larger rooms of Catherine and Annabelle along the south corridor. There were no bedrooms in the east corridor, only a few, small store rooms and the stairs leading from the kitchens to the servants' quarters on the second floor.

There was no sound from Annabelle's room, but the flickering candle-light beneath her door indicated that she was still awake. Parsons recalled Johnson saying that at night she frequently read alone in her room for hours. Perhaps, thought Parsons as he paused outside, she was not reading but had other thoughts to occupy her tonight. With an unpleasant chapter of her life closed, there were surely better times ahead. She was still young and beautiful and now had the prospect of a fresh start in her life.

Catherine's room was in darkness. For several minutes Parsons stood with his ear pressed against her door, straining to hear the slightest sound. But he could hear nothing. If indeed she was asleep, she slept quietly. For a moment he considered entering the room to see if she was there, but decided against it. Should she wake and report him to Howard he had no doubt the colonel would relish the prospect of accusing him of indecent assault and throwing him in a cell alongside Dunne.

Parsons could hear muffled voices in Montagu's room, but try as he might he could not distinguish the words. He found it somewhat ironic that while he was creeping around the castle like a thief, Alexander and Montagu were in all likelihood plotting the downfall of capitalism. It was a conversation he might have enjoyed at any other time. But for the moment there were other things for him to think of.

He entered Philip's room quietly and without knocking. As he had expected Philip was asleep, no doubt emotionally and physically exhausted by the day's events. The curtains were still open, and in the bright moonlight Parsons could see the boy holding his pillow in the manner of a helpless child. Seeing him so only served to strengthen Parsons' resolve to do everything possible to help his friend and the young groom. Even after his return to London he would not let matters rest, but would continue to do everything in his power to prove that Howard had made the wrong decision in arresting the groom. But quite how he would manage that remained to be seen.

The other rooms on the first floor were dark, silent and empty, their occupants, no doubt still drinking downstairs. But it was now getting late and they might retire for the night at any time. Before then Parsons needed a suitable vantage point from which he could watch.

When he had previously visited Lord Quentin's room he had noticed a narrow corridor running alongside the room. It was effectively a continuation of the main west corridor. During the day it was barely visible; and at night, with the nearest lamp at the top of the main staircase it was almost impossible to see.

At the end of this corridor, some twenty paces past Lord Quentin's door, there was a single narrow window. From there Parsons could see the stables. But of far greater interest were the narrow stone steps that spiraled upwards towards the second floor. Not until he had reached the window were they visible, and unless he was mistaken they provided an excellent and unobtrusive access to Lord Quentin's room from the servants' quarters above.

There would be opportunity for him to explore these stairs later, but for the moment the bottom steps provided an ideal spot from which to keep his eye on what was happening along the main west corridor. He settled down to wait, the only sound that of a loud grandfather clock some sixty or so paces away at the top of the main stairs.

Just after this clock had struck quarter to midnight Catherine and Montgomery came up the stairs. Parsons had not expected to see them together, but after the previous night's disagreements Montgomery might well have decided it prudent to avoid the company of the other men. They exchanged a final few words at the top of the stairs and then went their separate ways; she along the west corridor in the opposite direction to where Parsons was sitting, and he towards Parsons but then turning to his right towards his room on the north corridor.

After a discrete interval Parsons ventured back into the main corridor and crept towards Montgomery's room. For a while the candle-light flickered under the bottom of his door and he could hear Montgomery moving about the room. Then the candle was extinguished and the room fell silent. Parsons waited a few minutes longer to confirm that there was no further movements in the room and then returned to the cold steps, hoping that the others downstairs would not be long in seeking their beds.

It was after quarter past midnight before he heard raucous laughter on the stairs. By then he was wishing he had worn an extra layer of clothing, and hoped that the four men emerging into the corridor would not be long in dispersing. But they appeared to be in excellent humor and in no apparent hurry to retire.

"I'm sorry you're leaving us so soon, Ashton," he heard Lord Paul say as he lit a cigar from the lamp at the head of the stairs. "There's a meet at Chilgrove next week, and as I'm very keen to take over from Quentin as Master of Hounds I'm hoping for a good turn-out from the castle. I trust I can rely upon you others to put in an appearance."

There were enthusiastic grunts of agreement from Howard and Fitzherbert.

"Dashed bad luck I have to go," replied Ashton, "but business calls."

"Business be damned." There was no mistaking Fitzherbert's drunken slur. "It's a wench I'll be bound. Can't keep your hands off them can you, you old devil. All the same I never thought you'd choose a woman rather than attend your old friend's funeral."

"Nothing of the sort, Fitzherbert," said Ashton irritably. "No wenches involved. Just a long-standing engagement with a man with a spot of money to invest. Say no more, what."

There was a general murmur of understanding from the others.

"Will we see you in the morning before you leave?" Howard boomed heartily.

"Not a chance, colonel. Early start for me. Hope you don't mind, Paul, but I asked Johnson to make sure the stables have my horse ready."

"Not in the least, Ashton. That lazy beggar, Smith, will just have to get used to getting up early now that Dunne is otherwise engaged."

The other three laughed loudly at their host's joke, unaware that in the shadows there was someone who did not consider the matter to be so amusing.

"Well, I don't know about you, gentlemen, but that clock is telling me it's time for bed." Lord Paul yawned. "Ashton, your hand, sir. A pleasure to meet you."

The group split up after a general shaking of hands, Ashton, Fitzherbert and Howard moving off in the direction that Montgomery had taken. Lord Paul turned in the opposite direction. But when he reached his own door he waited there only long enough to see that the others were out of sight, before continuing along the corridor and turning in the direction of Lady Annabelle's room.

Parsons moved forward again and watched for any movement in the three rooms. Within five minutes Fitzherbert's and Howard's rooms were dark and silent. Ashton, on the other hand, appeared in no hurry to go to bed. He might well be preparing for his journey, thought Parsons, but on the other hand he could be biding his time and waiting for other people in the castle to go to sleep.

-23-

11th September 1880

By half-past midnight Parsons had become so cold that he was forced to pace up and down the corridor between the bottom of the spiral stairway and the door to Lord Quentin's room. At intervals he checked to see if there was still a light in Ashton's room and occasionally rested for a few minutes on the cold steps until he felt chilled enough to resume his perambulation. It was during one of his periods of rest, while he was debating how much longer to continue his surveillance, that he heard the noise. Magnified by the all-embracing silence and reflected by the curvature of the stairway, there was no doubting the sound of footsteps on the worn stone slabs, nor of the flickering light that grew brighter as each second passed. Someone was coming down the stairs towards him.

The nearest place for him to hide was in Lord Quentin's room. He scurried back along the corridor on tip-toe, searching vainly all the while in his pockets for the key. He cursed himself when he remembered he had returned it to Johnson, knowing then that he would be returning to London and not thinking he would need to enter the room again. But luck was with him. The door had remained open from when Mrs. Williams from the village had laid out the body.

Once inside the room Parsons gently closed the door, leaving only a narrow crack through which to view the corridor. His heart was racing, but in spite of what was happening in the corridor outside his eyes were drawn inexorably towards the bed. In the cold light of the moon and wrapped in its white shroud the body looked even more spectral, and he was grateful that the shroud at least hid the corpse's tortured expression and Lord Quentin's limbs had been returned to a more dignified position.

He shuddered involuntarily when he considered how Mrs Williams must have forced the rigored arms and legs into their present position. The thought of the sounds of the bones cracking in their sockets as they were manipulated made his stomach churn.

With an effort Parsons focused on what was now happening outside. He held his breath to stop his heart pounding, as it sounded louder to him than the approaching footsteps.

The shimmering circle of candle-light moved slowly along the corridor towards him, at its center a woman in a thin white night-gown. She drew level with Lord Quentin's door and for one desperate moment Parsons thought she would enter into the room; but she turned along the north corridor, her long chestnut-coloured hair swaying sensuously with the motion of her body. Parsons had seen similar hair the previous night glistening in the firelight in the Great Hall. O'Brien and Sweeney, the only two girls he had yet to interview, had hair like this. By a process of elimination the girl in the corridor was O'Brien. He could not imagine Sweeney voluntarily wishing to renew her acquaintance with Fitzherbert.

His deduction was confirmed a few seconds later when Ashton's door opened in response to the girl's quiet knock, and when Parsons pressed his ear to it after a discrete interval he could hear only loud sighs and amorous giggles. Fitzherbert was right. Ashton seemed to have only one thing on his mind.

Confident that he now knew the whereabouts of all the occupants of the first floor, Parsons ascended the spiral staircase to begin his search of the servants' quarters.

Without the benefit of curtains over the windows and carpets on the floor it was much colder on the floor above. Movement was noisier and sound traveled further. Parsons had no choice but to remove his shoes and carry them, ignoring the risk of splinters from the rough wooden floor-boards.

He inched forward from the top of the stairs in the darkness until he could see the flickering light of a candle some way off to his left. If, as he assumed, the layout was much the same as it was on the floor below, he was now standing at the point where the north and west corridors met. He watched the light closely for a few minutes, and as it came no closer he reasoned that it was probably a night-light, and keeping close to the wall in the shadows he moved slowly towards it.

The first doors he passed were all ajar and opened onto rooms much smaller than those on the floor below. By the light of the moon through the curtain-less windows he could see they were empty, although from what Johnson had said there was a time when there were sufficient servants to fill them.

Parsons had been correct about the night-light. It stood on a small table opposite the middle of three closed doors. These, he imagined, were where the Irish girls slept, two to a room. There was no mistaking the deep, rhythmic sounds of sleep coming from two of the rooms. The third was silent, and turning the handle quietly he opened the door and peered inside. Finding it unoccupied he entered, closing the door behind him.

There were curtains across the single window, but they were sorely in need of repair and allowed sufficient light for him to see the thin rug between two empty beds. A wash-stand stood against the wall on Parsons left and an assort-ment of clothing hung from nails hammered into the oppo-site wall. Other than these few meager items the room was empty. There was no fireplace, so the room must have been unbearably cold in winter.

He recalled the servants' sleeping arrangements. O'Mahoney shared a room with O'Halloran, Dwyer with Sweeney, and O'Brien with Claire Dunne. O'Brien he knew to be downstairs with Ashton, and on the assumption that she must be one of the occupants of this room, Claire must be the other. Where was she at this late hour and what was she doing?

Leaving the room quietly Parsons resumed his search, turning right at the end of the north corridor into the east. Leaving behind him the little light provided by the night-light he was fortunate not to stumble down a flight of stairs as he fumbled his way along the wall. Judging by their location they were the back stairs leading to the kitchen area. There would be time to investigate these stairs later.

There were three rooms beyond the stairs, all of them open and empty; and after a cursory inspection of each he continued until he reached the south corridor and two further inhabited rooms. Well away from the noise of the stairs and situated on the warmer side of the castle, these were, no doubt, the rooms occupied by Johnson and Mrs. Hughes. Only old servants with clear consciences and weary bones, thought Parsons, could produce such resonant snores.

It was not until he was half-way along the final corridor—the west—that he found another door that was closed. In such an isolated position it seemed unlikely that this room was used by one of the servants. In any event Parsons thought he had accounted for all the servants except Smith. And Smith, he had been led to believe, slept in the stables like Dunne. Unless, regardless of the strict rules of the castle and whatever the members of the family might think, Smith chose to sleep where he liked.

There was no sound from inside the room, but it was several minutes before Parsons plucked up the courage to turn the door-handle. If indeed it was Smith inside, from what he had heard about this unpleasant creature he would not take kindly to anyone disturbing his sleep, especially a person like Parsons with no recognized authority in the castle hierarchy.

To his dismay the hinge creaked loudly as he gingerly opened the door. But gritting his teeth and muttering a few silent prayers he pressed on, expecting at any moment to hear Smith's angry challenge. To his relief it never came. The room was unoccupied.

Like most of the other empty rooms, this one was also used to store oddments of furniture. But unlike the other rooms there were curtains of a sort across the window, so that what little light there was in the room came from the corridor.

Parsons edged forward slowly into the semi-darkness, holding his arms out in front of him and probing the floor with his stockinged feet. Towards the center of the room his feet made contact with what felt like a thick rug. Carefully kneeling, he placed his shoes on the floor and ran his hands across the surface of the rug. It was not a rug as he had first imagined, but a coarse straw mattress, with a pillow at one end and a rough blanket screwed into a ball at the other. There were indentations in the mattress, as though someone had recently used it. Someone with a strong body odor.

He closed the door gently and lit the small candle he had been carrying in his pocket. Then he examined the room.

The miscellany of furniture that had been stored in the room had been stacked against the walls to create space for the makeshift bed, and a length of sacking had been hung across the window to prevent any light from inside the room being seen from outside. Whoever had used the room had not wished to make it common knowledge.

On the floor beside the mattress he found a stump of candle, a small bottle and a dirty plate containing the remnants of a meal. It was difficult to be certain, but the dried-up food on the plate appeared to be several days old. The bottle was empty, but one sniff was enough to tell Parsons it had once contained brandy.

The room, it seemed, had been used within the past few days by an untidy person with a liking for brandy who was sorely in need of a bath. And from what Parsons had learned about him, and had indeed seen with his own eyes, that person could only be Smith.

-24-

*O*nly the muffled sounds of sleep broke the silence as Parsons retraced his steps to the top of the staircase leading to the kitchens. Still carrying his shoes he crept cautiously down the stairs. The deeper he went the darker it became, as the only light reaching the stairs came from a sky-light high in the roof. It was nearly two o'clock, from what he could tell the castle was silent, yet he still felt it imprudent to light his candle lest it attract the attention of anyone else in the castle who might still be awake.

A door opening onto the first floor enabled Parsons to make a quick inspection of the family and guest rooms to see if there had been any changes while he had been upstairs. No sound came from any of the rooms, and only in Ashton's—where the shadows of an ebbing fire flickered under the door—was there any sign of life. The only other movements in the corridors were the fitful quiver of the flames in the oil lamps, the only sound the remorseless ticking of the clock at the top of the main staircase. Reassured by what he found Parsons

211

returned once more to the back stairs and made his way down to the kitchens.

The stairs terminated on the ground floor in a dark passage, and before entering it Parsons waited for several minutes to allow his eyes to adjust to the gloom.

Three doors led off this passage. The first, on his left, was open and led into the Servants' Hall where he had earlier eaten his sandwiches with Mrs. Hughes. A second, further along the passage and on the opposite side, was locked. The third door was at the end of the passage, and from what he remembered from his earlier visit, it led directly into the main kitchen. This door was also closed, but if the chink of light underneath it was anything to go by he was not the only person in the castle still awake.

Claire Dunne sat alone at the large wooden table with a plate of food before her. She did not seem unduly surprised as the door first opened, but when she saw it was Parsons who emerged from the dark passage and not one of the other girls she became alarmed.

The events of the past twenty-four hours had left their indelible marks upon her youthful face. Shorn of its youthful innocence, she had been transformed overnight from a bashful maiden into a middle-aged drudge. Tears stained her cheeks and there were now dark sockets where once her bright eyes had been. The brown, curly hair, that had so radiantly reflected the flames of the log fire in the Great Hall, was now matted and disheveled.

"Whatever are you doing here at this time of night?" Parsons asked, in a voice that sought to combine authority with concern. "Don't you realize it's after two in the morning?"

"I couldn't sleep, sir," she answered pitifully, "and I haven't eaten much today. So when O'Brien left our room I came down here. And in case you're thinking badly of me, sir, Mrs. Hughes doesn't mind us having a bite of food during the night, provided we don't take too much."

There was no reason for Parsons to doubt her. Extra food for servants was not normally begrudged in large houses such as Beaumont. It was one of the few benefits the servants had.

"And where did O'Brien go?" he asked.

"Back to Captain Ashton, sir. Sure, she said he wasn't a bad gentleman. And he promised her some money if she went with him again."

Parsons' moral principles had taken such a battering since his arrival at Beaumont that nothing any more surprised him. And perhaps being paid for services given voluntarily was less an indignity than being chosen at random by one of Lord Quentin's drunken guests. Who was he to judge?"

"Are you worried about your brother?" he asked.

The concern showed so clearly on her face that even as he spoke he realized how foolish the question must sound to her. So he tried another tack.

"Do *you* think he killed Lord Quentin?"

'Sure, Brendan would never be doing such a thing," she replied, defiance adding a brief luster to her voice. "Isn't he the kindest and most gentle of God's creatures. How can anyone believe he could do such a wicked thing?"

It would have been too easy for Parsons to tell the poor girl that he had his own doubts. But to do so would be failing in his duty. Much as he believed in her brother's innocence, he was still a policeman investigating a murder, and such opinions were best kept to himself. He felt there was more he should ask her, but a sudden wave of tiredness swept over him. The tensions of the long day were finally having their effect. With a final entreaty that she get some sleep he left her to finish her meal.

After a brief inspection of the rooms on the ground floor, and after a final check of the corridors of his own floor, Parsons returned to his room. As far as he could tell, with the exception of Claire and himself, everyone else was asleep. That situation did not continue for long. Within a few minutes of entering his room, Parsons had joined the remainder of the castle in slumber.

In spite of his night-time activities Parsons was in the Dining Room before seven the next morning. Not wishing to dwell long over breakfast he ordered two boiled eggs and some toast. With the first available train at ten past eight it would give him ample time to make a brief report of his discoveries to Colonel Howard- or at least those he considered relevant—and be on his way. And with nothing more dramatic to reveal then a mattress in one of the second floor store-rooms, he had no expectations that Howard would change his mind and ask him to help with the investigation.

He was mid-way through his second egg when Catherine arrived, and judging by the dark shadows under her eyes she had slept as little as he. Had it been any woman other than she, he might have suspected she had been crying. But after seeing how she had reacted in the presence of her father's corpse, tears were the last thing he would have expected from her.

In Parsons' opinion Catherine's features were too gaunt and solemn ever to be considered attractive, but he nonetheless credited her as being someone who paid meticulous attention to her appearance. So it was with some surprise that he noticed the few extraneous strands of hair hanging from the elaborate locks she pinned so precisely, and the two unfastened buttons on her spotless white blouse.

She wished him a good morning and asked what time he was planning to leave.

"As soon as possible, Miss Catherine," he answered. "I've only to arrange transport to the station and make a brief report to Colonel Howard."

"A brief report about what exactly, inspector?"

The Chief Constable had entered the room without either of them noticing. In spite of his blood-shot eyes and high color the previous night's drinking seemed to have done little to dampen his spirits. On the contrary, Parsons would have described the colonel's humor as excellent, prompting him to wonder whether his own imminent departure might be in any way responsible.

After Howard had ordered his breakfast Parsons gave him a brief resume of his night's work, concluding with a suggestion that enquiries be made about the use of the mattress on the second floor. Howard said nothing, but his thunderous expression spoke volumes. It was clear that he was thoroughly displeased that Parsons had dared disregard his instructions to cease his involvement in the investigation.

"What do you know of this, Catherine?" he snapped. "Does Smith ever sleep in the castle?"

"Not that I know, Charles," replied Catherine coolly. "But you must realize that I rarely visit the store-rooms on the second floor. My instructions, and those of my father, have always been clear. Johnson is the only male servant allowed to sleep in the castle."

At this point her voice faltered, and much to the surprise of both men she began to cry. Her stoic image had shattered. Parsons watched in amazement as the tears flowed freely down her cheeks and Howard made clumsy attempts to comfort her.

"Whatever's the matter, Catherine, my dear?" he said, reaching across the table and offering her a large white handkerchief.

"I've been robbed, Charles," she wailed, taking the handkerchief and dabbing at her eyes. "The money was always my responsibility. Father trusted me, Charles. And now it's gone. Somebody has stolen it."

"Whatever are you talking about, Catherine?" asked Howard. "What money? Quentin always told me he kept very little money in the castle. He always said his credit was good anywhere in the county."

"That's just it, Charles," she said. "Father never paid for anything. He left all that to me. I settled all his accounts every quarter as well as paying the household expenses and the servants' wages."

The sound of her increasingly hysterical voice brought Howard rushing around the table to where she sat, but once there he seemed uncertain about what to do next, and stood awkwardly behind her with one large hand flapping gently on her shoulder.

"There, my dear, there, there," he said. "Try not to cry, there's a dear girl."

"You've got to help me, Charles," Catherine pleaded during sobs. "Please say you will."

"Of course, my dear, of course. How much money have you lost, and from where was it stolen?"

"There was over two hundred and fifty pounds, Charles," she said, her voice becoming more shrill with each word. "I kept it in a box in my desk. I always have done. The box was there after dinner last night. I know it was. I took some money to pay the musicians. But when I looked this morning the rest of it was gone."

Johnson had entered the room during Catherine's outburst, attracted, Parsons had assumed, by the sound of her increasingly distressed voice. But it was soon clear that he had not even been aware she was crying.

"Miss Catherine," he said, in his usual stiff and formal manner. "I regret to inform you that Dunne is missing. Her bed has not been slept in and a large quantity of food is missing from the dry larder."

Catherine's sobs slowly tapered away and Howard's expression changed from one of concern to surprise and finally to one of eminent self-satisfaction. He looked in triumph at Parsons. It was clear that this fresh development was a further confirmation of his earlier suspicions.

Parsons' emotions moved rapidly in the opposite direction. Money, food and a suspect were all missing. This was the last thing he had wanted to hear before leaving, especially as he had probably been the last person to see Claire Dunne before she had run away.

-25-

The look of triumph on Howard's face showed he had little doubt there was a connection between Claire Dunne's disappearance and the theft of the money. Not only did he now have a self-confessed murderer in custody, he also appeared to have evidence linking the suspect's sister with a robbery. Perhaps she was even an accomplice to the murder itself. Flimsy and circumstantial though this evidence might be, Howard seemed to be in no doubt that it would be more than enough to convince a local jury.

The news had an invigorating effect on Howard. His concern for Catherine's welfare rapidly evaporated, and even before Parsons had left for the railway station the Chief Constable was on his way to the police station in Petersfield to organize a county-wide search for the missing girl.

Philip had volunteered to take Parsons to the railway station. It was a somber journey, both of them aware that Claire's action had now made her brother's plight even more desperate. Parsons was unusually depressed. It had been less than forty-eight hours since he had arrived with such high hopes of spending a few enjoyable days at Beaumont. Little did he think then that he would be forced to leave so soon and in such unhappy circumstances, abandoning to their uncertain fate two people he considered to be innocent.

Tired, and in need of time in which to think, he was glad to board the train and be on his way. Not only was he struggling to make sense of what little inconclusive evidence he possessed, he also had been greatly shocked by the moral decadence and general apathy of those who laid claim to be leaders of society. Perhaps when he had put some distance between himself and Beaumont he would be able to view events more objectively.

The gentle rhythm of the train, his mental and physical exhaustion, and the warm autumn sun combined to act as a sedative. Within ten minutes of leaving Beaumont Station he had fallen into a deep sleep which not even the commuters boarding at stations closer to London could disturb. The next thing he knew was the jolt of the train arriving at Waterloo Station.

The sunshine and the usual jostling of the cabs outside the station were encouragement enough for him to decide to walk to his office. The September air in London was often the best of the year. The humidity of the summer had passed, and it was not yet cold enough for the inhabitants to light the coal-fires that permanently polluted the winter sky. And at this hour of the day the smoke of the evening hearths had yet to obscure the fragile Autumn sun.

As was often his habit when crossing Westminster Bridge, Parsons paused to admire the view, murmuring to himself the lines of poetry he had first learnt at school, long before he had ever visited London:

> *Earth has not anything to show more fair:*
> *Dull would he be of soul who could pass by*
> *A sight so touching in its majesty:*
> *This city now doth, like a garment wear*
> *The beauty of the morning: silent, bare,*
> *Ships, towers, domes, theatres, and temples lie*
> *Open unto the fields, and to the sky:*
> *All bright and glittering in the smokeless air.*

Much as Wordsworth had loved the countryside, thought Parsons, he had nevertheless found something of equal beauty in this splendid panorama. Nor had Wordsworth the added advantage of seeing the dramatic new Houses of Parliament in all their Gothic glory. Not for the first time Parsons found inspiration in the sight of the great river Thames and the imposing London skyline. There might be many things about England that offended him, but at heart he knew himself to be a proud patriot with a deep love for his country.

Even as he drank in the view he could feel the fog in his head clearing, and knew that once seated at his familiar desk it would become easier for him to think clearly. Squaring his shoulders he strode resolutely over the bridge, and turned along Whitehall towards his office in Scotland Yard.

It was a stroke of good fortune to discover that Superintendent Jeffries and Parsons' fellow inspectors were out of the office investigating a stabbing in Smithfield, and were not expected to return until much later in the afternoon. That would spare him—at least for the time being—from his colleagues' inevitable leg-pulling about his premature return. There would also no doubt be many ribald comments about the culinary delights he had described prior to his visit to Beaumont. If only they knew the truth. As for the superintendent, Parsons was more than happy to find that he had at least until the next day before facing him. It was not an interview he was relishing.

As there were no messages for him Parsons decided to spend the afternoon analyzing the events of the past two days. He settled down at his desk overlooking Northumberland Avenue and took a clean sheet of paper from the drawer. Then he began sifting through the notes he had made at Beaumont.

"Motive," he mumbled to himself. "You must find a motive."

He leant back in his chair, pressed the tips of his fingers together, closed his eyes, and concentrated.

It was unfortunate that he had had no opportunity to interview Lady Annabelle. On the one occasion they had spoken after her husband's death Lord Paul had been present. He assumed that, although she might not be aware of the sordid details, she must know something of Lord Quentin's abuse of the Irish girls. She had probably been aware of his perverted behavior for sometime, and no doubt had been appalled by even the little she knew. But was his behavior in itself sufficient motive for her to kill him? After many years of marriage it seemed unlikely, unless something recently had happened to change her attitude towards him.

It was conceivable that the prospect of a new will might have influenced her actions, but without knowing how her circumstances might have changed from one will to the next Parsons could only speculate. And what of the dashing figure of Paul? He, at least, was a new factor in her life. It was common knowledge, even among the servants, that their relationship was a close one. Paul had admitted as much, and Parsons had seen him going towards Annabelle's bedroom on the night after the murder. With her husband dead she was now free to marry whomsoever she might choose. Surely that was motive enough. In Paul she no doubt had a willing accomplice. Did that explain why, when Parsons saw her in the Drawing Room on the night of the murder, she was so anxious to know Paul's whereabouts?

Paul was, of course, the one person who had most clearly gained from Lord Quentin's death. He had arrived at Beaumont only recently with a wildly romantic explanation of his relationship with the family. And in that time he had not only persuaded Lord Quentin to make him his heir, he also appeared to have seduced his wife. With Lord Quentin now dead both the title and Annabelle were his. On the night of the murder he not only knew that Lord Quentin was drunk enough to be virtually defenseless, he had given himself the time and opportunity by dispensing with the services of Dwyer when the girl had visited his room. It was also likely that if he was ever accused of the murder, Annabelle would provide him with an alibi.

Catherine was something of an enigma to Parsons. Until her emotional outburst earlier in the day he had imagined her to be a woman very much in control of her emotions. Now he was less sure. Of all Lord Quentin's children she appeared to be the one closest to her father and the one who cared most for Beaumont. Perhaps she had hoped to follow in his footsteps. Had she, as Dwyer had said, been his heir in a previous will? If that was so she had much to lose from a new one.

It seemed inconceivable to Parsons that any daughter could murder her father, even when the father was a cruel sadist like Lord Quentin. But perhaps Catherine had harbored a long-standing hatred for her father's brutality. Was her's a hatred that had smoldered over years of faithful service to him, a hatred that had finally been spurred into action when she learned he was disinheriting her. If she was not the cool, detached woman she appeared on the surface, but one possessing her father's violent nature, the act of murder might have been easier for her than Parsons had originally thought.

But was there any need for her to commit the crime herself when there were others who might act for her? Her brothers, for instance. Neither of them had any affection for their father, and they might even have felt they owed Catherine a debt of gratitude for her attempts to protect them from his violence. There were also the servants. Smith was an obvious accomplice. Had Smith been using the room on the second floor on the night of the murder, and were Catherine's sudden tears at breakfast no more than an attempt to divert Howard's attention from Parsons' discovery? Perhaps the 'stolen' money was also a subterfuge and might miraculously be found later after things had quieted down.

The more Parsons thought about it, the more convinced he became that Catherine was capable of murder. And in Smith she had a violent accomplice who would no doubt do anything for money.

Alexander was also an obvious suspect. Not only did he dislike his father intensely he had also been disinherited by him. But did he know in advance what the new will contained? Montagu implied that he did. They had spoken about it after dinner on the night of the murder.

Montagu was an ideal accomplice for Alexander: a revolutionary anarchist with a strong dislike, even a hatred, for the Lord Quentins of this world. It was even possible he would goad Alexander into action. On the night of the murder they were both probably under the influence of alcohol and cocaine; indeed they might have taken drugs to bolster their courage. Did that account for Montagu's subsequent disappearance? Was that the result of a fit of panic after the murder had been committed?

Like many in Beaumont that night the two young men had the opportunity, but Parsons was less sure that they were determined or cruel enough to commit such a ghastly crime. In his experience young men of their sort were more inclined to play at being anarchists rather than actually follow through with their threats. He was inclined to agree with Paul. Even if Alexander was aware of the terms of the new will, did he really care? His outburst in the Library might imply that he did, but Parsons thought otherwise.

If Philip's story was to be believed he had an alibi. But it was a worthless one if he was unwilling to make his relationship with Dunne public. On the other hand, both of them had their own motives for the murder. Philip made no secret about hating his father, and Dunne could have been driven both by his affection for Philip and the desire to protect his sister. The more Parsons thought about Philip the more he was inclined to think him more capable of a crime of passion than his elder brother. During the past twenty-four hours he had learned things about Philip's state of mind that had led him to significantly change his opinion of the quiet young boy he had once known.

It was difficult to attribute any motives to Anne Hamilton and Elizabeth Rawlinson, Lord Quentin's two married daughters. They were unlikely to be greatly affected by any changes to their father's will, and at the time of the murder were not even in the castle. They might, of course, have had accomplices; but that was unlikely. Without further evidence, Parsons decided, any possible involvement of either of the women or their husbands was best ignored.

The same applied to the Howards and Joshua Harding, the vicar. As yet Parsons could see no possible reasons for them to be involved in the murder. In any event the three of them had left the castle long before the crime was committed.

Parsons considered the other guests: Ashton, Fitzherbert, Montgomery and Robertson. Any of these could easily have killed Lord Quentin. But Ashton and Fitzherbert were two of his few long-standing friends, and both had alibis of sorts. Ashton's admittedly relied on the word of a servant who could easily have been bribed, and Fitzherbert could only be ruled out if his drunkenness was considered such as to make him incapable of the crime. Parsons had seen enough of alcohol-related assaults and murders to know the violent effect that drink had upon some people. But having seen for himself Fitzherbert's condition the next morning and having heard the evidence of the servants, he found it difficult to believe that Fitzherbert was involved in any way.

He knew little about Montgomery other than what he had been told. He was allegedly a recent friend of Alexander's, with no obvious interest in the will, and he had never previously visited Beaumont. From what Parsons had seen of him he was a man of liberal opinions who was unafraid to speak his mind; qualities that could be relied upon to precipitate the sort of dispute that had taken place after dinner. But Montgomery was hardly likely to commit such a violent murder in order to make a political point. In addition, if O'Mahoney's story was to be believed he also had an alibi.

There was a large question mark against Robertson in Parsons' notes. He had learned very little about the solicitor, although his instincts told him that Robertson was over-qualified for a rural law practice. In Parsons' opinion something had attracted him to Beaumont beyond a desire to be the de Courcey's solicitor. But as the family solicitor Robertson would know not only the contents of the new will, but also the beneficiaries of any previous ones. And it was not unknown for such a professional confidence to be for sale.

That left the servants.

Parsons had ruled out Johnson. The old man had not only been a faithful servant of the family for many years he had also remained loyal to Lord Quentin regardless of anything he had done. And if Johnson had been the murderer, his acting performance the following morning had been nothing short of sensational.

It was also difficult to imagine Mrs Hughes committing the crime. Lord Quentin might well have forfeited her respect, but what had she to gain from his death? Like Johnson she had served the family long and faithfully, and neither of them had any wish to work elsewhere. What had either of them to gain by change? Any new master at Beaumont might well decide to dispense with their services. And at their ages where would they look for other employment?

Nobody had anything but ill to say about Smith. Even his fellow servants disliked him. He was the worst sort of bully, and only Lord Quentin or someone of a like mind would tolerate such a man as Smith in their service. Why was that? Was Lord Quentin merely providing employment for faithful old soldiers like Smith, or was there something in their past lives that formed a bond between them? Yet Smith was no respecter of authority. Parsons still remembered the look of contempt on his face when they had driven through the village on the first afternoon. He also remembered their conversation in the stables on the morning after the murder. Such a man's loyalty was easily bought. If the price was right he would be a ready accomplice for any crime, although Parsons imagined that it would need to be a substantial sum for Smith to murder his benefactor. And if large sums of money were involved that seemed to bring the motive back to the will.

Spencer, in contrast, seemed to be an upright sort of man. Parsons would have described him as a typical English yeoman, conscientiously going about his night duties while the feckless upper classes debauched themselves. But Parsons had only his word for that. Philip, for one, knew nothing about the nightly patrols of the grounds Spencer claimed to be making. Spencer could equally well have been inside the castle, or at least have interrupted his patrol to murder Lord Quentin. Like Smith, Spencer could have been working for someone who could pay well, and seeing Dunne leaving the castle had not only provided a fortuitous alibi it had also presented the police with an ideal suspect.

What of the other servants? Of the six Irish girls, O'Mahoney, O'Brien, Sweeney and Dwyer had alibis of sorts:

O'Mahoney had been with Montgomery, O'Brien with Ashton. The other two shared a room and could vouch for each other. That left Claire Dunne and O'Halloran, both of whom claimed they had spent the night alone in their rooms. On that basis either or both of them could have killed Lord Quentin. But were their motives any different from those of the other girls. Had Howard been right? Was the murder, after all, an Irish conspiracy. Every Irish servant at Beaumont was a victim of a system that exploited them both in England and in their own country. But that did not necessarily make them murderers, reasoned Parsons, any more than being Irish made them Fenian assassins.

The Fenian threat would always be a convenient card for the police to play. It always went down well with an English public that regarded most Irish as beyond contempt. The successful overthrow of an Irish conspiracy would therefore suit Colonel Howard admirably. In view of the recent spate of bombings in England and the murders of English aristo-crats living in Ireland it would make him a national hero. It would also divert attention from any involvement he and others might have had at Beaumont in the abuse of the Irish servants.

But the actual murder bore none of the hallmarks of a Fenian killing. Fenians invariably preferred the bullet or the bomb. And as far as Parsons could see a Fenian attack at Beaumont at this particular time did not make sense. Why choose to strike when the castle was full of people? There were so many more favorable opportunities. And why target the de Courceys? The family was not actively involved in British or Irish politics and over the years had probably misused or neglected their Irish estates no more than many other aristocratic English families.

Parsons opened his eyes and looked out of the window. In the darkening afternoon sky above Horse Guards a cloud of sparrows twisted and whirled as it made its way to St James' Park to join the countless thousands of others gathering there in the tall trees. The instincts that guided these sparrows were always right. In their world there was never any doubt. They knew when, as now, summer was drawing to a close and it was time to leave. If only, he thought, he could have their insight.

That will come, he promised himself, provided you don't miss the details. In matters of murder it's always the little things that matter. He had made a start, and he felt all the better for that.

Parsons read through his notes again, this time making a list of the more important questions he felt needed answering.

What were the terms of the previous will? Who gained and lost as a result of the new one?

Who had used the room on the second floor?

What was known about Smith and Spencer prior to their employment at Beaumont?

Had there been any recent Fenian activity that might be connected with this crime?

What could be learned from the backgrounds of the Irish servants?

What was known about Ashton, Fitzherbert, Montagu, Montgomery and Robertson?

After sucking the end of his pen for a few seconds longer he added two further questions to the list.

Who had placed the announcement in the Times?

Was there any significance to be drawn from Catherine recently deciding to wear red underwear?

He may have been removed from the investigation, but even from his desk in London Parsons felt he could find many of the answers to these questions; and armed with this information he might even persuade his superiors to take an interest in the case. If his duties allowed he would start work tomorrow after a good night's sleep.

"If the superintendent or any of the others come back tonight tell them I'll be in first thing in the morning," he shouted through the door of the clerks' office.

Then he hurried out of the building. Any embarrassing questions about his premature return from the country could wait until after his inevitable interview with Superintendent Jeffries on the morrow.

Parsons rented an attic room in the Baker's small terraced house in Camberwell. A dull middle-grade civil servant, Harold Baker worked in Whitehall with his two equally dull lower-grade civil servant sons. His wife, Alice, a frugal woman from Dunfermline, presided over the household. Parsons had reason to be grateful for her native Scottish thrift, as it was solely through her desire to avoid the expense of a living-in servant that the attic room in the Baker's house had become vacant.

In spite of the lack of intellectual stimulus within the household the situation suited his requirements admirably. In addition to it being an eminently peaceful house in which to live, he was provided each morning with a hearty breakfast and a substantial supper on every weekday evening; leaving him to indulge himself at weekends with more exotic dishes than generally fell within Mrs Baker's repertoire. And apart from the domestic convenience, Camberwell also offered relative ease of access to Whitehall by horse-tram, or even by foot whenever Parsons felt the need for exercise.

His unexpected arrival threw Mrs. Baker into an unaccustomed tizzy. She was full of profuse apologies about there being insufficient pork chops for supper and the butcher's shop being closed.

"You should've told me you were coming back so soon, Inspector Parsons," she said.

Mrs. Baker took a secret delight in having a detective-inspector boarding with her, and never referred to Parsons by anything other than his correct title. Apart from making her feel more secure in a part of Camberwell that had sadly become less genteel over the years, his presence also lent a little excitement to her otherwise uneventful life. His involvement in the recent Fenian arrests and subsequent trial had been the talk of the house for several weeks, much to the irritation of her husband and sons, who could offer nothing better in the way of supper-time conversation than anecdotes of interminable committee meetings or discussions on the merits of various methods of filing papers.

"Please don't concern yourself, Mrs. Baker," Parsons replied. "The fault is entirely mine. In any case, I feel in need of a walk. Strange as it may sound to you I've had little opportunity to stretch my legs while I was in the country, and a quiet stroll to the White Hart in Southwark for one of their steak and kidney pies will do me nicely this evening."

It also enabled him to avoid the close questioning about the grandeur of life at Beaumont that was bound to accompany his next meal en famille. Postponing that for the next twenty-four hours would be another small relief.

-26-

12th September 1880

arsons was at his desk the next morning just after half past eight, searching through the office newspapers for any report of Lord Quentin's murder. Surprisingly there were none. But news traveled much slower in the country, and it was easier for the local police to keep the press ignorant, if it was in their best interest to do so. In all probability Howard wanted to keep the affair out of the news until he could make a suitably dramatic announcement. Had he been in a similar position, Parsons mused, he would have used the publicity to help him find the suspect's fugitive sister and canvas the public's assistance in reporting any suspicious characters seen in the area.

It was generally Parsons' aim to be in the office before the arrival just before nine of Superintendent Jeffries from his home in Surbiton. And as he was anticipating an early summons from his superior to explain why the Chief Constable of Hampshire had found cause to demand the pre-

235

mature recall to London of one of his inspectors, today was no time to be late. But to Parsons' surprise it was not until after ten that he was called to the superintendent's office.

"Well, Parsons," said Jeffries, busying himself with the routine of lighting his briar pipe, "the last time I was called to the Commissioner's office twice in less than twenty-four hours there had been a threat on the life of a Cabinet minister. What have you been up to? You'd better sit down and tell me what's been going on at Beaumont.

Jeffries nodded towards a brown leather button-backed chair opposite his desk. The superintendent always sat with his back to the window, keeping his face in the shadows as much as possible whilst having a clear view of the people to whom he was speaking. It was a useful interviewing technique and one Parsons had employed often himself. But now that he was aware of the ploy he took the precautionary measure of moving his chair to a position where Jeffries was forced to concede Parsons at least a partial view of his face.

It was the determined face of a man who did not suffer fools gladly. For Jeffries there had been no favors in his career from influential friends or family. His steady rise through the ranks of the Metropolitan Police had been entirely due to his own hard work. The effort that had taken showed in the deep creases in his grim leathery countenance. He was called "The Judge" behind his back and, like his infamous namesake whose Bloody Assizes following the failed Monmouth Rebellion of 1685 had left three hundred rebels hanging from roadside gallows, he was a relentless pursuer of criminals. He was almost as hard on his own men, and particularly impatient with those who wasted his time unnecessarily. Aware of that, Parsons always made his reports as brief as possible, and it was a measure of his clarity of thought and expression that Jeffries had rarely found it necessary to question him until he had finished speaking.

As ever, Parsons admired the way in which the superintendent never allowed his expression to reveal what he was thinking. A successful detective needed to be a good card-player he always maintained.

"And what is your opinion of this Colonel Howard?" Jeffries asked, when Parsons had finished his report.

Those who did not know Jeffries better might have assumed the question invited a flippant response. But he had little to offer by way of a sense of humor. He dealt only in facts and sensible opinion. Knowing this, Parsons answered diplomatically and concisely. Sarcasm and exaggerated criticism of a superior were not an option for him at this moment. Jeffries could be relied on to make up his own mind about Howard from what Parsons had said.

"Then you can imagine how he'll react to this."

Jeffries pushed a paper across his desk towards Parsons. It was a telegram addressed to the Metropolitan Commissioner that had been sent from Beaumont Station at seven thirty-four that morning, and as Parsons read it he experienced a gamut of emotions ranging from surprise, to horror and finally to exhilaration.

The wording of the telegram was terse but nonetheless dramatic. It read:

'Lord Paul de Courcey shot dead at ten last night Stop Chief Constable wounded Stop Stables destroyed in fire Stop Request you release Inspector Everett Parsons to assist enquiries Stop Lady Annabelle de Courcey Stop

-27-

"*Well, young man,*" said Jeffries, "*what do I tell the* Commissioner? Do you want this opportunity to impress this Colonel Howard of yours and the rest of the Hampshire Constabulary?"

There was no doubt at all in Parsons' mind. He would like nothing better than a chance to prove himself to Howard by finding the real murderer or murderers. At least there was no doubt that the young groom was innocent of the second killing, and it also seemed that the murder of the two leading members of the de Courcey family within the space of forty-eight hours could hardly be the work of a few women servants. But if he returned to Beaumont it would be on his terms. He had no intention of playing second fiddle to the Chief Constable.

"Of course I'll go, sir." he replied. "But when the Commissioner replies I want him to make it absolutely clear to Colonel Howard that if I go the investigation is to be my responsibility alone. You must already know what I think of the Chief Constable's competence. He may have admirable qualities as an administrator, but as a detective he has none. If I go I must have complete charge."

Jeffries gave Parsons a long penetrating look from behind the cloud of pipe smoke, and when he replied there was a trace of admiration in his voice.

"You never cease to surprise me, Parsons," he said. "In spite of looking as though you couldn't say boo to a goose you've got more backbone than anyone else in this department. I don't know whether the Commissioner will support you in this, but for what it's worth you've got my backing. I'll give you half an hour to draft a telegram for the old man to send to your friend Howard in which you can spell out all your terms and conditions. Now don't just sit there. Get on with it."

"There's just one other thing, sir," said Parsons as he reached the door. "I need someone at this end to do some research for me. There's still a lot I don't know about some of the people down at Beaumont. Having someone here to investigate their backgrounds would be invaluable. For instance, someone like Sergeant Harris. I had a quick word with him this morning before coming here, and he tells me at present he doesn't have too much on his plate."

"Don't push your luck too far, Parsons," snorted Jeffries. "Requests for your services from the aristocracy don't automatically entitle you to the personal use of half of CID. You can have Harris, but only on the condition that I have first call on his services if I need them. And if he finds anything that could prove embarrassing to important people, I want to be the first to know. Is that clear? Now run along and get to work on that telegram."

Within twenty minutes Parsons was back in the superintendent's office.

"You haven't pulled any punches, have you," said Jeffries as he read the paper on his desk. "From what you've told me about Howard, when he sees this he'll probably have an apoplexy."

The telegram Parsons had drafted not only established his credentials it also attempted to set the investigation on a more professional footing. It read:

Personal for Colonel Howard. Hope your wounds not serious. As requested by Lady Annabelle de Courcey am releasing Inspector Parsons to investigate murders at Beaumont. Parsons has my full authority to take complete control of investigation. Grateful you give him all necessary assistance. Request minimum disturbance of scene of murder and stable fire until Parsons arrives. Please forward following information as soon as possible: home addresses of all house guests and Irish servants; address of Andrew Robertson; address of Harrison Montgomery in Canada and London and date of arrival in Britain; regimental numbers and service backgrounds of Smith and Spencer. Parsons arriving by train four fifteen pm today. Please arrange transport Beaumont Station with reliable police officer to brief him. Kind regards and best wishes for speedy recovery. Colonel Wilson, Metropolitan Police Commissioner.

"You're sure you haven't forgotten anything, Parsons," Jeffries asked, a wry smile revealing teeth stained dark by tobacco and misaligned by years of pipe clenching. "I'd hate to go back to the Commissioner later with another of your shopping lists."

"I'm sure I can manage with what I've asked for, sir," Parsons replied smugly. "But in case I encounter any problems later I've taken the liberty of drafting the Commissioner's reply to Lady Annabelle."

He handed a second paper to his superior.

"Regret to hear sad news from Beaumont," Jeffries read. *"Pleased to agree your request for Inspector Parsons to take over investigation. Parsons arriving pm today. Have asked Colonel Howard to arrange transport. Do not hesitate to contact me if further assistance required. Best wishes. Reginald Wilson.*

Parsons' smile was as angelic as a choirboys.

"If I need any further help I'm sure I can rely upon the Commissioner's weakness for a pretty ankle," he said, "especially one that comes so well-shod."

"Sometimes, Parsons, you're too clever for your own good," Jeffries declared. "Now get out of here before I change my mind and tell the old man this is all a big mistake."

But by then Parsons was half way across the room. He was enjoying being able to call the shots for once.

Leonard Harris was a slim, dapper man of thirty-two, with eager blue eyes and short, dark hair held firmly in place by the liberal application of macassar oil. He sported an immaculately-groomed and waxed moustache which he stroked continually, which together with the distinctive brown check suits he wore gave him the appearance of a mannequin and led frequently to him being the butt of office jokes. Having suffered in a like fashion himself when he had first joined the department, Parsons could empathize with Harris, and he soon realized that the rather prim exterior concealed an organized and methodical mind very akin to his own.

Had Harris' pedigree been other than a Board School in a Shoreditch back-street that he had left at the age of fourteen, his intelligence and dogged perseverance might by now have qualified him to be an inspector. As it was, as long as he remained a detective the social mores made it unlikely he would ever be promoted above his present rank. Parsons was sure that Harris was well aware of that, but in spite of his limited horizons the sergeant retained an infectious enthusiasm for his work. If there was one man in the department Parsons knew he could rely on it was Harris.

He listened carefully as Parsons briefed him on the background to the murders, and from the eager expression on his face it was clear he was delighted to be involved. Researching background information was an activity he particularly enjoyed, especially in a case like this involving such an interesting cross-section of people. Harris could be as deferential as the next man when it was necessary, but he also possessed a healthy skepticism for the airs and graces of those who considered themselves to be his betters.

"At this stage we must consider everyone at Beaumont as a suspect," said Parsons. "So I don't want any telegrams addressed to me at the castle where they might fall into the wrong hands. Send them care-of the station master at

Beaumont. From what I've seen of him he looks a reliable man. If Colonel Howard does what he's been asked, within the next few days you should begin receiving the information I've asked for. Start working on it as soon as it arrives. We've lost too much time already. And one last thing. On the day I traveled down to Beaumont there was an announcement about the reunion in the *Times*. No one at Beaumont seems to know anything about it, so find out who put it in the paper."

"Leave it to me, sir," said Harris enthusiastically, "I'm sure we can show these Hampshire gents a thing or two."

Parsons winked at him.

"I've every confidence we can, Harris. And remember, we've got the old man's full support in this. So if you've got any problems go straight to the Judge. No one else. Is that clear?"

Satisfied that Harris fully understood his requirements Parsons rushed to the cab rank in Whitehall, and was soon on his way to Camberwell to pack some clothes. The news of his return to Beaumont and the briefest outline of what had occurred there made a great impression on Mrs. Baker, who lost no time in telling her friends, family, neighbors and tradesmen alike the story of Inspector Parsons' dramatic recall. It was a story that her husband and sons would grow weary of hearing.

-28-

The station master was waiting on the platform when Parsons arrived at Beaumont Station, his ruddy features arranged with a gravitas appropriate to the occasion. He greeted Parsons with a salute as he had on his earlier visit.

"We've been expecting 'ee, Inspector Parsons," he said in his rich Hampshire accent, "Sergeant Brown's been waiting upon thee this past half hour."

He took Parsons' bag and marched purposefully beside him along the platform.

"I hope ye'll allow me to express my good wishes for your success in bringing these criminals to justice," he said gravely. "And I'd like 'ee to know thou can rely upon me for any assistance."

"That's just what I'd been hoping to hear, station master," replied Parsons. "For a start you can tell me your name."

"Carpenter, sir. Gabriel Carpenter at your service. A loyal servant of the London and South Western railway these past sixteen years."

245

"Well, Mr. Carpenter, I'm expecting a regular supply of telegrams from London, all of which will be addressed care of your good self," explained Parsons. "When they arrive I want them delivered to me and no one else. I cannot stress how important that is. Do you understand?"

The station master's expression of stout resolve indicated how well he understood the seriousness of this responsibility, and suitably impressed by this reaction Parsons continued with his instructions.

"It's possible these telegrams may come at any time of the day or night, and I would like your assurance that when they arrive they will receive the prompt attention of either you or a member of your staff. Can I rely upon that?"

"That 'ee can, sir. If I'm not on duty m'self I'll ensure my staff bring thy telegrams to my cottage."

He indicated the small dwelling on the opposite side of the railway line.

"Any time night or day, sir," he repeated gravely. "You can rely upon that."

"I knew I could, Mr. Carpenter. And you can be sure that a favorable report of your support in this matter will in due course reach your superiors."

The brass buttons on the stationmaster's brown uniform jacket strained as he straightened his back and pulled back his shoulders in a fashion that would have been a credit to the Brigade of Guards.

"My pleasure, sir," he said, his face flushed and glowing with pleasure.

And after placing Parsons' luggage on the back of the trap he gave a further salute, and remained at a position of military attention until the trap turned the bend and passed from his view.

In requesting that he be met by a reliable police officer Parsons had hoped for someone other than Sergeant Brown, an officer whose sole contribution as far as he could tell had been his manhandling of Dunne. But from his general demeanor and the methodical briefing he gave during the journey to the castle Parsons began to think more kindly disposed towards him.

Like many policemen, Brown was motivated primarily by the necessity of obeying orders and responding to the individual idiosyncrasies of his superiors. And it was easy to imagine what that could lead to in a force commanded by a person like Colonel Howard. Instant obedience and discipline would always be the order of the day rather than initiative and common sense.

"First I knew was when Mr. Alexander arrived at my house last night, sir. 'Twas just after midnight," Brown had explained, after being told by Parsons to start his story from the beginning.

"What took him so long? I thought Lord Paul was shot at ten."

"Mr. Alexander went for the doctor first," Brown explained. "his lordship was already dead. Colonel Howard was badly wounded, so they thought it best to get medical help first. From what I understand, sir, everything was at sixes and sevens. As well as the shooting, the stables was on fire, and the poor frightened horses was running loose around the grounds."

Parsons could imagine the scene and wondered who had taken charge. Had it been the wounded Howard, Catherine or one of the guests. His money was on Catherine. But it would have been no easy matter for anyone, faced with panic-striken servants and a situation such as Brown had described.

"It was past one by the time I arrived in the trap with my two constables," continued Brown. "By then the doctor had given Colonel Howard something to help 'im sleep and I was told not to disturb 'im. The fire was nearly out, the ladies and gentl'mun were in the Drawing Room and the servants in the Servants' Hall. That is all of them except Smith."

"And where was he?"

"Bless you, sir. 'Twas Smith that done it. 'Twas Smith that shot his lordship and set light to the stables."

Parsons had always thought that Smith would be involved in the murders in one way or another, but he cautioned himself for jumping to any conclusions. It was foolish to be thinking of anyone's guilt at this stage, with only Brown's second-hand account of what had happened as evidence.

"And what did you do for the rest of the night?" he asked.

"After everyone had gone to bed we mounted guard on the castle, sir. We'd no way of knowing whether Smith might return. Not that I figured 'twas much chance of that. Round about three we had a fair downpour, and I couldn't see anyone riding about in that. We never received any orders 'til this morning. That's when Major Fitzherbert told us a telegram had come and the investigation was being handed over to a detective from London. We was just told to wait and do nothing until you arrived."

As a professional, Parsons was dismayed by the inactivity and lack of initiative displayed by the local police since the time of the murder. But he was also relieved. Much of the evidence might still be intact, and it would suit him better to start the investigation from scratch. If the weather had been as bad as Brown had said Smith would probably not have got far. With luck little damage had been done by the delay.

East of the village the lane began its ascent through open countryside to the castle. On one side of the lane soft-eyed cattle grazed idly in the undulating pastures, offering the casual observer a romanticized image of rural life. The reality of life in the country-side could be seen in the wet fields on the opposite side of the lane, where the flattened wheat provided sad evidence of another disappointing harvest.

The land gradually thickened into copse, which gave way in turn to the mighty elms and oaks of the Great Park. From one such copse a group of village children stared at them as the trap passed, the recent drama at the castle seemingly of little consequence in their own small world of make-believe. The faces peering through the trees reminded Parsons of his own childhood in India. Frequently the only white child in a remote garrison, his Indian ayah had often taken him to play in the village with the children of her own extended family. And together with his brown-skinned friends, he had scrambled amongst the trees and the rocks and marveled at the kaleidoscope that was India unfolding around him.

But whereas his had been the only white face amongst many brown ones, unless he was mistaken amidst the grubby faces now peering at him from beneath the trees there was one that was a darker shade than the rest. It was but a fleeting sensation, perhaps a trick of the light, and the image had disappeared as quickly as the children, who vanished into the depths of the copse as he twisted round in his seat to get a closer view of them.

-29-

During his thirty-one years in the army, that had included service in Africa, India and the Crimea, Colonel Howard had seen action on many occasions. But he had never imagined that it would not be until he became the chief constable of a rural English county that he would be shot. He had been fortunate. The wound in his left thigh had been deep, but not one that threatened his life. But he had lost a great deal of blood during the initial panic after the shots had been fired, and in the hours since then the effect of delayed shock had been debilitating.

When he had seen it was Parsons entering his room he had attempted to sit straighter in his bed and strike a more authoritative pose. But the gesture was unconvincing. Howard's eyes seemed to have sunk into his face and the color had drained from it, and Parsons could tell that even without the Commissioner's instructions there was no way the Chief Constable would be able to control the investigation.

251

The tables had been turned dramatically in his favor, and as he offered his condolences, it was all Parsons could do to keep a smug expression off his face.

"Tell me all you can remember about last night, sir" he asked, after the polite formalities were complete.

In a little over an hour it would be dark outside, and while there was sufficient light Parsons wanted to examine the scene of the shooting and the remains of the stables. But before that it was important that Howard be questioned, regardless of his condition.

Howard's formerly dominating parade-ground voice had changed beyond recognition. Like the rest of his body it had aged and shriveled, and Parsons was obliged to move his chair closer to the bed to hear what the colonel was saying.

"We'd just finished our dinner," explained Howard. "The others had left the Hall, and Lord Paul, Fitzherbert and I were drinking our brandy."

Howard began to cough painfully and beckoned to Parsons for the glass of water on the bedside cabinet.

"A storm had been threatening all evening," he said, "and the air at dinner had been uncomfortably warm and humid. So as soon as the ladies had gone we decided to open the French windows."

Watched impatiently by Parsons he took another sip of water.

"Round about ten we heard what sounded like gravel being thrown against one of the windows, and Lord Paul and I went to investigate. Fitzherbert, needless to say, stayed with his brandy."

The ghost of a laugh at this scrap of humor precipitated another fit of coughing, and as Howard struggled for breath small beads of perspiration appeared on his forehead.

There might be justice in this world after all, thought Parsons, as he watched the swaggering bully of forty-eight hours before in such discomfort.

"Go on please, sir," he prompted, after a discrete pause. "What did you find?"

"Nothing," said Howard. "There was no sign of anybody. But once we were outside the two of us decided to take a few turns along the terrace to get some air. As I said before, it was a balmy night."

Howard raised his eyes upwards, as though the scene he was about to describe was projected onto the ceiling.

"There were only a few stars and not much light from the Hall, but it was sufficient to see where we were going."

"And which direction was that?"

"Patience, young man," Howard snapped, his voice displaying something of its former rancor. "I'll tell you what happened in my own good time."

Suitably admonished Parsons waited for Howard to continue.

"As I was saying, we were walking along the path towards the Drawing Room windows—for your information that's in a westerly direction—and we were about twenty yards from the corner of the castle when a figure appeared in front of us. He must have been hiding around the corner. Almost immediately there was a shot and Lord Paul fell to the ground. For a second I wasn't sure what to do for the best, whether to stay with his lordship or follow a soldier's natural instincts and charge the enemy."

"What did you do, sir?"

"I shouted for Fitzherbert and then ran towards the assailant."

Parsons questioned the wisdom of such an action but said nothing. In his opinion, discretion was always the better part of valor.

"I had only advanced a matter of a few yards when there was a second shot. It caught me in the leg and stopped me in my tracks. Fitzherbert appeared then, and seeing what had happened ran back to fetch help. I don't know how long that took. Probably no more than a few minutes. But at the time it felt much longer, especially when I was expecting the murderer to finish me off. After shooting at me he'd disappeared round the corner of the castle, but I wasn't to know he wouldn't come back. Then Annabelle arrived with Catherine, Alexander and Montagu. I didn't realize until later that Paul was still alive then and was able to say a few words. But I believe he died soon after that."

Colonel Howard paused, reflecting for a moment upon the horror of that moment.

"Catherine was magnificent," he said after a while, with a slight tremor in his voice. "She sent Alexander to fetch bandages and to bring Johnson and some of the girls. But before they arrived Philip came with the news that the stables were on fire. It's difficult to be clear about what actually happened then as there was a great deal of panic, confusion and shouting, and it must have been round about then that I lost consciousness."

Howard seemed embarrassed by that. Fainting, it appeared, was an unmanly act and one not expected of old soldiers.

"Did you recognize your assailant, sir?" Parsons asked.

"I can't be absolutely certain. Everything happened so fast. It certainly looked like Smith. He was wearing that filthy long coat of his and his wide-brimmed hat. According to Annabelle, Lord Paul recognized him because he mumbled his name before he died. One of the servants also thought they saw him soon afterwards riding away from the burning stables."

"What about the search, sir. Who's handling that?"

"Inspector Marsden. He's the station officer in Petersfield. He's also in charge of the search for that girl. But if you don't mind, Parsons. I'm feeling tired now. I'm sure you'll find other people to answer your questions. You can talk to me again later."

Even though he knew it would irritate the colonel there was still one question Parsons wanted to ask. In normal circumstances he would have thought twice before upsetting someone in Howard's condition, but in this case he felt justified.

"The Commissioner asked for some additional information about the people here, sir. Can you tell me whose providing it?"

He was right. At the mention of the Commissioner the blood momentarily rushed back to the colonel's face.

"Damned impertinence," he said. "I suppose you were responsible for that. You'd better speak to Catherine. I asked her to get the information. She wasn't too pleased, I can tell you, but in the circumstances there was no one else. Brown's never been too comfortable handling that sort of thing. He's a reliable enough chap, but he isn't very good at handling paperwork or dealing with his betters. He doesn't have much in the way of social graces. You know what I mean, Parsons."

Brown has probably more qualities than you give him credit for, thought Parsons as he left the room. But if he's never given any opportunity he can't be expected to demonstrate them.

Parsons found Johnson in the kitchen. The old man was exhausted. The lack of sleep and the dramas of the previous night were manifest in the dark rings under his eyes and in his drawn and weary expression. But the long years of service were standing him in good stead. Regardless of any physical tiredness he was still functioning as normal. It was unlikely that Catherine or anyone else had given the poor fellow a second thought, reflected Parsons. Or any of the other servants for that matter. As far as most of the family was concerned servants could keep going until they dropped.

"Find Sergeant Brown and his men and tell them to meet me at the stables in fifteen minutes," Parsons instructed, "and tell them not to touch anything until I arrive. Then ask Lady Annabelle, Miss Catherine and the gentlemen to gather in the Drawing Room at seven. If they ask why you can tell them I want a few words with them before dinner. Other than that you know nothing. I'll want to talk to the servants as well. Assemble them here as soon after dinner as possible. I'll try not to keep them waiting."

Satisfied with the arrangements he had now set in motion, Parsons set off for his own preliminary inspection of the scene of Lord Paul's murder. After that, if the light allowed, he would set Brown and his men the task of picking through the charred remains of the stables.

The previous night's glasses and china were still on the long oak table in the Great Hall. There were eight settings. Parsons counted those staying in the castle on his fingers. Including the family and guests there should have been nine for dinner the previous evening. Although the Commissioner's telegram had instructed that everything be left as it was at the time of Lord Paul's death, it would not have arrived at the castle until late morning or even early afternoon, which was well after the normal hour for clearing the room. It was not, therefore, a result of the Commissioner's wishes that the table was still uncleared, but more an indication of how much the normal routine of the castle had been disrupted.

Parsons walked slowly across the Hall to the French windows and opened them. Outside a short flight of lichen-covered stone steps led down to a wide gravel path. About seventy yards of undulating lawn lay between this path and the castle walls. From his previous visit Parsons knew there were only two entrances to the castle through these walls: the main west gate and the stable entrance in the north-east corner of the castle. But from where he stood on the gravel path he could see neither.

He turned to his right towards the south-west corner of the castle and began slowly walking along the path, retracing the steps taken by Lord Paul and Colonel Howard on the previous night. As he walked he examined the path for traces of blood. There were none. The over-night rain had washed away any there might have been.

On the grass ahead of him, at the point where the path turned north and disappeared from view, stood a large stone plinth. When he reached it he found it to be about four feet high and supporting an ornamental Greek urn draped with garlands and topped with an assortment of fruit. There was a similar artifact behind him at the other end of the path.

Parsons turned and looked back along the path, trying to imagine the scene through the eyes of the murderer. Where would he have stood to get the best shooting position? Would he have used the corner of the wall to steady his aim or the top of the plinth? The flat surface was an ideal place on which to rest a weapon, but the plinth itself was exposed to the view of anyone approaching along the path. On balance it appeared the wall had the advantage of better concealment for a marksman as well as offering a degree of support for a weapon. But he would need to ask Howard what he remembered. Howard was the only witness to the shooting, and Parsons was annoyed with himself for not asking him more questions about the position of the assailant when he had fired and whether he had used a rifle or a hand gun.

After searching in vain around the plinth and on the path for any discarded cartridge cases Parsons followed the path along the west side of the castle, past the Drawing Room and the Library, and the main entrance to the castle. Although he could see nothing that was relevant, he nevertheless considered it worthwhile for Brown and his men to search the area again later.

When he reached the north-west corner of the castle Parsons had his first view of the stable area. Had he not been there so recently he would never have imagined the stables had ever existed. The fire had completely destroyed the great gable-ended barn and its large wooden doors. Not even the massive timbers supporting the steeply-pitched roof had survived.

The storm had arrived too late to save anything. The timbers, the wooden stalls for the horses and the hay inside the building had burned like tinder. Under the weight of the slates the weakened roof had collapsed, and these slates now lay scattered amongst the charred embers like so many discarded playing cards.

A single section of the wattle-and-daub wall, that must have been close enough to the castle wall to be offered a degree of protection, had not been completely engulfed by the flames. But without the timber frame to provide support it had fallen onto the ground as a single entity.

Three tethered horses, homeless but otherwise intact, nibbled at the grass as though it was of no consequence to them that their former residence was no more. Close to them, Brown and his two constables stood waiting patiently, grey with fatigue and wearing the same mud-splattered uniforms they had worn since arriving the previous night.

Parsons had already decided not to keep them long. They were clearly dead on their feet and deserving of a good night's sleep. And in view of the fading light, there would probably only be time for a short preliminary search of the stable area.

Watched with mild curiosity by the horses, Parsons deployed the three policemen at equal intervals along the northern edge of the cremated building. He and Brown took up central positions with Chambers and Jessop, the two constables, on either side. The three policemen could not have been more different in their appearance: Brown was dark-skinned and thick-set with a heavy growth of side whiskers; Chambers, tall, spare and fair-haired with a fresh boyish complexion; and Jessop, the oldest of the three, clean-shaven on his upper lip, but heavily bearded over the remainder of his face. It was Jessop's surly face that had showed the greatest sign of displeasure at being kept on duty for so long.

"We're going to walk slowly along the length of the stables," instructed Parsons. "Keep in line and look carefully at the ground around you for any items you think might be connected with starting the fire or the shooting. By that I mean articles like oil lamps, cartridge cases and weapons. If you find anything you think is important don't touch it. Call me."

As they shuffled forward the shadows of the castle wall engulfed ever more of the area they were searching. Within half an hour the sun would be gone and there would be no point in continuing. There was always tomorrow, thought

Parsons, but he prayed that Fortune would favor them tonight with at least one useful piece of evidence.

They found several items of horse tackle and the remains of two oil lamps, which Parsons decided to leave where they lay. Tomorrow the men could carry out a more systematic search and produce a detailed plan and inventory of their finds. There was no time for that now and in any case he was hoping to find something more germane to the crime. A weapon, or at least some cartridge cases.

They had almost finished their sweep and Parsons was beginning to resign himself to another disappointment, when he heard Jessop's excited cry. Disgruntled at the long hours he had already worked and intent upon food and sleep, he had moved ahead of the others, anxious to complete his allotted area of search. It was in this area that the single section of wattle-and-daub wall to survive had finally collapsed across the floor of what had formerly been the stables.

For a moment Jessop had stared at the ground in disbelief, thinking that his tired eyes had deceived him. But they had not. From under the edge of a pile of charred beams, wattle and slates protruded what at first glance he took to be a black glove. But on closer inspection he saw he was wrong. Jessop had discovered the charred remains of a human hand.

-30-

Within a few seconds of Jessop's startled cry, Parsons and the other two policemen were carefully removing the debris from around the exposed hand. In less than five minutes they had exposed a complete body.

There was nothing about the posture of the corpse to indicate that the victim had ever been aware of the terrible fate that was over-taking it. The body lay on its back, with its charred face to the sky, strangely at ease in the remnants of the raging ferment that had engulfed it. There were no visible signs to suggest that whoever this was had been restrained in any way. There were no signs of a struggle nor anything in the position of the limbs to suggest that any attempt had been made to escape from the fire. The victim's legs were as straight as those of a soldier on a parade ground, with its arms spread evenly on each side of the torso.

Parsons recalled seeing hay stored in this part of the building during his previous visit, and it occurred to him that the victim might have chosen the spot as one suitable for a quiet sleep. But surely, he thought, that sleep could not have been so deep that this person could not have failed to notice the fire. Unless, of course, the victim was drunk. Could this be Smith's body? Smith, the man everyone thought to have been Lord Paul's killer.

Judging by its length the body was indeed that of a man. But identifying it was not going to be easy. The face had been burned out of all recognition and the clothing all but destroyed.

But one thing became clear as Parsons carefully turned the body onto its side. The cause of the death had not been the fire. The back of the victim's skull had been smashed.

It was possible, he thought, as he gently lowered the body back into its former position, that the victim had been struck by a falling beam. But in view of the position in which the body lay it was unlikely a falling beam could have inflicted such damage. On the contrary, there was every indication that a violent and unexpected blow had been struck from behind the victim, before ever the fire had started.

Parsons continued examining the body, and with a grunt of satisfaction noticed a ring on the little finger of the right hand. He removed it carefully, cleaned it with his handkerchief and peered at it through his small magnifying glass. It was the sort of signet ring popular with many gentlemen: often a twenty-first birthday present or a gift on becoming betrothed. Scarcely the sort of ring that Smith would have worn. Judging by the well-worn initials engraved on it, the ring was of some age, but the initials were too indistinct for him to read. But perhaps someone in the castle might recognize the ring and be able to decipher them.

A few feet from the body lay the remnants of a pair of saddle bags, the leather shriveled, twisted and split by the heat. Using his small pocket knife Parsons cut through what remained of the stitching and peeled the bags open. Like everything else around, most of the contents seemed burned beyond recognition. Everything except a small metal box.

The box was closed but unlocked, and judging by the charred contents it had once contained papers of some sort. But not just any papers, for as Parsons carefully sifted through them with the blade of his knife, he found to his delight that the box had provided some protection from the flames for a few of them. These few scraps, perhaps even all the papers in the box, had once been bank notes.

Parsons was thrilled by the finds. They had been a most profitable and unexpected conclusion to their search. But the light was now all but gone. Apart from that the men were exhausted. It was time to call a halt for the night.

"Sergeant Brown," he said, "ask Mr. Johnson to find something to cover this body and the saddle bags. I don't want anything moved until the doctor has seen the body. And that won't be until tomorrow at the earliest. Until then I want a guard on the stables and the immediate area of the castle. Sort out a roster between the three of you."

He could see from their downcast expressions that the thought of another disturbed night was not at all well received. But he had no option. Apart from the chance of the murderer returning he could not risk anyone disturbing an area that might yet reveal even more clues.

"I realize you and your men are all tired and hungry, Sergeant Brown," he said sympathetically. "But we can't afford to relax with a dangerous felon still at large. Give Mr Johnson my compliments and ask him to feed you all and find you somewhere to sleep. But tell him you're not to use any of the rooms in the west wing of the second floor. If he doesn't understand what I mean tell him to speak to me. Is all that clear?"

"Yes, sir," replied Brown. If there was one thing about which all Brown's superiors in the police force would agree, it was his ability to follow instructions to the letter.

"Good man," said Parsons. "I'm going to the Drawing Room now to speak with the family and the others staying in the castle, and I'm taking this box with me. After dinner I'll be in the Servants' Hall. So if any of you need me you'll know where I'll be. That reminds me, Brown. Ask Mr Johnson to arrange for some supper to be sent to my room. And thank you for your help, gentlemen. We've made an excellent start, but there'll be plenty more to do tomorrow. So make sure you get as much sleep as you can."

The temperature had fallen with the fading light, and as Parsons set off across the grass towards the path leading to the front of the castle he found himself hurrying to keep warm. Behind him the three tired policemen remained temporarily rooted to the spot on which they stood, basking in the unexpected but nevertheless welcome praise from a superior officer. Then they set off wearily towards the rear entrance to the kitchens and their long overdue meal.

-31-

s soon as Parsons entered the Drawing Room he sensed the strained atmosphere. It seemed to him as if the seven people in the room were strangers to one another. There was no longer any pretense at the normal house-party social conventions. No one was speaking. The only signs of life in the room were the log-fire hissing and crackling under the stern, stone mantle and the occasional rustle of paper as someone turned the pages of a magazine or a book.

Lady Annabelle and Catherine faced one another from matching settees at opposite sides of the fireplace, the bright ornamental design of the upholstery contrasting starkly with their black mourning-dresses. Montgomery shared the settee with Catherine, while Alexander and Geoffrey Montagu hunched disconsolately over a game of cards. Philip sat alone in a corner idly turning a revolving bookcase and occasionally selecting a book for a cursory examination, and Fitzherbert cradled a tumbler in a wing-backed chair in the center of the room.

Although no one acknowledged his presence by speaking, Parsons found himself the focus of everyone's attention

266

as he walked across the room. He also sensed an under-current of fear, curiosity and hostility, with the balance of these emotions inclining towards the latter.

"Thank you for waiting so patiently, ladies and gentlemen," he said, choosing a chair near Fitzherbert from where he could command everyone's attention. "I'm sure you're already aware that I've been given full responsibility for this investigation."

He paused briefly for a reaction. But none came.

"I've already been here for a few hours," he said, "but before I decided to speak to you all I thought it best to familiarize myself with the scene of last night's crime."

The uneasy silence continued. Whatever they might be thinking, each person in the room seemed intent on keeping it to himself. At least until such time as they had heard what Parsons had to say.

"I won't keep you long from your dinner," he continued, "but as you were all witnesses in one way or another to the tragic events, I'd like to hear your recollections about what happened. Colonel Howard has already given me his account, but as a result of his unfortunate wound I believe that he was unconscious for some of the time. In normal circumstances I would choose to speak with each of you individually, and indeed I may do that later; but in view of the unfortunate delay I'd like to start by talking to you as a group."

"Just catch that scoundrel, Smith," interjected Fitzherbert rudely, his speech as slurred and unfriendly as ever. "That's all you need do. Don't waste your time with us. We had nothing to do with it. Just find Smith."

"All in good time, Major Fitzherbert," said Parsons calmly, aware of the murmur of support from some of the others for what Fitzherbert had said. "But it's important for me to establish a few facts before I arrest anyone."

"The man's a disgrace to the regiment," Fitzherbert mumbled into his glass. "I would never have dreamt one of our men could do such a thing." He swallowed the remaining contents of his glass in a single gulp and reached for the decanter he had placed conveniently on the small table at his side.

Parsons opened his note-book and rested it on his knee.

"Can I start with you, major," he said, staring directly into the hostile blood-shot eyes. "I believe you were in the Hall last night with Lord Paul and Colonel Howard when a noise was heard outside. Can you tell me what happened after that?"

Fitzherbert's expression was anything but co-operative, and for a moment Parsons wondered what he would do if the major refused to talk. But to his relief support came from an unexpected source.

"For heaven's sake answer the inspector's question, George, or we'll be sitting here all night!"

Parsons' smile of gratitude for Catherine's timely intervention was met with stony indifference. In all probability she was more concerned at starting the meal on time than worrying about the progress of his investigation.

Like the good soldier he had once been Fitzherbert could recognize an order when he heard one. He grunted once then took a long swill from his glass.

"It sounded like gravel being thrown against one of the windows," he explained. "Howard and Lord Paul decided to investigate. I stayed behind in the Hall. A few minutes after they had gone I heard what sounded like a shot. Then someone shouted my name. Then there was another shot, but before that I was on my way outside."

He paused for another drink.

"What did you see?" asked Parsons.

Fitzherbert wiped some spilled drink from his moustache with a hand that was noticeably shaking.

"Lord Paul was lying motionless on the ground about fifty yards away. Howard was a few yards beyond that. He was rolling on the ground holding his leg, and when I saw what a bad state he was in I ran back into the castle for help."

"And what of Lord Paul? Didn't you see whether he needed assistance?"

"Of course I did, inspector. D'you take me for a fool? But I could see clearly he'd been hit in the chest, and as he was lying so still I assumed he was already dead."

Lady Annabelle's head slumped forward a little and she moaned pitifully. The movement was barely perceptible, but the sound of her quiet sobbing carried into the furthest corners of the room. Only Montgomery responded to the pitiful sound and crossed the hearth to sit by her side. No one else moved.

Before resuming again Parsons waited until she was more composed and he had regained everyone's attention.

"Did you see the assailant, major?" he asked.

"No. Whoever had shot them both had gone before I arrived."

Parsons made a few notes before continuing.

"From your army experiences, major, could you say whether the shots were fired from a rifle or a hand gun?"

This unexpected appeal to his past military service had an invigorating effect upon Fitzherbert. His face showed briefly an uncharacteristic sign of intelligence and the scowl that was normally such a permanent fixture gave way to a far more helpful expression.

"I was inside at the time," he explained, "so the sound of the shots was distorted. But I'd wager on it being a hand gun. A rifle shot is much louder."

"Thank you, major. That's very useful," said Parsons gratefully, hoping that Fitzherbert would continue in this co-operative vein. "Now can you tell me where you went looking for assistance."

"I came in here," Fitzherbert replied, reverting almost immediately to his usual belligerent tone. "Where else would I expect to find help, but here with the ladies?"

Parsons turned his attention to Catherine.

"Perhaps you will be kind enough to explain what happened then, Miss Catherine," he asked. "Who was with you at the time Major Fitzherbert arrived?"

"Annabelle, Alexander and Geoffrey," she replied.

"And had any of you heard the shots?"

The question was directed to all four of them, but it was Catherine who replied before any of the others had chance to speak.

"No, inspector, we didn't. The curtains were drawn and we were sitting at the end of the room furthest from the Hall. It was cooler there. We heard nothing of the shooting, although Alexander said later he thought he'd heard someone running across the grass outside. We'd opened the windows, you see, because it was so warm."

"And did you think you heard that sound before or after Major Fitzherbert arrived?"

Parsons' question was directed towards Alexander. But again it was Catherine who replied.

"Before," she said. "As soon as George arrived with the terrible news we followed him outside at once to where Paul and Charles were lying. Like Major Fitzherbert I thought Paul was already dead and gave my full attention to Charles. I could see he was badly hurt, so I sent Alexander back into the house to get bandages and to fetch some of the servants to help carry him inside."

"And was Lord Paul dead at the time as Major Fitzherbert had assumed?"

"He wasn't, Everett. He was alive when I arrived."

Annabelle's voice was scarcely audible, but there was no mistaking the accusatory tone. She looked directly across at Catherine as she spoke. But there was no sign of sorrow or regret from the woman opposite, only an icy glare and a hostile silence. Fitzherbert and the others remained equally unmoved, but Montgomery took the opportunity of holding Annabelle's hand and patting it sympathetically.

"And did he speak before he died, Lady Annabelle?"

"He did, Everett, though I'm afraid the words don't seem to make very much sense."

"Perhaps you'll let me be the judge of that, your ladyship. What did he say?"

"The poor man was barely alive, and he opened his mouth several times before he said anything. But he finally managed a few words. What he said sounded like 'Not left. Smith's not left.' That's all he said. It wasn't very distinct and I don't think he finished what he was trying to say. I asked him what he meant, but he never spoke again. There was only a strange noise in his throat—and then he died."

She began to cry quietly again, and this time with a pathos that touched Parsons' heart. Montgomery continued to take advantage of her distress and without any sign of self-consciousness retained a firm grip of her hand. He was more a lady's man than it had first appeared, thought Parsons, although in the circumstances it was a natural reaction for any man. What was more unusual, in his opinion, was the apparent lack of sympathy shown by everyone else.

"Smith's not left," said Fitzherbert cynically. "Whatever's that supposed to mean? Are you sure that's what he said, Annabelle? Are you sure he didn't say 'Smith's not right'? That would make far more sense. After all, Smith can't be right in the head, if you ask me. Only a mad man would behave like that. What did he hope to gain from it, I'd like to know? He had a comfortable enough life here looking after a few horses. Now he's got no prospect but the hangman's noose."

It was true, thought Parsons. There was nothing at all obvious about Smith's motive. Unless, of course he'd been working for someone else. Someone who would reward him well enough to make his desperate actions worth the risk of being caught and hanged. Someone who might even be able to arrange temporary concealment and eventually help Smith leave the country. Perhaps the same person who had wanted Lord Quentin dead.

"On the contrary, I think what Paul said makes perfect sense."

Quite unexpectedly Montgomery had released Annabelle's hand. It was he who had spoken.

"Paul had said several times after Lord Quentin's death that he intended to get rid of Smith," he explained. "He'd never be able to have a decent stables, he said, with a useless drunk like that in charge. And perhaps before last night he'd already given Smith his marching orders, and was surprised to see that he was still around. 'Smith's not left' might have been his way of trying to draw attention to the fact that Smith was still here."

"That makes perfect sense, Everett," said Annabelle, wiping her tears with a small lace handkerchief. "Dear Paul told me he intended to sack Smith. But I'd no idea he'd already told him to go."

"Where were you when all this was going on, Philip?" asked Parsons, suddenly changing the direction of his questions.

Philip had appeared to be in a world of his own throughout the questioning, scarcely paying heed to anything that was said. And it was not until Parsons had repeated the question a second time in a louder voice that he realized he had become the center of attention. When he did he became embarrassed and blushed profusely.

"I was in the L-library," he said self-consciously.

He then began to speak so rapidly that it appeared he was trying to get his information over and done with in order to escape back to his own thoughts. But it only served to worsen his stammer and to further embarrass him.

"The h-horses seemed unusually n-noisy. So I l-looked through the c-curtains. That's when I r-realised the stables were on f-fire. There was n-nothing I could do by m-myself, so I r-ran for h-help. I thought everyone w-would be h-here or in the H-hall. B-but they weren't in either p-place. B-both rooms were empty. Th-then I h-heard v-voices outside on the t-terrace. Th-that's where I found everyone. I t-told them about the f-fire. B-but they already knew by th-then. One of the s-servants had already s-seen it. Everyone except C-catherine was in a p-panic, b-but somehow she organized th-things and g-got C-colonel H-howard inside. Th-then she s-sent Alexander for the d-doctor. Major F-fitzherbert and I went to the k-kitchens to h-help with the f-fire and when we g-got there Mrs. H-hughes and the g-girls were f-filling buckets of water. B-but it was no g-good. There was so much w-wood in the b-building that once the f-fire got started there was n-nothing we could do."

Philip sank back into his chair, exhausted by his impediment and the torrent of words.

"Did you see anyone acting suspiciously, either when you were in the Library or at any time afterwards?" asked Parsons.

Philip shook his head. He seemed no longer capable of words.

"And what about you, Mr. Montgomery?" asked Parsons. "I don't seem to have heard your name mentioned at all."

Montgomery reluctantly turned his attention away from Annabelle.

"I'd been out riding," he said calmly. "I was intending to leave Beaumont soon, and I'd been talking to Catherine about it the other night. That was when she suggested I should take one of the horses and spend the day exploring the countryside before I left. It was good advice. To return to London without seeing the Downs would've been unforgivable."

"So it was you who was missing from dinner," said Parsons.

"That's right. I'd no idea what time I'd be back, so I told Johnson not to lay a place for me and to keep something cold for whenever I returned."

"And what time was that?"

"I couldn't say exactly, but it was after the fire had started. I was still some distance away when I saw the flames. Naturally I got back as quickly as I could. But as Philip has just explained, there wasn't much anyone could do by then."

"Did you see anyone on the road?"

"No one. After I left Midhurst I never saw anyone until I reached the castle."

Parsons turned finally to Alexander and Montagu.

"I believe you were both here at the time of the shooting," he said.

They both nodded, but it was Alexander who answered.

"Everything happened just as Catherine said," he explained impatiently. "It's true that I said I thought I heard someone outside, but after a few glasses of wine I couldn't really be sure. It could just as easily have been a gust of wind. So I didn't bother to look. I only mentioned it afterwards when I already knew what had happened."

"How did you manage to ride to Doctor Hamilton?" asked Parsons. "The horses must have been terrified, and I imagine the saddles and bridles were destroyed in the fire."

"How clever you are, Everett," Alexander said ironically. "But you're right. I had great difficulty in catching any of the horses and the prospect of riding bare-back didn't appeal to me at all. But as luck would have it, Harrison arrived back just then. So I took his horse."

"Wasn't the poor creature exhausted?"

"I suppose it was. But there wasn't an alternative."

"Which horse was that?" asked Catherine sharply. Even at such a time she seemed more concerned that Alexander's irresponsibility and thoughtlessness might have damaged one of the horses.

"The grey, Catherine," Alexander replied, sounding more like a guilty school-boy than a potential anarchist.

"Which grey?" she demanded. "We don't have a grey horse."

Alexander appeared confused by this revelation, and wilted under Catherine's interrogatory gaze. He clearly felt embarrassed at being publicly ridiculed, and foolish that he was ignorant about which horses his family owned.

"No, Catherine, you don't. But Ashton does."

All eyes turned in Fitzherbert's direction. He was pale, and suddenly more sober than at any time since his arrival at Beaumont.

Parsons took the ring from his pocket and handed it to Fitzherbert.

"Do you recognize this, major?" he asked quietly.

Fitzherbert inspected it closely, his blood-shot eyes half closed in concentration.

"My God, Parsons, I'd know this ring anywhere," he said. "It's difficult to see them now, but there are initials on it. CSEA. Charles Spencer Eustace Ashton. That was Ashton's father. Never got on well with his father, did Ashton. This ring's about the only thing poor old Ashton inherited when his father died. Where the devil did you find it?"

"All in good time, Major Fitzherbert. All in good time," said Parsons reassuringly. His next question was addressed to everyone in the room. "Did anyone see Captain Ashton before he left yesterday morning?"

After a few moments of silence Fitzherbert spoke.

"He said he'd be up early and would leave before breakfast," he said. "He'd said his good-byes to a few of us the night before."

The room was eerily silent, each person making his own assessment of the possible connection between Ashton and the events of the previous night.

Parsons stood up.

"Please wait a minute," he said.

Parsons went outside to the main entrance hall, where he collected the metal box he had concealed inside an oak settle before he had first entered the Drawing Room.

"I believe this belongs to you, Miss Catherine," he said when he returned.

"If you know that why do you ask, inspector," she replied coldly.

She glared at him, willing her cold eyes to gain mastery over his. But she failed. Nor did she manage in her vain attempt to conceal her shock at seeing the box.

"Unless I'm mistaken, Miss Catherine," Parsons said with measured tones, "this is the money box you reported missing from your bedroom. As I recall, Claire Dunne was being accused of stealing it when I left yesterday morning."

"And where did *you* find it, inspector," she demanded.

'Near the body we found in the stable area this evening. The body I have every reason to believe is that of Captain Ashton."

His announcement had a more galvanizing effect on the gathering than even Parsons had imagined. Fitzherbert sprang to his feet in genuine distress. Catherine looked furious, and even Alexander, Montagu and Philip were shaken out of their lethargy. Annabelle stopped crying abruptly and retrieved her hand from Montgomery, who was sufficiently startled not to know it had gone. They all looked towards Parsons in anticipation of some further dramatic announcement or some form of explanation.

But Parsons had already decided to abandon the group questioning. Based on the information he already possessed he knew enough to be able to concentrate later on individuals. Before that he needed to question the servants.

"Thank you, ladies and gentlemen," he said. "You've been very helpful, and I need not delay you any longer from your dinner. You'll forgive me if I don't join you, but I've arranged to eat alone in my room. I'll be in the Servants' Hall after that, and then I intend to examine Lord Paul's body. Am I right in assuming, Miss Catherine, that I will find it upstairs in his room?"

Catherine nodded. She made little secret of her anger. But it was impossible for Parsons to tell whether this anger was a result of her thinking that Ashton was a thief or for something else.

"If any of you have anything to tell me," said Parsons as he walked towards the door, "you know where to find me during the next few hours. But in any event I will probably speak to you all again individually within the next day or two. So please don't leave the castle without telling me."

"And do we need to seek your permission to attend my father's funeral, inspector?"

Alexander spoke with biting sarcasm, and with an exaggerated stress upon Parsons' title, which he had chosen instead of the more familiar Christian name he invariably used for his friend. There was an edginess and aggression about Alexander that had not been present even a few minutes before, and not for the first time Parsons noted how unstable his behavior had become. He seemed like a child at times, putty in Catherine's hands; but he could also be wild and unpredictable. But how much of his mood swings was attributable to the recent murders, and how much to the unsettling influence of Montagu and the drugs they were both taking was not at all clear.

"I'm sorry, Alexander, but I'd quite forgotten about the funeral," said Parsons humbly. "How can you think I would want to stop anyone attending? Indeed, I would like to go myself."

He turned to Catherine, assuming that it was she who would be in charge of the arrangements.

"Will it be possible for me to attend?" he asked.

"The funeral will be at twelve tomorrow in the village church, inspector," she said. "The cortege leaves here at half past eleven. And if you have omitted to bring a black tie I'm sure Johnson will find one for you. Now if you will excuse us we will take our dinner before it spoils."

This was more like the Catherine of old, thought Parsons, as with this final dismissive sentence she terminated the conversation. Gathering her skirts around her she swept past Parsons, followed demurely by the others. At first Annabelle seemed reluctant to join her step-daughter. But then she bestowed upon Montgomery one of her alluring smiles and left the room on his willing arm.

-32-

The silence in the Servants' Hall when Parsons entered was not altogether unlike that he had encountered in the Drawing Room. The normal bustle of activity was absent. Instead the servants sat around the table like fearful children awaiting the arrival of a strict schoolmaster. No longer evident to Parsons was the resentment and hostility he had previously encountered from Johnson and some of the girls. Had he chosen that moment to raise his voice and shout at them he had no doubt they would all have been terrified. That was the last thing he wanted. He had far more to gain by winning their confidence.

"May I join you?" he asked, moving towards a vacant space on one of the benches.

But he was prevented from sitting there by Johnson. The old man insisted that Parsons take the chair at the head of the table that he had been occupying himself.

A glance round the table confirmed that Parsons had their undivided attention. He had decided to speak to them all together to save time, he explained, but he would also

281

question each one individually later. For the moment he was simply trying to establish an overall picture of what had occurred on the previous night.

Parsons turned first to Johnson, who had sat himself self-consciously on one of the benches between two of the girls.

"Can I begin by asking you to explain where everyone here was during the evening," he said. "Start with dinner, unless you can think of anything before then that might be important."

After some deliberation Johnson decided that nothing that had occurred before dinner was of any significance.

"O'Mahoney and O'Halloran had been serving dinner with me, sir," he explained. "Dwyer, O'Brien and Sweeney were here in the kitchen with Mrs. Hughes. After dinner O'Mahoney served the coffee in the Drawing Room and O'Halloran came here for her supper before clearing the table in the Hall after the gentlemen had finished their brandy. Leastwise she should've done, but I regret to say she didn't complete that task."

Johnson gave O'Halloran a severe look, which in the circumstances Parsons felt was quite unjustified.

"I stayed in the Hall for a short while, sir, to see if his lordship and the gentlemen had all they required. Then I came here to have my meal with the others. That must've been at about half past nine, sir."

"You mean you all ate together about that time?"

"Yes, sir, more or less. Though we didn't all sit down at the same time. We rarely do."

"But were you all here when Mr Alexander arrived?"

"Yes, sir. O'Mahoney, O'Halloran and I were having our supper. The other girls were helping Mrs. Hughes."

"And did any of you hear any shots before then?"

Parsons looked around the table. They all shook their heads as though they dared not trust their voices.

"Who went with you to help Colonel Howard?" Parsons asked Johnson.

"O'Mahoney and O'Halloran, sir. There seemed no sense in us all going. I shouted through to O'Brien in the scullery to get some towels and sheets from the laundry-room. And that's the first we knew about the fire."

"Who saw it first?" asked Parsons.

"I did, sir," said O'Brien apprehensively. "As soon as I went into the laundry-room didn't I see there was something strange going on. There was this bright orange glow in the sky and a terrible shrieking. It was as if the Divil himself was outside. B'Jaysus, wasn't I almost too scared to look. Then I saw 'twas the stables on fire and the poor horses galloping around on the grass and neighing their blessed heads off. Sure I started hollering myself then, and didn't Dwyer and Sweeney come rushing in thinking that dirty feller Smith had his hands on me."

The fact that the horses were loose raised an interesting point. Alexander had explained how difficult it was to catch one. It confirmed that the fire was no accident. Had it been an accident, some or all of the horses would surely have perished. The fire had been a deliberate act, and the horses released by someone who had no wish to see them die.

"Did you see anybody?" asked Parsons. "Did you see who started the fire?"

The three girls looked at one another, unsure of which of them should answer. Eventually it was Sweeney who spoke.

"We saw Smith ride through the gateway, sir," she said nervously.

"How did you know it was him?"

"You couldn't be mistaking him, sir," Dwyer interjected. "wasn't he wearing that long coat and dirty old hat of his."

"But you didn't see his face."

"Nay, sir," said each of the girls, almost with reluctance.

"Did you see the horse he was riding?"

"Aye, sir," said Sweeney. "Sure 'twas the black mare."

The other two nodded in agreement.

"Tell me, Johnson," asked Parsons. "Does Smith generally eat here with the rest of you?"

"Not always, sir. Though we generally keep food for him. But more often than not he's down in the village inn at night drinking himself stupid. He only comes in for a meal if he's short of money or he's got nothing better to do."

"Not that we're sorry about that, sir," said O'Mahoney vehemently. "For a dirty, stinking, lecherous man he is, to be sure. And after a few jars he's the very divil himself."

The other girls nodded emphatically. It was clear that Smith was thoroughly unpopular with them all.

"Thank you all for your co-operation, ladies; and you, Johnson," said Parsons. "That will be all for now. But as I explained before, I'll speak to you all again if I think it necessary."

There was an audible sigh of relief around the table as he stood up. The reaction of the servants could not have been more at odds with that of the group in the Drawing Room. There was a sense of unease and apprehension in the Servants' Hall that could have been interpreted as guilt, but it was more likely the fear of how the powers that be might somehow implicate one of them, as they had Claire Dunne's brother. There had been indifference and barely concealed hostility in the Drawing Room from those that represented such powers.

It will be interesting, thought Parsons, to see if those attitudes change over the next few days.

"One last question," he said, turning to face them at the door. "Did anyone see Captain Ashton before he left yesterday.

As he spoke Parsons tried vainly to catch O'Brien's eyes, and he noticed that one or two of the other girls had also glanced in her direction. But she was too quick for them. She had suddenly busied herself examining her nails, too clever to allow any involuntary change of expression to reveal anything about her relationship with the gentleman in question.

Oblivious to the unspoken drama playing out at the table, Johnson answered.

"He left early, sir, before anyone else in the castle was awake. He gave me strict instructions to tell Smith to have his horse ready at six. He'd a long journey ahead, he told me, and he wanted to make an early start."

"But didn't he want a meal before he left?"

"I asked him that, sir. But he said no. He told me he'd stop somewhere on the way."

"Did you give Smith this message?"

"Yes, sir, of course."

The old servant seemed upset to think that Parsons should entertain the possibility that he would ever forget to carry out such a simple instruction.

"Then it would no doubt come as a surprise to you all to learn that the captain never left Beaumont."

Parsons watched the reactions around the table. Without exception there was nothing but genuine surprise. O'Brien showed it more so than the rest.

"Then where is he, sir?" she asked, her nails no longer the focus of her attention. "Sure, when I cleaned his room wasn't he already gone, and no one has seen him since."

Parsons refrained from commenting on the undue interest that O'Brien was suddenly showing in the missing guest. There would be time enough to pursue that with her later.

"Unless I'm mistaken," he said, "he was burned last night in the fire."

The news of Ashton's death had almost as profound an impact on the servants as it had in the Drawing Room. It was as though they considered the murder of a member of the family to be one thing, but the prospect of the killing spreading to others was quite another. That presented a far greater threat to everyone, rich and poor alike.

O'Brien's publicly declared interest in Ashton had even surprised some of the other girls, but her next outburst startled Parsons as much as everyone else.

"Smith!" she exclaimed venomously. "That dirty, robbing bastard, Smith. B'Jaysus, shouldn't I have known Smith would know all about that blessed money!"

-33-

*M*uted expressions of surprise and half-suppressed cries of 'whose money?' and 'what money?' sprang from several mouths at once, and it was with some difficulty that Parsons prevented himself from joining the chorus. He would, of course, be asking the same questions but that would be later and away from the prying ears of others.

"I'd like a word with you, O'Brien," he said, waiving aside Mrs. Hughes' protests about the girl's responsibilities in the kitchen. "Just wait there by the table while I speak with Johnson."

He took the old man to one side while the girls began reluctantly to busy themselves about their kitchen tasks. They would, no doubt, have preferred the opportunity of remaining at table and talking about what they had just heard. But Mrs. Hughes' routine took precedence over most matters, even those appertaining to life and death.

"Can you drive a trap, Johnson?" Parsons asked.

"I'm surprised you ask an old countryman like me a question like that, sir. Whoever heard of a Hampshire man who couldn't handle a trap?"

"Then you can take Sergeant Brown's trap and deliver some messages for me. But first of all I want you to come to my room. You as well, O'Brien."

To the surprise of the two servants Parsons took one of the candles from the table and walked purposefully across the Servants' Hall towards the door leading to the back stairs. It was a route that neither of them had expected him to know, and he took considerable pleasure in seeing their bewilderment. As he led them up the stairs and along the corridor to his room he hummed contentedly to himself. The long vigil during his last night in Beaumont was beginning to pay off in more ways than one.

Earlier that evening Parsons had written a note to Doctor Hamilton asking for his assistance and a telegram for Harris back in London giving him more background information about events at Beaumont. With Brown and his men already fully committed for the rest of the night, Parsons was reluctant to use the family or any of their guests for running errands. Of the servants he considered only Johnson to be capable or reliable enough. The old man, he knew, would also be tired, but if Parsons was to avoid going himself, there was no other option. And he had much better things to do with his time.

Once inside his room Parsons gave Johnson the two envelopes.

"This one is for Doctor Hamilton," he explained. "Be sure you wait for an answer. The other contains a telegram for London. Take it to Carpenter, the station master. If he's not at the station go to his cottage opposite the station. Ask him if there are any telegrams for me, and when you get back, whatever time it is, report to me. Do you understand? Good. Now be sure to wrap up warm, Johnson. It's cold outside."

With an encouraging pat on the old servant's back Parsons sent him on his way. Then he turned his attention to O'Brien.

Ashton was a good judge of a woman. Even in her black uniform dress and white apron, and fresh from her work in the kitchen, O'Brien was attractive. And Parsons knew how beautiful she could look in an evening gown or a night-gown.

When plaited or allowed to hang loose her long bright-chestnut hair was the girl's most striking feature, complementing large brown eyes and an inviting mouth. The hair was hidden now inside her white mob-cap and she stood demurely in front of Parsons, her head bowed respectfully and her slender hands clasped nervously over her apron. But her sequacious pose did not deceive him. Even had he not been aware of her nocturnal movements, her recent outburst raised questions enough.

"Well, young woman, what was all that about Smith stealing money?" he demanded. "And to save you wasting my time, let me explain to you from the outset that I know you were with Captain Ashton during his last night at Beaumont. I also know you were expecting money for your services."

The effect on the girl could not have been more dramatic had he slapped her full on the face. Her brown eyes opened wide in horror and the fingers that had so absorbed her interest in the Servants' Hall flew to her mouth to muffle an anguished cry. The shock drained the blood from her face and she appeared undecided whether to flee or to faint. She did neither. Instead she remained firmly rooted to the spot, and as Parsons watched her initial shock subside, she burst into tears.

"And who'll be telling you all that, sir," she managed to say at last, tending the corners of her eyes with the edge of her apron.

"Never you mind all that, O'Brien," Parsons said sternly. "What should be concerning you more than anything at this moment is the fact that you were one of the last people to see Ashton alive. Perhaps the last."

It took a few seconds for her to absorb the full significance of his last sentence.

"I didn't kill him, if that's what you're thinking, sir," she beseeched. "B'Jaysus, you must believe I wouldn't be doing such a thing."

Parsons beckoned her towards a chair.

"Then sit down, O'Brien, and pull yourself together," he said, not unkindly, "and then tell me exactly what happened."

Parsons could imagine the difficult situation in which she now found herself. She could only hazard a guess as to how much he actually knew about her movements that night and who had told him, but she could not afford to run the risk of being caught out in a lie. Any embellishments of the truth she might originally have planned would now be fraught with danger, faced with the prospect of what Parsons might know had occurred between herself and Ashton. Realizing all this, he hoped she would see little point in telling him anything but the truth.

From the uncertain way in which she returned his inquisitorial gaze he was sure she had reached the same conclusion.

"After the first night," she said nervously, "Captain Ashton asked me to go back to his room again. He told me he wouldn't be staying long at Beaumont, sir. Sure I hesitated at first, but he said he'd be giving me some money. B'Jaysus, I'm no whore, sir. But when a gentleman offers to give a poor servant girl a little of his money for something he'd already had for free, sure only a fool would be refusing."

O'Brien challenged Parsons to deny the wisdom and morality of what she had just said. He could see she was rapidly regaining her composure and her self-confidence was beginning to reassert itself. Who can blame me, she was saying, for trying to profit from a situation in which she had already been a victim. Better women than she had accepted similar offers.

"And did he pay you?" he asked.

"Nay, sir," she said bitterly. "He did not."

The disparaging look on her face implied that not only Ashton but Parsons and all men of his class could never be trusted to pay their debts.

"He told me he was leaving early that morning. And at five wasn't he up and packing his bags. Sure I expected him to pay me then. But he said he couldn't. Would you believe it, the bastard said he had no money."

She stared accusingly at Parsons.

"Sure now, aren't you people all the same," she said contemptuously. "Such fine ladies and gentlemen with your fancy clothes and your fancy ways. But none of you have two pennies to rub together. You'll all be living on credit. Well, the likes of poor people like us can't be doing that. People like the local tradesmen who have to come begging at the castle for the money that's rightfully theirs. And round at the back door too. And how many times must they be doing that before it suits the high and mighty Miss Catherine to pay them. Holy Mary, why are decent hard-working people treated so?"

Parsons thought of reprimanding her for her outburst. But then he had second thoughts. Not only did he share some of her opinions, but he would probably learn more about what went on at Beaumont if he allowed her to speak her mind freely.

"And was Captain Ashton like that?" he asked. "Did he promise to pay you later?"

"Oh, aye, indeed he did," she said sarcastically. "Wasn't he saying he was expecting a large sum of money before he went. Not that he'd be telling me who was giving it to him, or how much it was; but he seemed mighty pleased with himself. 'Come back at six, my sweet,' he said. 'I'll be having the money for you then.' And wasn't I believing him. Sure, what else could I do?"

Under the circumstances very little, thought Parsons.

"What happened when you returned at six?" he asked.

"Well sure he was gone. Hadn't that fine and dandy bastard upped and left. At first I was thinking he'd hidden my money. Sometimes the gentlemen leave a few coins under the pillows for us girls. But, sure, there was nothing there or anywhere else I looked. And B'Jaysus, didn't I look everywhere when I was cleaning the room later in the day. But I found not a thing. If I could've laid my hands on him then wouldn't I have half-killed him. But I didn't, sir. Sure I never saw him again."

She looked towards Parsons as though he were a Catholic priest, able to grant absolution to her for confessing her evil thoughts. Then she began to cry again. But whether the tears on this occasion were tears of rage, sorrow or contrition was beyond Parsons. And as he listened to the barely distinct words punctuating her loud sobs he wondered if even she understood the real reason she was crying.

"Sure he wasn't a bad gentleman," she wailed. "And maybe he didn't really mean to cheat me. Perhaps he was going to pay me after all. And then someone killed him. Surely to God after all he'd said to me during the night he wouldn't be leaving me without saying good-bye. Didn't he ask me for a piece of the pink ribbon from my night-gown as a keep-sake. He would tie it on his monocle, he said. That way he'd be remembering me whenever he wore it."

It was always possible, thought Parsons, that Ashton had intended waiting for O'Brien to return at six. But, if that was what he intended, why had he cleared his room before she returned? And why was his body found in the stables? Whatever she chose to believe about her dashing lover it looked very much as though he never intended to give her any money. But money was clearly involved. Ashton had talked about money, and someone had stolen money from Catherine. If the box found in the stables belonged to Catherine as he suspected, then there was clearly only one lot of money involved. But who had stolen it? Ashton, or someone on his behalf? Smith, for instance. Was it Smith who subsequently double-crossed Ashton and killed him? And what was the link between Ashton's death and the other murders?

"You still haven't told me why you think Smith stole the money, O'Brien," said Parsons, when she had finally stopped sobbing. "Why do you think he was involved?"

"Isn't it obvious, sir," she said. "Didn't Smith know Captain Ashton was leaving. Hadn't he been given orders to prepare the captain's horse. Captain Ashton had told Johnson the night before to give Smith the message. Smith must've seen the money. Maybe it was when he went to the captain's room to tell him his horse was ready. Or perhaps he saw the money later in the stables. Sure, one way or another he'd be knowing that Captain Ashton had money. And didn't he kill him for it. B'Jaysus, that Smith is capable of anything. If he was planning to kill Lord Paul, wouldn't it be easy for him to be hiding the captain's body somewhere in the stables. With Brendan Dunne in prison there'd be no one to find it, and wasn't he going to set the blessed place alight later on."

"So you think Smith had already planned to murder Lord Paul."

O'Brien sighed. In spite of her forthright description of what she thought had happened, she was clearly confused by the whole train of events.

"I wouldn't be knowing, sir. I'm only a poor wee girl trying to make some sense of it all. But I do remember Mrs Hughes saying that Smith and his drunken ways wouldn't last long with the new master. Didn't she hear Lord Paul shouting at him about being asleep when he should be cleaning the stables."

Being dismissed from one's job was hardly a motive for murder, thought Parsons. But as Fitzherbert had said earlier Smith had a comfortable enough life at Beaumont, and without a good reference from a former employer it would be difficult for someone like him to find alternative employment. The workhouse was generally the only option for men like Smith. And in the workhouse he'd be on the receiving end of the punishments. He wouldn't take kindly to that. So if it was true, and Smith had already been dismissed, then Montgomery was right and Lord Paul's dying words made perfect sense. And if Smith had been dismissed he would need money. So the two murders appeared to be linked; and the motives were revenge and robbery.

Events were still far from clear, mused Parsons, but it seemed whichever way he viewed them, Smith featured one way or another.

"So among the servants only Johnson, Smith and you knew that Captain Ashton was leaving," he said.

"Nay, sir. Sure everyone knew that. Didn't Johnson tell us all at supper."

"How many people knew you were spending the night with Ashton?"

"Only Claire Dunne, sir. We shared the same room. I had to tell her."

"Do you know why she left and where she might have gone?"

"She never said anything about leaving, sir. Sure, she was in our room that night when I left to go to Captain Ashton's room. But she was gone in the morning when I went back. She was terrified after they took her brother away. She thought they'd be arresting her as well, and she thought the English police would do terrible things to her. Just like they did to her grandfather. Didn't they beat him half to death, sir, for behaving like a man and telling the Protestant bailiffs to get off his land. All of us know that Claire would never harm a fly. But we all know better than to expect Colonel Howard to believe that. Sure, he only wants one thing from the likes of us. That's why she left. And God knows where the poor wee girl is now."

-34-

After he had finished questioning O'Brien and hurriedly eaten the cold dinner that had been provided for him, Parsons locked his door and went along the corridor to Lord Paul's room.

The curtains were drawn, the only light coming from a single candle on the table at the foot of the bed, the only sound the remorseless ticking of a clock on the mantel above the empty grate.

It was a room not unlike his own, furnished to meet the simple needs of a bachelor. There was a solid oak cupboard and a washstand against one wall and a dressing table against the other. A writing desk and chair stood beneath the single window, and there were easy chairs on each side of the fireplace.

When he had opened the door a draught of air from the corridor had accompanied him, setting the candlelight in the room dancing to the same rhythm as the one he carried. The shadows on the wall and on the ceiling echoed the movement in a silent *danse macabre*, momentarily breathing life into what had hitherto become the domain of Death.

297

The corpse lay on the large oak bedstead covered by a white sheet; and when Parsons gently drew the sheet from the body he saw a face wearing the peaceful mask of one who has suffered a swift, unheralded death. But no matter how tranquil the expression, there was no disguising the transformation of the once-handsome, animated features into the empty shell gazing sightlessly into space.

Lord Paul was still wearing the same evening clothes he had worn at the time of his death. The large bloodstain covering the front of his frilled dress shirt had dried and darkened, but must once have matched the color of the red sash around his waist. Whoever had killed him had either been skilled in his craft or fortunate with his aim. The single shot had struck straight at the heart.

Parsons recovered the body with its shroud and turned to examine the contents of the room. He began at the washstand. Each item of toiletry was arranged around the basin and jug ready for use, as though the body would rise next day and perform the time-honoured rituals of morning. The silver-backed hair brushes and cologne, together with the rows of fine suits inside the mirrored doors of the cupboard, confirmed Paul de Courcey as a man of excellent and expensive tastes. Judging by the tailors' labels inside the clothes, most of his purchases had been made in the expensive quarters of London. Either he was a relatively wealthy man in his own right or someone had been generous to him since his arrival in England.

Among the few books on the writing desk he found the one that Paul had given him at breakfast that first morning, just before Johnson had made his dramatic entrance; and he was still holding it when he crossed the room to answer the gentle knock on the door. To his surprise he found Lady Annabelle in the corridor.

"I hope I'm not intruding, Everett," she said, "but I hoped I might find you here."

She looked wistfully for a few seconds towards the body and then turned away.

"I've not had the opportunity before to thank you for responding so quickly to my plea," she said. "After the way you were treated I could well understand it if you had never wanted to see Beaumont again."

She paused to look around the room, as though seeing it for the first time. Then, refreshed it seemed by the aura of Paul's possessions, she continued.

"After Paul was murdered I remembered what you'd said to us both on the night before you left. You were right, and I should have said so at the time. Everything is not as simple as Colonel Howard first made it out to be. I've lived here long enough to know that."

Parsons crossed to the empty fireplace and returned with one of the easy chairs. He invited her to sit, ensuring that when she sat it was with her back to the bed. Then he fetched the other chair for himself and positioned it opposite her, placing his candle on the floor between them.

From such a low angle the candle-light cruelly accentuated the deep hollows that had formed under her eyes and the downward-sloping lines at the corners of her mouth. The face that Parsons had always found so captivating was now that of a tired and unhappy woman. Her next words reflected this sad metamorphosis.

"I know what it is to be an outsider here, Everett," she said sadly. "From the start of our marriage Quentin's children, especially Catherine, never accepted me. They had all been very close to their mother, for reasons I was to discover later. With Quentin's wild reputation and the difference in age between us, they distrusted my motives for marrying him. Perhaps they were right. When I look back now I'm confused by what those motives really were. It's all so long ago. I was only nineteen and flattered to be wooed by such a dashing and exciting man as Quentin. Of course, I'd heard about his reputation, as had every young girl within a hundred miles. But I flattered myself that I could change his ways. Of course he was twenty-seven years older than me, but that didn't seem important. He was so strong and full of life then. And there have been many happy marriages between people whose age differences were greater than ours."

She looked down at the candle, as though the flame would give her the strength to continue.

"I can't deny that the prospect of becoming Lady de Courcey was not unappealing. But believe me, Everett, that wasn't my sole reason for marriage. I truly loved Quentin then, and although that love died many years ago, if he had been more gentle with me things could have been so different."

She shuddered, as though reliving an unpleasant episode from her past. Then suddenly she stood up.

"I can't stay in this gloomy place any longer," she said. "The darkness only serves to stir up evil memories. You must come with me if you want me to tell you anything more."

Parsons understood as soon as he entered her room why it was that she spent so many hours there. Furnished in the curvaceous style of Louis XV, its finely-crafted French furniture, luscious drapes, Venetian mirrors, and potted plants gave the room an overwhelmingly feminine ambience, making it unlike any other room he had seen in the castle. It was indeed a refuge from her late husband and his family.

"I can see you're surprised, Everett," she said with some satisfaction. "But when we were first married Quentin could never do enough for me. He refurnished this room and the Drawing Room, and even began to make his own bedroom more inviting. I really thought my foolish hopes of changing his wild ways were beginning to work. But I was very wrong."

She walked across the room to the mahogany bookcase between the windows, and after a brief search selected a book.

"I have always loved to read, Everett. In recent years it has been my one great salvation. And poetry, Everett. What is there to match the romantic poetry of Wordsworth, Keats or Shelley? And can you imagine, Everett. I even tried to interest Quentin."

She laughed at what to anyone who had known her late husband must indeed have sounded a foolish notion.

"In the early months of our marriage he pretended to be interested, and we spent hours together in this room or in his reading aloud to one another. Those were the days when I imagined him as a great gentle bear that I had tamed. Then he gave me this."

Her voice had become cold and bitter.

"Read it, Everett," she commanded. "Read aloud the verses he marked."

She handed Parsons an anthology of verse. It was opened at a poem called 'Dolores' by Algernon Charles Swinburne.

The poet's name was not one with which Parsons was familiar. His own limited knowledge of poetry had been gleaned from what he had learnt at school and from his own dear mother's wish to share her love of literature with him. But as he began to read he realized that this poem was not one that either his school or his mother would have approved.

But as Annabelle had instructed he read aloud the three verses that had been side-lined with red ink:

"Oh lips full of lust and of laughter,
Curled snakes that are fed from thy breast,
Bite hard, lest remembrance come after
And press with new lips where you pressed,
For my heart too springs up at the pressure,
Mine eyelids to moisten and burn;
Ah, feed me and fill me with pleasure,
Ere pain come in turn.

There are sins it may be to discover,
There are deeds it may be to delight.
What new work wilt thou find for thy lover,
What new passions for daytime or night?
What spells that they know not a word of

Whose lives are as leaves overblown?
What tortures undreamt of, unheard of,
Unwritten, unknown?

Ah beautiful passionate body
That never had ached with a heart!
On thy mouth though the kisses are bloody,
Though they sting till it shudder and smart,
More kind than the love we adore is,
They hurt not the heart or the brain.
O bitter and tender Dolores,
Our Lady of Pain."

"That's enough, Everett," said Annabelle. "I'm sure you understand what Swinbourne meant. But can you believe that Quentin sought to woo me with words such as that. At first I thought he had misunderstood their meaning, but not when I saw his eyes as he read them to me. If you have been confused by the grotesque manner of Quentin's death, Everett, I think you will find the answer in the verses you have just read. They explain better than I ever could the beast that lay within him."

When Parsons could bring himself to look at her again he could see that there were tears in her eyes.

"He expected me to behave like *that,*" she said bitterly. "He expected me to tie him to his bed. To tie him to *this* bed, and do those terrible things. I wouldn't do it, Everett. I couldn't! I was only nineteen years old!"

It crossed Parsons' mind to remind her of the ages of the Irish girls—especially Claire Dunne—but he thought better of it. No doubt she imagined herself to have finer and more sensitive feelings than those of her servants.

"Since then no man has been in this room, Everett. Apart from you and the boys when they were younger. No one. Not even Johnson. Not for nine years."

"You will excuse my impertinence, your ladyship, but what of Lord Paul?"

"I said *no man*, Everett," she snapped, "and I meant it. I was a respectable married woman and Paul and I were good friends. He brought a sparkle back into my life and made me forget the long, lonely years of my marriage. Nothing more. And anyone who suggests otherwise is a liar."

At the mention of such happy memories the lines faded from her face and she looked as young as her portrait once more.

"I see you are reading Paul's book about the Civil War again," she said, glancing towards the book that Parsons was still carrying. "He told me he'd loaned it to you. But I can tell you he wasn't pleased to find some of the pages missing when it was returned."

Parsons flicked through the book, as though expecting to see the space left by the missing pages.

"It's true Lord Paul gave me the book during my previous visit, Annabelle," he said. "But I never had the opportunity to read it. I left it on the breakfast table when Johnson arrived with the news of your husband's death, and I never saw it again until this evening."

"Well, that's a mystery, Everett," she said sweetly, "and one I'm sure you'll enjoy solving. But you'll have to excuse me now. Reliving my past has not been a pleasant experience and I suddenly feel tired."

Until an hour ago Parsons had forgotten about the book. But someone else had seen it and for some reason had removed some of the pages. Did the pages have any bearing on the murders? There was only one way to find out, he thought, as he hurried back to his room.

-35-

It was just after eleven o'clock. After the dramas of the previous night everyone appeared to have retired to their rooms. Apart from the flicker of the lamps in the corridors and the metronomic sounds of the ubiquitous clocks there was no sign of life.

Parsons had decided against telling Howard about the discovery of Ashton's body. It was now too late to disturb him, and in all probability someone else would already have given him the news. Instead he decided to concentrate on the book.

'The Great American Civil War 1861-1865' had been written by Andrew Blake and published by Dickerman & Jenson of New York seven years after the war had ended. Like the Crimean War a decade before, the horrors of the American war had been brought closer to the imaginations of readers many hundreds of miles away from the battlefields by the use of photography; and as a war correspondent for the New

York Times, Blake had made good use of this new and exciting science.

It was a science that greatly interested Parsons, who could see many advantages in using it for police work. It was he who had persuaded his superiors to add photographic information whenever possible to their ever-expanding records of known criminals. Working with the Irish Special Branch, this information had proved especially important in the campaign against the London Fenian group.

It was his habit when first beginning to read a book with illustrations to turn first to the list of contents, using the page numbers in the front to find the pictures in the main body of the book. Almost at once he could see why Lord Paul had been so annoyed. Two pages of photographs had been removed; one between pages sixty-eight and sixty-nine and another between pages two hundred and six and two hundred and seven. As far as he could see these two were the only pages missing, together with the twelve photographs they contained.

He examined the stitching and the pages on each side of the missing photographs. As he suspected the photographs had been printed on double-sized pages, so that if the photographs between pages sixty-eight and sixty-nine were torn out of the book, the corresponding photographs between pages two hundred and six and two hundred and seven would also become loose. No doubt wishing to avoid any attention being drawn to this, whoever had decided to take the photographs had decided to remove both pages.

Parsons turned back to the list of contents and read the photograph captions, hoping they would provide some clue as to why any of the photographs might have been removed. But the twelve photographs seemed only to be a miscellany of subjects relating to the war, no different in their general content to any of the others in the book. The captions for the missing photographs were:

Opposite page sixty-eight:
Brigadier-General Beauregard, Confederate commander at the first Battle of Bull Run.
Confederate dead after the second Battle of Bull Run.
Some of the thirty thousand Confederate losses at Gettysburg.
Opposite page sixty-nine:
Boy musicians in the 93rd New York Infantry.
Black soldiers of the 4th United States Colored Infantry.
'Rushes Lancers' in Virginia.
Opposite page two hundred and six:
General Sherman outside Atlanta.
Members of the 1st battery of Light Artillery, Massachusetts Volunteer Militia
Sharpshooters from the 63rd Infantry regiment, Irish Brigade in West Virginia.
Opposite page two hundred and seven:
Union soldiers waiting to attack Confederate trenches at Petersburg.
Color party of the 7th Illinois Infantry.
Example of the Union's 'scorched earth' policy.

Parsons read the captions several times, but there was nothing he could see that might be connected in any way with anyone at Beaumont. But there was obviously something in one or other of the photographs that someone had not wanted Paul de Courcey, or even Parsons himself, to see.

He took a sheet of paper from his desk and wrote a telegram to Harris.

'For Harris from Parsons. Require copy of book entitled The Great American Civil War 1861 to 1865 by Andrew Blake. Published by Dickerman and Jenson of New York in 1872. Check if publisher has London office, try British Museum Library, American Embassy, and National Lending Libraries. Vital repeat vital that copy of book be obtained.'

It was not long after he had finished writing that Johnson arrived back from his errands. There had been no telegrams from London, he reported, but he had brought with him a note from Doctor Hamilton.

As Parsons would expect at such a late hour, the contents were brief.

'Dear Parsons,' he read,
'I will be at Beaumont in the morning before the funeral and will see you then.
Hamilton.'

It occurred to Parsons that the curtness of the doctor's reply might also reflect his irritation at being further called upon to assist the police. He hoped that was not true, as he was relying on Hamilton's professional judgment to confirm his own theory about Ashton's death.

"Thank you, Johnson," he said to the weary servant. "That will be all for tonight. I'm sure you can do with a good night's sleep. But I've one last favor to ask. I need a black tie for the funeral tomorrow. Do you think you can find one for me?"

"I'm sure I can, sir. Lord Quentin had several. I will give you one in the morning. Good night, sir."

"It's just as well I'm not superstitious," mused Parsons, as Johnson closed the door behind him. "Not many people would enjoy attending a funeral wearing an item of the dead man's clothing."

After Johnson had gone Parsons locked the door. He was a light sleeper and would normally wake if anyone entered the room. But there was no point in taking chances.

-36-

13th September 1880

Parsons was up early next morning and breakfasting before anyone else. O'Brien and Sweeney were on duty in the Dining Room, both of them wearing a short length of black ribbon pinned to the bosoms of their white aprons as a token of respect for the dead. Such emblems, thought Parsons as he ordered his breakfast, could scarcely reflect any genuine expressions of grief that the Irish girls might feel for the late Lord Quentin, but no doubt there had been a few tears shed for his successor, and perhaps even for Captain Ashton.

"Are the policemen awake yet?" he asked Sweeney, after O'Brien had gone to the kitchen to fetch the large cooked breakfast he had ordered.

"The sergeant and the young constable are up, sir," she replied, "but the grumpy old one's still asleep. Sergeant Brown says they were up all night guarding us. To be sure, I didn't know we were so valuable."

311

She giggled. Had Catherine, or indeed any other members of the family been present it was unlikely that she would have dared behave so, and it left Parsons to ponder whether he was pleased she felt able to relax in his company or concerned that she no longer felt in awe of his authority. On balance, he opted for the former. The servants knew more about what was going on in the castle than the family cared to admit, and it could only be to his advantage if they felt comfortable enough to speak freely in his presence.

But for the moment he was more interested in Mrs. Hughes' fine breakfast of mutton chop, kidneys and bacon. And after he had washed that down with two cups of cocoa he felt ready to face the day.

"My compliments to Mrs. Hughes for the breakfast," he said to O'Brien as he left the table. "And tell Sergeant Brown I'd like to see him upstairs as soon as he's finished eating. I'll be in Captain Ashton's room. I'm sure you know where that is."

"Yes, sir," she answered demurely, her color rising as Parsons left the room.

Ashton's bed had been stripped of its sheets and pillow cases, and the blankets folded and arranged in two neat piles. There were no toiletries on the marble top of the washstand, and the surface of each item of furniture was spotlessly clean. A quick inspection of the wardrobe and dresser also revealed them to be empty. If O'Brien indeed had been responsible for cleaning the room, she had managed to eliminate every trace of Ashton's presence.

The layout and furnishing of the room was similar to his and the other bachelor rooms in the castle. Although far from being as Spartan as a barrack room, there was nevertheless something distinctly regimental about the furniture provided; leaving Parsons to wonder whether this uniformity was a product of the military mind of the late Lord Quentin or the chastening qualities of his daughter, Catherine.

But a second glance revealed an incongruity. The hearth-rug in front of the fireplace was much larger, more luxurious and had a thicker pile than the one in his room or any of the other bachelor rooms he had visited.

As Parsons had hoped, it was Johnson who eventually answered his tug on the bed-pull at the side of Ashton's bed. Shortly before that Brown had reported for his day's tasks.

"Send one of your men to Mr. Carpenter at the railway station with this telegram," Parsons instructed the sergeant. "Then continue searching the stables and the area around the castle. Make a note of anything you find and draw a sketch to show where each item was located. I leave it to your discretion to decide whether anything you find is important enough to be brought to my attention straight away. Otherwise wait until I bring the doctor down to the stables. Is all that clear? Good man. I'll see you later."

Delighted at being encouraged to use his initiative for the first time in his police career, Brown had hurried away, and in his haste to start work had almost collided with Johnson in the doorway. Much to his surprise, Brown was beginning to warm to the young inspector from London; and in spite of his initial misgivings Parsons was feeling increasingly that the sergeant was a man he could rely on.

Parsons beckoned Johnson into the room.

"Unless I'm mistaken," he said, pointing towards the fireplace, "that rug does not belong there. It's altogether too grand for this room. Do you know where it came from and what happened to the rug that was here before?"

"Blest if I know where the rug for this room is, sir. It was here when I was last in the room. But that was several days ago, before Captain Ashton arrived. You'd better ask O'Brien. She was the last one to clean the room."

Johnson walked over to examine the present rug.

"I recognize this one sure enough, sir," he said. "It's one of Lord Quentin's."

"You mean it was previously in his room?"

"Yes, sir."

Parsons was silent for a few moments.

"Fetch O'Brien," he instructed. "I know she's busy waiting at table, but you'll just have to replace her with one of the other girls."

"I'll do my best, sir, but there may be a problem with Mrs. Hughes. That woman is a stickler for routine."

Johnson had reached the door when he stopped and took something from his pocket.

"I nearly forgot, sir," he said. "It was O'Brien that gave me this first thing this morning. She said I should have it, as I was likely to have a chance of speaking with you before she could."

The sealed envelope Johnson handed him contained a single sheet of de Courcey headed note-paper. It was folded into four, but from the web of creases visible on the paper, at some time previously it had been screwed into a tight ball. Prior to that a short note had been written on it in firm sloping writing. The note was undated and unsigned, and judging by the large ink blot at the end of the last incomplete sentence, it was probably discarded before ever it was finished.

'My dearest Paul,' it read,

'You have no idea how happy you have made me these last few days. Each minute with you is precious and every hour without you an eternity. I long to'

A few other words were obscured by the ink blot. Presumably the author had discarded the note at that point and started afresh on another sheet. Parsons held the note up to the window in an unsuccessful attempt to decipher the remaining words. But the author's identity was of far greater interest, and hopefully O'Brien would provide that.

She arrived five minutes later, her flushed face evidence of her haste. With the main stairs out of bounds to all servants except Johnson, the girl had been obliged to take the longer route via the back stairs. Although breathless, she otherwise appeared calm and ready for the questions that she knew would inevitably follow her summons to see the inspector.

"Do you recognize this rug, O'Brien?" Parsons asked.

The girl was surprised by the question. She had been expecting him to ask her about the note.

"Aye, sir," she said in a puzzled tone. "Sure, it's the one normally in Lord Quentin's room."

"Was it here yesterday morning when you cleaned the room?"

"That it might, sir. But if it was, I'd be thinking nothing about it. Wasn't I still feeling bad about Captain Ashton and his wicked deceit."

"Then was it here the night before, or at any time while the Captain stayed in this room?"

"Nay, sir. It was not."

Parsons was surprised by her certainty about this. For her part O'Brien was unsure whether she should explain why she had no doubt that the rug was there at one time and not at another. Then with a shameless toss of her head she decided to explain.

"Didn't we make love in front of the fire that night, sir. And wouldn't I be remembering which rug we lay on."

The words were spoken defiantly, but Parsons sensed that the girl was still more upset by Ashton's treatment of her and his subsequent death than she cared to admit. Nevertheless, she held Parsons' gaze as she spoke, and of the two of them it was he who was the more embarrassed by her revelation. He could even feel his color rising and was only too pleased to be able to change the subject.

"What about this note, O'Brien," he said. "Where did you find it and do you know who wrote it?"

"Miss Catherine wrote it, sir. I found it in her waste-paper basket."

"When was that?"

"About three weeks ago, sir."

"Why did you keep it?"

"To tell you the truth, sir, I'm not rightly sure. I don't make a habit of looking through her papers. It just happened to catch my eye when I was cleaning her room, and I thought it might come in useful one day."

On the face of it her answer was reasonable enough, but Parsons was not convinced she was being completely truthful.

"What do you mean, O'Brien? How could this discarded note be useful to you?"

She gave a long sigh. For a moment she seemed uncertain about what to say. In all probability what she had done could lead to her being dismissed. And what chances of future employment would she have, with an unfavorable reference saying that she was in the habit of searching through her mistress' waste-paper basket for anything that might be 'useful.' But if she told the truth, she had a feeling the young inspector would understand. So she decided to brave it out.

"To be truthful, sir, at the time I wasn't knowing how useful it might be. But I said to myself, what's the harm in knowing a few of your mistress' secrets?"

She challenged Parsons to deny such logic.

"None of us had ever imagined prim Miss Catherine to be the romantic sort, sir. If you know what I mean. If she was sweet on anyone wasn't it that stuffy solicitor, My Robertson. Sure, he didn't come to Beaumont often, but whenever he did they spent a deal of time together."

Parsons felt he was missing something. What had Robertson got to do with this note?

"I'm still not sure, O'Brien, why you thought this note was so important," he said.

O'Brien looked at him as though he was trying to make a fool of her. But she could find no trace of humor on his face.

"Well, sir," she said condescendingly. "Anyone could see that Lord Paul had eyes only for Lady Annabelle. After all what man with any taste would be finding anything attractive about Miss Catherine?"

She managed to convey perfectly through those few words that no matter what the advantages of her position might be, when it was a matter of basic human attraction, Catherine de Courcey compared very unfavorably with even the plainest of her servants.

"Don't you see what's so strange about the note, sir. It's as if Miss Catherine was living in her own dream world, imagining it was she that Lord Paul wanted and not Lady Annabelle."

The idea that the frigid Catherine ever wasted her time on extravagant romantic notions was not one Parsons had ever seriously considered. It seemed highly unlikely. But he had learned to have a healthy respect for a woman's intuition, and O'Brien might be right in thinking that the straight-laced Catherine was not all she appeared to be. After all, he'd had similar thoughts himself. Hadn't she used her feminine wiles on Howard, and wasn't there the matter of the red underwear.

"Who else knew about this note, O'Brien?" Parsons said forcefully.

"None of the servants, sir. But I did show it to Captain Ashton."

"To Ashton! Whatever for?"

Parsons was much surprised to hear Ashton's name mentioned in connection with Catherine's note.

"Wasn't he always asking me questions, sir. Sure he liked to be knowing about everyone who came to Beaumont, and what it was that they were doing while they were here."

"And what did you tell him?"

"I told him who the regular visitors were and which of them bedded the girls. And I told him about Miss Catherine and Mr. Robertson. I didn't need to say anything about Lady Annabelle and Lord Paul. Couldn't everyone see what was going on there."

"And what was his reaction when you showed him this?"

"He laughed, sir. Sure he laughed more than I've heard anyone laugh before."

"And why did you think he did that?"

"Sure, he said he couldn't imagine anything so ridiculous, sir. But I could see he was pleased in spite of all that. 'That's a good bet at long odds, my girl,' he said, 'and one that might be earning you a few guineas.'"

Much as Parsons might have wished to avoid seeing Howard, he felt obliged to make a gesture towards keeping him informed about what was happening. He need not have worried. Someone, presumably Catherine or Fitzherbert, had already told the colonel about Ashton.

"It's just as well there are other people here who tell me what's been happening, Parsons," Howard said, after he had been briefed about some of the recent developments.

"I'm sorry, colonel, but I'm sure you realize I've been busy."

Howard grudgingly accepted this excuse.

"This is becoming very serious, Parsons," he said, after they had spoken for a short while. "Do you want me to send for reinforcements?"

"I can manage with Brown and the two constables for the time being, sir. Your men will have more than enough on their hands searching for Claire Dunne and Smith. Have you received any news on their progress?"

"Not a word," said the colonel with a weary sigh of resignation. "I left Marsden in charge of that. I suggest you go and talk to him."

It was obvious now to Parsons that Howard's condition had caused him to lose much of his earlier interest in the investigation. That suited him admirably. There was nothing worse than a superior officer trying to interfere from a sick bed. But it was also clear that Howard's men in Petersfield were not keeping him fully informed about their progress. It was time he paid them a visit. While he was there he could see how they were treating Brendan Dunne. And after what Philip had said about their relationship he had plenty of questions of his own for the young groom.

"I'll probably ride over to see Marsden later today or tomorrow, sir," he told Howard. "Between us we can decide how to deploy the resources we have."

Parsons was keen to get back to work, but realized that he had still not broached the subject of the weapon with Howard.

"Just one more question before I leave, sir," he said. "What can you tell me about the weapon used to shoot at Lord Paul and yourself? Was it a rifle or a hand gun?"

"A revolver, Parsons. No doubt about that. The man was using the base of that stone vase to steady his aim, and from what I can remember of his position he was a left-hand shot. But I really can't be sure of that. Everything became a bit muddled then."

"I quite understand, sir. But you're certain the man used a revolver."

Howard scowled at Parsons.

"If you don't believe me Parsons, look in the drawer," he said irritably.

Parsons opened the drawer of the bedside cabinet. There was only one small item inside. A bullet. Parsons looked in disbelief at Howard and then removed the bullet between the thumb and index finger of his right hand and fumbled inside his coat pocket for his magnifying glass.

"Hamilton took it out of my leg while I was unconscious," explained Howard to the incredulous Parsons. "It's a point four-five. Probably fired from a Webley. There were plenty of those around in the army. Officers' weapons really, though Smith no doubt managed to get his hands on one somewhere. Probably stole one before he left the army, if the truth be told."

As Howard had said, the bullet was of point four-five inch caliber. The colonel's knowledge of the weapon used was crucially important, and even allowing for his injury Parsons was amazed that the colonel had not seen fit to mention it before. Had he not brought up the subject now, Parsons wondered how long it would have been before Howard told him.

"Thank you, sir," he said through gritted teeth. "I'm hoping that Doctor Hamilton will be able to confirm what you have told me when he takes the other bullet from Lord Paul."

Parsons met the doctor in the corridor on his way to see his patient. As a country physician he no doubt attended many funerals, and judging by his elegant attire he was well equipped for such occasions. His long black top coat was unbuttoned to reveal a handsome double-breasted morning suit. But it was scarcely appropriate dress for examining Ashton's body on the ash-strewn ground outside or for slicing open Lord Paul's chest.

His concern about the doctor's co-operation was unfounded. Hamilton was perfectly willing to assist him in any way. But he pleaded to be allowed to delay starting work until later. His wife would never forgive him, he explained, if he attended her father's funeral in dirty clothes. It was a point Parsons was reluctantly forced to concede.

The delay had its advantages. It would allow him the opportunity of speaking with Robertson, something he had intended doing for sometime. Not only would the solicitor have a detailed knowledge of Lord Quentin's wills, but Parsons also wanted to pursue another line of enquiry based upon Robertson's alleged relationship with Catherine.

-37-

*S*ince the previous evening the Drawing Room had been transformed into a temple of mourning. Black drapes masked the mirrors and every chair and table leg had been garlanded with a black bow.

O'Halloran and O'Mahoney stood solemn-faced on each side of the entrance, each with a silver salver of sherry glasses. As a sign of respect they had been instructed to remove their customary white aprons, and in their long black dresses looked like two large mythic birds guarding the entrance to an Egyptian temple. Inside the room, beyond the two servants, the family, close friends and local dignitaries gathered to pay homage to the late master of Beaumont.

They all glanced uneasily in Parsons' direction as he entered the room. Not only was he a stranger in their ranks, and like Fitzherbert, Montagu and Montgomery dressed inappropriately for the occasion; he was also someone they feared might unravel a dreadful secret and thereby bring dishonor upon the de Courceys. Perhaps others as well.

323

Parsons looked only for those faces that were familiar to him. In the short time available before the funeral he had no wish to be distracted by introductions to people who were strangers. Anne Hamilton and the Rawlinsons he could see standing in the center of the room with Mrs. Howard. And if their bored and distracted expressions were any indication, they were engaged in a conversation in which none of them had any interest. Alexander, Philip and Montagu hunched together near one of the windows; Montgomery stood alone at another looking vacantly into the distance, his back towards the dowager Annabelle, who was sitting alone by the fireplace. Catherine, the high-priestess of the solemnities, ignoring widow and guests alike, paced remorselessly to and fro, impatient for proceedings to begin. His knuckles white against the glass he held, Fitzherbert slumped ashen-faced on a chair in the far corner of the room. Robertson stood alone in another corner, his pretense at examining a large classical landscape painted in the style of Claude made unconvincing by the nervous movements of his hands and his frequent glances back into the room.

Taking a glass from O'Mahoney's tray Parsons made straight for the solicitor. Here was the opportunity he sought to ask a few questions before the funeral cortege left the castle.

"Good morning, Mr. Robertson," he said cheerfully, amused by the solicitor's feigned surprise at the interruption. "You'll forgive me if I discuss business on such a sad occasion, but we've had little opportunity of talking before now. So I thought I would take advantage of what little time we have before leaving for the church."

Anticipating conversation of a more mundane nature, Robertson was taken aback by this direct approach and searched across the room in desperation for a friendly face or a welcoming glance towards which he might retreat. Finding none he reluctantly conceded to Parsons' request.

"Of course, of course, inspector," he said in nervous irritation. "As you can plainly see, I'm at your mercy."

Robertson smiled feebly and gestured towards two vacant chairs a short distance away. He seemed to Parsons to be unusually distracted, the absence of the calm equilibrium Parsons had noted at dinner a few nights past betrayed by over-active hands and a tendency to fidget with the cuffs of his shirt and the creases in his trousers. As befitted a professional man he dressed conservatively, and were it not for the nervous mannerisms he was now displaying he would have looked distinguished in his dark suit. It suited his complexion admirably. Too swarthy to be considered handsome in an English sense, his dark-brown eyes and jet black hair resonated more of the Mediterranean seaboard than the Lowlands of Scotland from which he had originated. His overall appearance, however, was marred by several small patches of dried blood on his chin. He had been unusually careless with the razor during his morning toilet.

"These recent events will make life difficult for a solicitor," said Parsons.

"I don't follow your meaning, inspector."

"Well, no sooner is one man's will resolved than there is need for another."

"I see what you mean," replied Robertson with a wry smile, his hands stationary for the first time as he clasped them firmly across his stomach. "But in this case it's not that simple. No one could have anticipated that Lord Paul would die so soon. In consequence he has died intestate."

"So what happens to the estate now? Does it automatically pass to the next of kin?"

"In normal circumstances it might. But not in this case."

"Why is that, Mr. Robertson?"

Robertson's hands had become active again, the two thumbs rotating slowly around each other, and for the third time since they had sat down he recrossed his legs.

"You probably know something of Lord Paul's background," he said.

"Only from what others have told me," replied Parsons, "and the little I gleaned from my brief conversations with him."

Robertson straightened his legs and tugged gently at the creases in his trousers. Then he took a deep breath.

"Then you are probably not aware of everything, inspector," he said solemnly. "No doubt he told you how he arrived from America a few months ago claiming to be a long lost relative whose family had perished during the war in America. I expect he also told you their estates were confiscated or destroyed after the war by the Northern states."

Parsons nodded and waited in silence for Robertson to continue.

"From the start Paul's charm and good looks made a favorable impression on Quentin," he said. "I'm sure you can imagine how such a handsome out-going young man with a distinguished war record would appeal to him. He was just the sort of son Quentin had always wanted. But Quentin was no fool. After all he only had Paul's word that he was a de Courcey."

While Robertson was speaking Parsons had noticed that Doctor Hamilton had joined his wife and had bent to whisper something in her ear. Whatever he said made her smile. It was probably no more than an innocent comment about his patient upstairs, but the tiny ripple of laughter brought a welcome ray of sunshine into the gloomy atmosphere of the room.

"What action did Lord Quentin take?" asked Parsons, his momentary distraction abandoned for the more important information Robertson was offering.

"He asked me to employ Pinkertons, the American detective agency, to establish whether Paul's story was genuine. I regret to say it was not. The man's real name is Henry Longstaff. It's true he fought for the Confederates, but he was an infantry corporal, not the cavalry officer he claimed to be. Longstaff was taken prisoner at Gettysburg, where the real Paul de Courcey's regiment suffered terrible losses. All of their officers, including Paul, were killed. At sometime Longstaff must have stolen Paul's papers and taken the opportunity in the confusion of battle to acquire another identity. We'll never know exactly why he did it, it may simply have been that he decided that if he was going to be made a prisoner for the rest of the war he would rather settle for the relative comfort of an officers' camp rather than be sent to one for the rank and file. At that stage he could hardly have hoped to gain anything else from his new persona, as at that time he probably had no idea who Paul de Courcey really was. But if he had any ideas of exploiting his new identity after the war he would have been disappointed. He was being entirely truthful when he said the American de Courceys, like many other wealthy Southern families, lost everything in the war. The last chapter of his story also appears to be true. In the best traditions of a Southern gentleman he became a riverboat gambler and somewhere along the way heard about the English branch of his new family. And I guess it was at that point that he finally saw an opportunity to exploit his name."

"So he came over to England in the hope of establishing his credentials as a member of the aristocracy."

"We can't be sure exactly what his motives were. But he can scarcely have imagined he'd find such a favorable situation as the one at Beaumont, where the head of a distinguished family had disinherited his son."

"You mean that Lord Quentin had actually disinherited Alexander before Paul arrived."

"Yes, although Alexander didn't know that at the time."

"But if Lord Quentin knew that Paul was an impostor, why didn't he expose him?"

"At first I think he intended to. At least that's the impression I got when I told Quentin what Pinkertons had discovered. But it was also obvious that much that Quentin saw about Paul pleased him. If you don't mind I'll continue to call him that to avoid confusion. He was a dashing fellow right enough: a good horseman, a gambler and a man with an eye for the ladies. Quentin admired all that. So I think that the more he knew about Paul the more he saw him as the sort of new blood the family needed."

"You say he had an eye for the ladies. Was Lord Quentin aware of Paul's feelings for his own wife?"

Robertson appeared to be uncomfortable with the question.

"I don't think I can discuss that, inspector," he said. "As the family solicitor it's not for me to comment on Lady Annabelle's relationship with her husband or anyone else."

"Don't be evasive and try to hide behind your professional code of behavior, Robertson," interjected Parsons sharply. "There have been two murders here within the last few days, possibly three. So if you have any information you think is pertinent to my investigation you must give it to me. Do I make myself clear?"

The words were spoken quietly enough, but there was no disguising Parsons' determination. If need be he had a few trump cards of his own he could use to force the solicitor's hand. But he hoped he could hold them in reserve until such time he might need them.

Robertson took a clean white handkerchief from his pocket and wiped the palms of his hands and beads of perspiration from his brow. If it was a cry for help it did not go unseen. At the opposite end of the room Catherine interrupted her impatient pacing and looked in his direction with some concern. For a second she contemplated crossing the room to where the two men sat, but after catching Robertson's eye she turned away and resumed her perambulation.

With no possibility of help coming from that source Robertson was obliged to continue his narrative.

"What I say to you now, inspector, is pure conjecture and not something I'd be prepared to substantiate in a court of law. I hope you understand that."

Parsons nodded in acknowledgement.

"It was obvious to practically everyone that the relationship between Quentin and his wife was a very distant one. They rarely spoke to one another. But it's my personal belief that in spite of that Quentin still loved her, even if she did not return his affections. He probably also realized that even a strong constitution like his could not last forever, especially living the wild sort of life that he did. It may sound like an odd thing for me to say, inspector, but perhaps he saw in Paul not only a man able to provide a strong new line of de Courceys, but one who could also provide his wife with the sort of love he had been unable to give her himself. There was no doubt that he knew they were attracted to one another; but he never appeared to resent it, or show any bitterness towards Paul for his conduct. At least, not as far as I know. Believe me, inspector, the late Lord Quentin was a very strange and complex man."

"And what happens now?" asked Parsons. "Who inherits the title?"

"As I said before Quentin was no fool. The last thing he wanted was to have some American relative of Longstaff turning up some time in the future and laying claims to the family name. The terms of his last will are quite clear about that, although I didn't spell them out in full in the Library the other morning. In the event of Paul inheriting the title and dying without conceiving an heir, the estate reverts to the person named in the previous will."

"So Alexander inherits after all."

Robertson licked his dry lips and rubbed his handkerchief between his hands. Then he looked wistfully across the room.

"No," he said quietly. "The previous will did not name Alexander. After Alexander and before Paul there was someone else. Catherine is now mistress of Beaumont."

-38-

*J*ohnson's announcement that the carriages were ready to leave for the church gave Robertson the opportunity to escape further questioning. He rose hastily to his feet and joined the others already making their way outside. Still deep in thought Parsons joined the cortege a few minutes later.

Like many of his generation, Parsons' religious beliefs had been shaken by Darwin's revelations about the origin of Man. He found himself doubting the very existence of the paternalistic all-knowing God that had once been so much a part of his daily life at home and at school. But because there had been so much sincerity in this upbringing he found it impossible to discard these beliefs completely. Like Darwin himself, Parsons did not think that science alone could provide the answer to the great mysteries of life, and even though he disputed many traditional Christian beliefs he derived great spiritual comfort from attending an occasional service in one of the many beautiful old English churches.

He did not include in that number those of the older churches that had been internally redesigned in the recent past. Nor did he care much for services that focused upon preaching, as this invariably led to hideous tiered pulpits from which a flood of scriptural readings descended on a hapless congregation below. Those ill-favoured pieces of church furniture were invariably accompanied by unsightly rows of boxed pews, in which the wealth of some was flaunted over the poverty of others. For if the Christian message was seen to reflect the social inequities of the temporal world, it was hardly surprising that the size of church congregations continued to fall.

It was not that Parsons had developed an affinity for the Church of Rome. He merely regretted the actions of those Reformation iconoclasts who had destroyed so much of the wondrous interiors of the older English churches; churches whose beauty had provided such solace to worshipers over the centuries. For he argued that if indeed there was a God, he would surely choose to associate himself with buildings in which mankind had created something sublime, rather than those that merely reflected many of the less joyful aspects of Protestantism.

In this respect the village church of Saint James was a great disappointment. Having seen its square Norman tower on his previous journeys through the village, Parsons had imagined that much of its original character remained. But once inside he found there was very little left of the soul of this once-handsome building. Its stain-glass windows and rood-screen had at some time been removed, to be replaced by a plain altar, a grotesque pulpit and monotonous rows of drab oak pews.

The Union flag draped over Lord Quentin's coffin provided the only splash of color in the gloomy interior of the church among the black suits of the men and the long black dresses and veils of the women.

Even in death and in the house of God the family remained divided. Lady Catherine, the new head of the family, sat with her brothers in the front pew on one side of the aisle. Lady Annabelle sat alone on the other. Noticing Annabelle's isolation, Doctor Hamilton had attempted to persuade his wife to join her; but after some hesitation, Anne Hamilton squeezed into a pew with the Rawlinsons, directly behind Catherine. With Montagu and Fitzherbert and most of the remaining mourners also opting for that side of the church, it left only Montgomery to offer some form of moral support to the widow by occupying one of the many empty seats behind her.

Lady Annabelle seemed unaware that the bitterness that had accompanied her married life had continued into her widowhood. She sat silent and motionless, her head bowed and hidden from the world behind a thick black veil.

Parsons chose to sit at the back of the church. From there he could not only command a view of the congregation, he would also have the privacy to read the information that had just arrived from London. The admirable Carpenter had had the foresight to realize that Parsons would be attending the funeral and was waiting outside the church with Harris' telegram.

A few curious villagers and those servants that could be spared from their duties gradually filled the remaining pews.

The loyalty of the servants was divided. Johnson and Mrs Hughes, as befitted their status as long-serving members of the household, took their places a discrete distance behind the family; but O'Brien and Sweeney chose to offer their allegiance to Lady Annabelle. That was a much fairer reflection, Parsons thought, of the affection with which she was held by most ordinary people.

When the nervous, perspiring figure of Joshua Harding mounted the pulpit in his white surplice, Parsons turned his attention to Harris' telegram. In the short time since Parsons had left London the sergeant had not been idle, and it was unlikely that the vicar would have anything to say that would be as interesting as the information on the paper in Parsons' hand. After waiting for the congregation to resume its seats after the first hymn, Parsons placed the telegram on his open hymn book and began reading.

For Parsons from Harris.

Geoffrey Montagu son of wealthy banker Sir Jeremiah Montagu. Sir Jeremiah self-made man frequently in public eye. Known to keep several mistresses. Relationship between father and son never good. Deteriorated since Geoffrey sent down from Oxford during his first year. Sir Jeremiah threw Geoffrey out of family home and disowned him. Since then Geoffrey relied entirely on friends for financial support. At present living with woman friend Caroline Mayhew in artist commune at 82 Woburn Square Bloomsbury. Alexander de Courcey also staying there for past three months. House owned by Oliver Craig young painter with large private income. House appears to be refuge for bohemian artists.

Also occasionally used as meeting place for radical political group calling themselves anarchists. Local police aware of meetings but consider group ineffective and harmless.

Major George Fitzherbert retired officer 18th Royal Lancers. Bachelor. Lives alone in single rented room at 55 Lawford Road Camden Town. Three months rent owing. Known to be heavy drinker. Spends most of small private income in local ale houses. Frequently penniless. Other tenants say Fitzherbert has no real friends. Described as sad figure with no other interest in life other than drinking.

Captain Sir Cecil Ashton also retired 18th Royal Lancers. Rents two rooms at 38 Parker Street Holborn. Not seen there for several weeks. Owes two months rent. Bachelor but described by fellow lodgers as womanizer. Frequently absent from London especially during racing season. According to landlord Ashton once relatively wealthy with substantial private income. Disinherited by father just before death. Ashton's main income now from gambling. Anonymous letter to Wood Street Police May 1878 accused Ashton of blackmail but never sufficient evidence to start proceedings.

Andrew Robertson practiced law in Petersfield since October 1879. No other partners in firm. Prior to Petersfield worked in Winchester. According to Law Society has also worked in Oxford Edinburgh and London since leaving Magdalen College Oxford 1865. Never stayed anywhere longer than four years. Bachelor.

Address in Canada given by Harrison Montgomery still being verified. East Canada Shipping Line confirm he embarked Quebec on SS Ontario 14 July. Disembarked Waterford Ireland 27 July. Addresses given for stays in Dublin and Belfast still being checked. Also unable confirm date Montgomery sailed Belfast to Glasgow. Caledonian Hotel Glasgow confirm room booked 8 and 9 August. No other known addresses in Scotland. Since 23 August staying Queens Hotel Bayswater.

According to hotel manager Montgomery perfect guest who pays for board week in advance. Apart from Montgomery being Canadian on first visit to Britain manager knows nothing. Montgomery receives no visitors and goes sight-seeing most days. Before leaving for Beaumont Montgomery vacated room and put some luggage in hotel store. Manager expects Montgomery to return but unsure when.

Still awaiting information on Paul de Courcey from Pinkerton detective agency from War Office on John Spencer and Albert Smith and from Royal Irish Constabulary on Irish servants.

Announcement in Times regarding reunion placed and paid for by Ashton. No reason for newspaper to doubt Ashton's good faith. Established identity showed invitation to Beaumont and said was brother officer of Lord Quentin.'

Ashton being a blackmailer made perfect sense, mused Parsons. It would explain his relationship and close-questioning of O'Brien; a servant who was, fortunately for him, in the habit of searching waste-paper baskets for interesting snippets of information. Country houses like Beaumont provided the sort of idle gossip that blackmailers thrived on. It might also explain why he had placed the announcement in the newspaper. If he relied on regular invitations from wealthy families for free board and lodging as well as a source of information it would be in his interest to see that any important events to which he was invited were given the maximum publicity. Everyone who was someone—or wished to be—read the Court Circular in the *Times*

Like all blackmailers Ashton was playing a dangerous game. In this instance it had proved to be fatal. There was more to his death than at first appeared. Although it was likely that the motive for his murder was somehow linked to theft, there was also a chance that one of his blackmail victims had been present at Beaumont and had decided to silence him.

A perceptible change in the tone of Harding's voice interrupted Parsons' thoughts. The vicar's monotonous monologue had given way to the tuneless dirge adopted by churchmen when chanting the psalms. In this instance it was the Ninety-first Psalm, and as Parsons listened to the familiar words they struck him as being especially apposite for Lord Quentin: a military man struck down mercilessly without warning.

'Thou shalt not be afraid for the terror by night;
Nor for the arrow that flieth by day;
Nor for the pestilence that walketh in darkness;
Nor for the destruction that wasteth at noonday.
A thousand shall fall by thy side,
And ten thousand at thy right hand;
But it shall not come to thee.
Only with thine eyes shalt though behold
And see the reward of the wicked.'

The congregation bowed their heads for the final blessing. Instinctively Parsons followed suit, from the corner of his eye noticing that Montgomery and the two Irish girls furtively crossed themselves. How ironic, he thought, that in what was alleged to a be a house of God it was still necessary to be secretive about one's religion.

Almost with indecent haste Lord Quentin's sons and sons-in-law began struggling down the narrow aisle with the casket, as though desperate to escape from the oppressive gloom of the church into the cool September afternoon. Once outside the mourners shuffled across the courtyard to the family vault, and there after a brief ceremony the late head of the de Courcey family was interred with his forefathers. Parsons watched from a distance, speculating whether Lord Paul, alias Henry Longstaff, would ever join his predecessor there. He doubted that would happen if Lady Catherine was aware of his true identity.

The funeral party began filing back into the waiting carriages. Knowing that there was to be lunch at the castle there was little point in dwelling over-long amongst the grave-stones. But Parsons had noticed Robertson, and was not about to let him escape so easily a second time.

"Do you mind waiting a moment longer," he asked the solicitor. "There are still some questions I'd like you to answer."

"I'm sorry, Parsons, but you'll have to excuse me. I've pressing business in Petersfield this afternoon and need to return to the castle to collect my horse."

"You need not worry unduly about that," said Parsons. "I've asked Johnson to send it back with the trap when it comes to collect me. That gives us ample time to finish our conversation."

Accepting his defeat gracefully Robertson found a comfortable position on the low stone wall around the church, and with a resigned expression took out his tobacco pouch. If delay was inevitable he had very intention of making himself comfortable. It was after all not an unpleasant afternoon, and it was only with his landlord that he had business that afternoon. It was not a meeting he was relishing. The cost of his rented house was proving to be far above his means, and he was already several months behind with the rent. Initially it was an expense that had seemed justified and a gamble that had appeared to be paying off. At first Catherine had been greatly impressed. But that was before the arrival of Henry Longstaff.

"I imagine the de Courcey estate is worth a great deal," said Parsons, in a matter-of-fact voice, but aware that as he spoke a dark frown had suddenly clouded Robertson's face. "Would you say that was motive enough for murder?"

"No one who knew the true financial state of Beaumont would consider it worth the risk," replied Robertson. "The income from the estate has been falling over the years, owing to general neglect and the recent decline in the value of agricultural land. Were it not for the inflated rent paid by the London and South West Railway for the lease they have on a stretch of de Courcey land, the family would by now be bankrupt."

Parsons was surprised to hear how desperate the de Courcey finances were.

"How many people were aware of this?" he asked.

"Other than myself and Quentin, only one person."

"Catherine?"

"That's right, inspector. Only Catherine knew."

"And how many people, apart from Lord Quentin and you, knew about the different wills?"

"Two. Catherine and Paul."

"I can understand why Catherine might know, but why on earth did Lord Quentin decide to tell someone he knew to be an impostor."

"Quentin didn't tell him. I did."

Robertson smiled ironically at Parsons before dropping his eyes and busying himself with his pipe.

"If you don't mind me saying, Robertson," said Parsons, "that sounds very unprofessional, and I can only assume you had a very good reason for doing it."

Robertson struck a match and relit his pipe, hiding his face momentarily behind a plume of smoke. He smiled again at Parsons, but there was very little humor in his eyes.

"I don't know why I'm telling you this, Parsons. Perhaps it's because I think you're the only person capable of getting to the truth. And even though I may have done things that were foolish and, as you say, unprofessional, I never had anything to do with the other ghastly events. So why shouldn't I tell you the truth?"

"Why not indeed," said Parsons half to himself, and delighted by this unexpected and welcome turn of events. "Please continue. Why did you tell Paul about the different wills?"

"Because he was a cunning rascal, and through his scheming and my foolishness I was deeply in his debt."

He spoke with the bitterness of a man who has been betrayed.

"Not long after the so-called Paul de Courcey arrived at Beaumont he invited me to join his party for a day at the races," explained Robertson. "I'm not a regular race-goer, but like many I enjoy an occasional wager. And there's no finer place for that than at Epsom on Derby Day. I have to admit I was delighted to be included in such exalted company, as the de Courceys were not in the habit of inviting humble solicitors like myself to their social events. But of course, I was assuming then that it was a de Courcey that had invited me."

He paused for a few moments and sat morosely puffing on his pipe.

"It all started so well. I was lucky with the races and by the end of the afternoon was more than fifty pounds in credit. That's more than I make in a good month as a lawyer. During the afternoon we'd all been drinking heavily, so you can imagine I was feeling particularly pleased with the world. So when someone suggested we went to a drinking club in the town for a round or two of cards, I thought why not, this could indeed be my day. And by Heaven I was in need of a good day or two to sort out my financial problems. But perhaps you can guess what happened?"

Parsons nodded sympathetically. He could well imagine what was coming.

"At first I won a little money. Not enough to make me stop playing and sit on my winnings, but just enough to keep me interested and persuade me that there was more of it to come. And of course, the drinks kept flowing. Everyone cheered my good fortune and reckless play. I can still hear Paul's seductive voice: 'Well done, Robertson old man. What a bold player you are.' Of course, I knew nothing then about his former career on the Mississippi river boats. Nor did I realize I was in the hands of a bunch of professional gamblers. My brain was blurred by the drink and the more I lost the more reckless I became. At the end of the evening my winnings had not only evaporated, but I found myself several hundred pounds in debt. The sum I owed terrified me. It was almost a year's income! I had no way of ever paying it!"

His eyes were cold with hate as he looked across the peaceful graveyard.

"It was all very embarrassing. But that's just what that scoundrel Longstaff intended. He knew I couldn't pay, and that's exactly what he wanted. He knew he had me in his power. Even in my drunkenness I could see what was happening. He'd take care of the debts, he said. All I had to do was let him see Quentin's will. So I agreed. What else could I do? I couldn't see any other way out."

"Was Captain Ashton a member of this group?" asked Parsons.

"As a matter of fact he was. But how did you know?"

Parsons ignored the question.

"And can I assume that at this time Catherine was the main beneficiary?"

"That's correct."

"And was that before or after you began your affair with her?"

The solicitor's voice was flat when he replied.

"You're well informed, Parsons," he said. "I suppose the servants have been talking."

He had let his pipe go out, and tapped the bowl against the church wall before continuing.

"You're quite right," he said. "At that time I was attempting to court Catherine. And no doubt, having seen the relatively limited charms possessed by that lady you can guess my motive."

"I have a fairly good idea, Robertson. It was probably for the same reason that Paul suddenly found her so attractive."

"Right again, Parsons. We both wanted her for the money she would one day inherit. Although I knew better than he the true state of the family wealth. I think at one time she was desperate enough to have taken either of us. Me a penniless solicitor and he the impostor she knew him to be. Yes, Parsons, I made sure she knew he was an impostor. But she has no need for either of us now. With her newly acquired title, she can have her pick. Bankers, industrialists or property developers. Anyone with money who is attracted to the prospect of becoming master of Beaumont."

Not long afterwards Jessop arrived with the trap and Robertson's horse. The solicitor blew the loose tobacco from his pipe, returned it to his pocket and prepared to mount his horse. Before doing so he shook Parsons' hand.

"Good luck with your enquiry, inspector. If you think of any other questions you'll find me at this address." he smiled wryly. "At least for a little while longer."

He handed Parsons his card.

"There's one last question, Robertson," said Parsons, keeping firm hold of the horse's bridle. "Can you tell me where you were on the night Paul was murdered?"

Parsons felt the full animosity of the solicitor's cold stare.

"I've been expecting you to ask that, inspector," he said, "but I resent the implication nevertheless. Fortunately I can provide an alibi. I was doing what many frustrated bachelors of my age do most night's of the week. Drinking in the local hostelry. 'The White Hart' in Petersfield to be exact. Ask George Butcher, the landlord. He'll be able to confirm that for you. Now I really must go. Good-day to you, inspector."

Robertson touched the rim of his hat in a final salute and turned his horse's head in the direction of the village. Then he nudged its flanks with his heels and set off down the narrow lane. Parsons watched him until he had turned the bend and disappeared from sight before reading the card Robertson had given him.

Andrew Robertson Esq BA (Oxon)
Solicitor
Aspen House
Oak Drive
Petersfield
Hampshire

"All the trappings of rural respectability," he thought as he climbed into the trap. "and all for the love of a lady."

-39-

Doctor *Hamilton was washing his hands in the bowl in Lord* Paul's room when Parsons entered the room.

"I've found your bullet, inspector," he said, nodding towards a small metal tray on the bedside cabinet. "It was lodged in the heart. Quite a shot I'd say. Your murderer must be quite a marksman."

"But he only managed to wing Colonel Howard."

"Quite right, young man," Hamilton said with a twinkle in his eye. "But don't forget our gallant Chief Constable was a moving target. Wasn't he charging the enemy at the time. Paul, on the other hand, would have been easier to hit."

Parsons thought it was more likely that whoever fired the shot did not mean to kill Howard at all, but merely intended to stop any pursuit. Paul had always been the murderer's prime target. The murderer had always planned to kill him.

He examined the bullet. As he would have expected it was a point four-five caliber like the one that Howard had given him. Pistols of that caliber were, as Howard had said, commonly used by the army. But they were also used by the Royal Irish Constabulary; and as a result of occasional raids on police posts in Ireland, often the weapon used by Fenians.

"Have you been outside to examine the other corpse yet?" asked Parsons.

"You mean the remains of Captain Ashton."

"Everything seems to point towards it being him. But I'd still like you to examine the body and tell me when and how you think he died."

The two men made their way outside, where they found Sergeant Brown methodically searching the area around the stables. Judging by the sergeant's expression he was well pleased with himself, and as soon as Hamilton had begun examining the corpse Parsons walked over to join him.

"Well, Brown, how are you getting on?" he asked.

"Quite well, thank 'ee, sir. Jessop and Chalmers 'ave been searching the grounds. I've been concentrating 'ere in the stables. Let me show 'ee what we've found so far."

Brown led Parsons to a large sheet of canvas that was stretched on the grass.

"Like 'ee said, sir. I've drawn a little map to show 'ee where everything was found, and I've laid 'em out on the canvas for 'ee to see."

He proudly showed Parsons a rough sketch in his notebook and then pointed to the individual items on the canvas.

"'Tis mainly 'orse tackle from the stables, sir. Most of the leather work was destroyed in the fire, but the metal parts 'ave survived."

Brown pointed to what was left of several sets of smoke-begrimed stirrups and bridles.

" 'ee might find these interesting, sir."

The sergeant bent down and picked up two items from the canvas sheet and handed them to Parsons.

"These were in the saddle bags by the corpse, sir. As I remember it, after we found that box last night we didn't look at the bags again. We must've missed these."

Parsons was in no doubt as to whose fault Brown considered this to be. And Brown was right, the oversight had been entirely his. He had been too excited at finding the box and the scraps of money.

"Looks to me like the backs of two silver hair brushes, sir. And they got initials on 'em. See what I mean, sir. 'CA,' I think it says."

"Cecil Ashton," said Parsons. "Well done, Brown. There certainly doesn't appear to be any doubt now about the identity of the corpse."

Brown bristled with pride. But it was evident from his rather self-satisfied expression that there was still more he wanted to show Parsons.

"There are these as well, sir."

His tone had become that of an excited child hoping to impress a parent with an unexpectedly good school report. He watched Parsons' face expectantly as he carefully examined the two items Brown had handed him: two matching silver hip flasks, each with the initials 'QdeC' engraved on them.

"Where exactly did you find these."

"Just 'ere, sir."

He pointed to the sketch in his note-book.

"I've spoken with Mr. Johnson to get some idea of where everything was in the stables before the fire, sir," Brown explained, "and 'e says where we found these 'ere flasks was jus' below where Smith used to sleep. So Smith probably 'ad them up in the loft with 'im, and they fell to the ground in the fire. Looks like our man was a thief as well as a murderer, sir."

"I'd say Smith was capable of any crime, sergeant. But if he was planning on running away, why do you think he left such valuable items behind?"

"Panic, sir. Blind panic. If I'd just murdered someone and set a building on fire, reckon I'd leave one or two things behind in my rush to get away. Weren't no good to 'im after all. Man like Smith don't drink out of no 'ip-flask. And selling them with these 'ere initials would only implicate 'im in the murders."

"You're probably right. But we'll never know what Smith was thinking until we catch him. What about the rest of the grounds. Have you found anything there?"

"We found this rope at the bottom of the castle wall, sir. Over there."

Brown pointed to the north-west corner of the castle.

"Show me exactly where," said Parsons.

They walked over to the castle.

"It was just 'ere, sir. You can see where I made my mark on the wall."

Brown pointed to a line scratched in the surface of the stone, just under the Library window.

"How long is the rope, sergeant?"

Brown consulted his note-book again.

" 'bout sixty feet, sir. I got Jessop to pace it out."

More than enough to reach to the first floor, thought Parsons, looking upwards towards the windows of Lord Quentin's room. And perhaps even enough to reach the floor above that.

"I've finished here now, Parsons," shouted Hamilton.

The doctor was dusting the ash from his trousers when Parsons reached him. He had been right in thinking his wife would not have been pleased to see him arriving at church in such a state.

"What can you tell me about the body?" asked Parsons.

"Not a great deal I'm afraid. It's the body of a middle-aged man with a good set of teeth, about five feet ten and slimly built."

"That description matches Ashton pretty well, wouldn't you say? Have you any idea how he died and when?"

"I can't be precise about the time, but I'm sure he was dead before the fire. The cause of the death was a series of severe blows to the back of the head. But the position of the limbs is unusual. After blows like that I would expect a body to fall forward with the arms and legs splayed randomly. It would be very unusual to fall onto its back and arrange itself as neatly as this."

"Do you mean that somebody rearranged the body after death. Wouldn't that be a rather strange and morbid thing to do? And wouldn't it have to be done before the onset of *rigor mortis?*"

"You're right. It would have to be done very soon after this poor wretch died. But I don't imagine things happened quite like that. As I see it the normal way to move a lifeless body is to drag it on its back, and I was thinking more along the lines of someone moving the body to hide it."

"Are you suggesting that Ashton died somewhere else before the fire started and then was dragged here?"

"That's just what I think. I've no doubt that death took place several hours before the fire, but I can't say exactly when."

"So it's possible that Smith murdered Ashton when he came here in the morning to get his horse. Let's say that was sometime after six. He could hardly leave a body lying around for anyone to find, but the stables were still an ideal place to hide it. There's always plenty of hay around, and with Dunne in prison there was nobody likely to find it. It would be much safer to move it after it got dark, but if Smith had already decided to murder Lord Paul at around ten that night, a much better idea would be to set light to the stables as he was leaving. That would solve two problems at once. It would get rid of Ashton's body and at the same time cause a diversion as he was escaping."

"But as you can see bodies don't disappear in a fire, inspector."

"Smith probably didn't think about that. Maybe he didn't even care. If he was planning to murder Lord Paul, burn down the stables and make a run for it with stolen money, I don't imagine he'd be too worried if Ashton's body was discovered after he'd gone. After all his behavior doesn't appear to be that of a man trying to cover his tracks."

Parsons was pleased to find that Hamilton shared his general view of what had occurred. But it was a view that did not account for the rope.

"There is of course another explanation."

Parsons looked back towards the castle.

"How easy is it to move a body with *rigor mortis*, doctor?"

"That depends on where you're moving it. If you're dragging it along the ground it would be no more difficult to move than a live body, but in other instances it could be extremely difficult. What had you in mind?"

"I'm assuming that Ashton was killed early in the morning, not here in the stables, but somewhere in the castle. If that happened the body would have to remain hidden until it was dark. Moving it before then would be too risky. But by the time evening came the body would be stiff, and that would present the murderer with a problem or two he might not have foreseen. However, whatever state the body was in it would have to be moved. If it was left in the castle it wouldn't be long before it was found. Now, if I was trying to get a body out of the castle I would do it by lowering it through a window. From Lord Quentin's window, for instance, or even the one above. How easy do you think it would be for someone to attach a rope to Ashton's body after *rigor mortis* had set in, lower it to the ground and then drag it here to the stables? And could one person manage it alone?"

The doctor thought for some time before replying.

"I've no doubt it could be done," he said. "Ashton wasn't a heavy man and a reasonably strong person could manage him. But it wouldn't be easy. And what about his saddle bags? If they were lowered at the same time as the body the load would be much more awkward to handle. That would probably require two people or one very strong one."

"One strong person leads us back to Smith again. But I think I can see how it could be done relatively simply by any reasonably able-bodied person."

Parsons looked at his pocket-watch."

"I don't know about you, Doctor Hamilton, but this has given me an appetite. If we go now we'll just catch the end of luncheon."

-40-

By the time Parsons had reached the Dining Room the servants were already clearing the table. Everyone else had eaten Johnson informed him.

Hamilton had not been able to join him for luncheon. He had remembered there were other patients to see and had gone in search of his wife.

The main dish had been a large gelantine. A boneless meat dish such as this would have been far easier for the ladies in their heavy mourning dresses and thick veils to handle. Not that Parsons could imagine any of them eating much. A loss of appetite at funerals was an obligatory social convention. But as he was eating alone it was a convention he could cheerfully ignore.

"Would you give my compliments to Mr. Montgomery," he said as Johnson filled his glass with Burgundy, "and ask him to meet me in the Library at two."

Then putting his professional responsibilities to one side he gave his full attention to the loin of pork covered with layers of ham, seasoned sausage meat, game, pistachio kernels and mushrooms.

354

"Mrs. Hughes," he murmured contentedly, "you have indeed excelled yourself."

Montgomery was seated in one of the wing-chairs by the window at the far end of the Library. He was reading a book, but it seemed to Parsons that he had positioned himself where he could see what was happening outside.

"How are things going, Parsons?" he enquired good-humouredly. "I can see your men are still busy."

He rose from his chair and walked over to the bookcase to replace his book.

"Have you ever read Montaigne?" he asked, as he slid the book into its place on the shelf. "To my shame I'd never heard of him before today. His 'Essays' make fascinating reading. There's even one on drunkenness that poor old Fitzherbert might care to read. In ancient times, believe it or not, Fitzherbert's problem was described as a form of ecstasy. Montaigne, however, didn't agree with that, and after seeing Fitzherbert in action I'm inclined to see his point."

He chuckled loudly at his own wit, and Parsons politely acknowledged the joke. But he had not come for light-hearted banter, and made a great show of pulling out his notebook. Montgomery at once became serious and beckoned Parsons to an adjacent chair.

"Sit down, my dear chap," he said, adopting what was for him an unusually nonchalant manner. "I can see you haven't come to see me for social reasons. How can I help you?"

The Canadian had seemed a changed man since Paul's death, and it appeared to Parsons that in his own rather awkward way he was trying to emulate the dead man. It had been noticeable how much Montgomery had been seen in Annabelle's company, and it was possible he thought he had only to imitate Paul's charm to have the same success with her. But whether Montgomery would manage to impress the beautiful widow so easily was quite another matter. Such an easy and assured manner as Paul's was not acquired over-night, thought Parsons. Centuries of breeding also played their part. Then he reminded himself that Paul had managed the transition relatively quickly himself.

"You can start by telling me a little about yourself, Mr. Montgomery. When we first met you were described to me as a writer. But I would hazard a guess that you have tried other professions as well."

"You are right as usual, inspector. My claim to literary merit has a great deal to do with wishing to impress Alexander and his friends. Although I do write a little now, as you may have guessed, my earlier life was very different. I was not born into a cultured or educated family. My family left Scotland for Canada two generations ago. Some people would say they had chosen to emigrate, but as I see it they were driven off their land by a wealthy landlord who was clearing his tenants in order to graze sheep and provide a playground for his rich deer-stalking friends."

His tone was light enough, but Parsons sensed an underlying bitterness. It was as well for the de Courceys, he thought, that they had never owned land in Scotland.

Once he had begun with his family's history Montgomery seemed anxious to continue.

"Like a lot of Highland crofters at that time my family had no choice but to start their lives again in another country. In their case they exchanged a hard life in the Monadhliath Mountains south of Inverness for an equally hard one on a small farm in Saskatchewan. That's where I grew up. But to the disappointment of my father I didn't stay. I'm something of a free spirit, you see; and not one to be tied down to any particular place. Canada is a great country for people like me. In my life I've tried most things: lumber-jacking, fishing, even hunting in the remote backwoods. Now that I think about it, it must be pretty obvious to anyone with half an eye to see that I'm not a literary man."

"Did you never have the desire to settle down?"

"Marriage you mean. No, Parsons, that was not for me. Such a life as the one I'd chosen to lead was hardly conducive to marriage; and to be frank until I arrived in England I'd never met the sort of woman, or should I say *lady*, that I could ever imagine spending the rest of my life with."

Montgomery's voice trailed off at that point, and his eyes focused on some distant point at the end of the Library. Parsons waited in silence for him to continue.

"I make no claim to be an educated man," he said at last, "but I've always read anything I could get my hands on. My being a loner was probably one reason for that. A few years ago I began trying to put my experiences into words. Nothing fancy, you understand. Just a few short stories about life in the out-back. But when some of them were published I began to take myself a bit more seriously. As I think I told you when we first met, I've started gathering some material together to write a novel about the native Indians. From what

I've seen it's not a subject many writers have explored; and after all North America was the Indians' home before ever the Europeans arrived."

"Isn't that somewhat ironic after what you've told me about your ancestors. Weren't they the ones responsible for taking the Indians' land?"

"Not at all, Parsons. It was off-shoots of the same land owning class that took my grandfather's land who were mainly to blame for exploiting the Indians."

"I'm sure you're right," said Parsons, aware that Montgomery's lesson in social history was not contributing anything to his investigation. "But I'm more interested in hearing about the reason for your visiting England. Or should I say Britain, as I believe you were traveling in Ireland and Scotland before you arrived in London."

"There's nothing like travel for broadening the mind, inspector. Every writer should travel. And every man should try to trace his roots. We all need to do that, don't you think?"

Parsons had to agree with him. He had always wanted to go back to the India of his childhood. It was a place he had only the happiest memories of. One day he would, he promised himself. One day.

"And did you find them?" he asked, shaking himself out of his reverie.

"Unfortunately not," replied Montgomery sadly. "I spent several days searching that part of the Highlands where my family had lived for anyone who had known them. No one I met had even heard of them. It was as though they had never existed. And when I tried to find the spot where their croft had been, I was threatened by a game-keeper with a gun. That upset me I can tell you."

There was no disguising the bitterness in his voice now.

"But why did you go to Ireland," asked Parsons, eager to divert the questioning to a fresh subject. "You didn't mention you had family connections there."

"The Celtic Diaspora, Parsons. Every bar in Canada has at least one Irishman spinning romantic yarns about his homeland. Most of them have never been there and probably never will, but it doesn't stop them talking about it. That's what exiles do. They dream and romanticize about places they have never seen. Well, they certainly fired my imagination. When my ship docked at Waterford I thought it was too good an opportunity to miss. I spent a few days in Dublin—now that's a city a man can enjoy—then I traveled north to Belfast before crossing over to Scotland. And those Irish-Canadians were right. Ireland is certainly a wild and wonderful place."

All very interesting, thought Parsons, but it didn't seem to be leading anywhere. It was time to deflect Montgomery onto events closer to home.

"Tell me about your movements on the day Lord Paul was murdered," he said. "I believe you went riding."

"That's right. I'd arranged with Johnson the night before to have a horse ready for me that morning. And when I got to the stables I found Smith had harnessed the grey. I had no idea then that it was Ashton's horse, I can assure you."

"And Smith never thought to mention it?"

Montgomery laughed.

"When I arrived at the stables Smith was nowhere to be seen. For all I knew he'd been drinking as usual and had gone back to his loft to sleep. Either that or he was having breakfast in the kitchen. All I can say is that I saw that the grey was ready, so I took it. Tell me, Parsons, have you not had the pleasure of meeting Smith?"

"We exchanged a few discourteous words during my previous visit. Everyone tells me he drinks too much and by all accounts none of the servants like him."

"That's Smith, all right. As you say, no one liked him. It was only a whim of Quentin's that ever kept him here. I can only imagine he did Quentin some favor in the past. Heaven knows what that could have been. It's likely to be something that happened when they were both in the army, but for the life of me I don't see Smith playing the hero and saving Quentin's life. So how he came to be here is something of a mystery."

He smiled at Parsons.

"Perhaps you'll solve it one day," he said.

Parsons said nothing, waiting for Montgomery to continue.

"There was no doubt that things would change with Paul. Paul wasn't going to put up with Smith for long. He said he intended buying more horses, and he wanted someone more capable and personable to run the stables. There was no doubt in my mind that he intended to get rid of Smith sooner rather than later."

"So you think Smith murdered Paul just because he'd dismissed him."

"Who can say. It does seem an extreme action for anyone to take over such a relatively small thing. But who knows what goes on in the mind of someone like Smith. As

Fitzherbert said, Smith had a comfortable life here and the prospects of similar work elsewhere were pretty slim. Perhaps the thought of losing everything after so many years made him wild. I'm told he was never able to control his temper at the best of times."

"Did you see or hear anything of Ashton before he left?" asked Parsons.

"Not a thing, inspector. Like everyone else I assumed he'd gone hours before, and like them I was amazed by your announcement last evening."

"So you took the grey and went for a ride. Across the Downs, I think you said. Like yourself I don't know the area well, and I wonder if you can make a small sketch for me showing your route."

Parsons opened his note pad at a blank page and handed it to Montgomery.

The Canadian looked surprised, but took the pad and pencil and began sketching.

"You'll have to excuse my draughtmanship," he said. "I'm also ashamed to say I got lost at one stage. That's quite a confession from someone who claims to have lived in the back-country. But the tracks on the Downs all look the same and it can be confusing when you don't know them."

Noticing that Montgomery was left-handed gave Parsons the opportunity to test one of his theories. He believed he could determine whether a man was left or right handed by studying his side-whiskers. It was not a theory he would ever wish to submit to the rigors of the courts, but it was surprisingly accurate. Right-handed shavers, he maintained, invariably cut the ends of their side-whiskers sloping downwards from their right ear and upwards from their left. The opposite was true of those who were left-handed. Montgomery's whiskers supported his theory admirably. A line drawn from his left ear-lobe along the edge of the neatly trimmed side-whisker on the left-hand side of his face passed just below the left-hand edge of his mouth. On the opposite side of his face a similar line passed just above the right-hand edge of his mouth. It was merely a casual observation, but it was small things like that that gave Parsons great satisfaction.

"That's the best I can do, Parsons," said Montgomery, laying down the pencil. "I warned you I was no artist."

It was no more than a crude sketch with few landmarks, but it gave Parsons some idea of where Montgomery had gone."

"I rode east towards the edge of the Downs," Montgomery explained, indicating the route he had taken with his index finger, "and on my way back I turned north towards Midhurst. By then it was late afternoon and I was beginning to feel hungry. I suppose I reached Midhurst around five."

"Is that where you ate?"

"Yes. There's an old coaching inn in the center of the town. 'The Bull.' What a pretty place that is. I'll treasure the memory of my visit there. We don't have anything like that back home."

"What time did you leave Midhurst?"

"I couldn't be sure. I wasn't too concerned about time. But I suppose it was about half past six."

"You said earlier that you got lost. Where was that?"

"It was on my way back from Midhurst. By the time I turned off the road onto the bridle way over the Downs it was getting dark, and it wasn't until I reached a small hamlet I hadn't passed in the morning that I realized I'd taken a wrong turning. So I retraced my steps and eventually found the right track."

"Where were you when you saw the fire?"

"About here."

Montgomery put a cross on the map roughly half-way between the small castle he had drawn on the map to represent Beaumont and the elliptical shape representing the Downs.

"At first I thought it was a thatched roof in one of the villages or a haystack that was burning, but as I got closer to Beaumont I realized the fire was in the grounds of the castle. So I gave my poor tired horse a dig in the ribs and rode here as fast as I could. But as the others have already said, there was never any chance of putting the fire out."

"Alexander said that he took your horse to go for help."

"That's right. I told him the horse was tired but he would hear nothing of it."

"Did you see anyone on the road riding away from the castle?"

"No one. If anyone had come in my direction I couldn't have missed them. And if you're thinking of Smith, surely he would have been well away from the castle before I was anywhere near it. Don't forget the fire had already started when I was still some distance away."

"I'll leave you to your books, sir," said Parsons, rising from his chair. "But allow me to recommend to you a chapter in Montaigne concerning some lines from Virgil. It may not sound much like it from the title, but in that chapter Montaigne discusses the sexual instincts that motivate men and women. As I remember he is all for allowing women more freedom in that respect."

Parsons smiled to himself as he crossed the Library towards the door. Behind him he could hear the scrape of Montgomery's chair on the wooden floor and his footsteps moving towards the bookcase.

-41-

Parsons was surprised to find Lord Quentin's room locked. There seemed no reason for that now that the funeral had been held, so he went down to the kitchen to find Johnson.

"Why is Lord Quentin's room locked?" he asked.

"Lady Catherine's orders, sir. Until the period of mourning is over she wants nothing touched inside the room without her permission."

"And when will that be?"

Parsons found Catherine's adherence to a strict routine and punctilious protocol exasperating. And, for the life of him, he could see no reason for it in this case.

"Blessed if I know, sir. Whenever her ladyship sees fit I suppose."

"Well, Johnson, whether she sees fit or not I need to go into that room now, so will you please give me the key."

Johnson shook his head.

"I don't have it, sir. Lady Catherine took it from me when the undertakers arrived with his lordship's casket. That

365

would be the day before yesterday, sir. She said she wanted to spend some time with her father before they buried him. Quite emotional she was, sir. I have to say I was surprised to see her like that. She said if anyone wanted to go into the room they would have to ask her permission."

"Do you remember what time of the day it was when she asked for the key?"

"I couldn't say exactly, sir. It was sometime in the morning."

"And was the door locked before then?"

"No, sir, it wasn't. It's been unlocked since Mrs. Williams prepared his lordship for burial."

Having hidden inside the room the night before he left Beaumont, Parsons was well aware of that. But he wasn't going to admit that to Johnson.

"Isn't there another key?"

"No, sir. Lord Quentin never wanted anyone but me to have the key to his room."

Johnson spoke with pride, as though this small matter of trust between master and servant had meant a great deal to him. And though he pretended not to notice, Parsons could see the old man brush away a tear at the memory of it.

"Then I will have to ask Lady Catherine, Johnson. Can you tell me where I can find her?"

"You might try her room, sir. She's there more often than not these past few days."

Lady Catherine was at her writing desk when she bade Parsons enter her room. Although it was adjacent to Annabelle's, in style and taste it could not have been more different. There were no soft furnishings in the room and no visible feminine touches. Catherine's room had more in common with the bachelor quarters.

"Well, inspector. What can I do for you?" she asked, clearly none too pleased to see him.

Although the strain of burying her father and bearing the responsibility for the funeral had taken some of the edge of authority from her voice, it still remained as cold and un-friendly as ever; and Parsons could only admire the perse-verance of her former lovers for maintaining their ardor in the face of such obvious frigidity. But it was surprising what effect the prospect of a title and wealth could have on the patience of penniless bachelors.

"I was hoping you could tell me a little more about the theft of your money box, Lady Catherine. I'd like to know where you kept it and when you first noticed it was missing."

"You know perfectly well when I discovered it missing, inspector. I seem to remember you were having breakfast at the time."

"You will excuse me for saying, your ladyship, but that was when you reported it missing. That is not quite what I asked. When did you first notice it was missing?"

She gave him the frosty look of one whose authority is not normally questioned.

"I noticed it had gone just before breakfast, inspector, if that makes you happier. I had opened the drawer of my dressing table to look for something when I noticed the box was missing."

As she spoke she indicated a plain walnut dressing table in the corner of the room.

"May I look, your ladyship?" asked Parsons politely as he walked across the room.

"If you must, inspector," she replied.

The drawer contained only a few items: some hair combs, a box of hair pins, and some jewelry.

"I notice the drawer has no key," Parsons commented.

"As you can see, inspector, there is nothing of much worth inside," she replied.

"But there was, your ladyship. Did you not say at breakfast on the day you reported the box missing that it contained over two hundred and fifty pounds. To many people that would represent a considerable sum of money."

She bridled visibly at Parsons' reprimand. But she said nothing.

"And what of these? Surely they have some value as well."

He held up a pair of pearl ear-rings and a matching necklace.

"Did you not think that these and the money might prove a temptation for the servants?" he said accusingly.

She gave him another frosty glare.

"Even if they did, inspector, I use this drawer every day. Had the box or anything else been taken I would notice at once. As in fact I did. Whoever stole the money did not go unnoticed. And in this instance it was clear that it was the girl Dunne."

"Then how can you account for it being in Captain Ashton's saddle bag?"

"I'm sure I have no idea, inspector," she said dismissively. "Perhaps I was wrong about Dunne after all. Maybe one of the other girls was involved. O'Brien, for instance. I believe she shares a room with Dunne. Maybe they were both involved. Even Smith. I really don't know anymore."

A note of hysteria had crept almost imperceptibly into her voice, as it had on the morning Dunne and the money were reported missing; but on this occasion, somewhat to Parsons' disappointment, she managed to control her emotions. Had she lost her grip he might have learned a lot more.

"Judging by the state of the box when it was found," he continued, "it had not been necessary to force the lid open. So I assume it was not locked when it was in your drawer."

"Of course it was locked, inspector," she snapped. "Do you think I'd be so foolish as to leave an unlocked money box in my drawer for any of those girls to help themselves."

"It would indeed be foolish, your ladyship. On the other hand the box was unlocked when it was found. Can you explain that?"

It was clear to Parsons that she was unhappy with the direction that the questioning was taking. But her hostility was tempered by a touch of anxiety.

"I can't explain it, inspector," she conceded. "But it wasn't a very strong box, and surely there are other ways it might have been opened other than by using a key. You must know about these things, you're dealing with criminals all the time."

"You're quite right, Lady Catherine. Any thief worthy of his name would find such a box easy to open."

Catherine looked visibly relieved to hear that.

"Where is the key normally kept?" asked Parsons. "Do you carry it with you?"

"I do, inspector. The key always stays in my possession."

She shook the chatelaine on her belt, to which were attached a bunch of keys and a watch.

"I have the key to the box here and the keys for my room and the silver store."

"And your father's room?"

"Yes. I have that key also, if you must know. Who told you?"

"Johnson. I'd assumed that he would be responsible for all the keys in the castle, so I asked him for it."

"And why do you want it, inspector? Surely you've already seen all you want in that room. Have you no respect for the dead?"

"I mean no disrespect for your dead father, Lady Catherine. But I've a very good reason for wanting to see inside the room again."

"And pray what is that?"

"That, your ladyship, is my business. But I've no objection to you accompanying me if that will set your mind at rest."

She made little attempt to disguise her anger at his refusal to buckle under her authority. But she could do little to deter him, and his suggestion that she accompany him left her with no reasonable grounds for further objections.

"Very well, inspector," she said with a resigned expression. "It seems you give me little choice."

The room was very much as Parsons remembered it, with two very obvious exceptions. There was no rug in front of the fireplace and the portrait of Lady Annabelle was no longer hanging above it.

"Did you not approve of your step-mother's portrait being here?" he asked innocently as he strolled across the room to the two north-facing windows over-looking the stables.

"It had no right to be here," she replied, somewhat taken aback to hear Annabelle referred to as her step-mother. "She had ceased to be his wife in all but name many years ago. It was only an embarrassment to have it here."

Lady Catherine stayed near the door, but she followed Parsons' every movement closely.

"And where is it now?"

"The portrait? How should I know?" she replied impatiently. "I told Johnson to remove it, so I imagine he's put it in one of the store rooms on the second floor."

Her irritation gave way to curiosity as she watched him open one of the windows and look out. He looked upwards to the second floor and then down to the ground. Then he carefully examined the bottom of the window frame and the adjacent stone-work before closing the window and moving across to the second window.

"Is that somewhere you go often?"

"The second floor? Good heavens, inspector, why ever should I? There are only the servants' sleeping quarters there and a few dusty rooms full of old furniture."

Parsons opened the other window and looked down at the ground again, this time for much longer than before.

Then he looked upwards to the floor above, and as before, examined the window frame and the stone-work outside the window. Seemingly satisfied, he closed the window and dusted his hands.

"Is it true that you allow no other male servants into the castle other than Johnson?"

"That's perfectly true, inspector. An exception is made at meal times. We allow male servants into the kitchen for their meals. But it was always one of father's rules to forbid them to enter other parts of the castle. He said there were too many temptations."

"By that I imagine he meant the women servants, rather than the family silver," he said, amused by her struggle to control her temper at his blatant impertinence.

She nodded, words seemingly to fail her.

"Do you remember me telling Colonel Howard that I thought an unauthorized person was using one of the rooms on the second floor?"

"I remember vaguely, inspector. But you may recall I was rather upset at the time."

Parsons nodded sympathetically.

"Have you any idea who that might be?"

"I can only imagine that it was Smith," she said. "He's been getting far above himself these past months. And you can see where that has led."

"Indeed, Lady Catherine, I can," he said, slowly walking around the room. He examined the paintings and the books in the bookcase; then he opened the doors leading into the closet and the dressing room, and then closed them again. Finally he turned to face an increasingly impatient Catherine.

"I think I'll leave you now," she said. "The key is in the door. You can return it later when you've finished."

She had her hand on the door-handle when she spoke.

"Did the late Lord Paul go to your room often?" he asked.

For a moment she froze. Then she turned towards him with her eyes blazing with fury.

"How dare you, Inspector Parsons! How dare you! Charles was right. You're an impatient, vulgar young man!"

Parsons was quite unmoved by the outburst.

Merely servants' gossip, your ladyship," he said calmly. "But in my profession I can't afford to ignore gossip no matter what its source."

She hovered near the door, uncertain of whether to leave or remain to hear what else he had learned about her from the servants. Parsons sensed her dilemma and quietly enjoyed her predicament.

"So would I be correct in thinking that Lord Paul visited your room the night before he died? The night your money was stolen, and the night before you appeared at breakfast in such a disturbed condition."

For a moment Parsons thought she was going to strike him. She took a pace or two into the room and raised her hands towards him, with her nails spread like talons ready to tear at his face. Then, realizing what she was doing, she stopped and glared at him, her breast rising and falling rapidly as she struggled to control her temper.

"Have you nothing further to say, your ladyship?" he asked quietly, after several minutes.

"Only this, inspector. You'll regret ever speaking to me in that manner. I can promise you that."

Then she stormed out of the room, slamming the door behind her.

The noise reverberated through the room, rattling the windows and causing a ripple to run through the heavy drapes used to cover the bed. It was only a small movement, but it was enough to catch Parsons' eye, and it drew his attention to the unusual position of these drapes. Those on the side nearest the door had been drawn up towards the head of the bed, whereas those on the opposite side had been drawn down towards the foot. In normal circumstances, he imagined that both drapes would be drawn to the foot of the bed, so as not to obstruct anyone getting into the bed. His curiosity roused he raised the bedspread and peered under the bed.

It was not easy to see clearly, but there appeared to be a bulky object on the floor roughly mid-way under the bed. Much to his irritation it was just beyond his reach. It would mean crawling under the bed, an undignified action for a man of his stature. Nevertheless, it had to be done, and grunting with displeasure he wriggled along the floor with one arm out-stretched in front of him. His fingers finally came into contact with what felt like a rug, and with some difficulty he crawled backwards dragging it with him. He was right. It was an Axminster rug similar to the one in front of the fireplace in his own room. It had been rolled up, presumably in order to make it easier to push under the bed. Could this be the rug missing from Ashton's room?

Slowly and carefully Parsons unrolled the Axminster to reveal a brown candle-wick bedspread wrapped around a hard, thin object about three feet in length. There were dark stains on both the rug and the bedspread. With mounting excitement he unwrapped the bedspread to find that the thin object was a poker with a heavy brass handle. There were also dark stains on the handle.

Using his small magnifying glass Parsons examined the rug inch by inch. Near one of the edges he found two hair-pins caught up in the woolen strands of the rug. O'Brien's most likely, he thought. Evidence of her last night of passion with Ashton. But the poker, the bedspread and the rug itself and the accompanying dark stains were evidence of a passion of a far more sinister kind.

Parsons' elation was interrupted by the sound of someone knocking at the door. Outside in the corridor Brown and a young policeman Parsons did not recognize were waiting.

"Excuse me, sir," said Brown. "Cooper 'ere's just come from Petersfield with a note for Colonel Howard from Inspector Marsden. In the circumstances I thought it were best he spoke to thee first."

"You did right, Sergeant Brown," said Parsons, pleased at this display of initiative.

"Colonel Howard is still much too weak to be disturbed," he explained to the young constable, "but you may leave the note with me and rest assured I will inform the colonel of its contents in due course."

Cooper was confused. He had been given strict instructions before he left Petersfield to report only to the Chief Constable. But the authority in the young inspector's voice and the familiar figure of Sergeant Brown persuaded him he should do otherwise. As a relatively junior officer he felt in no position to insist on seeing the colonel, but he also had no wish to return to Petersfield without discharging his responsibility. So after the briefest of deliberations he handed Parsons the envelope.

The note inside was a model of brevity.

'Colonel Howard,' it said, *'Claire Dunne, the Irish servant, has been apprehended and is being held in the cells at Petersfield. Request you advise on further action. Inspector Marsden'*

Parsons had been planning to visit Petersfield to question Brendan Dunne. Now, with his sister also in custody, it was essential that he went as soon as possible.

"How did you get here, Cooper?" he asked.

"In a trap, sir."

"And how long did that take?"

"About two hours."

Parsons consulted his watch. It was ten to four. If he intended going to Petersfield he had several options. He could return with Cooper, or Brown or one of the other constables could drive him. Both would take longer than he would have wished. And if he went with Cooper he ran the risk of being stranded in Petersfield. The only alternative was to ride over himself on one of the horses. It was not an option he would normally have favored, as he was far from comfortable on horseback. But it was quicker than going by trap, and if the light held it had the added advantage of allowing him to see something of the surrounding countryside on the way back. Like Montgomery, he was ignorant of the area beyond the castle and the village.

"I'm riding over to Petersfield, Brown," he announced. "You're in charge while I'm away. If Colonel Howard asks what's happening you must, of course, tell him; but I'd prefer it if you kept out of his way. I'll bring him up to date with what's happening when I return."

He gave Brown a wink.

"What's far more important is for you to ask Johnson for one of Mrs. Hughes' special late suppers for when I return."

Parsons handed the keys of both Lord Quentin's room and his own to Brown. Then he pointed to the rug and its contents.

"Take these to my room and put them in my wardrobe. Lock Lord Quentin's room when you leave and lock mine as well. No one but you is to have either key. No one. And that includes Lady Catherine, Colonel Howard and anyone else. Is that clear?"

Brown nodded his head gloomily. He was never one to relish the prospect of an argument with authority.

"Don't look so solemn, Brown," said Parsons. We're making great progress. Unless I'm mistaken we've found the weapon with which Captain Ashton was bludgeoned to death."

-42-

The police station in Petersfield was a detached white-washed two-storey building in the High Street with a neat row of stables at the rear. Leaving his horse tethered to a post at the side of the building, Parsons returned to the front and climbed the three stone steps to the heavy black double-doors with their gleaming brass handles. The doors opened directly onto a large room, with bare walls painted as white as the building itself. A single wood bench standing against one of the walls was the only artifact in this room apart from a highly-polished brass bell that had been placed precisely in the center of a long counter. Parsons had never been inside a military guard-room, but he could imagine it would be very similar to this. The room spoke volumes about the manner in which Colonel Howard ran his force.

His footsteps reverberated on the waxed wooden floor-boards, and as he approached the counter he could see his own distorted and inverted image in the lustrous surface of the bell. But before he had time to grasp the handle and summon attention an elderly sergeant with large bushy whiskers appeared from a room at the back of the building.

"Good afternoon, sir. May I help you?" he asked, in a gruff unfriendly manner.

Parsons introduced himself and informed the desk sergeant that he wished to speak with Inspector Marsden. For a moment it appeared the sergeant was going to ask Parsons for some form of identification, but then he decided against it. There was a determined look in the young man's eyes that was an adequate credential.

"Yes, sir. Very good, sir," he said. "Will you please follow me."

He led Parsons along a corridor as empty and inhospitable as the room they had left, their footsteps on the bare floor giving due warning of their approach to anyone working in the rooms on either side. It was impossible to see how many that might have been as all the doors were closed.

Inspector Marsden's office was the last room in the corridor. There could be no doubting it was his, as there was a large brass plaque on the door bearing his name.

The sergeant knocked twice before a thin, lisping voice from within bade them enter.

The voice made a perfect match for the small weasel-faced man with thinning hair and a waxed moustache who sat stiffly behind a solitary desk. The desk itself had been positioned exactly mid-way along the wall opposite the door, with a single chair set to one side of it. What few items of stationery there were had been arranged with strict geometrical symmetry relative to the four straight sides of the desk. There was little in the way of paper-work to suggest that the inspector was busy, but he nevertheless managed to convey to a casual observer that he was a man dealing with matters of great importance.

An attempt to reinforce this sense of importance had been made by hanging a group photograph of the Petersfield police contingent on the wall directly above Marsden's head. Seated in a prominent central position in the photograph Marsden's face exhibited an identical expression of smug self-esteem to that which he now wore.

Parsons introduced himself again, and waited in vain for Marsden to offer him the hospitality of a seat.

"Well, Inspector Parsons, what can I do for you," he lisped, in a tone that managed to make the few words sound as unhelpful and unfriendly as possible.

"Colonel Howard sends his compliments, Inspector Marsden," said Parsons, clenching his fists tightly together behind his back, "and sends his congratulations on your success in capturing the girl. He say's you're to keep her here until you hear further from him, but in the meantime he wants me to interview both her and her brother."

"I see," replied Marsden, clearly pleased to hear his superior's praise, but less happy to allow Parsons access to his prisoners. "And may I see that request in writing."

Parsons had been half-expecting a bureaucratic response similar to this. Quite clearly the news that he had been given sole control of the investigation had not filtered down to Marsden. There was only one way to handle people like him, and that was to adopt the same tone as he had used with the young constable, Cooper.

"I don't know how acquainted you are with the nature of Colonel Howard's wound," he said. "He is making good progress but is still seriously incapacitated, and his condition is such that he finds difficulty in writing. That's why he asked me to interrupt what I was doing at Beaumont and come here with his message. I don't know whether you are truly aware who I am, but I have the authority of no less a person than the Commissioner of Police in London. I should not have to remind you of the importance of this investigation and the need for a rapid and successful outcome. We are, after all, dealing with the murder of two members of the aristocracy and a senior army officer, and the wounding of your own Chief Constable. So please stop procrastinating and allow me to do what I have been asked, so that I can report back to the Chief Constable before nightfall."

Behind him Parsons could hear a sharp intake of breath and the embarrassed shuffle of the desk sergeant's feet. Marsden turned even paler at the shock of being reprimanded in such a manner in front of one of his men. He glared at Parsons for a few moments and then nodded his head towards his sergeant.

"Take the inspector down to the damned Irish, Edmunds, if that's what he wants."

Marsden tried to sound dismissive, in an unsuccessful attempt to regain some of his damaged authority. But a glance at Edmunds was enough to tell Parsons that that authority was already seriously dented. Although the sergeant made a great pretense at stroking his expansive whiskers, it was clear to both inspectors that he was doing his best to hide a grin.

"You'll learn precious little from them I can tell you, inspector," Marsden shouted, as Parsons followed Edmunds out of the room. "The boy's guilty without shadow of doubt and the girl does nothing but cry."

-43-

A flight of well-worn stone steps led below ground level to a narrow corridor that was lit by an oil lamp at each end. Along each side of the corridor were six solid oak doors, each with a small grill at eye-level. Only two of the doors were closed; one near the bottom of the steps, on Parsons' left, and another at the far end of the corridor on the opposite side. It appeared that the Dunnes were the only prisoners, and that they were being kept as far apart as possible to prevent them from communicating.

"I'll see the girl first, Sergeant Edmunds," said Parsons, holding out his hand. "You can trust me with the keys. I won't steal them."

The fastidious cleanliness of the other parts of the prison did not extend to the cellar. Here the uneven earth floors were cold underfoot, the walls damp, and there was a strong smell of human excrement. The sergeant handed over the keys with alacrity. He required little prompting to leave the unsavory atmosphere below ground for the relative comfort of his room upstairs.

"She's the one at the far end of the corridor, sir," he said.

Then he left Parsons and went back upstairs.

Parsons took the lamp nearest him and walked slowly along the corridor until he came to the last door on the right. After spending some time finding the right key from the heavy bunch he had been given, he opened the door and entered Claire Dunne's cell. Frightened by the noise and blinded by the unaccustomed light, the girl struggled anxiously to her feet.

"It's me, Claire. Inspector Parsons," he said, with what he hoped was a reassuring voice. "Don't be afraid."

He barely recognized the young girl. Her hair was wild and unkempt and it appeared only her tears had cleansed the dirt from a face that it now seemed had grown prematurely old. Beneath the dirt her face showed signs of bruising. She was still wearing the same simple print dress she had worn on her last night at Beaumont, but it was now torn and spattered with mud

Apart from a coarse straw mattress, a wooden stool and the galvanized bucket that served as her privy, the room was bare. It was a frightening enough place for a hardened criminal, let alone a defenseless young girl. There was no natural light nor had she been provided with what small comfort of a candle. In normal circumstances only the feeble tendrils of light from the oil lamp seeped under the door and through the small grill.

Parsons picked up the stool and positioned it near the dirty mattress. He placed the lamp on the floor by the side of the stool furthest from the mattress, enabling him to use its light to make his notes, but preventing it from drawing undue attention to her distressed and disheveled appearance.

"It's important we have a little talk, Claire," he said soothingly, trying to dispel the look of fear he could see in her eyes. "I want you to tell me everything that has happened since we last met, and I want to know why you ran away."

The wretched girl sat on her straw bed, her arms folded around her legs and her chin on her knees. For several minutes she said nothing and gazed blankly at the door. The silence worried Parsons, and he feared that the tenuous bond of trust he had previously established with her had been destroyed by the rough treatment she had received from her captors. But, to his relief, she began talking.

"I'd already made up my mind to run away before you ever came into the kitchen that night, sir," she explained wearily. "Everything seemed hopeless. I was desperate sure enough, sir, and there was no one in the blessed world I could be turning to for help. But when you came into the room didn't I almost change my mind and tell you my problems. You had seemed such a kind gentleman when we had first spoken, and I thought the Blessed Virgin might have sent you in answer to my prayers. But didn't I know I was being foolish. What could you be doing to help me? Weren't you just another policeman like the rest of them."

It seemed to Parsons that her position that night had been no more desperate than that of the other girls. Admittedly her brother had been arrested on the charge of murder. But that, in itself, was no reason to run away. That would only make things worse for her when she was eventually captured. Unless, of course, she did have something to hide.

"What of the other girls?" he asked. "Aren't they your friends? Couldn't you turn to them for help?"

"They're all sweet girls, to be sure; and don't I love them all dearly. We're very close to one another at Beaumont, and b'Jaysus we need to be. But there's not much any of us can do against the likes of Colonel Howard. Sure, who'd be taking the side of poor Irish girls like us against a fine English gentleman like him. Look at what happened to poor Brendan. Not in a million years would that sweet boy ever do the terrible thing he's accused of. But aren't all these policeman convinced of his guilt, and that's the end of it. He'll hang to be sure, and not a single Englishman will shed a tear."

Her voice choked at that prospect, but she had wept so much since her capture that she had no more tears to shed.

"Don't be too sure about that, Claire," Parsons said reassuringly. "Not everyone believes your brother is guilty. I don't for one; and I'm determined to do all I can to see he doesn't hang."

She looked at him in disbelief, thinking that this was just another policeman's trick. Yet, although he was asking her questions like the others he was not rough with her. There saw something in his sensitive, intelligent face that offered her a faint glimmer of hope. Perhaps she could trust him. She reached out and grasped his arm, and even through the thickness of his jacket and outer coat he could sense the desperation in her grip.

"Bless you for saying that, sir," she said, trying to smile in spite of her misery. "B'Jaysus, if only there were more like you."

Parsons patted her hand.

"You still haven't told me why you ran away, Claire," he said quietly. "Surely you realized that would do nothing to help your brother and might even implicate you in Lord Quentin's murder."

"I know, sir," she said sadly, turning her face away so that he could barely hear what she was saying. "But with his lordship dead wasn't I even more than ever at the mercy of that wicked man, Smith. With Brendan gone wasn't I even more defenseless. Though God knows what my poor Brendan could do to help me. Wasn't Smith already beating the living daylights out of the poor wee boy?"

"What has Smith to do with all this?" asked Parsons in surprise. It seemed Smith was involved whichever way he turned.

"More than anyone else ever knew, sir. Didn't he have his eye on me from the first day I arrived at Beaumont. And didn't he threaten me that if I didn't give him what he wanted it would be all the worse for Brendan. He was a divil to be sure. He made a point of showing me what he could do every once in a while by beating my poor brother black and blue."

Parsons recalled what Philip had told him and remembered the bruises on the groom's face that first afternoon at Beaumont.

"And you let Smith have what he wanted?"

There was a small sad movement of her head in acknowledgement.

"When did this happen?"

"Sure, it had been going on for many weeks before you arrived, sir. Maybe once or twice a week when no one else was around he would let me know he'd be wanting me that night. Then after he'd been drinking in the village he'd wait for me in one of the empty rooms on the servants' floor. I always had to fetch him some food and drink. Sure, the man had a rare hunger."

She paused again, seemingly ashamed of what had happened to her, and in some foolish way holding herself to blame.

"There was a makeshift bed in one of the rooms, sir," she explained.

"I know, Claire. I've seen it," he said gently. "But at the time I didn't know its purpose."

Parsons tried to hide the rage that was now boiling up inside him. Was there no limit to the depths to which Smith could sink!

"Was that your first time with a man, Claire?" he asked, barely trusting himself to speak.

She nodded, and he shuddered at the thought of the innocent girl being forced to submit against her will to the demands of a man like Smith.

"But didn't you tell anyone?" he asked, aware of the sound of despair in his own voice. "Johnson or Mrs Hughes, for instance. Couldn't they inform someone in the family who might be able to help you? Surely even Lord Quentin might object to Smith taking advantage of what, you'll excuse me saying, he considered to be rightfully his?"

Parsons regretted his words as soon as they were spoken.

"I couldn't sir," she cried, tears once more pouring down her cheeks. "I was too ashamed. I couldn't tell a soul."

"Not even Brendan."

"Especially Brendan, sir. Sure, if Brendan knew what was happening wouldn't he try and kill the man. And wouldn't that only have made matters worse. If he failed, Smith would've half killed him. And if he'd succeeded wouldn't the police have hanged him. Just like they're going to do now!"

The note of shame and self-pity in her voice turned to despair, and her pitiful small body shook with loud sobs.

"Don't you see how helpless it was, sir?' she wailed. "Sure there was no other way out for me."

"But where were you going?" Parsons asked. "I don't imagine you had any friends in England, and even if you'd got as far as Ireland the authorities there would soon have found you."

"Didn't I know all that, sir," she howled. "But you must see how desperate I was. There was only Uncle Kevin left. He knew what was going on between Lord Quentin and us girls, and he always said if any of us needed help we could go to him."

"Who in Heaven's name is Uncle Kevin?" asked Parsons in amazement. The presence nearby of any relatives of the Dunnes was the last thing he'd been expecting. And why, if he existed, had the other girls never mentioned this man before.

Claire could see how this revelation had surprised Parsons.

"Sure, he's not really my uncle, sir," she explained. "It's just what we girls like to call him. He's just a harmless old Irishman with a wee red beard who comes to the castle once in a while looking for work. Not that he ever gets much, and then only the dirty jobs that no one else will do. But that doesn't stop him coming. Nor does being called a dirty Irish tinker by the likes of Mr Johnson. He's well used to that by now, like the rest of us."

"Where does this Uncle Kevin live?" Parsons asked, still aggrieved that he had not been told before about his existence.

"Wherever he can, sir. He and his people are always moving around looking for any casual work they can find. They set up their wee benders on the common land outside the villages. But there's precious little work for them these days, and more often the village people drive them away."

"What do you mean by their 'benders'?" asked Parsons, unsure now where this was leading.

"Their tents, sir," Claire said, surprised by his ignorance of what for her was a common expression. "Have you never seen them? Well you should go to Ireland. You'll see plenty of them there. The people there use them when they're moving from place to place, or when they've no proper home to live in. They just stick the ends of long sticks in the ground, bend them over to form a wee hoop and drape their tarpaulins over them. That's where they sleep."

"But if Uncle Kevin is always moving around, how did you know where to find him?"

"It was something he said when he was last at Beaumont, sir. That would be the week before you came. They'd found a good spot just north of Midhurst, he said, and he hoped they'd be staying there a wee while. Sure, he said we'd be welcome there anytime. It was really a joke, sir. We only get but one free day each month and none of us would ever dream of spending it walking all that way to Midhurst, even to be with our own people."

"Is that where the police found you?"

"Aye, sir."

"Was that why you stole food from the castle before you left, Claire? Was it to give to your friends?"

For the first time Parsons saw signs of her former spirit.

"And what if I did, sir. What's a few crusts of bread, some cheese and some cold meat to the de Courceys. Nothing but scraps."

"But what about the money?"

He studied her face carefully. Judging by her puzzled expression she had no idea what he was talking about.

"What money is that, sir?" she said indignantly. "Sure I took no money. Who's been spreading such lies about me?"

"Money was stolen from Miss Catherine's room on the night you left. In the circumstances some people concluded that you were the thief."

"I swear to God I know nothing about Miss Catherine's money, sir. B'Jaysus," she said, almost to herself, "don't they have us for thieves now."

"I know you didn't take the money, Claire," said Parsons reassuringly, "and I believe you've committed no other crime. I can't promise you anything now, but I'll do my best to see you released from here as soon as possible. That won't be for a day or two. For the moment you'll just have to be brave."

Parsons looked around at the grim surroundings.

"I hope no one's mistreating you," he said.

She shook her head.

"In that case, I'll leave you now and go and speak to Brendan."

"Give him my love, sir," she said, as he stood at the door of her cell.

"I will, Claire," he said softly, and as he locked her cell he found he had tears in his eyes.

-44-

Brendan Dunne was lying on his back on a straw mattress when Parsons entered his cell. In such a twilight world as he and his sister shared there was little else to do.

"Claire is well and sends her love, Brendan," Parsons said, hoping that as the conveyer of such good wishes he would at least get the groom's attention.

Parsons was only too aware that in Brendan Dunne's mind he would still be associated with Colonel Howard and the beating he had received in Lord Quentin's room. It was unlikely those memories would have faded during his time in prison, as even under the accumulated grime Parsons' lamp revealed fresh bruising on the boy's face.

But Parsons had stuck the right chord. The effect upon the groom of the mention of his sister's name was dramatic. His surly defiant look disappeared and was replaced by one of concern.

"You've seen her," he asked anxiously. "How is she? Are they ill-treating her?"

393

"She's as well as can be expected," said Parsons. "And she's worried about you. But I've told her I'll do all I can to help you both."

Dunne looked at him with even greater suspicion than his sister had done but a short time before.

"You're a policeman, aren't you," he said sourly. "What help can you be to the likes of us?"

"We'll come to that later," said Parsons. "But first I'd like to know more about you and your family back in Ireland. Apart from Claire, do you have any other brothers and sisters?"

The question surprised Dunne. No other policeman had been interested in his family, other than to imply that they were all filthy Fenians. Although this might be a trick, he thought, there was nothing to be lost in humoring the inspector.

"I did once, sir," Dunne answered bitterly. "There were so many of them I almost lost count. My poor mother, God rest her soul, was pregnant all the blessed time; thanks to that drunken brute of a husband of hers. None of them lived except Claire and me. And in the end it was the death of my mother."

The more Parsons listened to the sad tales of the Irish, the more he comprehended their frustration and bitterness. He had no qualms about sending Fenian murderers to the gallows, but some of the things he recently learned about the Irish helped him to understand how it was they had acquired their fanatical zeal.

"How old were you when your mother died?" he asked.

"Twelve, sir."

"So who brought the two of you up?"

"My Aunt Claire. She's my mother's only sister. That's where my sister got her name."

"It seems you were very close to your mother."

"She was a living saint, sir, and that's God's truth. Didn't everyone say so. Always scrimping and saving and going without to feed Claire and me, and all the time living in fear of what my daddy would do in his drunken rages. B'Jaysus, many's the time she's stood between me and a good thrashing."

The boy paused, lost for a moment in the dreadful memories of his childhood. For his part, Parsons pondered the story that was unfolding. He had heard a similar one not long ago.

"The punches and the bairns finally wore my poor mother down. She couldn't take any more. Just two days before her thirty-first birthday she died, and her last words to me were to beg me to look after my sister. And didn't my daddy—the wicked man who put her in the ground—cry like a baby. As though it had nothing to do with him. B'Jaysus, if the drink hadn't killed him, sure wouldn't I have done so myself. That I would."

They were strong words, thought Parsons, and similar to those he had heard before from both O'Brien and Philip.

"It seems you've little time for your fellow countrymen," said Parsons.

"There's good and bad in us all, sir. But there's very little good in a drunken Irishman, and that's God's truth."

In spite of being born hundreds of miles apart and in very different worlds, the similarity between the lives of Philip de Courcey and Brendan Dunne were remarkable. Both had brutal fathers, and their adored mothers had died tragically young; leaving them to grow up in a harsh world in which there was little affection. Strange though it might seem there was probably more love in Brendan's deprived world than in Philip's world of privilege. But it was easy to see why a bond between the two could have grown so quickly.

"I had a long conversation with Philip the day after his father's death," Parsons explained, "so I know about your friendship."

The grieved expression on Brendan's face that had accompanied the story of his mother's tragic life abruptly changed to one of uncertainty.

"I'm sure I don't have to tell you that you are both committing a criminal offense," said Parsons. "But it's one I'm prepared to overlook for the time being. My enquiries concern matters that are far more serious. However, if what Philip has told me is true, and you were with him that night, it would be impossible for you to have murdered Lord Quentin. I'm inclined to believe him, but I still want to hear your account of what happened."

At first Dunne had stared at Parsons in disbelief. But by the time he had finished speaking his expression had turned to one of hope.

"Sweet Jaysus," he murmured to himself. "So Philip cares enough for me to risk prison."

Parsons knew better than that. Prison was one thing that Philip did not intend to risk.

"You can think about that after I've gone," he said, "but I'm still waiting to hear your version of what happened. You can start by telling me what time you entered the castle, and where Smith was at the time."

"It was late when I went in, sir. Just after one. Wasn't Philip always warning me to be careful about being seen, and wasn't I extra careful knowing there was a dinner taking place and that extra people were staying for the night. Smith was asleep. He'd been down to the village that evening and the man had got himself drunk as usual. Sure, I could hear him snoring up in the loft while I was watching the windows up in the castle."

"Why did you do that? Surely all the curtains were drawn."

"It's always possible to see wee chinks of light through the curtains, sir. Especially when it's dark outside."

"That's interesting," murmured Parsons, as much to himself as to Dunne. "But why were you doing that in the first place?"

"So's I know who's awake, sir, and when it's safe to go inside."

"Which rooms can you see from the stables?"

"I could see Lord Quentin's room and the four other rooms on the first floor, and the girls' rooms on the floor above."

"Now I want you to think carefully, Brendan. This is very important. Can you remember in which rooms you could see lights, and then the order in which these lights went out."

Dunne thought for several minutes before answering.

"It's difficult to be certain after all this time, sir. But I'll do my best. As I remember, the light in the room furthest from Lord Quentin went out first. Then the one at the other end. Not Lord Quentin's, but the room next to his."

That would account for Robertson, thought Parsons. He was the first along that corridor to go to bed. Fitzherbert would have been much later, and it would not have been until around midnight that Sweeney had gone to his room and had extinguished his lamp when she found him in such a state.

"There was a light in Lord Quentin's room well after that," explained Dunne. "I knew my sister was there. Hadn't Smith taken pleasure for days in telling me it was going to be her night with Lord Quentin. 'He always breaks in the new girls' he had said. How I hated him for telling me that!"

He looked towards Parsons in desperation.

"I remember praying to God all the time that she was with him that it wouldn't be long and hoping he wasn't hurting her. I felt so helpless. And all the while I kept hearing my mother's dying words: 'Look after Claire. Look after your sister. Keep her away from men like your father.'"

Dunne put his hands over his ears in an attempt to shut out the memory of his mother's voice. For a while he was silent.

"So I was pleased when I saw the light in Claire's room," he said at last.

"What time was that?"

"I can't remember exactly, sir, but it was before one. I went inside myself at one."

"How could you be sure of the exact time? Do you have a watch?"

"I don't have one of my own, but Philip gave me one of his. He said if anyone ever found me with it I was to say he'd lent it to me. Otherwise, wouldn't they be accusing me of stealing."

Parsons nodded.

"I understand," he said. "But how could you be sure it was your sister? How do you know it wasn't O'Brien going to bed? Doesn't she share the room with Claire?"

"Because Claire waved her candle in the window, sir. Sure, she waves to me every night. When it's summer we can see one another. But it's too dark at this time of the year, so she waves a candle once or twice. Then I light my candle and wave back."

Parsons found the idea of the brother and sister waving to each other in the darkness very moving, and he could only imagine the loneliness and affection that lay behind such a simple act.

"What about the other servants' rooms? From what you could see had any of the other girls gone to bed before you went into the castle?"

"I'd seen a light in Dwyer and Sweeney's room and then one in O'Mahoney and O'Halloran's. But that was before I saw Claire's."

"What about the first floor?"

"There were still lights in two of the rooms, sir. Lord Quentin's room was in darkness. But I thought I'd waited long enough by then. So I went into the castle."

So Ashton and Montgomery were still awake at one, thought Parsons. Or at least there were lights in their rooms. But what of Lord Quentin? Was he murdered before one, in the time after Claire left his room and some time before one o'clock, or did the murderer return later?

"Which way did you go into the castle, Brendan?"

"Through the scullery, sir. The door there's always left open for anyone working outside late to get themselves a bite to eat. Then I went up the back stairs to the first floor and along the corridor past Miss Catherine's and Lady Annabelle's rooms to Philip's."

"Did you see anybody or hear anything?"

"Lady Annabelle's room was dark, but there was a light under Miss Catherine's door. I thought that was unusual. From what I know she was normally in bed early. But I suppose with the dinner and everything she was later that night."

"What about the room between Miss Catherine's and Philip's?"

"Someone was awake in there. I could see the candle-light and hear voices. I asked Philip later who they were, and he said it was his brother and his friend. Philip said they always stayed up late drinking and talking politics. As though there aren't enough politics in this blessed world."

"About what time did you leave Philip's room in the morning?"

"About five o'clock, sir. Normally that was long before anyone else was awake. But neither of us knew that Spencer would be patrolling the grounds that night."

Parsons decided to embark on a new line of questioning.

"Tell me something about Smith," he said. "From what I've heard he seems to have had a considerable degree of freedom at Beaumont to do as he pleased. It was almost as though Lord Quentin had little control over him or simply could not be bothered about what he did. Would you say that was true?"

"You're right about that, sir. Even in the short time I've been at Beaumont there's been no one trying to control him. His drinking was something fearful, and he was doing little or no work around the stables. It may be presumptuous of me, sir, but were it not for me the horses would've been sorely neglected. I know in his heart that Smith really loved the horses, sir. They were the only thing he ever had any affection for. But his drinking was getting the better of the man. I know about that, sir. Hadn't I seen it all before with my own daddy."

"So you think it likely that Smith would have been dismissed when Lord Quentin was no longer there to protect him."

"That I do, sir. Sure who in their right mind would want to employ a man like that."

"Did you ever see Smith with any large sums of money or items of value that Lord Quentin had given him?"

"Oh aye, sir. Wasn't Smith always boasting to me about that. His lordship was always giving him money and small bits and pieces of his. Like cuff-links and sometimes an old watch. Smith sold them in Petersfield. How else could he afford to be drinking the way he did."

"Did he ever show you a pair of silver hip flasks with Lord Quentin's initials engraved on them?"

"Nay, sir," said Dunne. "As far as I could see the master was careful not to give Smith anything of a personal nature like that.

Parsons decided it was time for him to leave if he was to be back at Beaumont before nightfall. His time with Dunne had confirmed much that he already knew, but it had also provided him with fresh and useful information about Smith's relationship with Lord Quentin.

"I think you've told me the truth, Brendan," he said. "Perhaps I shouldn't say this, but I believe that you are innocent. You'll have to be patient and trust me, just as I've asked Claire to be. But I'll do all I can to get you out of here as soon as possible."

And with that vague promise Parsons left, with the gratitude of the young groom echoing around him as he climbed the stone stairs.

Marsden was seated in much the same position as when Parsons had left him, and it appeared he was still working on the same duty roster.

"Well, Parsons," he said with a sneer. "How did you find the prisoners?"

"I find them innocent of any crime," Parsons replied calmly, "and intend to inform Colonel Howard accordingly. When I have his agreement I'll send word for you to release them. In the meantime I don't want you or your men man-handling them."

"I won't take your word alone for their innocence, Parsons," Marsden said defiantly. "And they won't leave here without Colonel Howard's written authority."

"Then give me a piece of paper and dictate your terms," said Parsons, by then thoroughly irritated by Marsden's bureaucratic manner.

Marsden opened one of the drawers in his desk and produced a single sheet of white paper bearing the crest of the Hampshire Constabulary. Then he dipped his pen into the ink-pot and offered it to Parsons.

"Anything you say, old boy," he lisped, and began dictating.

"I hereby authorize the release of Brendan and Claire Dunne from the custody of Inspector Marsden at Petersfield Police Station."

"Just get Colonel Howard to sign that," he said, with a humorless grin on his sallow face, "and I'll be happy to let you have those vermin downstairs."

He produced an envelope from another drawer, addressed it to Colonel Howard and handed it to Parsons.

"Put your note in there," he said. "I wouldn't want you to lose it."

The light was fading fast as Parsons left Petersfield, but with a full harvest moon to guide him he could see his way well enough. The air was fresh, the night still, and in spite of his discomfort in the saddle he began to enjoy the ride along the narrow country lanes towards Beaumont.

About a mile north of Beaumont village the lane veered away from the railway line it had been following from Petersfield and dropped down towards a lake on the north-west edge of the Great Park. All around him the outlines of the great trees stood silently silhouetted against the dark sky. At one point he reached a clearing and stopped to enjoy the tranquility of the scene and to admire the reflections of the trees in the surface of the still waters of the lake. There was such a sense of peace in the natural world that it seemed difficult to believe that the filthy prison cells in Petersfield and the scene of three gruesome murders were but a short distance away.

A small movement on the surface of the water caught his attention, at a point where a small copse jutted out into the lake. Within the shadows cast by the copse, something was astir, causing slow-moving ripples to radiate out across the surface of the lake. At first, Parsons imagined some sort of animal to be the cause, but the shape that gradually emerged from the shadows was too large to be an animal and moved with none of the effortless grace of a duck or a swan. Then to his surprise, he realized he was looking at a human head. Someone was swimming in the lake at this late hour.

There was nothing unusual in finding people swimming alone at night. But it was late in the year and the water was cold. His curiosity aroused, Parsons dismounted and led his horse quietly around the lake, keeping in the trees to conceal his movement. When he was about a hundred yards away from the swimmer he tethered the horse and continued alone.

He soon reached the edge of a small clearing close to the spot where he had seen the swimmer, and crouched down in the bushes. On the opposite side of the clearing he could see a pile of clothes and a white towel resting on the trunk of a fallen tree. This was clearly the point at which the swimmer had entered the water.

Parsons did not have long to wait. With slow powerful strokes the swimmer approached the shore and waded from the water towards the pile of clothes. Only then did he realize his mistake. This time his curiosity had got the better of him, and what he saw made him draw back further into the shadows. The swimmer was a woman, and she was naked. And as she toweled herself in the moonlight Parsons could see that her skin was as dark as the shadow in which he hid.

Cursing himself for being drawn into this potentially embarrassing position, but unable to extricate himself without attracting the woman's attention, he crouched down in the darkness and waited. Hardly daring to breathe, he nevertheless found himself hypnotized by the sight of the woman's body. He had seen few enough dark-skinned women since his childhood in India, but even there he had never seen an adult woman naked. Indian women were far too protective of their modesty to ever allow that.

In spite of his better feelings he found himself all too easily accepting the role of voyeur, admiring the firmness of the woman's limbs and the grace of her movements as she dried herself and dressed. To such an extent did this mysterious woman and the ritual of her toilet absorb his interest that he was unaware of the movement in the trees behind him, and unprepared for the heavy blow on the back of his head that precipitated his swift fall into unconsciousness.

-45-

London, 13th September 1880

*S*ergeant *Harris' horse-drawn cab drew up outside 82 Woburn* Square. He could have walked from Whitehall in half the time the cab had taken in the dense London traffic, but with the rain as it was he had little option. He disliked interviewing anyone when he was wet, especially when he was anticipating being at somewhat of a social disadvantage.

The Bloomsbury address had warned him of what he might expect, but even so the four-storey houses with their well-tended private communal gardens in the center of the square made a striking impression on him, even on a thoroughly wet and miserable September afternoon. It was a very different world from the narrow streets of back-to-back terraced houses in Mile End where he lived. But he was not one to be intimidated by external appearances, and straightening his brown bowler hat he trotted up the steps to the black front door, leaving behind him a steaming horse

406

and a rain-sodden cabby still protesting the inadequacy of the few small coins that Harris had left as a tip.

The heavy brass door-knocker in the shape of a naked woman gave an early warning of what might await him inside, which was further reinforced when his thrice-repeated knock was eventually answered by an attractive dark-haired young woman dressed in a flowing white toga. She smiled vacantly at him.

"Is Mr. Oliver Craig at home?" he asked politely, repeating the question twice more before realizing to his disgust that the girl was drunk.

"Oliver Craig!" he shouted, managing finally to extract from her a vague gesture in the direction of the stairs.

Inside, the house presented itself in quite a different fashion to its respectable Georgian exterior. Black carpets in the hall and on the stairs and dazzlingly-bright white walls, created a backdrop of startling contrast to the gold-painted moldings of cherubs and cornucopia, and the garishly-colored zodiac on the ceiling. This disconcerting color scheme was further confounded by a crimson balustrade on the stairs.

It was not at all to Harris' conservative East End tastes. Leaving the girl to rejoin her fellow revelers in one of the rooms in the back of the house, he made his way somewhat apprehensively to the first floor.

He passed several bedrooms, their doors unashamedly open to reveal states of untidiness that thoroughly offended the cleanliness-is-next-to-Godliness principles upon which Harris had been raised. Even worse, to his way of thinking, was the fact that at three-thirty in the afternoon two of the beds were still in use by occupants who seemed little ashamed of their indolence.

A man's voice drew him towards a large room in the front of the house, which he took to be the main sitting-room overlooking the square. The door was ajar, but Harris nevertheless felt obliged to knock before entering. Regardless of his politeness, the three people inside paid little heed to his entrance until he had coughed three times, each time louder than before. Only then did he manage to attract the attention of the man who was talking. This creature—as Harris was later to refer to him—wore a green velvet suit and a white silk shirt that was extravagantly ruffed at the collar and cuffs. His long blonde hair lay cradled on his shoulders with several loose strands hanging loosely across his face. As Harris entered the room the man casually removed a long cigarette-holder from his mouth and sipped languidly from his wine glass, revealing to the horrified policeman that not only were there rings on each of his fingers but also that his lips were painted red.

Dressed in a long painter's smock, a second man was engrossed in painting the third member of the group, a partially-naked red-headed woman draped in an emerald sheet. She was lying in such a position on a chaise-lounge that the light from the window accentuated every curve of her body.

Harris found his feelings equally torn between those of revulsion at the sight of the creature with the painted mouth, embarrassment at his unexpected exposure to female nudity, and disgust at seeing that the woman was smoking a cheroot.

But while he was struggling with these emotions the man in the velvet suit addressed him.

"What a divine moustache," he said, prompting Harris to self-consciously stroke the unexpected object of admiration. "Oliver, have you ever seen anything so exquisite? And such a heavenly choice in tweed. Brown is such a masterful color."

The second man interrupted his painting and regarded Harris with evident distaste.

"If you've brought a bill, leave it on the table on your way out," he said curtly, and returned to his easel.

Harris' initial surprise and confusion gave way to irritation and indignation.

"I'll have you know, gentlemen, that I'm a Metropolitan policeman," he said, mustering as much authority as he was able, and drawing his slim figure up to its full height of sixty-seven and a half inches. "The name is Detective-Sergeant Harris. And I wish to speak with Oliver Craig, whom I understand to be the owner of this house."

The painter placed his brushes on the easel.

"I'm Oliver Craig, sergeant," he said, "and this is all becoming rather tiresome. We've already had one of your uniformed colleagues here."

"And a divine young man he was," interjected the velvet suit.

"Behave yourself, Sebastian," retorted Craig. "I'm sure the sergeant has no desire to know about your penchant for policemen and their uniforms. What is it you want, Harris?"

Harris managed with an effort to turn his gaze away from Sebastian, who was alternatively winking and blowing smoke rings in his direction. He coughed once or twice more to allow himself time to regain what little composure remained and begin his questions.

"The colleague to whom you are referring has confirmed that a Mr. Geoffrey Montagu resides here with a lady-friend, Miss Caroline Mayhew. I would very much like to see their rooms."

"Rooms, my dear Oliver," chortled Sebastian. "Did you hear that. Isn't this man blissful?"

"Be quiet, Sebastian," snapped Craig. "You're becoming tiresome."

Sebastian pouted, then poured himself another glass of champagne from one of the two bottles in an ice-bucket on a table next to the easel.

"Why pray, do you wish to see their room, sergeant?" enquired Craig.

"That's my business, sir. But suffice to say there has been a murder in the house where Mr. Montagu has been staying."

"A murder? Whose?"

"Lord Quentin de Courcey, sir."

"How simply gorgeous," giggled Sebastian. "Geoffrey has executed a stuffy old lord."

"Why did you say that, sir?" demanded Harris. "And do you mind telling me your surname."

"Jefferson-ffoukes, my dear sergeant. With a hyphen and two small 'ff's.'"

Harris looked confused.

"The name is hyphenated, sergeant, and the name 'ffoukes' begins with two small 'ff's,'" explained Craig, as though he were teaching a stupid child.

"Thank you, sir," said Harris, blushing with embarrassment. "But you still haven't answered my question. Why do you think Mr. Montagu committed the murder?"

"Just my little joke, sergeant dear. The dear boy couldn't possibly do anything like that."

"Then please don't waste my time, sir," Harris said, his patience beginning to fail him.

"I'm getting cold, Ollie. If you've finished can I get dressed?"

The question came from the woman in the emerald sheet, and much to Harris' surprise she spoke with an East End accent not unlike his own.

"You're not going anywhere while the light lasts, Vicky," said Craig. "Sebastian will show you the room, sergeant. Now, if you'll excuse me I have work to do."

Craig returned his attention to his canvas and at once became oblivious to Harris' presence.

"This way, young man," purred Sebastian. "Follow me to the love-nest."

Harris followed the tall figure of Sebastian Jefferson-ffoukes at a discrete distance to the floor above and along a narrow corridor to the back of the house.

"Behold the bridal suite," Sebastian announced, standing at the open door of a room at the end of the corridor. "Not a particularly romantic view," he said, waving in the direction of the backs of the houses in adjacent Gordon Square. "But the two dears had each other, and the added compensation of having me as a neighbor."

Harris entered the room. Like others he had seen in the house it was a complete mess, with papers and articles of clothing strewn haphazardly everywhere. Two head and shoulder portraits of a young man and a young woman hung askew on one of the walls, and these he assumed to be the occupants of the room.

"Where is Miss Mayhew now?" asked Harris, pointing towards one of the portraits.

"Gone, my dear, gone. Several days before young Geoffrey took himself off to the country. A lover's tiff, I believe. But who am I to know about such things?"

He smiled suggestively at Harris.

"Would you know what the quarrel was about?" Harris asked.

"Oh, the usual boy and girl things, my dear. And money, of course."

Harris was already aware of Montagu's parlous financial position from his earlier briefing from Parsons.

"Do you know how Mr. Montagu supports himself?" he asked. "I assume he has no full-time employment."

"Geoffrey is a poet," said Sebastian theatrically. "Like all of us here he is a creative artist. That surely is employment enough for anyone."

"But how do you all manage to eat, and," Harris paused to give full effect to his next words, "clothe yourselves so magnificently."

Sebastian simpered with pleasure.

"Thank you for the compliment, my dear," he coo-ed. "Dear Oliver is very generous. And, of course, there is always papa."

"But not in the case of Mr. Montagu."

Sebastian did not at first appear to understand what Harris was referring to, but then he smiled knowingly and walked over to one of the chests of drawers. He picked up a photograph in a silver frame and flounced back to Harris.

"You are no doubt referring to Sir Jeremiah," he said, handing Harris the photograph. "What do you think of the old sod?"

Harris looked at the fierce features swathed in a mass of hair and whiskers.

"He seems a formidable gentleman," he said.

"Formidable. That's the word, my dear," said Sebastian. "Formidable. He was certainly formidable the day he came here. The shouting, my dear. You've never heard anything like it."

"He was here. When?" Harris asked in surprise.

"Just before Geoffrey went away. Oh, what a terrible argument they had. I thought I would wet myself next door."

"Did you hear what they were arguing about?"

Sebastian simpered.

"Now that would be telling, sergeant dear."

Harris advanced towards him in a threatening manner.

"Don't look so cross, my cherub," implored Sebastian. "It doesn't suit you. You're really not the masterful kind. But I'll tell you," he squealed. "I'll tell you."

He walked over to the wall where the two portraits hung.

"Do you notice anything about this divine pair that they have in common with the monster in your hand?"

Harris looked from the photograph to the paintings and back again. He shook his head.

"Nor would I, unless I had heard it with my own ears," said Sebastian. "But look at the dark widely-spaced eyes in all three of the faces. Do you see what I mean. Aren't they all gorgeous. And that isn't surprising, seeing they are all related. Believe it or not, my dear sergeant, the hairy ape in the photograph is the father of both Geoffrey and Caroline."

-46-

Ireland, 13th September 1880

"*God save us from this fecking Irish rain,*" muttered Constable Maguire through clenched teeth, as he urged his horse through the downpour along the mud-track to Westport. When Inspector Paisley had given him the task of checking a few names and addresses in Ballycara, it had seemed a great chance for a day out in the country; especially as the inspector had told him to take the chestnut mare rather than the cart.

"You'll get yourself bogged down in that country in a cart, Maguire," the inspector had said. "I know it well. You can take my horse, but by Christ I'll have your hide if she comes to any harm."

Maguire had set off from Castlebar early that morning in high spirits. The sun was warm on his back and he could smell the Atlantic salt in the fresh northerly breeze blowing into his face. It would be a rare chance to see something of the Sheeffry Hills and perhaps have a jar or two. And the locals would pay less heed to him in the village bars dressed as he was in civilian clothes instead of his Irish Constabulary uniform.

The day had not gone as planned. He had got lost several times in the bleak bog-ridden country, and it was after mid-day when he reached Ballycara. To his disgust there was nowhere there for a man to drink, and instead of getting his business done in the comfort of a bar he was forced to ride around the neighboring countryside finding the homes of those whose names appeared on the inspector's list. Not that any self-respecting Christian would ever consider living in these stinking hovels, amongst such dirty ill-mannered papists.

He was greeted everywhere with suspicion, and only by brandishing his police identity card threateningly in their faces could he persuade anyone to talk. So it was well into the afternoon before he had established that all the people on his list were indeed natives of these parts, and were all at present working for the de Courcey family over the water in England.

Without exception the mention of that name had prompted blasphemies, torrents of abuse, and showers of phlegm. Absentee English landlords were an accursed breed in this abandoned and loveless place, and he soon realized that in the eyes of these people his own status as a servant of the Crown placed him in a parlous position. So as soon as he had completed his mission he headed homeward.

The storm hit Maguire five miles short of Westport at a point where the track turned to the north. It was here he felt the full force of the gale blowing off Clew Bay, and even his thick riding cape offered scant protection against the biting wind. He strained his eyes, narrowed against the rain battering his face, for his first glimpse of the only ray of hope that lay between himself and his warm bed in Castlebar. O'Connell's Bar in Westport. If ever he had looked forward to a glass or two of stout and a few wee chasers, it was now.

"Have you come far then," asked O'Connell, as he placed the welcome glass of dark liquid on the bar in front of Maguire.

"Just riding around, admiring your beautiful land," replied Maguire, still conscious of the necessity of concealing his identity in Catholic bars. Policemen were not the most popular of God's creatures in County Mayo. The Famine may have been more than a generation ago, but the evictions of penniless tenants continued to this day; and landlord's agents and policemen had to be careful in whose company they drank.

"To be sure you've picked a fine day for it, and that's a fact," said O'Connell with a grin, nodding towards the rain-blasted window. "Now sit yourself down by the fire. I'll be putting a match to the peat and we'll soon be drying those wet clothes of yours."

And what business is it brings the law into these parts, thought Joseph O'Connell, as he busied himself with the fire.

Even without the Queen's uniform anyone could recognize a bastard Protestant policeman. Not that he was about to turn down the chance of some trade. Business had not been good lately and that was God's truth. The men in these parts had little enough money for even a jar to cheer themselves. Policemen, on the other hand, had money to spare; and with any luck this one would be hungry enough after his day in the Sheeffry Hills for a bowl of stew.

"You're a fine man, Joseph, that you are," said Maguire, as the landlord struggled to help the drunken policeman onto his horse. "I'll be back one day for another crack at your fine stew."

"You're a grand fellow yourself, John Maguire," replied O'Connell, as he gave the mare's flank a gentle pat to help it on its way. "Be sure now you keep a firm grip of your horse's head. I wouldn't want you spending the night in a wet ditch."

O'Connell had been sorry to see the rain stop, and had done his best to delay Maguire's departure by plying the policeman with the lethal combination of potheen and stout. Not that the man needed much tempting. A rare drunken fellow he had turned out to be, and not the bastard that so many policemen were. His takings for the evening were the best they had been since the American had passed through Westport a few weeks before, and O'Connell was almost ashamed of himself for spitting in Maguire's stew and short-changing him.

But it wasn't often he had the chance to get the better of a fecking Protestant, and a policeman at that.

"I think that calls for a drop of the Irish yourself, Joseph," he said, as he made his way into the bar to finish the half-empty bottle that Maguire had already paid for twice over. "It's been a rare day, that it has."

-47-

14th September 1880

Parsons was scared. Fear, like a cold sea mist, enveloped him. His body floated weightlessly in some dark void, in which the only movement was the light from a guttering candle somewhere way beyond his field of vision. He strained the muscles of his neck in a vain effort to turn his head towards this light, but found he did not have the strength.

The candle offered little by way of warmth, but as long as there was light he felt that there was hope. But that hope was short-lived. After a brief struggle for survival the flame spluttered and died, leaving the cold fear to gnaw at his flesh. He tried to shiver to warm himself, but could not. His body was in the grip of some invisible force.

He sensed a diabolic presence, and able only to move his petrified eyes in their sockets he waited in dread as the evil forces gathered around him.

420

A panic seized him when he sensed movements at the edge of his peripheral vision. He wanted to cry out for help, but was terrified lest the sound of his voice drew the forces towards him. But he knew that silence alone could not save him. The movements were metamorphosing; they were taking shape and they were moving closer.

A man in evening dress emerged from the mist, his white tie and shirt blindingly bright against the dark cosmos. His face was a mask, and the mask was a skull. The man slowly advanced upon the defenseless Parsons like a specter, opening his arms in an engulfing embrace.

Hysteria welled up inside Parsons like nausea. His mouth opened in a soundless scream. The skull was just inches away from his trembling face, when as if from nowhere a hand appeared and tore away the mask. The face beneath was Quentin's. A face contorted and racked by his tortured struggle for life. A face wearing the same expression that Parsons had seen on his death bed.

But this Quentin was not dead. The eyes of this monster did not stare sightlessly towards the ceiling. These eyes bored deep into Parson's soul.

Like an avenging wraith, Annabelle appeared behind her husband, the mask she had snatched from his face still clutched in her hand. Disdainfully she tossed it deep into the abyss, then wrapped her long sinuous fingers around his neck, digging them deeper and deeper into his flesh like the talons of a hawk piercing the soft fur of a defenseless rabbit. Her triumphant leer waxed as his struggles waned, and Parsons watched in horror as Quentin's body slowly disintegrated, gradually merging into the endless night from which it had sprung and leaving behind it the bewitching smile of his wife.

The cold alabaster that was Annabelle's face gradually faded into that of O'Brien: a fawning whore with rouged cheeks and crimson lips. She coiled around the naked Ashton like a serpent, stroking his body and whispering siren-like to him. He smirked evilly at Parsons, mouthing obscenities and reveling in the skills of his seductress. A look of pleasure born from pain spread across his face as she seized his hair and twisted his face towards her upward-tilting breasts. But his ecstasy was short. O'Brien turned her long, pointed red nails against his face, stripping his flesh. Blood oozed between her fingers as she peeled away his skin, each layer darker than the one before. He writhed helplessly in the firm grip of her strong thighs, screaming in agony as she flayed him. At last he lay still, stiffened by death, his skull parched like leather and black as night.

O'Brien and her lifeless prey faded slowly into the distance, replaced like actors in another scene by Catherine and the prone and helpless figure of Paul. She straddled his chest as though astride a horse, insensitive to his pain and the blood spreading slowly across his white dress shirt. Rocking slowly backwards and forwards and humming quietly to herself she slowly removed her hair-pins, allowing them to fall like autumn leaves into the red pool forming beneath her. When finally her long tresses covered her naked shoulders she bent forward and grasped him in her arms, squeezing her body against his. As her grip tightened around him his blood flowed like a stream in flood, engulfing them both like a thick layer of treacle. His mouth opened and closed in despair as his life ebbed away. "Smith's not left, Smith's not left," he screamed. But she paid him no heed as she carried him off.

Joshua Harding floated down, as though descending from the very heavens. White-cassocked and clutching a bible to his breast, he raised his hand in blessing, repeating over and over the words of the psalm he had read at Quentin's funeral: "A thousand shall fall at thy side, And ten thousand at thy right hand." His voice became louder, filling Parsons' head with a noise like a hammer smashing against an anvil. "Ten thousand at thy right hand. Thy right hand." The words battered his brain, but he was unable to raise his hands to his ears to block out the noise. With every word Harding's face grew uglier and more distorted. Foul-smelling sweat saturated him, pouring in torrents onto his cassock and falling in an endless stream upon Parsons, such that he feared he would drown in its vileness.

But now it was Smith leaning over him, a satyr with such rancid breath that Parsons wanted to vomit. Smith grinned vilely down at him, with blood-shot eyes and a mouth of broken teeth and rotting gums. From the darkness behind him Smith dragged the helpless Claire, who struggled and beat at him with her fists as he began tearing the thin dress from her body. In desperation she called to her brother. But Brendan was no match for Smith. A single pulverizing blow from Smith's right hand smashed into the boy's face. "Smith's not left handed. Not left handed," whimpered Claire, as Smith's arms closed around her.

Parsons returned to consciousness with a start, the last words of his nightmare echoing through his head. For a moment he thought he had died and gone to Hell, before gradually and gratefully realizing that he was still alive. He moved his limbs gingerly. He was not paralyzed as he had feared. It had all been a terrible dream.

But the momentary relief faded as he gradually realized his predicament. He was in a strange bed with a throbbing pain in the back of his head. He sat up slowly, delicately exploring the source of the pain with his fingers to discover that someone had bandaged his wound.

With a great effort his memory began sluggishly to unscramble the memories of the past evening, and he recalled with horror the circumstances that had led him to his present condition. He had been caught spying on a naked woman and someone had struck him. Suddenly he felt very awake and frightened. Where in God's name was he, and how had he got there?

Through the flowery curtains over the one small window he could see that the sun was low in the sky. Whether it was in the west or the east he could not tell, but judging by the growth of stubble on his chin it was long past morning. That must mean it had been almost a day since he was knocked out.

The darkened room was small and claustrophobic. There were rough wooden beams and a low sloping white ceiling. The uneven walls were also painted white and other than a small pine dresser under the window the room was bare. It looked like the upstairs room of a cottage. But whose cottage? One thing was certain, he would not find an answer by staying where he was.

Throwing back the bedding he tried to struggle out of bed, only to discover to his dismay that he wore only his under-clothes. He became even more alarmed and a feeling of panic swept over him. Where were his other clothes and who had undressed him?

With increasing desperation he looked frantically around, and to his relief saw what looked like a pile of clothes on a chair in a corner of the room, at a point where the ceiling and the floor seemed almost to meet. He struggled to his feet, but became dizzy with the effort and fell back onto the bed, hearing as he did a voice from the shadows at the edge of the room calling to someone who was outside.

"Ma. Ma. Come quick. The man's awake."

The speaker moved across the room and opened the door, revealing himself in the light from the corridor to be a small boy of about seven or eight years of age, dark in complexion and curly haired. It was a face Parsons had seen before, but one he was unable to place at that moment while his brain was still struggling to deal with the reality of his predicament. As he sat helplessly on the bed he could hear the person to whom the boy had called coming up the stairs and along a short corridor towards the room. To his utter dismay he recognized the boy's mother when she entered the room. Even in the poor light he could tell she was the same person he had seen swimming in the lake.

"Well, Mister Inspector, how is you today?" she asked in a soft Caribbean accent. "Solomon, draw de curtains and let de man see where he is."

She wore a high-necked print dress with three-quarter length sleeves, and in view of what had occurred, her calm matter-of-fact way of speaking came to Parsons as something of a relief. There appeared nothing but concern for him in the large dark eyes, and only a good-humoured expression on her wide mouth. Were he not so certain that the round close-cropped head was the same one he had seen gliding over the surface of the lake the previous evening, he might have been tempted to think his hostess was entirely ignorant of the whole episode.

She repeated her question.

"I'm well, thank you," he replied tentatively, "although my head still hurts a little."

"That's hardly surprising," she said with a laugh. "My husband sure give you a mighty blow. A jealous man, my husband. He no like anyone looking at his woman naked."

She laughed again, as though what had happened was of little consequence to her. Parsons was greatly relieved to hear the laughter. Although it in no way excused his behavior, at least it seemed she bore him no malice.

"Where am I?" he asked. "And how did I get here?"

""You're in my cottage, Mister Inspector. We brought you here on yo' horse. It was a struggle I don' mind telling you."

"I'm grateful for your trouble," he said humbly. "It's more than I deserved in the circumstances. But how long have I been here?"

"Almost a day," she replied. "It's half past five now."

Then she turned away towards the door at the sound of movements downstairs.

"That will be my husband," she said.

Parsons' temporary peace of mind evaporated and the fear welled up inside him again. This was the man he had so offended that he had found it necessary to resort to physical violence. He might easily strike again. But almost as though she had sensed his concern the woman hastened to reassure him.

"Don' worry yo'self, Mister Inspector. My husband's gentle most of de time."

She went to the door and called out to the man below.

"We're upstairs, John."

Parsons waited apprehensively as the footsteps ascended the wooden stairs and approached the room along the short uncarpeted corridor. He visualized the jealous husband as an Othello figure, with vengeance written large across his dark brow. But to his horror and amazement the man who had entered the room had a familiar white face. It was the face he had last seen on the morning of Brendan Dunne's arrest. The face was that of the game-keeper, Spencer.

Parsons was momentarily dumb-struck. The situation, if anything, had worsened and become even more embarrass-ing for him. To be caught peering at the naked wife of a stranger was bad enough, but it somehow felt worse when the husband was someone he knew, no matter how remotely.

"Spencer," he managed to splutter at last, the words pouring rapidly from his mouth, "I don't know how to explain my behavior last night or to know where to start apologizing. You may find it difficult to believe, but I'm not in the habit of skulking in the bushes late at night peering at naked women. To be perfectly honest I was so surprised at seeing a black person in the lake, particularly at that time of night, that I became mesmerized. That doesn't excuse my actions in any way, but I hope you will accept it as some sort of explanation."

Before Spencer had chance to reply his wife burst into laughter. Laughter so melodic and spontaneous that it was one of the most beautiful sounds Parsons had ever heard.

"Enough of dis nonsense," she said, "you'm already paid enough for yo' sins."

She laughed again, discounting once again the gravity of Parsons' offense.

"But you'm right," she said wistfully, "there are few black women in dese parts, more's de pity. And dat's one good reason why I swim in de night. By day I stand out like de sore thumb and people stare at me. But at night I become invisible. No one sees de black face in de night. Sometimes John joins me when I swim, but he's like many of you English. He thinks it not healthy to wash himself too often."

Her laughter overcame any offense her husband might have been caused by her comments. But her remarks about cleanliness drew Parsons' attention for the first time to the spotlessness of the room he was in. Having only previously seen the filthy exteriors of some of the cottages in the village, he had expected all of them to be as dirty inside. It was a foolish and unjustifiable assumption.

"Do you swim, Mister Inspector?" she asked.

"Like a walrus to your porpoise, madam," Parsons replied.

"Madam," she repeated, as though enjoying the sound of the word. "Madam. No white man has ever called me dat before."

Much to Parsons' embarrassment she stared intently at him for quite some time before speaking again.

"Fetch another chair for yo'self, John," she said at last. "I think I like dis man, and I have a curious feelin' he might like to hear my story."

Parsons readily agreed. Under the circumstances it would have been churlish to do otherwise.

-48-

John Spencer and his wife sat themselves at the side of Parsons' bed on small pine chairs that had been brought from their own bedroom. Solomon sat on his father's lap. Both they and Parsons waited patiently for Mrs. Spencer to begin her tale.

"My name is Grace," she said. "Grace Humphries once, but now Grace Spencer. I come from de island of Jamaica. And much as it was against de will of my people to go dere in de first place, so it was against my own wishes to leave."

The broad smile she gave her husband was evidence enough that she in no way held him responsible for anything that had precipitated this latter event.

"But maybe I come to change my mind about dat now I got me a good man," she said affectionately.

She turned her attention once more to Parsons.

"I'm sure an educated man like yo'self don' need me to tell him where de blacks in Jamaica originally come from," she said, with an underlying note of criticism in her voice.

Parsons shook his head, embarrassed to find himself discussing slavery, no matter how obliquely, with someone whose family had suffered its indignities and cruelties at first hand.

"My family come from Africa," she said proudly. "I don' know from where or in what year, and whether it be de Spanish or de British dat bring us. All I know is dat my daddy's bible show dey been in Jamaica since 1692. Perhaps dey bin dere longer."

She looked at Parsons with a mocking half-smile on her face.

"Do you know why de white man want us in Jamaica, Mister Inspector?"

"To work on the sugar plantations," answered Parsons, in a subdued voice.

He was not entirely happy with the direction this story was taking. His position in the cottage was awkward enough as it was, without the added indignity of a lesson from a black woman about the immorality of the slave trade.

"You is right," she said. "We worked on de sugar plantations; man, woman and chil.' Generation after generation, breaking our backs cutting de cane. And den in 1838, glory be, de British government abolish de slavery and make de black man free."

She laughed ironically.

"Make de black man free," she repeated. "Free to do what? Free to go where?"

Parsons hoped she intended the question to be rhetorical. If not, she would be disappointed. There was nothing he felt able to say in reply.

The twinkle in her eye told him she was aware of his discomfort.

"Many blacks try to become farmers like de white man. But de white man control de price of de sugar, de rum, de pimento and de coffee. So slowly, slowly, de black man find himself workin' for de white man agin. Not as slaves, you understan,' Mister Inspector. We now free people."

She had spoken the last words slowly and cynically with her eyes fixed firmly on Parsons. It was illogical, he knew, but he felt himself feeling guilty for the sins of others.

"De white man control de wages and de hours we work," said Grace. "So we slaves agin in all but name."

Parsons interrupted her, "You'll forgive me for asking, Mrs Spencer," he said, "but how do you know this? Who taught you?"

"You seem surprised dat a black woman know anythin,'" she said coolly. "But we ain't so dumb, you know. Ma daddy taught me. An' a fine educated Christian man he was. God rest his soul."

Parsons felt ashamed of himself. She was right. He had wrongly assumed her to be as ignorant as the most ill-educated beggar on the streets of London.

"My daddy was a Methodist minister," she explained proudly. "Educated in one of yo' fine Church schools. That was thanks to his own daddy, a white plantation manager. Oh yes, Mister Inspector, you needn't look so surprised. My daddy's daddy a white man. And my mammy's daddy. You may not think so to look at me. But I is half white."

She smiled beatifically at Parsons, and he bushed. He was receiving an education in life in the British colonies he had not been anticipating.

"But dey was sure different kinds of white man," she said. "My grandaddy Humphries was a good Christian gentleman who loved my granmammy. He never marry her, but he bring up her children to know him as dere daddy. I never know my mammy's daddy. He take her when she jus' a pretty young girl, an' when de baby come he throw her out. Dat's a lesson I learn early. Dere are many sorts of you white men in dis world, Mister Inspector. An' not all of you is bad."

She broke into another of her delightful peals of laughter, inviting her husband and Parsons to share her joke.

"I still don't understand how you came to be here," said Parsons.

"All in good time," Grace said. "Dat much all of you white men have in common. You all impatient. Even dis good man here."

She smiled warmly at her husband. John Spencer had said nothing since he had first come into the room, but it was obvious to Parsons from the way he watched his wife's every movement that he adored her.

"I hope you're not growing tired of my story, Mister Inspector," said Grace.

"Not at all," replied Parsons politely. "It's very interesting. But I'm sure your husband will have told you that I'm currently engaged in important police business. And much as I appreciate your hospitality—especially in view of what happened last night—I'd like to return to the castle as soon as I can."

"Patience, man," said Grace, for the first time allowing a tone of irritation to creep into her voice. "I know all about de murders at de castle. Everyone in de village know. But you may learn something from me to help with your so important investigation. You mus' jus' learn to be patient."

Suitably admonished, Parsons lent back on his pillows. What difference, he thought, did another half hour matter.

Grace continued her tale.

"I was telling you dat even after de slavery in Jamaica abolished dat de white man still de master," she said. "And from what I learn since, dis is true in all de parts of de world dat de white man rule. But in Jamaica when I was young we all t'ink dis will change. We hear about de civil war in America to free all de slaves dere. So de Jamaican workers start askin' de white bosses for a fairer share of de profits dat de white man make."

This was hardly anything new, thought Parsons. There had been more than enough industrial unrest throughout Europe in the nineteenth-century. What was so special about the Jamaican workers.

Grace's next words made him think she had been reading his mind.

"You're thinking dat you don' see anything unusual about dat," she said. "De workers always ask for more. I know dat. Even here in England de workers have been hanged or shipped to Australia for demanding more from de bosses. But what happened in Jamaica was different. What happened dere was murder. When de Jamaican people make dere peaceful protests de governor set de army loose on dem like a pack of hounds. De government give de soldiers de freedom to hang innocent people without trial. Good men like my daddy died for using de words of de Bible in his church to support de demands of de workers. And dose they don' hang dey flog. Even de women and young children. Dey flogged my mother. Fifty lashes dey laid on her back before my very eyes. I still hear her screams to dis day."

Tears of anger flashed in her eyes as she spoke, prompting her husband to lay a comforting arm round her shoulder. Even Solomon went over to his mother and put his arms round her waist. All three looked towards Parsons as though it was he who stood accused of such terrible crimes.

Parsons realized then what she was saying. The man ultimately responsible for the crimes, the acting governor at the time, had been Lord Quentin. The man who had himself been brutally murdered but a few days before.

"What of you, Grace?" he asked quietly, almost afraid of what he might hear.

"I was fifteen at de time," she answered. "A pretty young girl, innocent of de ways of men. I could've been raped by one soldier after another like many of my friends. But I was lucky. De sergeant save me from all dat. De sergeant save me for himself."

Parsons looked towards Spencer, expecting some acknowledgement from him for what he had done to spare his wife.

"No, Mister Inspector. It wasn't John. I not dat lucky. De sergeant's name on dat day was Smith. Yes, inspector, de same Smith. De same wicked man. As wicked a man as de one he served. Even before de rebellion we all know 'bout dis Smith. Smith, de procurer of de young girls for his master, de great Colonel Lord de Courcey. But dis time it different. Dis time Smith decide to keep one for himself."

This explained why it was that Lord Quentin had continued to employ Smith, thought Parsons. And not only to employ him, but also to ensure he had money enough to fund his drinking. Smith's loyalty and silence were important. The secrets he knew about Lord Quentin could have caused him further public ignominy.

Parsons recalled how public opinion at the time of the Jamaican rebellion had divided about the way it had been handled, and how Lord Quentin had been fortunate to escape criminal charges for what had occurred under his command. In the end nothing was done. Apart from a slur on his name in some quarters he was left to retire quietly to the country. But there was no doubt that had his appetite for young black women become common knowledge, opinion might have swung dramatically against him. When it came to a question of morals the English did not forgive men who were indiscrete, especially with women whose skins were of a different hue. Smith's silence at the time and later was important to Lord Quentin and his good name.

But Lord Quentin knew Smith well, probably as well as he knew himself. He knew what it required to keep him quiet. They were both sadists with a similar taste for young girls.

But Grace was not finished. Her story was not yet done.

"One year after dis, de governor and de soldiers involved in dis massacre were recalled to England. An' much against my will Smith take me with him. What choice had I?

De white man say I go to England with him. So I go. Dere was no one to say anyt'ing different. An' when Smith leave de army and come to work at Beaumont he bring me here with him. But he soon tire of me an' t'row me out. Maybe he see de chance of young Irish flesh."

The hatred burned brightly in her eyes as she spoke, but her tone softened when her husband gently patted her hand.

"Fortunately for me dere are men like John in dis world. Without him I don' know what I do. Either I starve or I sell my body like some dirty whore."

How could you work with a man like Smith," Parsons asked Spencer, "knowing how he'd treated your wife? For that matter how could you work for a man like Lord Quentin?"

"There were times when I could cheerfully have killed them both, sir," said Spencer. "It was only Grace's strong Christian beliefs that stopped me. But as you say, I need not have stayed. Maybe we could've made a new life somewhere else. Perhaps we should've tried. But it isn't that easy when you've got a family to feed. I'm an old soldier, like Smith, and finding another job is difficult at my age. We've a home here thanks to the de Courceys, and we've each other; and that's all that matters."

"From what you've both said, and from what I've heard many other people say, Smith seems capable of committing the foulest crimes," said Parsons. "But do you think he would murder Lord Quentin? After all he provided Smith with employment and much besides that. And if *you* felt uncertain about finding another job, Spencer, what hope had Smith?"

'Dat evil man was capable of anything," said Grace. "He could've killed both de masters. But if he did, he not act alone."

"What do you mean," Parsons exclaimed, surprised by the confident with which she spoke. "What do you know about all this?"

Spencer and his wife exchanged a quick glance. The game-keeper clearly felt uncomfortable. Perhaps he thought his wife had said enough. She, on the other hand, seemed anxious to tell Parsons all she knew.

"Do you feel strong enough to make a short journey, Mister Inspector," she asked.

Parsons nodded, his curiosity well and truly roused by what Grace had said and what she might have to show him.

"Den," she said, "we'll go back to the lake."

-49-

The ground floor of the Spencer's cottage consisted of a large single room. This room adequately accommodated the basic requirements of a small family, and like the bedroom Parsons had been sleeping in, it was spotlessly clean. There was a refreshing aroma in the room; one that was caused, as Grace Spencer explained, by herbs strewn amongst the rushes covering the beaten earth floor. It was a common practice in the country, she said, and one Parsons found most agreeable. With the low-lying evening sun shining through the pretty flower-patterned curtains, the overall effect created a delightful homely atmosphere in this simple dwelling.

The cottage had been built to allow the best use to be made of the natural elements: the only two windows on the ground floor faced south and the sun, and the large open fire-place and chimney breast had been incorporated into the east wall to allow the prevailing wind to blow the smoke away from the building. The thatched roof reached almost to the ground over the north wall, ensuring there was maximum insulation on the side of the cottage that would never see the sun.

Like the room itself, the furnishings were simple. There was a small wooden table with three pine chairs under one of the windows, and a kitchen dresser against the north wall, complete with cups, dishes and plates. There was also a small bookcase; an item of furniture that, until his experience in the Spencer's cottage, Parsons would not have expected to find in such a humble abode. He knew better now than to make such hasty and unreasonable judgments. The Spencers possessed few enough books, but he had no doubt the few they had would receive greater use than any in the library at Beaumont.

Parsons' outer coat, like those of the Spencers, hung in the warm air near the fire; suspended from nails hammered into the single wooden beam that ran the full length of the low ceiling. As he put his own coat on, he could not fail to notice the devoted way in which Spencer assisted his wife with hers. There was as much consideration and good manners in that single gesture as he had noticed in all the time he had spent at Beaumont.

It was not until he felt the envelope in his coat pocket that Parsons remembered Marsdens' note. Had the unexpected events of the previous night not occurred, Colonel Howard might by now have signed the authority to release the Dunnes, and Brown or one of his men would have been dispatched to Petersfield to collect them.

It was important that their release was not further delayed. Even one extra night in those cells was an injustice that Parsons did not wish to countenance. Spencer, Parsons decided, must take the note to Beaumont at once. The later it was left, the more chance there would be that the Chief Constable would be asleep. Knowing that Howard would be unlikely to sign the release note without a good reason, Parsons spent another fifteen minutes presenting the facts in a way he hoped would convince the colonel of the Dunnes' innocence. Aware that Howard would also question his overnight absence, he made a point in his note of explaining that he had stayed in the village to make further enquiries. The story was bound to raise questions, but Parsons would deal with them when the time came.

"Give these notes to Sergeant Brown," he instructed Spencer, after a brief explanation of their contents, "and tell him the importance of obtaining the Chief Constable's signature on the release note. I want Brown or one of his men to go to Petersfield in the morning to collect the Dunnes. Is that clear?"

Spencer nodded.

"I hope I can rely on you not mentioning last night's events to anyone else," said Parsons sheepishly.

He need not have been concerned. Grace Spencer well understood his predicament.

"Dis episode last night am between de t'ree of us, John," she said. "You is not to go spreading tales 'bout how you struck de inspector."

Parsons had no doubt as he watched Spencer bid a fond farewell to his wife that her instructions would be followed to the letter.

ゆゆゆ

It was agreed that Spencer would join them at the lake after delivering the notes. Young Solomon—whom Parsons had by now remembered as the dark face he had seen in the copse during his ride from the station—was also given an errand. He was given a note for the station master asking for any telegrams or parcels for Parsons that had arrived from London.

"An' when you get back you are to stay in, Solomon," Grace told her son as she planted a kiss on his forehead. "We won't be long. While you're waiting I want you to finish reading yo' book."

"Yes, Mama," the boy said dutifully before running off down the lane in the direction of the station.

Parsons had pleaded to be allowed to walk, but the Spencers insisted he take his horse.

"You're bound to be a bit dazed still, sir," Spencer had said, and his wife had agreed. So to mollify them both he rode, with Grace Spencer walking along the lane beside him.

As they left the village he could not fail to notice the inquisitive yet unfriendly faces peering at them from within the few cottages they passed. No voices wished them a 'good evening' or engaged them in any of the forms of conversation common to life in a small community. Even in so short a journey he realized how lonely life must be for a person of a different race in such an inward-looking society, and why it was that Grace chose the cover of darkness to go swimming. It also explained the deep affection she had for her husband.

Without his company and support her life in the village would have been unendurable.

But even had they decided to leave the village, he thought, where else in this racially prejudiced land would they ever find a welcome?

The lane took them almost due north. On one side, some hundred yards away across the fields, Parsons could see the railway line to Petersfield perched above them on the embankment; on the other side, lay a dense forest. The lane climbed slowly until it reached the level of the railway, then after a further half-mile it began its steep descent towards the lake. As they moved deeper in the shadow cast by the embankment the last rays of sunlight faded from view, and near the lake the air was noticeably colder. Apart from the muffled sound of the horse's hooves on the grassy track, there was silence.

Parsons' enquiries as to the purpose of their journey had gone unrewarded.

"Patience, Mister Inspector. All in de Lord's good time," was the only response he had been able to elicit from Grace.

There was nothing for it, he decided, but to allow this good woman to do things at her own pace.

They reached a fork in the lane he remembered from the previous night. To their left lay Petersfield; and to the right the ill-fated spot where Parsons had decided to watch his companion swimming. It was towards this self-same spot that Grace now led Parsons' horse.

"On de night of de fire at de castle I was swimming," she explained, after they had reached the clearing where he had seen her dressing. "It was later dan usual. An' while I was in de water I see a man ridin' slowly along de lane."

She pointed back in the direction from which they had come.

"He come dat way," she said. "An' when I see him I swim very quiet. I know it not John. He tell me he no come dat night. An' it not usual for anyone from de village to use de lane late at night. It was dark and de trees made it difficult to see, but I watch de man carefully until I no see him anymo.' When I sure he gone, I carry on swimmin.' Maybe ten, maybe fifteen minutes after I hear de noise of a horse again. It come from along de lane from where de man go. I not like dis. I not like strange men near me in de night and I not like men on horses. Dey remind me of de soldiers in Jamaica. So I swim towards de shore, very quiet, keeping in de shadow as much as I can. Den I get my towel and my clothes and hide.

She led Parsons a short distance into the trees.

"I hide here," she said.

"What did you see?" Parsons asked.

"I no see anythin.' Like I say, it very dark. But I still hear de noise of de horse's bridle. So I keep very still. Like I say, I no like men who come on de horses in de dark."

"Where does that lead?" asked Parsons, pointing in the direction from which the noise of the horse had come.

"In maybe one hundred yards de lane divide in two," she explained. "One way it go to Midhurst, de other towards de castle. Dat part of de lane divide again furder on: one way go to de stable entrance of de castle, de other to de Downs."

"How long would it take to ride from here to the castle?" Parsons asked.

"I not sure," Grace replied. "I no ride horse. But if I walk it take twenty minutes, maybe twenty five."

On horse-back, in the dark, it would take about ten minutes at most, Parsons thought.

They had been so engrossed in their whispered conversation that they had failed to notice a man coming along the lane from the castle. It was only the apprehensive movement of Parsons' horse in response to the sound of a breaking twig that attracted their attention. Instinctively they both crouched low to avoid being seen, and watched in silence as the figure approached.

About twenty yards from where they hid the man stopped and gave a low whistle.

"Don' worry, Mister Inspector," Grace said, greatly relieved. "It only my John."

She stood up and whistled in response.

Spencer joined them in the bushes. He had delivered the notes to Brown in the kitchen, and the sergeant had said he would give them to Colonel Howard that evening. Brown had one other piece of news for Parsons. Mr Geoffrey Montagu had left Beaumont suddenly sometime during the day.

Grace Spencer waited patiently while her husband delivered this information to Parsons. But she was anxious to finish her business at the lake and be away. She did not like leaving her son alone at this time of night.

Parsons now realized what she had meant when she had said she became invisible at night. She was standing only a few feet from him, but in the gathering gloom against the dark background of the trees, it was becoming increasingly difficult to see anything of her except occasional flashes of her teeth and the whites of her eyes. Not for the first time he felt she was reading his thoughts, and he wondered if she had any of the special powers he had heard were possessed by people from the Caribbean,

"Even though I know dat it difficult to see me in de dark," she said, "I feel afraid. I get dressed quietly den I crouch down very low an' keep quiet. Sometimes I t'ink de man and de horse go, but den I hear de bridle, like when de horse shake its head. I t'ink there not one horse, but two. So I wait and I wait. I no want any strange man to find me alone here or in de lane."

"How long did you wait?" Parsons asked.

"I don' know. I no have watch. Maybe half hour, maybe more, maybe less. Time go slow at night when you is alone and afraid in de dark. But if need be I wait all night. Den I hear de noise of another horse. Dis horse come runnin' fast. I t'ink it come from de castle. Den it stop, but not for long. De horse go de other way, around de lake towards Midhurst. Maybe five, maybe ten minutes it come back. Den I hear voices. Lordy, lordy I mighty scared now. I t'ink dere are two men now and dey come dis way towards me.

Parsons waited patiently for Grace to continue. Even now, with two other people for moral support and with nothing to fear from the darkness, he could appreciate how scared she must have felt as she crouched alone in the bushes.

"Two men come and three horses," she explained. "An' dey stop dere."

In the gloom it was difficult to see exactly where Grace meant, but Parsons thought she was pointing to a spot about twenty or thirty yards from where they stood, and in the direction of the castle.

"Dey talk quietly and I no hear what dey say. Den one of dem ride his horse into de water right near me. I nearly sick with fright. S'posing he see me."

"But he didn't, Mrs Spencer," Parsons said, more impatiently than he had intended. "You were safe in the bushes."

He had expected her to admonish him for that. It was no more than he deserved. But she continued as if he had not said anything. She was still reliving her terrible experience.

"De horse wade into de water a few feet, den de man throw somethin' in de lake. I hear it splash like a stone and I see de ripples in de surface of de water."

"What color was the horse?" asked Parsons excitedly.

"White, Mister Inspector," she said. "De horse was white like you."

"Did you see the man? Would you recognize him again? Did he wear a big hat?"

"No, sah," she said. "I don' know dis man. I don' t'ink he wear a hat. But it was dark and I was scared to look much at de man in case he feels my eyes on him. I jus' pray to de Lord dat dese men go away."

"Did you see what the man threw into the water?"

"Not den," said Grace. "But later I find it."

"Go on, please," said Parsons, thinking that Grace may have come to the end of her tale.

"At last de Lord hear me and de men go away. De one on de white horse go towards de castle. De other come dis way. Dis man I t'ink is de first man I see. Dis man ride one horse an' lead another."

"And the color of the horses, Mrs Spencer. What color were the horses?"

"Dey no special color, mister inspector. It dark. But I t'ink one horse darker dan de other."

"I suppose you wouldn't recognize this man either," Parsons said, exhilarated by what he had learned, yet still frustrated by having no clear descriptions of the people involved.

Grace shook her head.

"No Mister Inspector, I don.' I just wait here until I no hear de horses go. Den I t'ink it safe to go home."

"Where were you during all this?" Parsons asked Spencer.

"At home asleep, sir. I'd been on duty the night before and I was tired. So I went to bed straight after supper. I didn't know anything about any of this until Grace came home that night and told me about the fire."

"How did you know about that, Mrs. Spencer?"

"When I got back to the village I could see a big glow in de sky, and by den I could smell de smoke."

"Did you see either of these men again?"

"No. Dey go. I no see dem again."

"Now what about this thing you say was thrown in the lake. You said you found it later."

"Next day I went back to de lake. I feel more brave. I also curious. So I go early de next night, before it get dark and I swim to de spot where I t'ink de man throw it in de water. De lake not deep dere. I dive many times, but at las' I find it."

"You never told me this," said Spencer in surprise.

His voice displayed his growing concern. From the beginning he had not been happy that his wife had decided to confide her story to Parsons. He feared she might be unwittingly involving them both with the authorities, and he was unsure where that might lead.

"I t'ink it best you don' know, John," she said quietly. "Until I spoke with de inspector tonight, I no have any intention of telling you or anyone else. But den I change my mind."

Without any further explanation she left them and walked to the fallen tree where Parsons had seen her clothes on the previous evening. She climbed over it and disappeared into the bushes beyond. When she returned she was carrying a small bundle of rags, and without saying a word she handed it to Parsons. Inside the bundle was a revolver.

-50-

ontgomery had been in the Library when the boy had arrived from the station with the mail. For the sake of appearances he had taken several books out of the shelves and scattered them over the long table that had been used for reading the will. But much of the time he had spent pacing restlessly backwards and forwards, pausing occasionally to peer anxiously through the windows overlooking the stable area and the front of the castle. At other times, though he read not a word, he sat hunched over the books with a furrowed brow, trying to decide upon his best course of action.

But without knowing what Parsons was doing it was like trying to complete a jigsaw with only half the pieces. And Parsons had disappeared.

So when Montgomery saw the boy coming through the barbican in his chocolate-colored uniform he rushed to the Hall. He wanted to see what was in the afternoon mail before anyone else had a chance. It was unlikely, he knew, but there was a slim chance of something arriving that might help him to reach a decision about his next move.

It had been Carpenter's day off, and he had received orders from his wife to accompany her on her regular monthly shopping trip to Petersfield.

"Be sure ye arrange for any telegrams for that Inspector Parsons to go straight to the castle," the station master had told Emerson, one of the young porters. "And if for any reason ye can't find 'im, bring 'em back here and give 'em to me. No one else is to have 'em. That's the inspector's strict instructions. Do I make myself clear, Emerson. Good. I'll be back before six."

And with that he had joined his wife in Joshua Harding's trap. Mrs. Carpenter, a regular churchgoer, and one of the village ladies who arranged the flowers in the church considered it a great honor to go shopping with the clergy. Her husband was not of that opinion. The idea of several hours of the vicar's pious platitudes was not his idea of an enjoyable way to spend his well-earned day off.

Emerson had relished his temporary stewardship of the station. Although there had been no passengers for Beaumont, all the trains between Waterloo and Portsmouth stopped at the station; and that had provided opportunities for him to supervise Seaman while he checked the carriage doors. He had also derived enormous satisfaction from setting the great steam train in motion with a single blast on his whistle and a wave of his green flag.

The telegram for Parsons had been sent down the telegraph line running alongside the railway just five minutes before the four fifty-eight was due; so there was no time for Emerson to do anything about it until after he had seen the train safely on its way. There had been mail for the castle on the train. It was the correct procedure for all mail to go to Petersfield for the Royal Mail to deliver, but it had become customary for the guards on the trains to sort out anything for the castle and drop it off at Beaumont for the railway staff to deal with.

Emerson had not thought twice about the parcel for Parsons amongst the other mail for the castle. Mr. Carpenter had not told him to make any special arrangements for parcels.

"Take the mail to the castle and be quick about it, Seaman," Emerson had instructed, "and remember Mr. Carpenter's instructions about this telegram for Inspector Parsons. You're to give it to no one but 'e."

It had given Emerson great pleasure to send the clumsy youth lumbering along the lane to the castle. Seaman had always been a bully at school. But like many of those who rely upon their brawn, he had little in the way of brains. And it had always been Emerson, three years Seaman's junior, that Mr. Carpenter had chosen to deputize for him in his absence. There was nothing like a little power, thought Emerson, as he watched Seaman's broad back receding down the lane.

Seaman was about to tug at the bell-chain to summon one of the servants when Montgomery arrived.

"I'll take the mail, boy," he said, so delighted at seeing the parcel for Parsons that he gave Seaman a tip.

"Thank 'ee kindly, sir," Seaman replied, equally delighted by this unexpected largesse. In the four years he had been delivering mail to Beaumont no one had ever tipped him before. "I've a telegram 'ere for Inspector Parsons. Would ye know where I can find 'im?"

"The inspector's away from the castle on duty at the moment. If you leave the telegram with me I'll be sure to give it to him when he returns."

Montgomery smiled invitingly and jingled the loose change in his trouser pocket. The prospect of another tip was tempting, thought Seaman, but if Mr. Carpenter ever found out he'd disobeyed an order there'd be hell to play. He might even lose his job.

"I'm sorry, sir," he said with obvious reluctance, "but my orders are to give it only to the inspector."

Montgomery quietly cursed the boy as he watched him leave the castle grounds. Having sight of the contents of that telegram would have been an unexpected bonus. But at least he had the parcel, and that might provide some clue as to how Parsons' mind was working. He quickly checked the remaining mail, but there was nothing other than a magazine for Annabelle and two letters for Catherine. Leaving them on the chest in the entrance hall Montgomery made his way upstairs to his room.

-51-

There was little by way of conversation as the trio made its way along the silent lanes to the village. Parsons was deep in thought on the back of his horse, allowing Spencer to take the bridle. Only Mrs. Spencer seemed in any hurry. Now that night had fallen she was anxious to be home with her son.

Grace Spencer's information had shaken the kaleidoscope of evidence into an entirely new pattern. If what she had told him was true, both Smith and Montgomery were involved in Paul's death; perhaps the other murders as well. And Parsons had no reason to disbelieve her. After all, why should she invent such a fantastic tale? Until the previous night she could have no idea she would ever meet Parsons, and he was convinced she had only spoken so openly to him because she trusted him. Had it not been for the unfortunate episode by the lake he would know nothing about Grace Spencer or what she had seen on the night of the fire.

Smith had always been a likely suspect. His violent nature was beyond doubt, and in many people's opinion he was

454

quite capable of murder. Paul's murderer had apparently looked like Smith, and if Paul had indeed dismissed him, he had a motive of sorts.

Although it was dark, Parsons was fairly certain that the pistol given him by Grace Spencer was a point four-five Webley. That was the caliber of the weapon that had been used to shoot Howard and Paul.

According to Howard there was a good chance that the murderer had held the weapon in his left hand. Was that what Paul was trying to tell Annabelle as he lay dying? Had he been saying that Smith could not be the murderer, in spite of the hat and the long dirty coat, because Smith was not left-handed?

If evidence was required of that, there were the bruises Parsons had seen on Brendan Dunne's face when he had first arrived at Beaumont. They had almost certainly been caused by a man with a solid right hook. His dream had reminded him of that. But Montgomery was left-handed. Apart from the observation Parsons had made about his side-whiskers, Montgomery had also drawn him a map showing where he had ridden. There might, of course, be others in the castle who were also left-handed; but none like Montgomery with such corroborating evidence against them.

Then there were the horses. When he had left Beaumont on the morning of Paul's death Montgomery had been riding Ashton's grey. When he had returned after the fire he was still riding the same horse. But this was after Paul's murder had taken place and the murderer had been seen riding away from the burning stables on a black mare. If indeed it had been Montgomery that had shot Paul, he would need an accomplice to help him change horses. That would account for the man waiting by the lake. But was this man Smith?

Parsons ventured an hypothesis: Supposing Montgomery had arrived from his ride to Midhurst while Grace Spencer was swimming. That would have been much earlier than he had previously said. He could then have left his horse with Smith and walked to the stables—a walk of less than half an hour, according to Grace. Smith would not have been wearing his familiar coat and hat, as by prior arrangement with Montgomery he would have left them in the stables for Montgomery to wear. Montgomery would know the normal procedure after dinner. He would be fairly confident that Alexander, Philip and Geoffrey Montagu would join the ladies in the Drawing Room, leaving Paul, Fitzherbert and Howard to enjoy their brandy and cigars. All Montgomery had to do was throw gravel against the windows of the Great Hall to attract their attention.

Montgomery would no doubt have been delighted to see that only Paul and Howard took the bait. That would mean that after shooting both of them there would be no one else to pursue him. He could then run back to the stables, cause a diversion by setting them ablaze and ride away on the black mare, that had no doubt already been saddled for him by Smith. That, Parsons considered, fitted the sequence of events extremely well.

Parsons thought that his hypothesis had much to recommend it, but it did not throw any further light on the murders of Ashton and Quentin. If Montgomery or Smith were involved in either of these murders, what were their motives? Ashton's death might be a case of robbery with excessive violence, in which case Smith could well be involved. But if Ashton's murderer had been one of his blackmail victims, it was hardly likely to be Smith; although there was nothing to suggest that Smith would not have carried out the murder for money. The same could be said about Quentin's death. Smith could have done that on behalf of someone else, someone who now appeared to Parsons to look increasingly like Montgomery.

But the only solid evidence relating to Paul's murder was based on what Grace Spencer had said. And here Parsons had to admit that his hypothesis had some weaknesses. Smith might well have agreed to help Montgomery with the horses, but why would he implicate himself by agreeing to let Montgomery wear his clothes. And if Grace's story was to be believed in its entirety, the man arriving first had come from a different direction to the one Smith would have taken. This mysterious man, so crucial in the order of events, had not come from the direction of the castle.

"Are you certain that you understood Brown correctly when he said that Mr. Montagu had left Beaumont," Parsons asked Spencer as they reached the Spencer's cottage. "Are you sure he didn't say Mr. Montgomery?"

"No doubt about that, sir," Spencer replied. "Brown described him as the long-haired bohemian. I knew who he was at once. He was the young man I saw the night Lord Quentin was murdered."

"Where did you see him, for heaven's sake, and why haven't you told me this before?" said Parsons, angry that such an important piece of information should have been kept from him.

"You'll pardon me, sir, but the first opportunity I had of speaking to you after young Dunne was arrested, was in the bushes last night. And at that time I didn't know who I was addressing."

Grace Spencer's laugh was a reprimand in itself. Parsons realized he was in no position to accuse her husband of lacking responsibility. He could hardly blame Spencer for not coming forward before, after he had witnessed the sort of summary justice that was being handed out by Colonel Howard. And no doubt his experiences with senior officers in the army had taught him to keep his own counsel. That much was evident from the worried glance he had given his wife when she had decided to take Parsons to the lake.

Suitably admonished Parsons moderated his tone.

"Where did you see Montagu that night?" he asked.

"In the Park, sir. As I think I explained in Lord Quentin's room I was out looking for poachers that night. At first I thought the young gentleman might be one. I'd no idea he was a guest in the castle. So I followed him for sometime before I realized he was unlikely ever to catch any game."

"Why was that?"

"He was drunk, sir. He kept falling over and babbling a lot of rubbish. Sometimes it was poetry and sometimes it was something or other about the rights of workers. That made me laugh I can tell you. Workers' rights at Beaumont. Now that would be something."

"What time was all this going on?"

"I don't know for sure, sir. Probably between three and four. I know I followed him for sometime. To be honest it was an amusing diversion for me from what is usually a long lonely night's work. But I gave up on him eventually when he lay down on the ground and went to sleep."

It was scarcely the behavior of someone who had just committed a murder, thought Parsons. Unless the combination of drink and drugs had confused Montagu to the point that he no longer knew or cared what he was doing. But why had he decided to leave Beaumont so suddenly?

By the time they had reached the Spencers cottage it was after nine. Solomon had gone to bed, but had left the envelope containing Parsons' telegram on the table.

To Parsons from Harris,' it read. *'Royal Irish Constabulary confirm all servants' addresses in Ballycarra correct.*

Army records of Smith and Spencer: Both joined 18th Royal Lancers for service in Crimea. Spencer remained in regiment, serving in India and finally in regimental depot in Aldershot. Retired as sergeant in 1871. Service conduct described as exemplary. Smith court-martialled in 1862 for striking superior officer. Reduced to the ranks. Transferred to Hampshire Light Infantry in 1863 for service in Jamaica. Retired as sergeant in 1870. Service conduct described as satisfactory.

Montgomery's address in Toronto only temporary. There only three weeks. No police record in Toronto. Checking other known addresses.

Have ascertained Geoffrey Montagu's girl friend, Caroline Mayhew, is his half-sister. Daughter of Sir Jeremiah Montagu and Victoria Mayhew. Will investigate further.

Forwarding civil war book direct to you at Beaumont. Put on one forty pm train today. Take care of it, borrowed on my ticket from Central Lending Library.

'*She walks in beauty as the night,*' mused Parsons. The words were those of the poem by Lord Byron he had found in Montagu's room. The verse that had the words '*I will be in touch with you soon*' appended to it.

Byron's famous lines had been dedicated to his own half-sister, Augusta Leigh, with whom he had a notorious affair. It would appear that someone else in the castle knew of Montagu's incestuous relationship. Could that be the reason for Montagu's abrupt departure?

"I expect you've seen one or two of these before, Spencer," said Parsons, when they were sitting at the table in the Spencer's cottage. The pistol found in the lake lay on the table between them.

"It looks like a Webley, sir, but it's got a longer barrel than the ones we used in the army."

"You're right. This one is the model used by the Royal Irish Constabulary. And if this is a police weapon I'd like to know where our murderer obtained it. And why are there three empty cases in the cylinder. From what Colonel Howard and others have said, only two shots were fired. What I wonder happened to the third?"

"All guns are evil in de eyes of de Lord," said Mrs. Spencer from the fire-place, where she was preparing a deliciously-smelling broth. And then almost as an afterthought she said, "I hope you'll take some supper with us before you leave, inspector."

"I'd like nothing better, Mrs. Spencer," Parsons said. "But before that I want to write a telegram for my sergeant in London, and I'm going to prevail upon your good husband again and ask him to take it to the Mr. Carpenter at the railway station first thing in the morning."

'To Harris from Parsons,' he wrote. *'Require service history of Webley R.I.C. pistol serial number 8763. Urgent. Believe weapon may be stolen from Royal Irish Constabulary. Also double check movements of Montgomery since arrival, especially possibility of longer stay in Ireland than previously thought.'*

-52-

Montgomery assumed that the official-looking insignia on the red wax seal on the parcel was that of the Metropolitan Police. He turned the package over in his hands several times hoping to find some way of opening it that would allow him to reseal it without anyone noticing it had been tampered with. There was no way he could see that this could be done, so he tore the wrapping paper off, screwed it into a ball and threw it into the waste basket. The time for unnecessary caution had passed.

As he had feared from the weight of the parcel it contained the book. There was also a brief note to Parsons from someone called Harris explaining that the book had come from the Central Lending Library. In spite of his predicament Montgomery could not help smiling. Only a damn-fool pen-pushing bureaucrat would make a comment like that.

One thing was clear. Now that they had the book it was only a matter of time. Sooner or later Parsons would discover the truth. Even if he removed the incriminating photograph from this book, there would always be others.

He paced impatiently up and down the room for several minutes with the book in his hand before reaching a decision. He would get rid of it. At least that would give him a breathing space. For a start Parsons had no proof the book had ever reached the castle. No doubt his London office would have told him they had sent it, but there was always a slim chance he would think it had been mishandled or lost in transit. And Montgomery doubted whether the stupid yokel from the station would ever remember what was in the mail he had delivered to the castle.

For all Montgomery knew Parsons might already suspect him. But where was his proof? Apart from that fool Howard, there were no other witnesses to the shootings; and as far as he could tell his disguise had worked. Everyone it seemed blamed Smith. Parsons, he knew, was a methodical man, and would not be content until he had established a strong motive for the murders. And without the photograph what could he presume the motive to be?

That reminded him. He would need to speak with the Chief Constable before he left. But before that he had to destroy the book. There was only one sensible option. The book had to be burned.

Montgomery considered summoning one of the servants to make up a fire in his room, but decided against it. Not only would that take time, it would also look suspicious. It was too early in the day for bedroom fires to be lit, and it was also out of character for him to have one at all. Ever since his arrival he had never allowed a fire to be lit in his room, and had made it clear on several occasions to both the servants and the others in the castle that as a

Canadian he considered himself too hardy for such comforts.

But at this time in the afternoon there was always a fire in the Drawing Room. He could burn the book there. Before that he would spend a few minutes sorting out some clothing in readiness for his departure.

Montgomery entered the Drawing Room quietly, not wishing to attract attention to himself. He could not have planned things better. Apart from one of the servants the room was empty. Everyone else appeared to have already taken their afternoon tea.

"Is there any cocoa available?" he asked Sweeney, knowing full well that at that time of day there never was.

"Nay, sir. But I'll be getting you some straight away."

It irritated and embarrassed Montgomery to see the girl curtsy to him before she left the room. If only he could tell her, he thought. But even at this stage that would be foolish.

He crossed the room to the fire and poked at the logs to ensure there was a good flame. Then he carefully placed the book in the middle of the blaze, waiting impatiently for it to light. But even as he crouched over the fire, he heard a deep-throated snore from somewhere behind him. He had been mistaken. There was someone else in the room.

Montgomery's nerves were now on such an edge that the unexpected sound made him drop the poker. It fell with a resounding clatter onto the marble hearth.

Fitzherbert had been dozing in a wing-backed chair in the middle of the room. After drinking since mid-morning he was feeling nauseous and had chosen to sleep with his back to the fire. The sound of the falling poker woke him, but he was momentarily unsure of his whereabouts.

Montgomery panicked. He had no wish to be caught in the middle of what must appear to be a foolish act of vandalism. He rushed out of the room, leaving the book to burn unattended. But as he left, one of the logs he had previously disturbed by his impatient prodding, slipped forwards in the fire and ejected the partly burned book onto the hearth.

Fitzherbert was now wide awake. He stood up and turned in the direction of the fireplace trying to establish what it was that had disturbed his slumber.

"That's odd," he mumbled to himself. "I could've sworn I heard something."

Seeing what he took to be a log burning on the hearth he swayed over towards the fire. At that moment Sweeney returned with Montgomery's cocoa.

"Put that log back on the fire, girl," Fitzherbert ordered, in a voice made hoarse by an excess of alcohol.

The girl put down the pot of cocoa with the other beverages and hastened to obey his instruction.

"'Tis a book, sir," she said in surprise, when she reached the fireplace. She blew on the flames that were burning around the edges of the book.

"That's no good, you stupid girl," shouted Fitzherbert. "Get some water."

Sweeney knew there was precious little tea or hot water left. But there was the pot of cocoa she had just brought into the room.

"It's as well Mr Montgomery didn't want his cocoa," she said, as she doused the book with the hot drink.

"What is going on George?"

Lady Annabelle had come into the room without either Fitzherbert or Sweeney noticing.

"Some damn-fool put this book on the fire, Annabelle," Fitzherbert explained. "We were trying to rescue it."

Fitzherbert took the book from Sweeney.

"That's all, girl. You can go now," he said.

"Yes, sir. Thank you, sir. Thank you, your ladyship," Sweeney said, as she curtsied and left the room.

Fitzherbert examined the book. It had been badly burned around the edges of the black leather cover and down part of the spine, and it was also badly stained by the brown cocoa. But other than that little damage had been done.

'The Great American Civil War,' he read.

"Good heavens," said Annabelle, as much to herself as to Fitzherbert. "That's the book I saw Inspector Parsons with the other evening. Whatever was it doing on the fire?"

"Blessed if I know, Annabelle," said Fitzherbert. "I was just having a doze when I heard something fall out of the fire."

Annabelle looked at Fitzherbert in disgust. His breath smelt abominably. It was really time he left Beaumont. They had all endured his company long enough. She would speak with Catherine about it immediately after dinner.

2222

Colonel Howard was surprised to see his visitor. It was the first time Montgomery had deigned to visit him since the shooting. Perhaps he was leaving and had come to say good-bye. He couldn't say he liked the man. Never had; from the first evening when he had made those ridiculous remarks about the way gentlemen were supposed to behave. Still, as Paul had said, what could you expect from a Yankee. Except he wasn't a Yankee, he was a Canadian. Canadian, Yankee, American, they were all the same nowadays as far as Howard was concerned. There were few enough southern gentlemen like Paul, more's the pity.

"How are you feeling, colonel?" Montgomery asked.

"Much better, now that you ask," Howard grunted, implying by his tone that he felt it a little late to be asking such a foolish question.

He took a closer look at Montgomery. The man looked on edge. He'd always thought him to be a quiet, self-controlled sort of a fellow. But he was clearly agitated about something. Perhaps it was Annabelle. He had heard from Catherine what a fool Montgomery was making of himself over her. No doubt she'd finally put him in his place.

"Are you leaving us then, Montgomery?" Howard asked, surprised by the expression of guilt that had suddenly appeared on Montgomery's face.

"Leaving? No, sir. Whatever gave you that impression?" replied Montgomery, surprised by Howard's unexpected perception.

"Just that I haven't seen you before. So I assumed you'd come to say good-bye."

Montgomery laughed nervously.

"You're right, Colonel," he said. "I've been rather remiss in that respect. Truth is I've been a little preoccupied these last few days. These terrible deaths have made me feel quite depressed.

"Depressed, my eye, sir. I hear you've been giving all your attention to Annabelle."

The colonel winked at him.

"She's a fine catch, young man," he said. "But you'll have to be patient. It'll take her a long time to get over Paul."

Howard had decided he might just as well play Montgomery along. There seemed little point in telling him the truth about Annabelle. He'd find out soon enough for himself.

Montgomery nodded, as though accepting the advice of one older and wiser in matters of the heart. But it was not as simple as Howard thought. His play for Annabelle had all been part of an act at first. It was an attempt to make himself look less of an outsider, and deflect any suspicion he might have attracted after Paul's murder. But it had been the wrong ploy. Like others before, he had found himself falling under the spell of this beautiful and gracious woman. His emotions had become confused. She represented a social order he had come to despise, but he had nevertheless found himself falling in love with her. He knew he had no recourse but to leave Beaumont. Sooner or later Parsons would get another copy of the book and put two and two together, but the thought of never seeing Annabelle again was a hard cross to bear.

"How's the investigation going, Colonel?" he asked, concentrating as best he could on the purpose of his visit.

"How the hell am I supposed to know," Howard retorted in exasperation. "I never see anything of Parsons, and even my man in Petersfield seems to think I'm entirely dispensable. All I can say is that having got the Dunnes where I want them I now have a note from Parsons telling me to release them."

If Parsons was confident enough to want the Dunnes released he must be on to something, thought Montgomery. If only he knew what that was.

"Where is Parsons?" he asked, trying to curb his growing impatience. "No one's seen him since yesterday."

"God knows where the little upstart is. All I know is that he was in Petersfield yesterday. This note was written in the station, but it wasn't given to me until just before you arrived. I asked Brown if he knew what Parsons was playing at, but the fool didn't know. All he could tell me was that Parsons had spent the night in the village following up a line of enquiry. What he was doing there, God only knows. Here, Montgomery, read this. What would you do if you were in my shoes?"

Howard handed the release note to Montgomery.

"Don't you think it's possible the Dunnes are innocent after all, Colonel?" Montgomery said, giving the contents careful consideration; and at the same time trying to hide his pleasure at being made privy, even in the smallest way to developments in the investigation. "After all they couldn't possibly be involved in the deaths of Paul and Ashton."

"Everyone knows that was Smith's work," snorted Howard. "And it's only a matter of time before we catch him. Someone like that hasn't the brains to elude the police for long. But I still feel sure that one or other of the Dunnes was involved in Quentin's death. Perhaps they both were. But that's just my instinct."

"Then I should trust your instincts and leave the two of them where they are for the time being, sir. If Parsons is so sure they're innocent, let him catch the real murderer first."

"Spoken like a man after my own heart, Montgomery," said Howard, suddenly warming to the man. "After all I've been in the game longer than Parsons, and I told him from the start I had a nose for such things. What a damned cheek of Brown, telling me I should sign this note at once."

Montgomery watched with satisfaction as Howard tore up the note and put the pieces in the large glass ash-tray on the bedside table. Then he took his leave.

"Good-bye for now, Colonel," he said. "I'm truly glad to see you're getting back to your old self."

Montgomery walked along the corridor to his own room. Once inside he locked the door. Within an hour or two it would be dark enough for him to leave, but until then he had no wish to be disturbed or to see anyone.

It was fortunate that Howard had decided to show him the release note and that he had been able to persuade him to leave the Dunnes where they were. It could hardly be pleasant for them in police custody, but from his point of view they were much safer there for the time being. Until he had made his getaway they were best kept as far away from the castle as possible.

From his room he could see the stable area where the horses were tethered and the policemen patrolling the grounds. He had watched the men carefully over the past two days and knew how regular their movements were. There was only ever one man on duty at any time, and once he was on the other side of the castle Montgomery knew it would be safe for him to go down to the stables. Once there he would take Ashton's grey and set the others loose in the Great Park. There was no point in making it easy for anyone to follow him. But before he did all that he had a note to write.

-53-

There was little sign of life at Beaumont when Parsons returned. Even the trees in the Great Park stood motionless under the bright moon, but two days into its wane; and like a great ship of state cast loose upon a dark and empty sea the castle waited, becalmed and silent.

Parsons went first to the Servants' Hall. He felt certain he would find Brown and Johnson there mulling over their evening mug of cocoa. To his surprise and embarrassment they both expressed concern at his absence, and he could only hope that he was not blushing when he repeated his story about pursuing other lines of enquiry in the village. For once he was grateful for their subservience, neither of them being bold enough to enquire as to the actual nature of those enquiries.

He had taken the precaution of removing Grace Spencer's bandage from his head. Not only would it have taken some explaining, it was also a reminder to him of an incident he would prefer to forget. But from Brown and Johnson's credulous expressions, it was clear that Spencer had followed his wife's instructions, and had been economic with the truth when explaining his family's involvement in whatever Parsons had been involved in during the past twenty-four hours.

However, although Parsons was relieved at the lack of awkward questions, he was more concerned at the absence of the book that Harris had sent from London.

"I was expecting to find a parcel on my return," he said, not without some irritation. "Have either of you seen it?"

Both men shook their heads.

"What about the other servants?" he asked Johnson. "Do they ever remove the mail from the Hall?"

"Only if they are asked, sir," Johnson replied. "Sometimes one of the ladies wants her post taken to her room, but more often than not they collect it themselves. Living quietly as we do down here, the arrival of the mail is quite an event in the day."

Parsons was puzzled. It was unusual for Harris to be careless. He had been sure the book would be awaiting his return; and could only assume that in his absence from the castle, Carpenter had decided to keep it until later. In which case it would come with the next post. To some extent consoled by this thought, he put the book out of his mind.

"What's been happening while I've been away, Brown?" he asked briskly. "I'm told Mr. Montagu left yesterday."

"Yes, sir," Brown replied, rather sulkily.

The sergeant was still put out at finding Spencer running errands for the inspector.

"He received a telegram from London on a private matter," Brown explained, "and left straight away."

"And didn't you ask what this private matter was?" demanded Parsons.

"No, sir," replied Brown, rather shamefacedly.

Parsons was becoming angry, and all his previous doubts about Brown's ability and initiative began to surface again.

"What about my note for the Chief Constable? Has he signed it?"

"Not yet, sir. He told me to report back tomorrow morning at nine. He said he wanted to think about it first."

Parsons was beginning to think he was surrounded by incompetents. Harris in London and Brown here. Could no one do what he asked!

"I suppose I'll have to see Colonel Howard myself," he snapped. "and no doubt I'll have to waste more time convincing him as to why he should sign the release paper. Now before I go to my room do you have anything else to report?"

"No, sir," said Brown. "We've finished searching the grounds, and the men are at a bit of a loose end at present."

"We'll soon sort that out, sergeant. Yes, Johnson, what is it?"

For several minutes the old servant had been trying to say something.

"There are two things, sir," he said. "Mr. Montgomery did not appear for dinner and Lady Annabelle wishes me to give you this book."

Johnson opened one of the dresser drawers and handed Parsons a badly charred book.

"Her ladyship asked me to give you this when you returned," Johnson said. "She said I was to tell you that it was rescued from the Drawing Room fire this afternoon. She says she has no idea who was responsible for putting it there, but thinks it is the same book she saw you with a few days ago."

Ignoring the criticism implied in the message from Annabelle, Parsons took the book from Johnson. He knew full well that this book could not be the exact copy that Annabelle referred to. That had been locked in his room and Brown had had charge of the key. But if this was the copy Harris had sent, how had it ended up in the fire? And why had the station-master not arranged to deliver it to him personally?

He carefully turned the burned book over in his hands and then gingerly opened it. The fly-leaf confirmed it was not Paul's copy, but the book from the Central Library in London. They would not be pleased to see its condition when it was eventually returned.

The leather binding had been badly charred and the edges of most of the pages were singed. But miraculously the book had survived.

Parsons could only assume the book had been closed when it was put on the fire. Had it been open the damage would have been far more serious, perhaps irrecoverable. So, if it had been someone's intention to destroy the book, they had not been very thorough. This, and his meeting with Grace Spencer, were two exceptionally good pieces of fortune.

Parsons put on his spectacles and began examining the photographs, skimming past those he had seen before and scrutinizing the ones that had previously been missing from Paul's copy of the book.

There was one of General Beauregard, a Confederate as handsome as his name and twice as haughty looking. Then two photographs of Confederate corpses: at Bull Run and Gettysburg. As if to mock the dead the next photograph showed a group of Yankee boy-musicians, smiling with all the innocence of their youth and the vain hope of the brave adventure they were about to embark upon. There was also a photograph of some black soldiers in the Northern Army. If they had intended fighting a war to bring freedom to their people, then the group of heavily armed Confederate cavalry soldiers in the next photograph would no doubt have been intent upon disabusing them.

But when Parsons reached the photograph opposite page two hundred and six, his heart missed a beat. This was the clue he had been seeking since Lord Quentin's death. The missing piece of the jigsaw that enabled him to understand a murderer's motive. This was the photograph the murderer had set out to prevent him or anyone else at Beaumont from seeing, in order to hide his identity and his background.

He fumbled in his pocket for his magnifying glass, but there was no doubting the identity of the man in the photograph The face might have aged over fifteen or so years, but there was no mistaking Montgomery among the contingent of sharpshooters from the Irish Brigade. The man who claimed to be a Canadian had fought for the Northern states, appeared to have Irish connections and was apparently a marksman.

He turned the book towards Brown and Johnson and put his finger on the photograph.

"Do you recognize this man?" he asked them both.

"Mr. Montgomery," they replied in unison, clearly surprised by what they saw.

"I have a feeling his name wasn't Montgomery in those days," said Parsons. "Something a little more Irish I'd say. I hate to say this, but Colonel Howard may have been right. There *was* an Irish connection all along, tenuous though it may have been. It certainly explains why Montgomery was so anxious to prevent anyone seeing this photograph. Especially anyone who would seize upon the smallest piece of evidence to link the murders with the Fenians. Somehow Montgomery got his hands on this book, and it's just our good fortune that he made such a mess of destroying it. But he must be desperate if he resorted to this. He must know that it's only a matter of time before we discover his identity. And if he didn't appear at dinner tonight he's probably already on the run. What time was he last seen?"

Neither Brown nor Johnson had seen Montgomery recently. Brown had not seen him since the day before and Johnson had last seen him at luncheon.

Parsons paced up and down for several minutes, deep in thought. Then he gave his orders.

"Brown, come with me to Montgomery's room. I think we can assume that he's already left the castle, but if we know what he took with him, it may help us decide where he's gone. After that I want you to take a telegram to the station-master to send to the Metropolitan Police and all the surrounding police stations. Colonel Howard may be able to help us with some of the addresses. Johnson, I want you to check the horses. I'm sure you'll find one of them missing. I want to know which one. And I want to see O'Mahoney. I don't think that girl's been entirely truthful with me in the past, and I want to know why.

There was little sign in Montgomery's room of his departure. His clothes and his shoes were still in the cupboard and his toiletries were arranged neatly on the washstand. The drawers in the chest revealed much the same story. A dressing-gown lay stretched across his bed, and under the pillow, when Parsons looked, was his neatly-folded night-gown. Either he had decided that he didn't have time to pack before he left, or most of his clothes were inappropriate for the place he was going. The clothes he had left behind were those of a gentleman, and Montgomery may have decided that in his new persona he didn't need them. If, as it now appeared, Montgomery had fled, he had taken few clothes with him.

The chair had been pulled out from his desk. Sometime during the day Montgomery had sat there. There was string and crumpled brown wax wrapping paper in the waste basket, and ink stains on the blotter.

Parsons picked up the blotter and held it in front of the mirror over the washstand, trying to read what Montgomery had written, and so engrossed in this task was he that he ignored Brown's attempt to attract his attention.

"There's a letter for you here on the mantelpiece, sir," he said for the third time.

Parsons seized the envelope from Brown. Montgomery may have left the castle in a hurry, but there was nothing to show that in the firm strokes with which he had addressed the envelope.

The note inside was brief.

'Inspector Parsons,' it said. *'I believe you to be a man of honor. You may not choose to believe it, but I also consider myself as one. Even if you have not seen the book by now, my sudden disappearance must place me under suspicion, and I know you will eventually discover my secret. My sole reason for writing to you now is to tell you that neither Mary O'Mahoney, nor the Dunnes, nor anyone else knew anything of what I was doing. I swear that on my mother's grave, Parsons, and there is no greater oath I can make.'*

The note was unsigned, but only Montgomery could have written it.

Shortly afterwards O'Mahoney arrived with Johnson, who explained that she had been reluctant to come by herself. He also informed Parsons that all the horses were missing from the stables.

"So much for your security precautions, Brown," said Parsons to the crestfallen sergeant. "He's got such a head-start on us now it would be foolish to think of following him. But he'll soon have more than a few of us to contend with."

Parsons then turned to the two servants.

"You've both been in this room before and you've seen what Mr. Montgomery wore while he was here. I want you to take a good look round the room and tell me what is missing."

With O'Mahoney's half-hearted assistance Johnson began sifting through the clothes in the cupboard and the chest.

"I'd say he was wearing the same clothes he wore when he went riding on the Downs, sir. That day he was wearing a green Ulster coat with a cape and a brown worsted suit. As far as I can see he's taken little else. Perhaps a shirt or two and some fresh under-clothing. I don't think he ever wore a hat, sir. At least I never saw him with one."

Only on the night he shot Lord Paul, thought Parsons.

"Did you ever see a hat in this room, O'Mahoney?" Parsons asked fiercely.

"Nay, sir," she said quietly, almost as though she were afraid of the sound of her own voice.

"Thank you, Johnson," Parsons said. "You can go now. I don't think there's much more you can do for me tonight."

O'Mahoney attempted to leave the room at the same time.

"Not so fast, my girl," said Parsons. "There are still one or two questions I want to ask you. Come over here where I can see you better."

She made her way slowly and reluctantly across the room to where Parsons stood and waited demurely in front of him with her hands clasped over her apron.

"Before he left Mr. Montgomery left me a note in which he as much as confessed to the murders," Parsons said dramatically. "He also implied that you might know something about the events on the night Lord Quentin died. What have you got to say about that?"

It was a slight exaggeration of what Montgomery had actually written, but O'Mahoney was hardly likely to know that.

"I know nothing, sir," she said, clearly frightened by Parsons' unexpected revelation.

"Come now. You've already admitted to me that you were with Montgomery all that night. I even seem to recall you being quite sarcastic when you answered my question as to what you were doing."

The girl lowered her head, avoiding Parsons' eyes.

"You admitted that you tied Lord Quentin to the bed," he said quietly, "and yet you still expect me to believe that you know nothing about his murder. Even though the man you slept with that night admits he killed him. Do you expect me to believe you?"

Parsons' voice had gradually been getting louder, so much so that Brown had taken one or two steps towards the girl, half expecting to be asked to repeat his earlier treatment of Brendan Dunne. But Parsons held up his hand to stop him, and when he spoke again his voice was quieter but still as menacing.

"Well, Mary," he said. "I don't want to have you taken away to Petersfield to join your friend, Claire, in jail. But you leave me no option. You are a very foolish girl if you think, like O'Brien, that falling in love with a common criminal is an answer to your prayers. He may have been your lover, but a man like Montgomery isn't worth going to prison for."

The effect on the girl was more dramatic than even Parsons had expected.

"To be sure, he was never my lover, sir," she said, the desperation in her voice as clear as the tears in her eyes. "And his name isn't Montgomery. It's Larkin. Thomas Larkin. And may God help me, he's my uncle."

-54-

*P*arsons sat the girl on the edge of the bed. Then he poured a glass of water from the jug on the washstand and made her drink it. He waited until she had stopped crying before speaking.

"Tell me about your uncle," he said gently.

O'Mahoney's large brown eyes, brimming with tears, looked up at Parsons.

"I'd never seen my Uncle Thomas before the day he came to Beaumont, sir," she said. "And to be sure, even if he'd been using his real name, I'd never have known who he was. But he showed me a letter from my Ma. It was, he said, her way of telling me who he was."

She paused to take another sip from the glass.

"Uncle Thomas said he'd just been over to Ireland trying to find his kin and the place where he was born. He said it hadn't been easy. Sure, wasn't he only a wee boy of four when he went to America with his Daddy. And wasn't that during the Famine. God knows, there are few enough people alive in Ballycarra today who can remember those terrible times. His own Ma had died then, and he had always believed that all his brothers and sisters had died as well. But one of them survived, sir. His youngest sister, Claire. She's my Ma, and Claire Dunne's aunt."

"How many brothers and sisters had he?" asked Parsons quietly.

"Eight, sir, including my Ma."

Parsons remembered Montgomery's story of Irishmen abroad romanticizing about their homeland. There would have been few such happy memories for him.

"You can imagine, sir, how he felt after all these years when he found the sister he had always believed was dead. And he told me how angry he was when Ma told him how we girls were forced out of necessity to go over the water to England and work for Lord de Courcey. The self-same man that owned most of the land around Ballycarra, and who did as little for our people today as his family had done when the potatoes failed. My uncle said that after listening to Ma and seeing how badly our people were faring in Ireland, he decided to come to Beaumont and judge for himself how we were being treated over here.

"And what did he say about what he saw?"

"He said the English gentry were no better then the Southern slave-owners. And hadn't he fought a war against them. Sure he was in no position to start a war in England, but he would do what he could to see that justice was done."

"Was murder his idea of justice?" asked Parsons.

"We know little about your English justice in Ballycara," O'Mahoney replied angrily, challenging him to answer her criticism of the authority he represented.

And I am in no position to allow a murderer to go unpunished, thought Parsons. Even though I may understand his sense of injustice and his anger at finding how nothing had changed during the years of his absence in the country of his birth.

"Tell me what happened the night Lord Quentin died," he asked.

She placed the half-empty glass on the bedside table and crossed herself.

"May God forgive me for speaking ill of the dead," she said. "When I went to his room Uncle Thomas made me explain what it was we had to do for that lecherous old man. My uncle knew that it was wee Claire who was with him, and it was all I could do to stop him going right then into Lord Quentin's room and killing him. But then Claire came into my uncle's room to say his lordship had fallen asleep, all trussed-up as usual. My uncle said he wanted to see for himself, but when I said I'd go with him he wouldn't let me."

"How long was he gone?"

"I couldn't say, sir. But it seemed like a long time."

"And what did he do when he came back to his room?"

O'Mahoney covered her face with her hands, so that Parsons could barely hear what she said.

"He lit eight candles. He said that was one for his Ma and one for each of brothers and sisters."

She lifted her white apron to her face and wept as though her heart had been broken, leaving Parsons to speculate whether it was the wickedness of her uncle's deed or the tragedy of his family that caused the tears.

He could imagine what Montgomery had thought that night when he reached Lord Quentin's room. Lying helpless before him on the bed was the powerful head of the family he held responsible for the deaths of so many of his own kin. A man who would have forced himself upon an innocent young girl, but for the fact that he had drunk himself into a state of unconsciousness. This man had abused Montgomery's own niece and others besides, and had felt no shame for it. On the contrary he had boasted of his exploits. But the man was now completely at Montgomery's mercy.

It was little wonder Montgomery had chosen to act in the way he did. And when he had satisfied his desire for revenge, he had drawn the curtains over his shameful act. No matter what it was that had driven him, his act was not one that any self-proclaimed man of honor could ever be proud of.

When pressed by Parsons, O'Mahoney claimed that she had no idea whether her uncle was involved in any other murders. Like most other people she assumed that Smith had been responsible for the deaths of Lord Paul and Captain Ashton. But she could also see the possibility that her uncle would want to revenge himself against the whole de Courcey family. He might well have decided to kill Lord Quentin's successor. But she could think of no reason why he might want to murder Ashton. Perhaps her uncle had worked with Smith, and it was Smith who had killed Ashton. She didn't know what to think. She had only known her uncle a few days, and couldn't be expected to explain how his mind worked. And after what he had done to Lord Quentin, she was too frightened ever to speak to him again.

When she had finished speaking she was emotionally drained, and Parsons sent her to bed. There was no question of her doing any more work, he said, and if Mr. Johnson or Mrs. Hughes objected to that, she was to tell them to speak with him.

Even Brown appeared to be moved by what he had heard.

"I feel real bad now that I ever hit that boy," he said, after O'Mahoney had left the room.

Colonel Howard had finished the small decanter of brandy that Catherine had brought him after dinner, and was snoring contentedly when Parsons and Brown entered his room.

"What in God's name is it now?" he asked, making no attempt to hide his irritation at being woken.

At first he was disbelieving when he heard the explanation for Montgomery's disappearance. But his objections were silenced when he was told of the photograph and the murder weapon, and heard about the events at the lake on the night Lord Paul was murdered.

"Always knew there was something suspicious about that fellow, Montgomery," he snorted. "Trying to pass himself off as a gentleman. I can always spot an impostor a mile off."

Parsons refrained from mentioning that the Chief Constable had failed to do so in the case of a certain Henry Longstaff. But he had no wish to upset the colonel, especially as he was going to keep him from his sleep a while longer. Howard's help would be necessary in compiling a list of the police stations in Hampshire and the neighboring counties; and Parsons needed these to start the man-hunt.

While Howard was engaged in this task, Parsons composed the telegram he wanted sent. Brown would take this and the list of police stations to the station-master's cottage for immediate dispatch. When Brown pointed out that there were now no horses, Parsons told him to walk. The lack of horses was Brown's fault, and one way or another the telegrams must reach their destinations before daylight.

There being nothing else he felt he could usefully do that night, Parsons went to bed; leaving instructions for Brown that either he or one of his constables should wake him if there was anything to report.

-55-

15th September 1880

Sergeant Rory Campbell was sitting at the station officer's desk in Portsea Police Station. He was feeling especially pleased with the world. With the inspector away on sick leave Campbell was in temporary charge of the station in the tough dock area of Portsmouth. He liked being in charge. It gave him more opportunity to throw his substantial weight around, and a greater degree of freedom to act without any questions being asked.

Campbell loved living and working close to the sea and associating with the tough men who made their livelihood by it; and he was a familiar figure, both on duty and off, in the dockside bars they frequented.

For the second time he carefully perused the telegram that had arrived early that morning while he decided upon a course of action.

'From Inspector Parsons Metropolitan Police Criminal Investigation Department attached Hampshire Constabulary.' he read. *'To officers commanding stations in Hampshire, Surrey and Sussex. Wanted for Murder of Lord Quentin de Courcey of Beaumont Castle: Thomas Larkin alias Harrison Montgomery. Dark haired clean shaven slim build approximately five feet nine inches tall. North American accent. Last seen wearing green Ulster coat and cape and brown suit. Possibly armed extremely dangerous. Possible Fenian connections. Last seen at Beaumont afternoon 14 September. Thought to be attempting to leave country. Left Beaumont by horse. Request watch roads but also request vigilance at railways stations and ports. Report sightings or suspicions of sightings to Parsons care of Petersfield police station.'*

Parsons had hesitated before using the word 'Fenian' in relation to Montgomery. Although his Irish ancestry was now established it did not automatically follow that the man was a rebel. He had chosen the word more as a warning of Montgomery's dangerous nature than as a statement of his political affiliations. Parsons knew only too well from his own experience that policemen were more inclined to be vigilant when dealing with fanatical Fenians or mass murderers than with other forms of criminals; and in this instance that was exactly what Parsons wanted. At all costs, Montgomery had to be prevented from escaping back to North America and avoiding justice. There was, however, always a danger that some policemen might over-react.

It was policemen like Sergeant Campbell that Parsons had in mind. A tough Glaswegian, he had been twelve years a Royal

Marine before becoming a policeman. His strict Presbyterian upbringing and the disciplines of his military and naval careers had left him with little time for most Irishmen. In his eyes they were dirty, lazy and troublesome. This had grown into something of a personal crusade since the previous year, when his brother-in-law, a sergeant in the Royal Irish Constabulary, had been shot dead by Irish republicans while on patrol in County Sligo, leaving behind a widow and five bairns.

"So we have a Fenian bastard on the run," he growled at the constable who had brought him the telegram. "An Irish-American fox by the sound of it, trying to make a run for its lair. Well he won't make a run through this port. Not if I've anything to do with it."

Campbell drew himself up to his full seventy-five inches, reaching for his helmet and the thick walking stick that was his trade-mark in the port. It was made of ash and the knob that served as a handle had been hollowed out and filled with lead. Over the years it had proved a particularly effective close-combat weapon, as many a drunken sailor could testify.

"Evans! Foster!" he yelled. "Follow me. We may have a murdering bloody Irishman loose in the docks, and I know how much you boys would like to get your hands on him."

It was clear from the malevolent grins on the faces of the two burly policemen who broke into step behind Campbell that they would like nothing better.

By late afternoon the trio were beginning to think that their prey had decided to avoid Portsmouth. None of the bar-owners or sea-captains in the numerous drinking haunts they visited knew anything of a man answering Montgomery's description trying to gain a passage out of the country.

In the course of their search they had accepted numerous free tots of rum; and although their initial enthusiasm for the chase had long since gone, the dark Jamaican spirit still kept their blood pounding and their hunting instincts alive.

'The Jack Tar' was tucked away in the corner of a dark alley at the edge of the docks. With its reputation for out-of-hours drinking and gambling, any sailor who had just been paid off after a spell at sea was well advised to ignore it if they wished to retain their hard-earned money. Needless to say such advice was rarely heeded, and when the sergeant and his two cohorts arrived the bar was full. There was a brief lull in the conversation at the sight of the uniforms of the three large policemen, and at several tables playing cards were hastily concealed. But when the regulars recognized Campbell's familiar face the serious business of drinking and card-sharping quickly resumed.

Bert Smailes had already poured three large glasses of rum before the policemen reached the bar. With fights between drunken seamen a regular feature in his establishment, it was well for him to keep on the right side of Rory Campbell.

"Compliments of the house, gentlemen," Smailes said. "I can see by your uniforms that this visit isn't entirely for pleasure."

Campbell tossed the brown spirit down his throat with one swift and effortless movement of his left hand before answering. With the other he grasped his stick.

"Any strangers through here today, Bert?" Campbell asked. "Especially ones looking for a spare berth."

"You mean like the American in the corner?"

Smailes inclined his head towards the darkest corner of the room where a lone figure sat with his back to the bar. The man had removed his thick green outer coat and draped it over an adjacent chair while he sat warming himself by the fire.

Campbell nudged the two other constables and took a firmer grip on his ash-plant.

"We may be in luck, my lads," he whispered. "But watch your step. The bastard may be armed."

The three men moved quietly through the drinkers until there was but a few yards of sawdust-covered floor between them and their prey.

"Montgomery! Or is it Larkin!" bellowed Campbell in a voice that had in previous years instilled fear into the hearts of the young Marines in the Portsmouth Division. It now brought an expectant silence to the crowded bar.

The man spun round in his chair and sprang to his feet, surprise and fear written plainly across his face at the sight of the three large policemen.

"So it is you, you murdering Fenian bastard," hissed Campbell. "Well, we're taking you in mister. Which way is it to be? The easy way or the other?"

Montgomery had no intention of finding out the difference between the two options, and flung himself towards the gap between Campbell and the policeman to his left.

They were both too quick for him. With the experience of many years of dockside fights they waited for their victim to reach a suitable position midway between them before landing their blows on each side of his head. Once on the ground they continued to strike him, fired by the rum in their bellies and encouraged by the cheering crowd in the bar. After several frenzied minutes Montgomery lay motionless, with both collar-bones and several ribs broken, and severe brain damage caused by the business end of Campbell's stick.

Montgomery clung to his life for a further sixteen hours, although for most of that time he remained unconscious. After being half dragged and half carried to the station by Campbell's men, a local doctor was eventually summoned with reluctance from his rounds; and after a summary examination in the police cells declared the victim beyond saving.

Parsons arrived later the next morning, in response to Campbell's jubilant telegram; and spent the few remaining hours of Montgomery's life with him in his cell. Towards the end his patience was rewarded and Montgomery regained consciousness. It was only briefly, but in those fleeting minutes he seemed in full control of his senses. When he recognized Parsons he beckoned him closer.

"You have my note?" he said with difficulty.

Parsons nodded.

"I meant what I said. No one else was involved."

Parsons nodded again.

"Don't worry," said Parsons, his head bent over towards Montgomery's ear. "I've known for some time that none of the Irish servants were involved."

Montgomery said nothing, but Parsons could see a brief glimmer of satisfaction cross his battered face. But there was still one question Parsons wanted answering.

"Why after all this time," he asked, "did you still feel it necessary to murder Lord Quentin?"

Though his eyes were now closed Montgomery twisted his mouth into the ghost of a smile.

"An old Indian saying, my friend," he said, his voice now even fainter than before. "Vengeance is a dish eaten cold."

They were his last words. Not long after that he died.

-56-

17th September 1880

Parsons had returned to London the day after Montgomery's death to Superintendent Jeffries' approbation. The dour Jeffries was unusually delighted with the outcome of his young inspector's investigation, especially after the Commissioner had shown him the grateful letters from both Lady Annabelle and Lady Catherine praising Parsons' hard work and perseverance. It was a very satisfactory state of affairs for all concerned. Even the Hampshire Constabulary could afford to be pleased with themselves. It was, after all, one of their officers who had arrested Montgomery.

Subsequent information from America, Canada and Ireland had substantiated Parsons' own deductions and much of the anecdotal evidence about Montgomery. Born in County

Mayo in 1843, Montgomery—or Thomas Larkin as he then was, and as Parsons now preferred to think of him—had emigrated with his father to America in 1847 and settled in an Irish community in Rochester, a small town in New York State near the Canadian border. Those that still remembered him, had said that young Thomas had grown up believing that he and his father were the only members of his family to survive the dreadful famine in Ireland.

Reports from the Rochester police revealed that as a young man Larkin was no lover of authority, and Parsons was not surprised to learn that his name had been linked with Fenian sympathizers in that area. But there was no evidence of him doing anything other than distributing anti-British leaflets.

It was not until he joined the Union Army in 1862 that there was further record of him. Not surprisingly he had volunteered to fight against the Confederacy. A young man schooled in the tales of the inhumanity of the absentee English landlords would readily choose to fight a war against the plantation owners ruling the slave-economy of the southern states. His remarks at dinner the night before he murdered Lord Quentin had made his feelings on that score abundantly clear. But the ultimate irony was that this involvement, captured in a single photograph, was more instrumental than anything else in destroying his bogus identity.

After the Civil War Larkin had disappeared. There were rumors in Rochester that he had been involved in Fenian skirmishes on the border with Canada, and that he had subsequently gone to live in that country. No one knew for certain where he was. But he was never seen in Rochester again. Perhaps, thought Parsons, he had become disillusioned with post-war America and the failure of the Fenians to achieve any significant success either in Canada or back at home in Ireland. Maybe, as he had told Parsons, he had simply become a drifter. But whatever the life was he had chosen, there were no police records of either a Thomas Larkin or a Harrison Montgomery in New York State or any of the major cities in Canada during the late eighteen-sixties and eighteen-seventies.

It was impossible to say whether a man called Harrison Montgomery had ever existed, or whether Larkin had simply invented him. After all, there were thousands of Scotsmen in Canada who had been driven off their lands during the Highland Clearances, and from the many stories Larkin would have heard as he traveled around there would have been ample scope for him to create a persona and a convincing ancestry for himself. He did, after all, have a writer's imagination, and any apposite story would have been convincing enough to deceive most Englishman.

Parsons had no doubt that Larkin had never forgotten his home in Ireland and the family that had so tragically perished there. When he had spoken of the Celtic Diaspora he was clearly voicing his own feelings, and not merely echoing the stories he had heard in Canadian bars. And it was clear from what he had told his niece, Mary O'Mahoney, that visiting Ballycara to find his roots had finally set his mind upon revenge. What he found in Ballycara must have appalled him. His people were still forced to live in abject poverty, and absentee English landlords like the de Courceys continued to take every possible advantage of them.

It was probably while he was in Ireland that Larkin had decided to arm himself. The Webley revolver he had used to murder Lord Paul was one of several stolen during a raid on an isolated Irish Constabulary post in County Cork some months before Larkin had come to Britain. The Irish police had assumed the raid to be the work of Fenians operating out of Cork City, but links to a group in Dublin were established later when one of the revolvers was subsequently used to assassinate Lord Blakewell, an Englishman living in County Meath. With Fenian credentials of his own Larkin would have found it easy to make the necessary contacts and obtain a weapon; indeed the international success and recognition accorded to Fenian groups operating in England and Ireland in recent years might well have been an additional incentive for Larkin to visit Britain.

Using Alexander as a means of gaining entry to Beaumont was a master-stroke. As a member of a house-party, Larkin's pedigree would never be questioned, especially as he had concocted a story about being a writer. It was assumed, even by the Howards, that all Alexander's friends were creative in one way or another. And what did the average Englishman know or care about North American writers? Only Paul had been sufficiently concerned to point out, with some irritation, that there was a difference between America and Canada. As far as everyone else was concerned the man with the gauche accent was just someone from the other side of the Atlantic.

But Larkin was no fool. He knew that if he used a Webley revolver stolen from the Irish police to shoot an English aristocrat with Irish estates, the murder would almost certainly be construed as a political assassination. And he knew that in those circumstances suspicion would fall on any local Irish people. That would include the servants, among whom was his own niece. If he was going to kill Lord Quentin he would have to be more subtle.

From what Mary O'Mahoney had said Larkin had not planned his crime in any detail before he arrived at Beaumont. He merely took advantage of whatever situation presented itself. Finding his intended victim defenseless as he did, was a bonus he could never have expected, and was an invitation to him to act. From what his niece had told him he knew that Lord Quentin's sexual perversions were no secret, so it may have crossed Larkin's mind that the manner of Lord Quentin's death might even be construed as a masochistic sexual gambit that had badly misfired. Had that been his intention he made one vital error. Before Larkin left the room he had closed the curtains around the bed. Johnson had found them that way in the morning, but Claire Dunne had said they were open when she left the room. Larkin's motive in closing the curtains would never now be known—perhaps at the last moment he was ashamed of what he had done—but the drawn curtains around the bed had always suggested to Parsons that Lord Quentin's death was neither suicide nor misadventure.

The arrest of Brendan Dunne must have come as an unpleasant surprise. In spite of his careful precautions Larkin had failed to keep suspicion away from the Irish servants. It was scarcely his fault. He could never have anticipated that the investigation would initially be led by an incompetent police officer like Colonel Howard, with such a blinkered approach to the crime and such a misdirected sense of justice.

Larkin had not communicated with Mary O'Mahoney after Lord Quentin's murder, so it was impossible to say at what point he decided to kill Paul and why. It was abundantly clear that Larkin found Paul's superior southern ways thoroughly objectionable, especially in the way in which he held Yankees, blacks and Irish in equally low esteem. In itself this was hardly a reason to kill Paul; but Larkin could not have foreseen that Paul would not only unexpectedly become head of a family that he despised, but also possessed a book containing a photograph that was an embarrassing link with his Irish past. Larkin may not have known about the book before his visit to Beaumont; but when Paul had given the book to Parsons who in turn had left it on the breakfast table he might have been curious enough to glance through it. And finding the incriminating photograph he had removed it. If, indeed, the book had been one of the reasons behind Larkin's decision to murder Paul, there was a delightful irony about it. Paul was, if anything, a greater impostor than Larkin himself; and he had confessed to Parsons that he had never opened the book. Larkin, of course, would not have known that. He was only aware that the book existed and that more curious people, like Parsons or even Ashton, might decide to read it and see his photograph.

Apart from all that, a second murder while Brendan Dunne was in custody would hopefully cause the authorities to question Dunne's involvement with the first. But that, thought Parsons, was probably wishful thinking on Larkin's part.

But at what stage had Smith become involved? And for what reason? These were questions that exercised Parsons' mind late into the night in his attic room in Camberwell.

He doubted that Smith was involved in any way with Lord Quentin's murder. He had far too much to lose from the death of his patron. But Paul's death was another matter. If Smith was in danger of losing his job as a result of Paul inheriting the title and Larkin had money with which to bribe him, Parsons could well imagine that Smith would have willingly agreed to be an accomplice.

From what Grace Spencer had said Smith's involvement in Paul's murder was a minor one. He had merely stood by the lake with Larkin's horse while Larkin walked to Beaumont to commit his crime. By then Smith was in all probability already a murderer. By then Smith had battered Ashton to death.

It was far from clear whether Larkin was involved in Ashton's death or Smith had acted alone. There was every good reason why Larkin should have chosen to set fire to the stables. It created an excellent diversion and it also destroyed Ashton's body. But if burning Ashton's body was the main reason for the fire that idea must have been Smith's. Larkin could not have known of Ashton's death. Had he known he would never have returned the grey horse to the stables. The fact that Ashton's grey had remained at the castle was proof that he had never left.

Larkin was dead and Smith was missing. It was all very neat and tidy, and it satisfied both the police in Hampshire and Parsons' superiors in London. But there were still too many unanswered questions for Parsons liking. Was it Ashton who stole Catherine's money? If so, when did he take it? O'Brien would surely have known if he had left his room during their last night together; and if Ashton had waited until O'Brien had left his room he would have run a greater risk of finding Catherine awake. As Parsons knew, she was an early riser.

But even if Ashton did steal the money, the evidence for Smith killing him for it was entirely conjectural. Everything pointed towards Ashton being battered to death in his room and his body moved to the stables later by way of Lord Quentin's room. The rug under Lord Quentin's bed and the rope at the bottom of the castle wall was clear evidence of that. So why would Smith run the risk of killing Ashton in his room, knowing full well that he would have the problem of moving the body? It would be far more likely that Smith would wait until Ashton had reached the stables.

And there was another very significant factor which did not fit easily into this scenario. On the morning that Ashton was murdered Lord Quentin's room was locked and only Catherine had a key.

As far as Colonel Howard and the Hampshire Constabulary were concerned the case was closed. Even Superintendent Jeffries had tired of Parsons' all too frequent references to the unanswered questions at Beaumont. He had far more pressing problems closer to home.

But that was before Parsons had received a letter from Victoria Mayhew and another body was discovered at Beaumont.

-57-

t the time of Geoffrey Montagu's disappearance Parsons had telegraphed from Beaumont instructing Sergeant Harris to call at Oliver Craig's house in Woburn Square, Sir Jeremiah Montagu's mansion in Sloane Square and Victoria Mayhew's small cottage in Highgate. Harris had drawn a blank at each one. Montagu's whereabouts were unknown at any of the addresses, although both he and Caroline Mayhew had been at Craig's Bloomsbury home on the day before Harris' visit. He was also unfortunate not to have seen one or other of them at either of the other two places, as Caroline had visited her mother and Montagu his father but a few hours after Harris had called. These unfortunate coincidences, even had they been known, would have appeared of relatively minor importance at the time; but they became of increasing significance to Parsons during the coming weeks.

The letter from Victoria Mayhew had arrived a week after Parsons' return to London. It had been addressed to him at

505

Scotland Yard and said only that Montagu had given her an envelope addressed to the inspector. But it was enough to make him cut short his day at the office and jump into the first available cab to Highgate.

Victoria Mayhew was a petite lady in her mid-forties. She was as dainty as the small airy sitting-room in which she received Parsons, with its views over Hampstead Heath and mementos of her profession on the pale pink walls. Tight dark curls like bubbles and large brilliant azure eyes complemented her small round doll-like face. This apparent desire to remain forever young was also reflected in her choice of clothes. She wore a white lace cotton dress, with a large bow tied in the wide band of pink ribbon that was tightly fastened around her tiny waist.

By profession she was an artist's model, she explained to Parsons, noticing his immediate interest in the uneven rows of paintings around the walls, recording her career from the cupidity of youth to her present more rounded middle age. It was a career that had been followed both by her own mother and her one daughter, Caroline. The face in the paintings appeared never to have changed, and had Parsons had the opportunity to see the portrait of Caroline at Woburn Square he would at once have seen the remarkable similarity between Victoria and her daughter. Caroline might have inherited her father's eyes, but there was no mistaking the delicate bone-structure of her mother.

There was nothing therefore about Victoria Mayhew's demeanor that afternoon to prepare Parsons for the news that her daughter was dead. Brief reports of the discovery of Caroline's body and her subsequent funeral had appeared in the *Hampstead and Highgate Gazette*, but that was a newspaper neither Parsons nor any of his colleagues had reason to read.

It was not until they had exhausted the polite small-talk and Parsons had finished his second cup of tea that she spoke of more serious matters.

"I saw little of Caroline over the past few years," she explained in a small coquettish voice that grief had weakened to a point where it seemed scarcely to exist. "She moved out of this house into the bohemian world of Bloomsbury just after she was nineteen, and she seldom came home. When she did she never spoke of her relationships. Perhaps she thought I would disapprove. In all probability I would have done. You see, I had a very good idea of the kind of people she was mixing with. I had entered a similar demi-monde at much the same age, and that had resulted in my bringing up a child on my own."

Parsons found his gaze drawn towards the paintings on the walls of the room.

"Yes, inspector I think you understand what I mean," she said. "Once a woman's body becomes a commodity she can expect few favors from men."

During the long silence that followed Parsons found himself trying to reconcile her child-like appearance and the professional use to which she put her doll-like body. Sitting chastely as she did on the chaise-longue with its lapis-lazuli fabric, it seemed impossible to think that she was the same woman whose naked body appeared in many of the paintings around her.

"I knew nothing of Caroline's relationship with her half-brother," she said. "Believe me, if I did I would have done my utmost to end it. Caroline only told me of it just before she died. That was when she told me she was pregnant. Naturally I wanted to know who the father was, and when she told me I had no choice but to tell her the terrible truth. It was more than the poor girl could bear. At one moment she was delirious with joy at the prospect of bearing Geoffrey's child, and at the next she was terrified at the thought of the child being born physically deformed or with a mental handicap. I didn't know what to do for the best. When I learned from her where Geoffrey was I sent him a telegram asking him to return to London. But before he arrived she had left the house. Neither of us saw her again, and she didn't even leave a note of explanation. Two days later a policeman called to tell me her body had been found in the Thames."

The two brilliant pools of blue shimmered and slowly filled with tears. Almost imperceptibly her eyes over-flowed, causing a tiny stream to trickle down her cheeks and fall silently onto her lace dress. After several minutes, during which Parsons watched awkwardly and helplessly, she stopped crying and dabbed her eyes gently with a small lace handkerchief. Once composed she got up and took a white envelope from the drawer of a small lacquered Oriental table.

"Geoffrey gave me this letter for you at Caroline's funeral, inspector," she said. "He asked me to wait for a week before giving it to you as he hadn't then completed his plans to leave the country. Quite why he chose me to carry out this errand I couldn't say. Part of me was still angry at him for what he had inflicted upon Caroline, but the other part realized that the poor boy's heart was as broken as mine. From what I saw of him and from what he said it was obvious to me that he loved my daughter, and until very recently had been as ignorant of their blood ties as she. So in spite of everything I forgave him.

"Where has he gone?" Parsons asked.

The briefest of smiles crossed Victoria Mayhew's face.

"Greece," she said. "Where else. He told me he was going to follow the footsteps of Byron and hoped to settle eventually in Salona, the town where Byron died. I'm no judge of these matters, inspector, but I'm sure the foolish boy has no talent as a poet. No doubt he's been filled with the false flattery of his friends in Bloomsbury. There's nothing worse than artistic conceit. I should know. I've sat for enough second rate painters.

"How is he managing to support himself?" Parsons asked.

"His father, of course. At the last moment his father relented and gave him money to get out of the country. Perhaps he eventually felt a touch of remorse about a situation for which he was partly responsible. But if that man thinks that by paying his daughter's funeral expenses he has exonerated himself in my eyes for his complete lack of interest in Caroline's welfare he is very much mistaken."

Her words were so bitter it was difficult to imagine she was talking about a man who had once been her lover.

"What ever did I see in that ape?" she asked, gazing wistfully around at her meager possessions and absentmindedly strengthening a crease in her dress. "Nothing, inspector. I saw nothing. And I wasn't foolish enough to think I'd ever find anything. To be perfectly honest I was more concerned about having some financial security and somewhere comfortable to live. Isn't that what we all want?"

After a moment's further contemplation she turned again to Parsons.

"But I'm delaying you from your business, inspector," she said. "And I must confess I'm as curious as you must be to see what Geoffrey has sent you."

Parsons opened the envelope. There were three items inside. A brief hand-written note, a receipt from a goldsmith in Hatton Gardens, and a monocle with a pink ribbon attached to it.

-58-

Parsons turned first to the note and the now familiar lines of poetry.

*'She walks in beauty as the night
Of cloudless climes and starry eyes;
And all that's best of dark and bright
Meet in her aspect and her eyes.'*

The verse was followed by two terse paragraphs.

'You will need no reminding that the man who wrote those lines was disgraced for impregnating his half-sister; and I need hardly remind you how your father will react when he knows. My silence will cost five hundred guineas.

We have never met, but you will know me when I contact you again.'

The note, like the previous one Parsons had seen in Montagu's room at Beaumont was undated and unsigned. But this time he had no doubt as to the identity of the author.

511

It was Ashton. The man who had told O'Brien that he was expecting to receive a tidy sum of money before leaving Beaumont, and who had been bludgeoned to death before he could go.

The invoice was from one A Jacobson of 48 Hatton Gardens. It was made out to Catherine de Courcey of Beaumont Castle, Hampshire, for the sum of twenty guineas for the purchase and engraving of two silver hip flasks. It was dated the fifteenth of August eighteen-eighty.

Parsons had little doubt that these flasks were one and the same as the flasks found in the stables after the fire. The question was, how had they arrived there? In Brendan Dunne's experience—limited though that might be—Lord Quentin had never given Smith anything of a personal nature, and these flasks plainly bore his initials. Not only that, they were a recent gift from his daughter. It even seemed unlikely that Smith would actually want the flasks, as selling or pawning them could lead to some awkward questions.

Smith, of course, may have stolen them. But that also seemed unlikely. He was already receiving money and other small items from Lord Quentin, and it would have been foolish of Smith to resort to stealing and thereby run the risk of souring his relationship with his patron. But it was quite another matter if the theft had taken place after Lord Quentin's death.

Another possibility was that Smith had been given them in payment for a service he had performed. A murder, for instance. And if that was the case, who had paid him?

But whatever the reason and however he may have come by the flasks, Smith had nevertheless left them behind in the stables. And that seemed strange, for a man who was a fugitive from justice and in need of all the money he could get.

Parsons had no doubt that the monocle was Ashton's, and the pink ribbon fastened to it the one O'Brien had given him. She had explained that it was his last request of her before she left his room. If O'Brien was telling the truth Ashton had the monocle when she last saw him. And that was in his room shortly before he died.

These three items created more questions than they provided answers. But now there was a new and over-riding question. How had Montagu come into possession of the monocle? Was he present when Ashton was killed? Was he Ashton's murderer? And if so, why had he presented Parsons with such an obvious clue to his guilt?

-59-

Arnold Jacobson's small shop in Hatton Gardens jewelers' community was one of the few still remaining open when Parsons arrived. Business that day had been slow, and Jacobson had decided to stay open an hour longer than usual in the hope of attracting one or two of the clerks from the nearby law courts, banks or insurance offices on their way home after they had visited the public houses in Holborn. Who knows, he thought, a pint or two of strong ale might loosen their wallets.

When the small bearded jeweler saw Parsons striding determinedly towards his shop his hopes rose at the prospect of a late sale, only to be dashed when the inspector explained the reason for his visit.

He remembered Catherine de Courcey well. She had haggled long and hard over the price of the flasks in a manner most unusual for a Gentile, and had been most annoyed when told the flasks could not be engraved immediately. She had even wanted the price reduced because of that.

Jacobson chuckled to himself at what was clearly an enjoyable memory of a fiercely contested barter.

He was able to tell from his ledger when the flasks were collected. It had been on the third of September, and he recollected the pale young man with the long hair who had collected them. He was quite a literary-looking gentleman.

That evening Parsons wrote letters to Johnson and Montagu. The first he sent care of the station-master at Beaumont; the second to the main Post Office in Athens. It was to the latter address that Montagu had instructed Victoria Mayhew to send any of his mail.

Next morning before going to Whitehall, Parsons called at the Post Office on Waterloo Station and posted both letters. He was delighted to learn that a letter sent registered delivery via the continental railways could expect to reach Athens within four days. If Montagu responded reasonably quickly a reply might arrive within ten days, two weeks at the most. That was always assuming that Montagu was still in Athens.

While awaiting replies to these letters Parsons rehearsed the possible arguments he would use to persuade Superintendent Jeffries to allow him to return to Hampshire. He had no intention of discussing the case until all the relevant facts were available, as he knew only the most conclusive evidence would convince the superintendent.

Parsons need not have concerned himself unduly. A week after he visited Victoria Mayhew, Smith's swollen corpse was found by two local fishermen in the thick reeds in the lake at Beaumont.

-60-

8th October 1880

The *White Hart in Petersfield might be less outwardly* impressive than Beaumont Castle but the accommodation was equally as comfortable. It also suited Parsons' requirements admirably. There was little chance that the de Courcey family would know he was in the area; even the Hampshire Constabulary were unaware of his presence. However, Superintendent Jeffries had made it abundantly clear to Parsons that it was the local police who would decide whether matters should proceed to the courts, and for that reason Parsons had not made any arrangements to see Colonel Howard until the following day. By then he hoped to have tidied up all the loose ends.

After a substantial supper of steak and kidney pie Parsons was comfortably settled with a mug of local ale in front of a crackling log fire in his snug back bedroom. Like a good advocate before a trial he was planning his strategy, reviewing the facts and marshaling them into the form of persuasive argument he hoped would win the favor of a court. And in this case the court—in the shape of Colonel Howard, now fully restored to his former robust health—was strongly biased against him.

The first item of evidence was Dr Hamilton's report. In normal circumstances it was unlikely that a medical opinion would have been considered necessary for a drowning, but such was Smith's notoriety that Inspector Marsden had unexpectedly taken the initiative to authorize a post-mortem. A copy of this report, as a result of Parsons' persistence, had eventually been sent to the Metropolitan Police.

According to the report Smith's body had been in the lake for a considerable time. Hamilton could not be sure for how long, but it was likely to have been several weeks. But of one thing Hamilton was sure. Smith had not drowned. His death had been caused by a point four-five bullet entering the back of his skull—the third round fired from the pistol that Grace Spencer had retrieved from the lake.

For once Parsons was of the same opinion as the local police. He had no doubt that it was Larkin, alias Montgomery, who had murdered Smith. After two murders, what difference did another one make. The motive seemed clear enough. Smith had to be silenced. With someone like Smith as an accomplice, Larkin could never rest easy, even had he managed to reach Canada. Under the influence of drink Smith was the sort of man who would open his mouth once too often.

But there were still some puzzling aspects about this particular explanation. There was the matter of the stolen money. Larkin would have needed as much money as possible for his escape and subsequent passage to North America. If Smith had money Larkin would surely have taken it. But Larkin had little money when he was apprehended in Portsmouth, and the captains of the various ships he had approached in seeking a berth had said it had been Larkin's intention to work his passage.

Parsons took a sip of the excellent ale from the pewter mug and for a time contemplated the flickering shadows of the fire. Not only was the disappearing money an unresolved issue, there was also the matter of the disappearing black mare. And most critical of all, the timing of Smith's death.

There were several discrepancies over Smith's death. If Larkin had shot Smith before killing Paul, who then was the man at the lake tending the horses? But if the man at the lake was Smith then Larkin would have had to kill him when he returned to the lake after setting fire to the stables. But Grace Spencer had not heard any shot, and according to her evidence the man thought to be Smith had left the lake with two horses—one of them being the black mare—when Larkin rode back to the castle on the grey. And if that was the case Larkin would have had to kill Smith later. And that was most unlikely. As far as Parsons knew Larkin had never left the castle again, and Smith would hardly have been likely to return. The most likely solution was that the man at the lake was not Smith. At the time of the fire in the stables Smith was already dead. He had been shot by Larkin either just before he murdered Paul or at the time he set fire to the stables. On balance Parsons favored the latter explanation. The noise of a third shot would have been lost against the background noise of the burning wooden stables.

Larkin would have needed to remove Smith's body. If it was found in the stables it would have destroyed the fiction that the murderer was Smith. The simplest solution to this problem was for Larkin to take the body with him on the black mare. In the panic of the moment no one would be likely to see the body draped over the horse, especially with Smith's long coat that Larkin was wearing to cover it.

This hypothesis also fitted Grace's story. She had heard a horseman returning from the direction of the castle. This was Larkin with Smith's body on the black mare. Then she heard a horse going back in the same direction and one returning in about five or ten minutes. She was unable to see where this horse went, but Parsons surmised that this was Larkin taking Smith's body somewhere to dispose of it. What could be easier for him than to ride around the lake until he found some thick reeds in which to dump Smith's body. It was even possible that Larkin had reconnoitered the spot earlier in the day during his ride.

The scenario fitted the facts well, but there still remained the question of the black mare. A valuable animal like that does not just disappear. If Parsons had asked the local police to find it they might have eventually have done so. But more likely they would have ignored his request.

But someone else had seen the mare. The answer to the mare's disappearance had come to Parsons from an entirely unexpected source. It had come from Robertson. The solicitor had written to Parsons just two days before Smith's body was found.

Dear Inspector Parsons,

I have decided to cut my losses in Petersfield and move onto new pastures and in the process have been obliged to sell one of my horses. Not wishing to draw that fact to the attention of my friends and business acquaintances in Petersfield I recently attended a horse auction in Haslemere.

During the proceedings a black mare was auctioned which I believe to be the horse Smith stole from Beaumont the night Paul was shot. But when I made enquiries I was surprised to find that the vendor was a red-bearded Irishman called Kevin O'Neill.

At first I thought of reporting the matter to the police, but as I have said I had no wish to draw attention to my own reason for being at the auction. I also thought that Colonel Howard and his merry men would probably over-react at the mention of an Irishman and a stolen horse. So I thought it best to inform you. You can follow up the matter as best you see fit.

Should you wish to verify this information you should refer to the auctioneers, Mabbett and Cutler of Haslemere. Mention lot fifty-four on 29th September.

Delighted you managed to see fair play in matters at Beaumont. Perhaps we shall meet again one day.

Yours most sincerely,

Andrew Robertson

There was no address on the letter and when Parsons had called at Robertson's home in Petersfield he had found it reoccupied by the landlord. It appeared that the solicitor had gone without leaving a forwarding address or money for the previous quarter's rent.

From what Robertson had said Uncle Kevin and Kevin O'Neill were one and the same man. Robertson's description tallied with that of Claire Dunne. But how had the horse come to be in his possession. He could have stolen it or bought it, but from whom? It was far more likely he had come by it in a less dishonest fashion.

Parsons recalled that Larkin had made no secret of visiting Midhurst during his ride over the Downs. Was that to visit O'Neill? Had Larkin learnt of the Irish community living there from Mary O'Mahoney or one of the other servants? On the assumption that he had, Larkin could well have visited O'Neill at Midhurst and arranged for him to take charge of the horses at the lake. His reward would be one of the horses from the stables, the black mare as it turned out.

Parsons had some initial doubts about identifying the mysterious man at the lake as Kevin O'Neill. Grace Spencer had described the direction from which that man had approached the lake, and it was not from the direction of Midhurst. Although that fact worried Parsons he accepted that without interviewing O'Neill he could never be sure. He also accepted that he was now unlikely to be able to find O'Neill by himself, and he had no intention of involving the local police. Maybe the man had simply chosen to cover his tracks by going to the lake and leaving it in a less direct way. What could be more reasonable than that?

But there were two issues about which Parsons was quite clear. Larkin had said that no one but he was involved in any of the murders—once in a note and the second time on his death bed—and O'Neill had been in the possession of the black mare from the stables.

If all this was true and Smith had never been Larkin's accomplice, why did Larkin chose to kill him? Parsons thought there were two motives. Larkin needed to adopt Smith's identity for Paul's murder, and in consequence Smith had to disappear; and Larkin would have had no doubt that in killing Smith he was removing a thoroughly unpleasant creature from the face of the earth, a man who had tormented and indecently assaulted the Irish servants, including Larkin's own blood relatives, Mary O'Mahoney and the two Dunnes.

Parsons folded Robertson's letter and put it back in his pocket. If Robertson had no intention of mentioning the sale of the black mare to the local police then nor had he. Larkin and Smith were both now dead, and if the Hampshire Constabulary were content that only they had been involved in Lord Paul's death and the assault on their Chief Constable, who was he to disabuse them. There seemed no point in looking further. The Irish, he felt, had already suffered enough in this matter. The matter he wished to discuss with Colonel Howard was far more important. This matter concerned the brutal murder of Captain Ashton.

-61-

lthough Colonel Howard might rely upon his gut instinct, whim or fancy as a modus operandi, Parsons knew that in this instance circumstantial evidence alone would not spur the Chief Constable into action. Nothing less than proof of a substantial nature would do. And much much of that had hinged on what Johnson and Montagu had said in their letters.

At the time he had written to them Parsons could not have anticipated the discovery of Smith's body, nor that it would lead to another strange twist in the Beaumont saga. He was therefore relieved to find that in convincing himself of the identity of Smith's murderer he did not have to alter his opinion as to where the ultimate guilt lay for Ashton's death. And in their own way the letters he had received from Robertson, Johnson and Montagu served to set the whole series of tragedies into context, as well as answering many of the questions he had wrestled with since Larkin's death.

Neither Johnson nor Montagu were aware when they wrote that Smith was other then alive; Montagu's letter arriving in London only a few days before Parsons had traveled to Petersfield.

It was to that letter he turned first.

Dear Parsons

After the terrible events that have recently overtaken me, your letter saying you believed me innocent of murder came as a great relief. I was already beginning to feel like an exile from England, with little prospect of ever returning and facing the future with any confidence of remaining a free man.

I had hoped the items I left with Caroline's mother would lead you to the truth, but I realize now that in themselves they were not enough. You were right to ask me how I came by them and to ask me to explain in greater detail my part in all this.

You will by now have visited the jeweler in Hatton Gardens. Whether or not he remembered me is probably irrelevant, but suffice to say it was I who collected the two hip flasks that had been engraved for Catherine to give to her father. She had written to Alexander in London to ask him to collect them and he in turn had asked me. I can't remember now why it was that he did this, but that probably is not important. Suffice to say I delivered the flasks to Catherine when Alexander and I visited Beaumont for that dreadful reunion.

As you already know Captain Ashton was blackmailing me because of my relationship with Caroline. Somehow or other he had discovered that she was my half-sister. How he knew I will probably never discover, but as you say men such as Ashton make it their business to find out such things. However, it was my misfortune that Ashton had assumed that my father's wealth would either guarantee me a substantial private income or make it easy for me to ask for a large sum of money. As you know neither of these things is true.

The first note I received—the one I gave to Victoria Mayhew—was posted to me at Oliver Craig's house. I had no idea then who had sent it, but it was clear from what the note said that I would soon be told.

You can imagine my distress when I found the second note—the one you found in my room—pushed under my door at Beaumont. I was shocked to think that my blackmailer was in the castle, though at the time I still did not know who he or she was. It did not take long for Ashton to identify himself, nor for him to tell me that before he left Beaumont he wanted my assurance that the money would be paid to him before the end of the month. I think you know that my foolish response to that threat was to wander around the Great Park in the middle of the night in a drunken daze.

On the morning that Ashton was leaving Beaumont I went to his room early to beg for more time to pay—although I still had no idea how I would do that. To my amazement Catherine was already there, and to my utmost surprise I found that she was also one of Ashton's victims. As far as I could make out it was all to do with an affair of hers, though with whom I never discovered.

She had brought with her a small money box. That, of course, was the one you later found in the stables. She gave it to Ashton and we both watched him as he counted the money. I don't know how much he was expecting from her, but what she had given him was clearly not enough. He demanded more, and he wanted it before he left. That's when she gave him the two silver hip flasks. Or should I say she took them out of the cloth bag she was carrying and threw them at him. They bounced off his chest and fell on the rug where he was standing. I can still hear him laughing as he bent down to pick them up.

It was at just that point that she hit him with a poker. God knows where it came from. I can only assume she was carrying it in the bag. But once he had fallen to the floor she hit him again and again in a wild frenzy, until his head was a mass of blood. I was nearly sick at the sight of it.

I tried to leave the room, but she stopped me. She said I was as involved as she, and she would tell the police as much. Colonel Howard would never doubt her word, she said. In fact she said that it would be very easy for her to convince him that I had killed Ashton. But if we worked together, she said, no one need ever find out what had happened. Everyone knew that Ashton was leaving that morning, so no one was expecting to see him again. Then she calmly picked up most of the bank notes and put them back in her bag, leaving only a few in the box. She put that in one of Ashton's saddle bags. Then she told me what she wanted me to do.

She said I was to wrap the blood-stained poker in the bedspread and roll it up in the rug together with Ashton and his saddle bags. Then I should drag the rug into her father's room and push it under the bed. She said that Johnson had the only key to the room, and once she had got that she could ensure that no one could enter the room without her consent.

When I had done that, she told me I should do nothing more until it got dark. Then I should go back to her father's room and lower Ashton's body and the saddle bags out of the window and hide them in the stables. There was always plenty of hay there, she said, and the body and bags could easily be hidden. In a day or two it would be safe to dispose of the body. I asked her how we would do that, but she said she didn't know. But she was sure she would think of something.

I did what she asked and moved the body to Lord Quentin's room, and later that morning we met in my room and went over the rest of the plan in more detail. She convinced me that there was little chance of my being seen. Dunne was in prison and she would ensure that Smith was asleep. All she had to do was give him a bottle of brandy and tell him to drink it in memory of her father.

At first she said that she wanted people to think that it was Ashton that had stolen the money. Then she changed her mind. Smith would make a better and more obvious suspect. At one point I thought she was losing control and becoming hysterical, but somehow she managed to control herself. But it was clear to me that in many ways she was as confused and frightened as I was.

Finally she decided I should hide the money box and hip flasks close to where Smith slept. That way the police would assume Ashton had initially been the thief but that Smith had then murdered Ashton and robbed him. She said a few words from her to Colonel Howard would be all that was necessary to make him believe that story. I have to say it all sounded very unlikely to me, but I couldn't think of a better solution.

I did just as she told me, and that night after dinner I made a pretense of going to my room. Catherine had given me the key to her father's room, and during the day when Smith wasn't around, I had taken some rope from the stables and hidden it in my room. I was scared I can tell you. You can imagine how terrified I was as I struggled to lower Ashton's body and his saddle bags through the window with Lord Quentin's coffin still in the room. The rope was long enough for me to attach one end of it around Ashton's shoulders and lower him to the ground, and then attach the saddle bags to the other end. When the bags had reached the ground I dropped the rope and ran outside. Fortunately I didn't meet anyone on the way.

By the time I had untied the rope and dragged Ashton and the bags to the stables I was exhausted. Thankfully, as Catherine had said, Smith was asleep. I could hear him snoring, but I was still frightened he might wake at any minute. I dared not use a lamp, so I struggled in the dark, burying Ashton and the bags as best as I could with my bare hands. At first I forgot about the money box and the hip flasks in my panic and had to go back to the stables. By then I was sure Smith would wake at any moment so I was afraid to climb the ladder to where he was sleeping. Instead I threw the hip flasks up into the loft. One of them must have hit him because I heard him grunt and his snoring stopped. That was enough for me. I just wanted to get out of the stables as fast as possible. I didn't know what to do with the money box, so I put it back in one of Ashton's saddle bags.

That's when I saw the monocle. It must have dropped out of Ashton's clothing when I was moving him. It was lying there on the ground in a shaft of moonlight. It seemed to be staring at me, accusing me of the terrible crime I had become a party to. On an impulse I picked it up and put it in my pocket, and after cleaning myself up as best I could I rushed back to the Drawing Room; and I was there when the news came that Paul had been shot.

I wasn't sure I'd ever be able to lie convincingly about what I'd been doing that night. I'm surprised you didn't see how nervous I was when you were questioning everyone in the Drawing Room. But you made it easy for me, Parsons, you only asked us what we were doing at the time of the shooting. You never asked what we were doing before.

As you know I received a telegram from Victoria Mayhew while you were in Petersfield telling me that Caroline was distraught, although she didn't say then that she had told Caroline that she and I had the same father. You know what happened before I ever reached London. Caroline had fled and I never saw her again. It was all dreadful, the worst thing that had ever happened to me. At first I contemplated suicide myself, but I didn't have the courage. So I ran away. Leaving the country seemed the only sensible thing to do.

I had little time to think of Ashton during those terrible last few days. But while I was packing for my move to Greece I found his monocle. At first I thought of throwing it away, but something stopped me. I felt I couldn't discharge my guilt so easily. That's when I thought of you, Parsons, and gathered those few items together that I hoped would help *you understand what had happened. We may have exchanged heated words in the past but I trusted your ability to unscramble this terrible mess. And hopefully in doing so you won't think too badly of me.*

I can only wish you every success in your endeavor.

Your friend,

Geoffrey Montagu

It had been an extraordinary coincidence that the events surrounding the murders of Paul and Ashton should have over-lapped in the way they did. While Montagu was struggling to get Ashton's body into the stables Larkin was riding there from the lake.

Montagu's view of events had confirmed one thing. It could not have been Smith that Grace Spencer had seen by the lake. At that time he was either asleep or he was dead.

Evidence that Catherine was also a victim of blackmail had come not only from Montagu but also from O'Brien. She had told Parsons that Ashton had made it clear to her that he intended using Catherine's unfinished letter to Paul to earn himself some money. It also seemed likely that he was already blackmailing her about her previous relationship with Robertson. Ashton had been involved in helping Paul cheat Robertson at cards. He might not have known then why it was that Paul wanted the solicitor in his debt—although he could probably guess—but knowing Ashton's interest in scandals of any sort Parsons was certain he would have made it his business to probe more into Robertson's private life. Catherine was a proud and haughty woman, and one prepared to go to any length to protect her reputation. To his cost Ashton had thought he could exploit that.

During his long vigil the night before Ashton's death, Parsons had seen Paul entering the corridor leading to Annabelle and Catherine's rooms. At the time, from what had been said and from what he had seen, he had imagined that Paul was going to Annabelle. But she had vehemently denied that. Paul was going to Catherine's room. It was hardly a lovers' assignation. Paul's amorous relationship with Catherine extended no further than her proximity to the de Courcey title, and now that that was his, his interest in Catherine was over. No doubt he had gone to her room that night to gloat. He might even have told her the sad truth about their relationship, and now that he had the title, if it pleased him he could also have Annabelle. Catherine could return to Robertson. But without any prospect of a title, Paul might have told her, he doubted whether even a penniless lawyer would want her.

Parsons could well imagine how Catherine would have reacted to that. He had witnessed her volatile temper at first hand. Paul's taunts that night might well have tipped the balance and accounted for the violence with which she subsequently attacked Ashton.

Catherine would have known that Smith could not possibly have murdered Paul. At the time Paul was shot she knew Smith to be lying in a drunken stupor in the stables. A stupor she had herself induced by the gift of a bottle of brandy. As another apparently motiveless attack on the de Courcey family Paul's death might have concerned her. But she was pragmatic, and the truth of the matter would not have been her main concern. The idea of Smith's involvement in Paul's murder suited her admirably as it could only encourage the general belief that Smith had also killed Ashton. By a miraculous stroke of fortune the title was hers again and in Smith she had a convenient scapegoat for her own crime.

Parsons knew that much of this line of thought was speculative, and could only be used to prepare the ground and sow the seeds the doubt in Howard's mind about his previous view of events. But, in Johnson's letter, there was evidence that was more factual and persuasive.

Dear Inspector Parsons

I was surprised to receive your letter by way of Mr Carpenter at the station. I have done what you asked although I was not happy at invading her ladyship's privacy.

You asked me some questions about the Silver Room at Beaumont and about the silver hip flasks. I'll do my best to answer them

Lady Catherine first showed me the flasks the day before the Sevastopol Dinner. She told me that Mr Montagu had brought them with him from London and said she'd bought them for Lord Quentin's birthday. September 23rd that was. I visited his grave on that day.

Lady Catherine put the flasks in the Silver Room. She always kept the key. No one else was ever allowed to have it except on the day we cleaned the silver. That was every Friday. The silver was always looking good for the weekend then. The last time I saw the flasks was the afternoon before Lord Paul was shot. That was the same day she asked me for the key to her father's room. The flasks were in the Silver Room then. I remember asking her what she wanted to do with them now that her father was dead. She said she wasn't sure, perhaps she would put them in his coffin.

I was surprised when Sergeant Brown told me where the flasks had been found. I didn't know what to think. I assumed that her ladyship had done what she said she would do and taken the flasks out of the Silver Room and somehow Smith had stolen them. Perhaps he had asked permission to pay his respects to his lordship before he was buried. And seeing the flasks he had decided to take them. Smith was well capable of that. Stealing from his master's coffin was not the worst of his crimes. But I never said anything to her ladyship about that. It wasn't my place. I assumed she would tell you everything you wanted to know.

Parsons was surprised to learn that Johnson had thought that his mistress would be so forthcoming. After all his years at Beaumont he should have known better.

Catherine had indeed collected the flasks. As Johnson had said, she had the key to the Silver Room. But the flasks were not intended for her father's coffin. Now that he was dead she could offer them to Ashton as a blackmail payment. Only she knew if he would ever be allowed to keep them.

Catherine had also taken the key to her father's room from Johnson. Parsons remembered how upset the old man had been at that. But taking the key had nothing to do with preventing her father's corpse from becoming a spectacle for the curious, it had everything to do with hiding Ashton's body.

But there was more in Johnson's letter.

I asked one of the girls to take a few of the items you asked for from her ladyship's room and I am enclosing them with this letter. I hope they are the right ones.

I can also confirm that the poker in her ladyship's room does not belong there. As you suggested I have carried out an inspection of the other rooms, and it appears that it came from one of the bedrooms in the north wing. I'm afraid I can't explain why that should have happened.

Thank you for asking whether we were paid in full at the end of September. I am happy to confirm that we were. Lady Catherine paid us as usual. I believe she uses Lloyds Bank in Petersfield.

Your obedient servant,
Matthew Johnson

PS I nearly forgot to answer the question you asked me to ask O'Mahoney. She told me that her uncle, the man we thought was Mr. Montgomery, did know about the Irishman the girls call Uncle Kevin. She said Mr. Montgomery was always asking her questions about what went on at Beaumont and in the countryside around.

Parsons tipped the three black tortoise-shell hair-pins from Johnson's envelope into his left hand. They were similar pins to those he had seen in the drawer in Catherine's room. There had also been a set of matching combs. He remembered thinking at the time what good use she made of them, as her hair was always so immaculately groomed. There never seemed to be a hair out of place. But there was at breakfast on the day he left Beaumont. That morning there were several loose strands of hair and two buttons of her blouse were unfastened. That was the morning she reported her money was missing. The morning Ashton was murdered.

He took two other hair-pins from the right-hand pocket of his jacket. They had small brown labels attached to them to indicate that they were the pins he had found enmeshed in the blood-stained rug under Lord Quentin's bed. The rug that had previously been in Ashton's room, and on which he and O'Brien had made love. When Parsons had first found these pins he had assumed they were O'Brien's. A poignant memento of her last night of passion with Ashton.

But even had O'Brien possessed such expensive pieces she had not worn them that night. That night she had allowed her long beautiful chestnut hair to hang loose. On that night there were no pins in her hair. Even now, as he closed his eyes and concentrated, Parsons could see her long hair swaying sensuously down the back of her white night-dress as she made her way along the corridor to Ashton's room.

The pins that Parsons had found in the rug under Lord Quentin's bed had not come from O'Brien's hair. They had fallen from Catherine's carefully coiffured locks as she was smashing Ashton's skull with her poker.

The three pins in Parsons' left hand were a perfect match for the two in his right. Even Colonel Howard would be able to see that.

There was one other important matter. That afternoon Parsons had visited Lloyds Bank in Petersfield and spoken with the manager. It was not a large bank, but like many minor officials of his kind, William Troughton had an over-inflated opinion of his own importance, and much of the petty officiousness of an Inspector Marsden. He was also a snob. At first he had refused to allow Parsons to see the de Courcey accounts, and only reluctantly conceded when told that the family solicitor had recently disappeared and the Metropolitan Police were investigating the possible misuse of the family finances. Troughton's features had grown noticeably paler at the thought that this might reflect in some way on a lack of supervision on his part.

The bank administered four de Courcey accounts. Three of these had been in existence for all of the eight years that Troughton had been manager. There was one in the name of the late Lord Quentin, which Troughton regretted to say was still overdrawn; one in Lady Annabelle's name; and a third, in Lady Catherine's name, that was also used for the general running expenses of the castle. Each of these accounts received regular quarterly transfers of funds from the main trust account at the Winchester branch of the bank, which managed the income from the estate and from other sources such as government bonds and the London and South Western Railway Company.

The fourth account was in the name of Paul de Courcey. This account proved to be very revealing. It had been opened only recently in mid-July with a balance of a few pounds, but during the past six weeks over three hundred pounds had been transferred into it from Lady Catherine's account. The money had no sooner entered Paul's account than it had been withdrawn, and Parsons could hazard a guess as to where it had gone. He had seen Paul's expensive wardrobe and knew of his interest in gambling.

Over the years Lady Catherine's account had been a model of consistency, with a regular pattern of withdrawals each quarter of between two and three hundred pounds. These, Parsons imagined, were for the settlement of the servants' wages and other domestic bills, and for other personal expenditure. Troughton confirmed that only she ever had access to this account.

But recently that had changed. Apart from the money being transferred to Paul's account, a sum of one hundred pounds had been withdrawn in the middle of August. There was no possible way of knowing where it had gone, but Parsons would have been prepared to bet that it had found its way to Ashton.

Catherine's account was now overdrawn, and from the papers available to Parsons this was a state that had never previously occurred. There was nothing more foolish, Parsons mused, than a plain woman of means who is persuaded of her beauty by handsome men without any. In the case of Paul it had led her to unusually extravagant expenditure, and with both Paul and Robertson it had led also to blackmail. And blackmail had led to murder.

On the morning of the Sevastopol Reunion a sum of two hundred and fifty pounds in cash had been withdrawn from Catherine's account. Since then no other money had been withdrawn from the account and no checks cashed.

It followed, therefore, that if Lady Catherine had paid the servants in late September as Johnson had said, she had used money already in her possession. Her claim that over two hundred and fifty pounds had been stolen from her was a lie. As Montagu had witnessed, only a few notes had gone missing. Those that she had left in the money box in Ashton's saddle bag in order to fabricate the robbery. The remaining notes, as Montagu had said, had been scooped back into her cloth bag.

Parsons returned the hair-pins Johnson had sent him into the envelope with Johnson's letter and placed it together with the letter from Montagu in the inside pocket of his jacket. Then he returned the other pins to his right hand pocket. He could do no more now to prepare for his interview with Colonel Howard.

Lady Catherine might feel confident that she could use her strong personality and feminine wiles to persuade the colonel that it had been Montagu and not she who had murdered Ashton. And there was no doubt that Montagu had been involved. If he ever returned to England he would undoubtedly be charged as an accomplice. But to Parsons way of thinking any jury would regard Montagu's foolish attempt at trying to conceal a crime far more leniently than Catherine's cold-blooded and premeditated act.

It was always difficult for a policeman to avoid being judgmental. It was his role to bring evil-doers to justice, and then to let justice take its course. But in the case of the Beaumont murders, Parsons felt it difficult to be so detached. Thomas Larkin, an impostor, had murdered three times. Most fair-minded Englishmen would doubtless agree that two of his victims—Lord Quentin and Smith—had deserved to die. Although they had both served their country on the battlefield, they were nevertheless villains of the worst kind; treating those least able to defend themselves in the most vile and abusive manner. Larkin's family had been but one of many in Ireland and Jamaica that had suffered at the hands of one or other of these two. By removing them from society, Larkin was merely performing a task that the public in general would surely endorse had they known all the true facts. Such facts, however, were never likely to become public, as long as the vested interests of the de Courceys and their kind were protected by incompetent and corrupt policemen such as Colonel Howard. But by taking justice into his own hands, Larkin had forfeited his own life. It was rough justice of a kind that Parsons would not normally have subscribed to; but in this instance he was not ungrateful for it, as he would have regretted having to bring Larkin to justice himself for these two murders.

The murder of Lord Paul, alias Henry Longstaff, was another matter. Admittedly Longstaff, like Larkin, was an impostor who had used his gambling skills to entrap foolish men like Robertson. But Longstaff had charm and a love of life that appealed to many besides Parsons. Unlike Lord Quentin and Smith, his was a life that did not deserve to be prematurely ended. Had Larkin but known the full truth about Longstaff, Parsons could not help but feel he would have recognized a kindred spirit and would have stayed his hand.

But Ashton's murder was different. In this case Parsons felt sorrow for neither the murderer nor the victim. A blackmailer like Ashton was a leach on society, pressing his victims for payment regardless of their ability to pay. He was also a swindler and a man whose word could never be trusted. O'Brien, Parsons was sure, was but one of many young working women who had been beguiled by Ashton's soft words and had been left with nothing but the memory of his broken promises. Ashton assuredly deserved to be punished for his crimes; but he did not deserve to die. Even the Ashton's of this world were entitled to justice under the law.

There were, however, two aspects of the investigation that Parsons found especially gratifying. The first was his action in obtaining the release of the two innocent Dunnes; the second the gleaning of sufficient evidence to prove that Catherine de Courcey was a murderer. His failure to do either of these would have troubled him sorely.

The Dunnes were still servants at Beaumont, but they were at least spared the outrages previously imposed upon them by Lord Quentin and Smith. Parsons could only hope that without such indignities, their lives would improve at least a little. Lady Catherine, on the other hand, was still free and continuing her life of privilege; and before she was arrested, brought to trial and sentenced there still remained some work for him to do.

The situation had been spelt out quite clearly to him by Superintendent Jeffries. The authority to take the matter further rested firmly with the Hampshire Constabulary. For Lady Catherine to face the full consequence of her actions Parsons would have to persuade Colonel Howard of her guilt. But he had every confidence that what he had to say to the Chief Constable and the evidence he could now produce would be convincing enough to lead to Lady Catherine's arrest.

-62-

London, 22nd December 1880

The deep pile of the expensive burgundy-colored carpet in the small Bond Street art gallery and the freshly- falling snow in the street outside muffled the sounds of the late afternoon traffic and the bustle of Christmas shoppers. Within this comforting cocoon of silence Parsons had for the last hour been standing in enraptured contemplation of Dante Gabriel Rosetti's 'Monna Vanna.' It was the portrait he had been mindful of that first evening in the Great Hall at Beaumont Castle when he had met Lady Annabelle.

He had heard only that afternoon that the gallery was offering the portrait for sale and had hastened to see it. He had not come to buy it—it was way beyond his means—but he was hoping it would help exorcise the demons that had haunted him since the trial and execution of Catherine de Courcey.

Parsons had been the principal witness at her trial in Winchester. It had been a great ordeal for him. Catherine's

541

fierce dark eyes had never left his face while he gave evidence, and she continued to fix him with her glare even as the judge pronounced the death sentence upon her. Never had he felt such intense hatred from a pair of eyes.

He had never before attended an execution. At some time—for the sake of his conscience—he knew he would have to, as it was through actions such as his and those of his colleagues that other human beings were put to death by the State. It was only right that he should know exactly what that meant.

Even though it had been his investigations that had led to Catherine's arrest it had never been his intention to see her die. But the day before the execution a powerful impulse prompted him to board a train for Winchester and with much trepidation book into a small hotel near the prison. As dawn broke he had stood in the darkest corner of the execution yard when the small group accompanying the prison governor had led her to the gallows. Yet even then she had sensed his presence and had screamed his name as the executioner covered her head and placed the noose around her neck. When the trap door had opened and he heard her neck snap he was violently sick and had caught the first available train to London.

That had been two weeks ago, and since then his nightmares had been filled with the sights and sounds of that dreadful morning. In desperation, he had turned for solace to this sweet reminder of the other woman he had met at Beaumont Castle, the beautiful Annabelle.

"I'm afraid the gallery is closing now, sir."

Parsons had not noticed the approach of the young woman attendant.

"Thank you," he said quietly, his words directed more

towards the *Monna Vanna* than the attendant; and turning reluctantly away from the full red lips, the large green eyes and the lustrous chestnut hair of the woman in the portrait he moved with a gladdening heart and a lighter step towards the festive scene in the street outside the gallery.

Printed in the United States
68639LVS00007BA/2

9 781589 399334